W9-AXP-242

BANQUO'S GHOSTS

BANQUO'S GHOSTS

RICH LOWRY and KEITH KORMAN

Vanguard Press
A Member of the Perseus Books Group

New York

Published by Vanguard Press
A Member of the Perseus Books Group

Books published by Vanguard Press are available at special discounts for
bulk purchases in the United States by corporations, institutions, and other
organizations. For more information, please contact the Special Markets
Department at the Perseus Books Group, 2300 Chestnut Street, Suite 200,
Philadelphia, PA 19103, or call (800) 810-4145, ext. 5000, or
e-mail special.markets@perseusbooks.com.

Designed by Maria Fernandez

Library of Congress Cataloging-in-Publication Data
Lowry, Rich.
Banquo's ghosts : a novel / Rich Lowry & Keith Korman.
p. cm.
ISBN 978-1-59315-508-7 (alk. paper)
1. United States—Politics and government—Fiction. 2. Middle East—Politics
and government—fiction. 3. Political fiction. gsafd I. Korman, Keith. II. Title.
PS3612.O93B35 2009
813'.6—dc22
2008040420
10 9 8 7 6 5 4 3 2 1

To mom and dad,
with love and boundless gratitude
                    —Rich Lowry

For my Fathers, Mr. Raines and Mr. Korman,
the two wise men, the real Banquos
                    —Keith Korman

A Time Like the Present

God, whose law it is that he who learns must suffer. And even in Our sleep pain that cannot forget, falls drop by drop upon the Heart, and in our own despite, against our will, comes wisdom to Us by the awful grace of God.

—Aeschylus

PART ONE

VALLEY OF SHADOW

CHAPTER ONE

The Drunk

He sat in a ramshackle office chair staring at the little red light in the video camera and let the little red video light stare right back. Sounds trickled into his head from the earpiece, the familiar theme music of the cable news show six thousand miles away and then that raspy voice from the guy who never missed the chance to ask a cream-puff question:

"And joining us live from Tehran, the daring journalist Peter Johnson. The same Peter Johnson who has an opinion about everything and now boasts exclusive access to the Iranian government, its officials, its mullahs, its power brokers. Every beard and every turban." The raspy familiar voice *did* like its own sound. "So tell us, Peter, how're they treating you over there?"

"Fine, Larry. Fine." Johnson smiled. God, he could feel how pasty and blotched he looked. His skin a moist rubber mask. And the strands of hair he tried to comb onto his forehead from his scalp hinted at the merest plausibility of bangs. A suave geek. The perfect intellectualoid. "I think they're glad to have someone over here *listening* to them for once."

An awkward pause due to satellite delay, then Larry King's disembodied voice slid into Johnson's ear like sand. But it was too late; Johnson had already started to talk again. He couldn't help it, a natural reflex to fill any dead air. Chat show guestitis. When he finally became disentangled from Larry, the host got out, "I noticed you're growing a beard—does it help you fit in over there?"

"Not much can help a sophisticated New Yorker fit in over here, Larry." Johnson looked unshaven, with blue circles beneath his eyes. He could guess what anyone familiar with his reputation must have been thinking—hung over, maybe barely sober. If only they knew how hard it was to get a drink in this crummy town. Dry mouth, dry streets.

The dingy studio room at the Ministry of Culture and Islamic Guidance–Foreign Press and Media Department smelled of unwashed feet; a faded cityscape poster of "exotic" Tehran hung on the wall behind him, his backdrop for the CNN setup. An evening shot, streams of cars, the fairy lights of Scheherazade, all frozen. It might have been snatched from an Iran Air tourist office—about the time of the Shah. Along with the table, the chairs, the grime on the walls. Nothing here was new.

A bearded technician crouched behind the camera, impossible to make out from the glaring single spotlight aimed straight at Johnson. He smelled of tobacco and French cologne. A nice enough fellow when he had introduced himself, helping with the earpiece and mike. Soft, gentle hands; clean, manicured nails. Johnson had already forgotten his name. Was it Mohammed-Muhammed, first name and last?

The gravelly voice came again. "Now tell us, Peter—nuke or no nuke?"

This was easy. He hoped no one thought the moisture tickling his shiny forehead was panic sweat—oh, what he'd give for some powder right now.

"Unequivocally, no nuke, Larry. What can I say, except what everyone else knows? This is another put-on, another confabulation by the same people who always lust after another good war. What people don't realize is that Iran's oil reserves aren't inexhaustible, and that this government is planning for the future by developing an alternative source of energy. I am told by my sources in the Ministry of Energy that by the year 2015 nearly 20 percent of Iran's domestic power will be nuclear, and this will preserve oil, this country's most important source of revenue. Larry, some powerful people in America apparently believe they are the only ones who should be allowed to get rich off of oil."

Huh-han-huh—Larry bleated out his practiced laugh that was something between a chuckle and a smoker's cough. Now the tough question, or what passed for it: "Okay, you know this is coming. We've got those bloggers claiming you took money from the Hussein government in Iraq back before it fell."

"But who's paying them to make those accusations? Web loggers? Why don't we just call them what they are. Web *Liars*. Let's see the proof, Larry. Otherwise it's just a smear."

"So no Cypriot vineyards in your portfolio? No stock from the Nigerian Parking Garage Corporation in Lagos?"

"I don't think so, Larry. I don't even own a car. And . . . to quote Dracula, 'I never drink—*wine*.'"

Larry harrumphed again. "We'll leave it right there, with Peter Johnson, the controversial journalist, live from . . ." The earpiece went dead. The light switched off. Mohammed-Muhammed emerged from behind the camera and gave him thumbs up, then chuckled and shook his head.

Johnson wiped his forehead and looked at the technician with an open-palmed gesture. "What?"

"You don't take Saddam's money?" the technician asked, as he walked beside Johnson toward the door. Then, incredulous: "Why not? Everyone take Saddam's money. *But not you?* Hah." Mohammed-Muhammed threw him an easy, gracious smile, before opening the door and stepping aside to usher his journalist out with a broad sweep of the hand. "I don't believe you."

Join the club, Johnson thought.

The door shut behind him, and Johnson was out in the stuffy hallway, staring at his bare dry hands. His fingers trembled ever so slightly. From lack of drink? From the daggers of the man's smile? Or from thoughts of the test to come?

Didn't matter. He remembered the promise. It seemed long ago and far away, made by a man sitting at a well-appointed desk. *We'll provide a gun when the time is right.* When the time is right. Sheesh.

He stuffed his dry, shaky hands in his pockets and left the building.

CHAPTER TWO

In the Tar Pool

Stewart Banquo's office in 30 Rockefeller Plaza overlooked the skating rink and the spill pools of the promenade. The sounds of midtown Manhattan evening traffic, coursing down Fifth Avenue, drifted through the thick glass of the window into his wood-paneled office. The chiseled lettering in gold on the double oaken door read

Banquo & Duncan
Investment Banking

Or so everyone was told. As for Duncan, a pure cutout, dead as Jacob Marley, since no such personage ever existed at all. Tonight Banquo sat at his desk, a man alone. The bare, polished surface gleamed at him from a green-shaded banker's desk lamp, his own murky reflection featureless, like a face staring up from the vast deep. The rest of the room in shadow.

The large plasma TV screen across his darkened office showed its pretty, high-definition colors, way too effective for the grainy moving images coming through the military satellite broadband feed. Jerky shots as if coming from a small hand-held camera, now posted like YouTube for general dissemination in the intelligence community. A Middle Eastern locale: "Southern Lebanon, town of Bint Jbeil" read the white caption. A daytime street scene: hovels, rubble, apartment buildings. A dozen men marched three prisoners out into the street, the jerky video following them along. The prisoners stumbled toward a bullet-riddled wall, wearing knock-off jogging sweats, Michael Jordan wear, an Ice T-shirt—hopelessly out of date. Clumsily, they kneeled. The dozen men—executioners with hoods—let fly with AK-47s into the prisoners' backs and heads. The closed captioning–style line of type at the bottom of the Langley feed read:

> . . . *Presumed Hezbo execution, presumed members of Tazloum or Gemayel clan, opponents of Iranian-Nasrallah organization . . . humint ops Lang cnt confirm . . .*

So Hezbollah was knocking off some local opposition, while some dung beetle taped it all for posterity and propaganda—"presumably." Was it a sign of weakness or of strength, of an impending operation or of business as usual? Well, Human Intelligence Operations at Langley "cannot confirm." In other words, situation normal: nobody knew jack.

The image on the plasma monitor smoothly dissolved and reformed. No more jerky YouTube propaganda but the real deal: a spy satellite enhanced image. A new feed from Langley's C-SPAN. The military had what it called "happy snaps," satellite pictures famous for mesmerizing any civilians sitting around a table at a meeting. This stuff put happy snaps to shame. Southern Lebanon again. Though the only way you could tell would be by reading the captions. The satellite's name: Long Eye; longitude and latitude: 35° 28' E 33° 54' N; time: 0932Z; place: LEBANON Iranian Embassy, Bear Hasan, Beirut. Four men in turbans came out of the Iranian Embassy and got into a waiting Mercedes sedan. The Mercedes drove off. The image jumped again, back to the men walking to the car, and zoomed in closer and closer until it seemed you were standing ten feet over one of the turbans. Now the turban began to turn yellow-green, as though to identify itself. *See? This turban. Here I am.* The caption on the feed read: "Nasrallah leaves Iranian Embassy: 0932Z." Ah, so some clever PhD at Langley had figured out how to paint the Shiite's turban with some low-grade uranium dioxide, once used in ceramic glazes. Then a kind of black-light filter on the satellite teased out its color. You see? We can see him from space.

Banquo pursed his lips and thought: Not bad. Probably bribed the man's turban-winder. Yes, such men existed, earning their bread in Oriental countries, winding turbans for a living. Countless thousands of such men, as common as barbers in the West, from London to Bangkok. And easily enough bribed if you could find them. Just one problem: if the client was smart, and Nasrallah was smart enough, he'd be bribing his turban-winder too. Ensuring loyalty. Now another fellow could be wearing the turban, maybe his brother-in-law, or some unrelated poor sap, or even the local administrator of a Red Crescent Hospital whose untimely demise at the hands of the geniuses who thought up this turban-dying scheme would give rise to international outrage. Not that Nasrallah even needed to know about Langley's clever fabric-tagging system. Assassins had been poisoning people's garments in that part of the world for a thousand years. It paid to be careful. A paranoid might wear a new turban every day.

Or Nasrallah might leave his *fidai*—his body double—to wear the hand-me-downs in the ancient Oriental practice of employing a look-alike. The Sheik's 7th century answer to his 21st century problem. All done with a little baksheesh. Six thousand Lebanese pounds to be exact, the princely sum of *four whole U.S. dollars* in cold cash. It could trump $20 million plus in hardware, software, and satellite time. All so some clown at Langley could write the line in the president's daily brief tomorrow morning: "Nasrallah Leaves Iranian Embassy, Beirut: 0932Z." Whether it was true or not.

"We're losing," Banquo whispered to the walls.

Had he made the problem even worse? The thought nagged him. Risking disaster by sending a gin-soaked scribbler to do a man's job?

One of Banquo's associates knocked on the office door, opened it a crack, and muttered, "Our guy's on *Larry King*; we've got it on in the conference room. Wanna watch?"

"No, thank you."

He already knew what Peter Johnson would say. After all, they had deliberately recruited the man for his solid leftist credentials and his easy way with fashionable agitprop. That's exactly what made him useful. That, and his reputation as a drunk. Banquo had put an extra pair of eyes on Johnson's Lufthansa flight to watch their man safely through Tehran customs. During the flight Johnson pounded back enough First Class bourbons to embalm a horse. Now, two days in-country the fellow must be feeling pretty shaky. But not so shaky as to miss a TV appearance. Well and good—the firm didn't pick him for his uprightness.

His associate stood at the door and seemed to be waiting for something more. "Glad he made the show," Banquo told him. "Means he hasn't gone off the rails."

The door closed without reply. And the shadows engulfed him.

Banquo & Duncan. Some twenty-five years ago they let him pick his own name for the outfit, back when people had a sense of humor and Stewart Bancroft—his real name, long forgotten—had a little clout. No more. Now it was dog and pony shows for the congressional committees and frightened rabbits out in the field jumping at their shadows. But not much human intelligence. Banquo had watched the technology get smarter and smarter, the results weaker and weaker. With no real-life human eyes to spy.

Instead the powers-that-be gravitated to other priorities. "Voluntary" sexual harassment and racial sensitivity seminars. Bureaucrats wrote memos about memos. And if anything went wrong, they denied it had gone wrong, or blamed someone else for it going wrong, and resolved never ever to actually *do* anything ever again, lest someone somewhere construe it as having gone wrong.

Crises erupted over family-friendly construction projects. Delays and cost overruns had slowed the Men's Bathroom renovations—an installation of two hundred quality Care Bear® changing tables "for your convenience." When what—Mr. Mom *wet* himself? No matter. In case of emergency at a sensitivity seminar, there'd be a changing table for his convenience. And when the brutal workday came to a close at 4:30 PM, the Agency employees lined up in the Langley parking lot, shuffling off to their minivan carpools for their suburban commute home. To travel in herds.

If they ever saw the rare file photo of him in some forgotten file drawer, they might have glanced at it like a curiosity, a faded news picture from the time before bitmaps and jpegs. *How quaint. A dinosaur in a tar pool. Oh, that's what spies used to look like.* Every damn one of them smugly oblivious to the fact this dinosaur's offspring roamed the world at his bidding. He might be stuck in a New York office, but his ghosts— collected over a lifetime—slipped beyond borders and barbed wire into every dark hollow. Last of a vanished breed, an anachronistic rebuke to the self-protective nappies in a nanny's world.

Well into his mid-fifties, Banquo still owned a full head of hair, with a distinguished touch of gray around the sideburns. His features were handsome and regular, with the kind of strong jaw image-conscious male business types got chin implants to try to duplicate. A harder, lined face that didn't need to ingratiate itself with anybody or smile all the time. Still, he paid attention to his appearance and was partial to striped suits and shirts with French cuffs. Like a sober, solemn judge in chambers, without his robes. He knew all the staff on the third floor of the 44th Street Brooks Brothers on a first-name basis. A wise old wolf in dandy's clothes. Stern and unforgiving.

He was conscious of the effect his looks had on others: men either subconsciously deferred to him or succumbed to envy. Yes, the way it should be. His good looks gave him that extra measure of persuasiveness with women. But in dangerous situations, both his allies and his enemies underestimated him as a pretty boy. In the case of the latter, to their mortal peril.

Banquo's Cold War had been pretty hot, in El Salvador, in Western Pakistan, in Lebanon. Every plot, every betrayal, every death or near-escape never seemed to go away. Each left a vapor trail across his consciousness. His memories the undead, still walking the earth, restless spirits, rattling chains, slamming doors, and touching cold hand to shoulder in lonely moments. Faulkner would have understood. Banquo's past wasn't truly past.

It had pointed the way forward, providing an education in everything from the deepest recesses of the human heart to the most profound grasp of the obvious *in how the world worked.* Or had pointed the way forward until recently.

Until the intellectuals and policymakers called off history about five minutes after the end of the Cold War. Until U.S. intelligence agencies were directed to monitor environmental degradation of the ozone layer and facilitate a nonexistent "peace process." Until his tradecraft of a lifetime was left to molder away by less talented, less committed, less imaginative people, who didn't understand that their well-meaning indulgences would bring the most gruesome consequences: the death of innocents and smoky ruins soaked in blood. A vapor trail that wasn't a ghost of the mind. Thousands obliterated under a smoke-smudged sky falling back to earth the merest three miles from his office, on an innocent September morning.

So very quietly, all alone, Banquo hatched a plan no one else would understand or dare. Send a sodden, fashionable journalist to slay the Monster in his lair—before another September morning came to pass.

All from the comfort of an obscure office. Banquo & Duncan.

Forgotten even to the sublime powers that be. Forgotten to a succession of White House Chiefs of Staff, Special Advisors, heads of the National Security Agency, and a parade of agency directors who could barely organize their pencils on their desk. Same outfit. Same mission. Democrat or Republican administration, corrupt or honest. No matter who was in charge, Banquo & Duncan existed to execute unspoken decisions and deniable intentions. In every administration the same bloody mission:

Win the War.

Didn't matter which.

Now merely the upstairs maid's room of a monstrous bureaucratic mansion. Where the technocrats sent forlorn plans to curl up and die. Where they sent missions they had no intention of carrying out, so they could tell some congressional committee a given nettlesome problem was being "handled with all due dispatch."

Banquo got up from his desk, closed his office door behind him, and went to the conference room to see who was still around. Nobody. Everyone had left for the evening, but Larry King still talked to a lonely conference table, a mess of take-out Chinese food boxes, empty soda cans, and paper plates. The custodial engineers of Synch Office Cleaning, under the command of Mr. Synch, would get it later. A quiet grayish man, who once served previous regimes and administrations and therefore possessed clearance. Officially retired, no doubt—but still needing a job to perform. He glided like a phantom in a gray custodial uniform in and out of the offices when the lights were dark and desks empty, once a kind of spy, now a janitor. An old soldier who Banquo treated with the grave respect and deference due any warrior, a survivor of battles only he remembered.

And if their new man, Johnson, came through all right—he would be entitled to the same respect. For his own battle in Iran, never to be forgotten.

A couple of years back one of Banquo's staff hung a framed replica of Fox Mulder's famous Alien Saucer poster on the wall above the bank of televisions. Except this poster showed Saddam's noble profile superimposed over a mushroom cloud. The caption stayed the same though, a comment on the Agency's egregiously wrong "slam dunk" insistence that Iraq had WMDs when none could be found:

"I Want To Believe."

So for the good of the firm and reasons of professional grit the senior and *only* partner of Banquo & Duncan had left it there.

To hang forever as a warning.

CHAPTER THREE

A Free Hand

Peter Johnson's driver waited for him outside the studio, in a pink Yugo with "MahdiCab" stenciled on the side. His Information Ministry guide opened the cab door while Johnson kept his unreliable hands safely at his sides. Those bourbons on the plane still beckoned him. If anyone noticed, they didn't let on, and the two men drove him back to the Azadi Grand Hotel across town, a white concrete monolith that boasted "Lobby Coffy shop available 24 hours" on all its brochures.

Like every cab in the Middle East, the interior was tarted up in the latest Islamic Fashion, which hadn't changed in fifty years. Nauseating light green or pink surrey fringe along the inner windshield; large air freshener in the shape of minaret capstone; golden lines from the Koran in Farsi script on miniature scrolls hanging from every surface. The radio blasted music into Johnson's brittle ears that sounded like chanting with a lot of feedback on the sound system—just like back in New York. Even in this terribly sober moment, Johnson imagined what the script on the hanging scrolls said—just to amuse himself:

Don't Like My Driving?
Dial 1-800-ALLAH.

13

Or:

Hang On and Pray.

Or:

All Destinations are Final.

He resisted trying these lines out on the Ministry man sitting beside him, knowing full well that discretion is the better part of valor anywhere east of the Danube and south of Venice. Kahleed, his Ministry of Information guide, was an incurious fellow with a close dapper beard, Armani shirts, and the clean manicured nails any professional seemed to have in this part of the world. Johnson had asked him to dinner at the hotel several times, but each time Kahleed politely refused, appearing content to pick him up, drop him off, and make sure he didn't wander too far. Once again, Johnson offered the fellow a meal at the hotel, but once again Kahleed demurred, as he always did, with the words, "Perhaps tomorrow."

The air conditioning in the hotel chilled the shirt on his back, lovely and cool and making him think of gin and tonics at sundown on Cape Cod, of evenings hanging out on a front porch with Giselle, his daughter and only child. They took their most recent vacation together, and Dad marveled at his girl, ladylike and all grown up. At least as grown up as any kid could be racing through her twenties.

As usual, Johnson headed for the concierge to check his messages, but before he was halfway across the lobby, his cell phone chimed. Coverage was spotty in Tehran, and he was always pleasantly surprised when it worked. A voice message beeping in. A woman's voice: Josephine Parker von Hildebrand. His first ex-wife from Oxford days. *And* his Boss. How did a fellow's life turn out like that? To mangle the words of a great man: *an enigma wrapped in a mystery inside a riddle.*

"You were *mah*velous, *dah*ling." Purposely mimicking Billy Crystal in the old *Saturday Night Live* bit called Fernando's Hideaway— although with her you never quite knew what was playacting and what was just her. She meant his appearance on CNN's King, obviously.

Jo von H was editrix and part owner of the nation's oldest "progressive" weekly, named after the old abolitionist yellow rag of the 19th century, *The Crusader*. Even the mullahs knew of Jo von H's famous sway and weren't going to let the unfortunate name of the magazine stop them from giving Johnson special access. This was one Crusader they knew was against the cross.

The publication was a multimedia empire, with millions of dollars of Soros backing, a $100,000-an-issue budget, its own book imprint inside a mainstream publishing house, and its very own aged-in-wood genuine Hollywood icon front man selling his brand of Arizona Hot Sauce, called Crusading Fire. Even if they only paid their scribblers $1,000 per article, they had more true believers hitting their website than *The New Yorker* and the Grey Lady combined. That was exposure, raw *power*, a kind of intellectual invincibility that couldn't be bought for love or money. When Jo Parker von Hildebrand said you were clean, no smear went unpunished, even a smear that was true.

The voice message went on:

"After King trotted out that bribery business—*nonsense on stilts, darling*—our friend from *Newsweek* called—something about a 750-word sidebar to their Radical Right Wing Blogosphere cover. Wanted you especially. And I told him 'of *course*,' you'd be *delighted*, just as soon as you got back. But make it *just as soon*, darling; they're hoping to run it two issues up. Maybe we'll do it at the apartment. After all, who can resist a von Hildebrand private supper in her exclusive salon?"

Nobody. At least not since Oxford days. Back when a couple of smart, ambitious intellectual climbers thought they could have it all, romance, lust, politics, and life. Youth's delusion, soon set straight. Life's struggle casting the lust and romance aside—at least for one another—and leaving the politics, which occasionally still lit them up the way it did when they were twenty-one-year-olds.

Yeah, Jo Parker von H would cover him all right. And yes, it had been alleged—*alleged, mind you*—that some dirty money changed hands. Problem was, a touch of it was traceable, just enough for Banquo to hang him, to keep his man on the straight and narrow. But most of the money was not. Not from the late Hussein at any rate, except by extension. Johnson, like many another, let the late Lion of the Desert cross his palm with silver as Saddam tried to buy Iraq out of a war. A futile attempt, but the Lion's largesse spread around quite a bit of oil contracts, under some

United Nations criminality called Oil for Food: scores of billions of dollars in graft to ensure French, Russian, and Belgian bureaucrats, even whole governments and NGOs, would always give him the benefit of the diplomatic doubt, no matter how many Kurds he slaughtered or other people's wives he gave to his voracious sons, or children he fed into the wood chippers of his state security police.

Peter Johnson's cut, a measly $75,000, came not from the Lion of the Desert but indirectly from a man named Benon Sevan. Whom Johnson had chatted up and admiringly profiled whenever he could. Once the UN's executive director of the Oil for Food Programme, he was fired from Kofi's staff at the United Nations when the investigators came sniffing too close to the chump change in Sevan's own bank accounts. So he stopped running the UN's Grease for Dough Payola racket. Instead Mr. Benon Sevan fled abroad and was living large in his homeland of Cyprus. Fleeing beyond the reach of extradition, running home to his Aunt in Nicosia, claiming the hundreds of thousands of dollars—mere skim of billions, mind you—were simply his Aunt's money, his *Aunt's*, you understand. Of course, that poor bureaucrat's elderly Aunt curiously fell down an elevator airshaft and took a few inconvenient days to die. But as a Nicosia resident and Cypriot patriot, both Mr. Sevan and his bank accounts cowered under this flag of convenience, safe as Fort Knox. That's where the crack about Cyprus vineyards came in—but not before the tuition bill for Peter's daughter's years at Harvard was somewhat defrayed.

Johnson had read somewhere that the elevator shaft where the poor Auntie met her maker had long ago been repaired. His cell phone blinked: a text message.

Speak of the devil, his own flesh and blood. Fruit of his loins from his *second* ex-wife. Giselle, reacting to his *Larry King* appearance too. He scrolled down:

dad, I kno u.

yr so lyyyyyyyyyyyyyyyyying.

luv me.

He smiled: You couldn't kid the kid. There was some divine justice in that.

The concierge smirked as Johnson reached the desk. That amazing Oriental smile hovering somewhere between sincerity and servility. And where never the twain shall meet. His name was also Kahleed—his English marvelous and his French impeccable.

"Ah, Monsieur Johnson, that was a very fine broadcast. The manager let us watch it in his office. I have one message, the local producer for Al Jazeera—his name is Jazril Mahout. In fact he's here now, waiting in the tea lounge. Waiting with an emissary from His Eminence."

The lovely chill from the hotel air-conditioning tingled on the back of Peter's neck. That promised next step had finally arrived. He shrugged on his suit jacket and tugged at his cuffs. Then with a pang of satisfaction Johnson glanced at his hands—steady as a rock.

The Golden Martyrs of the Revolution May-They-Ever-Be-Blessed Tea Lounge was the official place of unofficial business, of promises that would never be kept and lies that told the truth. But with no gin to cut the tonic. Two men waited for him at a low coffee table surrounded by low, deep couches.

The shill from Al Jazeera, Mr. Jazril Mahout—or the Jazz Man, as Johnson nicknamed him—wore a suit, open shirt, no tie, hand-sewn Ferragamo loafers. The suit was an expensive one, $2,000 at least, the cloth impregnated with threads that made it shimmer slightly.

He stood up to greet Johnson, extending his hand—the grip firm, not the banana handclasp that made you want to wash your hands.

"Mr. Johnson, thank you for coming. I'm sorry we're so late tonight, but His Eminence, Sheik Kutmar, could only see His Holiness in the interval between prayers and therefore could make time for us only now."

The more forbidding figure of the two was Sheik Kutmar, little sheik to the big mullah who would decide matters of access. Johnson tried not to stare at the dark prayer callus directly in the middle of the man's forehead. He was in the presence of the next line of eyes, the next level of ears. Sheik Kutmar sat at right angles to the American, neither looking him directly in the eye, nor getting up to shake his hand, nor even speaking. His presence was enough. A thin, wiry, and arrogant man deigning to appear and listen like some carved stone idol waiting for his due offering.

The Jazz Man went on as if he and Johnson were alone, eyes directly on the westerner, "Our Washington, DC, bureau chief has expressed his desire to do the story as a large special, twenty-five to thirty minutes. He would do the wrap-around, the context. You'd be reporting on the ground."

"That's fine, but that doesn't avoid our primary problem," Johnson said. "Your network is widely recognized as one-stop shopping for beheading videos, ransom demands, and goons in black hoods sitting beside guys in turbans muttering about Zionist pigs and monkeys. As you know, I'm not under contract to any one news service, but if you want your story to get legs and credibility, if you want the story to go beyond chanting and ranting, I've got to be able to draw a Western network into the reportage. Since no one has a bureau here any more, that's not as difficult as it seems, but that might leave your DC man out of it. Everyone recognizes me as a partisan figure, but the mainstream networks have a way of overlooking such matters when exclusive access is involved."

The Al Jazeera producer sighed, his liquid brown eyes veiling themselves for a moment. "We were so hoping to make the segment our premier, signature breakthrough."

"Who says it can't be?"

The veils went away. "Explain."

"Rome wasn't burned in a day, my friend. On this story we start as a western network exclusive, CNN or MSNBC. But since none of the cable or big three networks have bureaus here, Al Jazeera should handle the tactical aspect, getting our road show from point A to point B, filming, and translation. A significant obligation. Now, imagine we do two reports—two separate pieces. The first: 'The Mullah Bomb: Fact or Fiction?' And as we know the answer already, this will come as something of a disappointment to those who want to see an underground test sometime soon. Peaceful uses, brilliant scientists, yawning energy needs in a country beset by American sanctions. For the second segment we do a teaser. We call the second piece 'The Scimitar of Faith.' We show the military strength of the Republic of Iran, how futile it is to attack or resist it. In this way we actually give the world something to see. Footage of secret military exercises and tests. Top defense officials talking candidly about their power to slaughter the infidel. Fortress Iran. Invincibility. Certain defeat at the hands of the Mahdi's Army. And this second piece is all produced, directed, and released through Al Jazeera. With exclusive, breaking news the major networks can't afford to ignore." He broke into an anchorman's standard standby, "'As Al Jazeera is now reporting—'" Then clapping his hands to his knees for effect. "You're at the table whether they like it or not."

The Jazz Man was silent for a moment.

"That's larger than anything we anticipated. But I see what you mean."

Johnson hoped so, because he wasn't sure what he explained even made sense to him. He took a piece of paper out of his jacket pocket. "I made a tentative list of sites that I'd like to visit. And that, of course, is the bulk of our first effort, regarding your peaceful nuclear program. We can leave the military aspect out of this for now."

Jazril took the printed list of sites and, without glancing at it, folded and put the paper in his jacket pocket. "Do you have any other concerns?"

"First, that we should start soon for obvious reasons. The U.S. could go either way now. Secondly, I want a free hand. Nothing impresses the West more than a free hand. So obviously a forced or willing conversion of this reporter to Islam would not work in your favor." He waited for some laugh or smile or even a curling lip from one of his listeners. Nothing. No sign of recognition. "In any event I'm not what they call . . . a churchgoing man."

Johnson extended his hand to the Sheik, rising to leave with these words of farewell: "I seem to recall the word *Kumtar* means 'Herald' or 'Messenger' in the Albanian language. Why I know this absurd fact can be laid at the feet of a liberal education, as well as some time spent on the Adriatic in the Dardanelles. Perhaps Sheik Kutmar's name means something similar in Farsi? Herald or Messenger? In any language, an auspicious name."

The soft, moist cough from Sheik Kutmar stopped him in his tracks. The man spoke, still not looking directly at the American.

"Do you know the Muslim mind, Mr. Johnson?"

After a breath, Johnson said, "I don't claim to know anyone's mind, Your Eminence."

"It's well that you don't. Do you know why we are going to win, Mr. Johnson, *'daring reporter'*?" Using Larry King's line with a touch of sarcasm, as though he knew how very little Johnson dared in life. He cleared his throat again.

"I shall tell you. The Jews and weaklings of the West love life. So that is what we shall take away from them. We are going to win because you love life and we love death. The war is as simple as that." Then with a smile in his voice. "As to the matter of your conversion, forced or willing—I think we can leave that in the hands of Allah. Though the prospect of you kneeling beside me in a mosque has the aspect of a farce even Allah could wish on no one."

Johnson went silent for a moment. "Right," he said, standing. "*Inshallah*, I suppose." He nodded to the Jazz Man and made a small bow to the Sheik, who did not meet his gaze, before retreating across the Golden Martyrs Tea Lounge. Once at a safe distance Johnson felt the urge to mutter some invective, but nothing sprang to mind.

All the same he sensed it was *them* playing him, not the other way round, and his mouth felt dirty as if used in unmentionable ways.

CHAPTER FOUR

Night Sweats

Dinner was a lonely, desultory buffet of chicken, tabouli, and tahini in a nearly empty dining room. The high spot of the buffet table was the large chilled bowl of caviar, surrounded by limp toast, hardboiled egg whites, egg yolks, chopped onions, and sour cream. Iran was the last place on earth still swimming in cheap and plentiful beluga, ossetra, or the even more rare sevruga. Johnson, an unapologetic Roe Ho, loaded up his plate.

A group of four middle-aged upper-class women in full chador ate silently in a far off corner, covering and uncovering their faces as their forks went first to their plates, then to their mouths. They exchanged the occasional word, then quietly went back to their meal, as if at a funeral. Johnson ignored them.

Opposing tables of Chinese and Russian trade-representative types squared off across the room. The Russians were sober and agitated. A Russian-made Tu-154 commercial jetliner of Iran AirTour had crashed at Meshed Airport that very afternoon, with thirty or so dead. After the spectacular crash and burn of Karl Marx, crappy planes doing the same just added insult to injury. One of the Russians was talking nonstop and using his hands as "wings" trying to explain what happened. Russian commercial aircraft had been crashing all over the world since the end of the Cold War, so this wasn't exactly "news"—but being sober didn't make it any better.

From his table seat Johnson thought the Chinese, for their part, seemed pleased with themselves. As representatives of the new master race, they had come to conquer and were deep in the process, drunk on power, the true nectar of the gods. Sales of Red Chinese missile parts to the Iranian Ministry of Defense: $1.3 billion. Import guarantees of light crude from a newly renovated Kharg Island: $750 million. A twenty-five-year bargain to develop natural gas: $100 billion.

On top of all that, a table full of grumpy Russians spilling caviar onto their ties and trying to explain why Soviet-designed planes kept falling out of the skies—priceless.

Johnson finished and headed upstairs. When he opened his suite door and flipped on the light, the first thing he saw was the set-up on the table. A large silver bucket of ice, a bowl of limes, a wooden cutting block, a knife, a bottle of Schweppes Tonic, and a blessed liter of Tanqueray. The green bottle smiled at him like a long lost friend. He reached out to touch it, savoring its sexy emerald curves. The little white note said, "Compliments of Al Jazeera." Compliments indeed, *Praise Allah*. He was saved.

And then from around the world Banquo's schoolmaster's voice warned, *Go easy, Peter* . . . It took a full moment to get the insistent voice out of his head and back to its proper place in the old man's spartan Rockefeller Center office.

The room smelled of must and rosewater but soon filled with the aroma of gin and tonics. He stood at the window overlooking the city, idly sucked the lime juice from a rind, and stared across the hot expanse of air dotted with those Scheherazade fairy lights, but this time with the traffic moving. Miles and miles of snaking cars, white lights coming and red lights, blinking brighter on and off, going the other way. The muezzins were calling the faithful to prayer. *Someone somewhere was always praying in this country.* He took a long draught that went down without complaint, stringent and quenching. Looking across the city at night, he felt as if he were standing on a great precipice, the immensity in front of him prompting the sort of contemplative reverie you get on a mountaintop or looking out over the ocean.

Knowing that for better or ill he was stepping off into some irrevocable chain of events from which there was no way back. He thought of God, or the idea of God, and suddenly wished that for *once* in his life he believed. How he might have given the gift of faith to his daughter. Even faked it for Giselle's sake. Let her grow up and decide for herself, whether to believe or not. Instead of breaking the notion of God like every other childhood fantasy—leprechauns, the Easter Bunny, the Tooth Fairy—*no, Giselle, there is no Santa Claus.* The thousand little ways adults wring the magic out of a child's life.

He looked down at the ice cubes, marooned, and stacked one on another at the bottom of his empty glass. Chances were excellent he was going to drink too much.

No, not tonight. One more, a stiff one, but not four more. Empty out most of the bottle just for show. With the taste of grit in his mouth and a touch of sadness, the better part of the liter vanished down the toilet and into the Euphrates River as Crocodile Cocktails. Cheers.

An hour of pacing, of looking at his sad reflection, jowls and drinker's veins, in the glass window, of wishing he could find a woman here to share his loneliness with, if just for one night, of finally imagining the incredible piece he'd really write if ever given the chance, about what was *really* going on now. All the ice had melted, the second glass long finished, and the bed found him.

As he lay there with the lights dimmed, love handles spilling over his boxers, something nagged him. Nagged him like the embarrassing regrets that usually splintered through his drunken hazes back home, over a rude pass at a woman too young for him, or a cruel remark to some slovenly sot as liquored up as himself in a forgotten dinner table debate. Something the clever Sheik had said, something knocking at the back door of his brain.

"Do you know why we are going to win, Mr. Johnson, 'daring reporter'? I shall tell you. The Jews and weaklings of the West love life. So that is what we shall take away from them."

It wasn't the fact that the imperious snob had actually said it— the sentiment was common enough out here—but because Johnson had heard it before, in other terms. Something much like it . . . long ago at a fancy New York dinner party. Dinner hosted by Jo von H. Years had passed between that party and tonight's meeting, as he methodically drank so many of his old memories out of his mind. But that night stood out. As clear and cool a September evening as you could ask for, the lights going on in all the apartment buildings, the traffic moving elegantly along the trees of Central Park, and Tavern on the Green bejeweled in white lights against the growing darkness of the park.

Josephine Parker von Hildebrand's apartment overlooked Central Park West, Number 151, The Kenilworth, a French Second Empire–style building with a magisterial entrance flanked by banded columns. Past the liveried doorman, he met Neville Poore, former theater critic at the *Times*, in the marble lobby, and they took the elevator together. Poore had recently strayed from the Great White Way, haughtily gliding onto the national scene.

Lately, he had written three straight columns about a Republican embroiled in a sex scandal after getting caught having affairs with both young men and women staffers in his congressional office. "I'm a bi American," the politician declared at an August press conference, at the end of which a cameraman accidentally knocked him over in the media crush. Neville Poore excoriated the country for its supposed fixation with the flap, even though he had written about nothing else since it happened and read the broadest possible meanings into it, like in today's number: "Democrats were quick to maneuver for advantage in the scandal, making it truly an exercise in *bi*partisanship. But the real story is Red State America's repressed obsession with sex that lashes out at any departure from an Ozzie and Harriet dream world at the same time it forces the desires of its own representatives into the shattering contortions entailed by the closet. Perhaps the nation will finally wake up: polymorphous perversity now, polymorphous perversity forever—for the sake of our emotional, political, and spiritual health, if nothing else."

And so it went. Neville lived the editorialist's dream, gassing on in blissful ignorance, seemingly unable to learn from the spectacularly extensive corrections buried near the front of the paper days after his columns ran.

"CORRECTION: Spiro Agnew was governor of Maryland, not Mississippi, prior to becoming the vice president of the United States.

He resigned in a scandal related to bribes taken as governor, not over the outrage after the bombing of Cambodia. He was Greek, not Italian."

Details, details.

"Nice bi-line today," Johnson said, relishing his pun, though Neville couldn't see it. He and the columnist still locked eyes, anticipating something fun and the taste of that first drink. Jo's parties always had that effect. As the elevator man opened the gated door, Johnson waved the exalted Nevillian out ahead of him, smiling, "It's just a simple supper party, but let's not keep the little woman waiting. She's been slaving all day."

Poore laughed. "If I had your ex-wives, I wouldn't have to work."

Johnson caught a glimpse of himself in the gilt-edged hallway mirror: the dapper drake with a receding hairline, in standard pinstripe blue and open collar, smiled gravely back. They heard the sounds of the party, the staccato clinking of glasses like a monstrous wind chime, then the sonorous murmuring of a gossipy theater crowd during an intermission at a Broadway opening. A long, tall, and narrow hall like the entranceway to a cathedral marched off ahead. The walls lined with paintings: a Caravaggio, a Dürer woodblock print—both darkly lush and worth more than $10 million; framed covers of *Crusader* issues; and black-and-white news file photos of Jo von H in various Edward R. Murrow poses. There'd been a lot of water under the bridge since those Oxford days, the briefest of marriages, a short detour on Josephine's march to glory. Vanity, thy name is suffragette. And to make it all perfect, one portrait, an oil painting, lit from above: the late Mr. Josephine Parker von Hildebrand. *Her* second Ex.

Also known on the oilfields of Texas as Big Joe Hill. No relation whatsoever to the Wobbly legend of Woody Guthrie fame. Josephine's great conquest and now dead ex-husband. A trim black bit of crepe crossed the corner of the portrait. The likeness showed the hard, unrelenting face of an oilman, emphasis on the man, many years older than his pretty wife.

Sure, she divorced him. Who wouldn't? Sure, she took him for everything—what was wrong with that? But it was pure Josephine to honor the old wildcatter's memory with a serious, sympathetic, and heroic likeness. She took his money, despised his Texas ways, and fled to more sophisticated climes, but damned if she didn't make him the poster boy of that long elegant hallway and every luxury that followed. After all, in every sense of the word, he was the founder of the feast.

Still, you couldn't feel too sorry for the old geezer. After Josephine put the touch on him, others lined up for the same treatment. She wasn't beautiful, but people thought she was. Tall, in as good shape as a fifty-year-old could be, with platinum blonde–dyed hair and the best breasts money could buy; Johnson had nicknamed her lesser charms from those Oxford days "our little secrets."

Her wardrobe took up closets that four or five families from Queens would be happy to live in. No one noticed her plain features. The force of her personality overwhelmed all else. Witty, shrewd, magnetic, and kind when she wanted to be, Josephine had practically every desirable personal characteristic, except wisdom and mercy. She was always dating very wealthy men fifteen years younger than herself, who adored her and eagerly did her bidding. She called them her "Lancelots."

The von Hildebrand hallway opened up into a grand oval foyer with rooms radiating from its center and a staircase rising to fainting heights. Every catered affair had its tone, some informal, some black-tie, but Josephine preferred the starched white blouse and gray apron types, a uniform commonly seen in the 1950s on pale Irish maidservants and reserved Spanish butlers fresh from Cuba.

Large silver platters of hors d'oeuvres circulated among the privileged, and Johnson never doubted his place among them: the hors d'oeuvres and the exalted both. In those days, he knew what he was supposed to think and duly thought it, although not without a dollop of ironic detachment. Whether he was chatting up the famous director of the Zyklon-B movie trilogy or whether he stopped and admired the footwear of a frail but winsomely vulnerable young woman wearing finely crafted wooden boxes on her feet instead of pumps to accessorize her little black cocktail dress. Yes, he knew how to ooze approval.

The boxes were about the size of women's cardboard shoeboxes, but fitted together with finely carpentered slats, plain and unvarnished. Her ankles emerged from their little sarcophagi through circular holes that rubbed her skin raw as she wore them. Like Hindu or Christian ascetics mortifying their flesh with metal collars or shackles. But what was she punishing herself for? A mystery.

The wooden boxes on the frail woman's feet turned out to have something to do with urban poverty or the rain forest, but as Johnson was on his third Knob Creek, the difference between the two causes had become immaterial to him. He just knew to nod at whatever she said and be sure to get her number. Rain forests or poor yobbos, it was all the same to him.

Then something even more curious happened. He overheard two men holding forth to a half circle of admirers. The word "Jews" said with a particular twist, veiled condescension. He knew the men, and he listened as each academic trumpeted his pedigree. One from the Kennedy School of Government at Harvard, a Belfer Professor of International Affairs. The other academic was from the Institute for Policy Studies, a Wendell Harrison Professor of Political Science at Chicago.

Professors Deerwood and Lenzheimer had recently worked together on a foreign policy white paper of some note, the thrust being that U.S. foreign policy was twisted on the fingers of . . . well, *you know*. What struck Johnson was the use of the phrase "the Jewish question"—those exact words, with an academic's sneer, bringing him up short.

Knowing he was too tight to join the magic circle of admirers he listened from afar until Professor Deerwood said, "Look at the numbers, 1.5 billion Muslims, 5 million Jews in the Holy Land—yet we dance along to their every whim."

Johnson felt a surge of anger crawl up into his throat. Yes, he could admit, he was a little dishonest, a little greedy, and even a little corrupt. Add to that a lush, a womanizer, and three times divorced. You could even throw in manipulative and selfish for good measure.

But he could honestly hate a thing as well as any saint or sinner. And the thing he reviled more than any other thing—honest to God—were Jew-haters. Jew-haters in every form and guise, from the toothless rube to the well-heeled WASP. But of all the Jew-haters he despised—more than any neo-Nazi skinhead—were the pointy-headed intellectuals, the sophisticated, sleight-of-hand Jew-haters, the let's-adopt-the-Saudi-peace-plan, and gosh-aren't-these-people-awfully-pushy-and-greedy-for-such-a-little-country? Jew-haters. The covert Jew-haters, covering their slimy tracks with position papers for think tanks and "peace" conferences in Belgium. "Look at the numbers, 1.5 billion Muslims, 5 million Jews." Yeah. That said it all. *Never again?*

Johnson decided to join the circle, spouting a bit of poetry at them, knowing the chances of making an ass out of himself ranged from quite high to near certain. He felt a good stab of regret coming on for later, but what he had to say came out coherently enough:

"As the journalist and good Commie William Norman Ewer said back in the 19th century,

'How odd of God

To Choose

The Jews.'"

He got a few nervous smiles. No one was quite sure where he was going with this. They didn't know the reference to Ewer-The-Obscure. At least Johnson had broken their moment. And so out of sheer spite he kicked the shards across the room:

"But many feel Norman Ewer lost the poetry battle to Cecil Browne, who replied,

'But not so odd

As those who choose

A Jewish God

But spurn the Jews.'"

This got a general chuckle, and suddenly, drunk as he was, Johnson realized that not one person in this circle, including himself, believed in God at all. That the idea was as foreign to them as a plague of frogs falling from the sky. It wasn't piety they despised, but sheer pluck. And the power of belief. Any race that had survived five thousand years was an insult. Any race that survived five thousand years and *thrived*—after being scattered to the four winds by Caesar, raped by Cossacks, and nearly liquidated by Germans—was to be reviled. Such history shattered that myth called "equality of man," and anything that threatened the common safety of common failure was to be repelled at all costs. Along with the God Who chose them. What was despicable wasn't that the Jews had made the ten common rules for living in a civilized society, but that they had the audacity to still expect the world to adhere to them.

One professor attempted to bring the conversation back along the lines he intended. "It's not like Jews have a monopoly on suffering, but they play it like a violin at Dachau, and the world is tired of that concerto—"

Johnson knew full well that might have been the fellow's drink talking, but he had an urge to toss the remainder of his Knob Creek at that filthy mouth. He raised his glass—

But a hand restrained him, drawing him away from the circle. He was looking into a pair of very sober gray eyes. A strong and handsome fellow, mid-thirties, not the type to be at this kind of party at all. Such a Boy Scout. Former military? And something else about the man—Johnson glimpsed the sharp edge of a human dagger. A ruthlessness narrowed the corners of his eyes. The kind of man who could take a punch and give one back, stick an ice pick in your eye just to leave it there.

"Orwell said, 'Only an intellectual could say something so stupid.'"

And that made Johnson smile. He looked into the tough gray eyes, then down at his half-finished drink. "You're right. And maybe I'm too tight to suffer intellectuals gladly tonight. Let me know who wins."

And with that he went home to Brooklyn.

Nobody missed him.

But that very next morning after the party, Johnson discovered who won. Nobody. Instead, *everyone lost*. He awoke on the living room couch about 9:30 with the fish hook of a moderate hangover under one eye, still wearing his suit jacket but no pants, and the phone ringing in his ear. He picked it up.

"Look out the window, Mr. Johnson."

"Who the hell is this?" But he went to the window anyway. His Brooklyn Heights condo faced straight across the East River near the Brooklyn Bridge, and there he saw what everyone saw that morning. World Trade Tower One was burning, and there came another plane.

At first he couldn't grasp what he was seeing. "Who the *hell* is this?" Then, "What the . . . ?" into the phone, having no idea who he was talking to, and not caring as he watched the second jetliner from a mile away sail silently into the side of Tower Two. A gleaming missile sailing purposefully into a building, almost floating on its irrevocable glide path to hell. "What the . . . ? What?" he kept on saying, until it came back to him that he was still on the phone with the mystery caller. "Who the *hell* is this?"

"We met last night." A vague memory began to surface in his brain: Yeah, the voice with the sober gray eyes. But that meant nothing. Not now.

He hung up, tossing the telephone onto the couch, transfixed by the shimmering towers—so otherworldly even on a normal day, now with plumes of smoke pouring into the unbelievable blue of that September sky.

Then he remembered yet another nagging thought—his life a long, haphazard habit of forgetting and regretting. Giselle. She worked at Salomon Smith Barney right beside the towers. The ice pick under his eye went from crappy hangover to mortal wound, slid sideways, and then dipped toward his heart. Fear. He dialed her cell. No signal. Work number? In his Blackberry. Where was his Blackberry?

And then the plume of smoke across the river widened and began to spread downward, and the whole building cascaded toward the ground in a grainy gray umbrella of smithereens, and nothing was left but a lighter colored smoke, air and empty space. The Tower was *gone*. Gone?

Where was Giselle?

The coffee pot was plugged in, the way Giselle always left it for him when she went to work. Where the hell was the damn Blackberry? He got down on his knees and tore at the sagging cushions of the couch. The stupid thing was lodged down a crack. He searched for G and dialed the work number. Busy signal. Bizzy-bizzy-bizzy.

He didn't know what to do.

One last hope. Maybe she didn't go to work today. Maybe she was still in bed. He stumbled to her room. Of course, he let her live with him. What father wouldn't? Monstrous New York rents, taxes, food, taxis—besides loving to see her every day. He yanked her bedroom door open, desperate to see the lump in bed, the tousled head. He almost shouted, *Giselle!* But the G died on his lips.

An empty unmade bed, no Giselle. In his frightful state he pawed the covers. No Giselle. He knocked on the bathroom door, no answer, then yanked it open. The empty tub and toilet sneered at him.

Out the apartment window the Single Tower was barely visible through the smoke and seemed to be beginning to tilt. The hallway quiet and still, but the chaos across the river ran riot in his mind, the screams, the sirens, the sinister patter of falling debris. He started to weep. Tears of pure bourbon coming, the whole of last night running from his head. Nostrils, eyes, from his slobbering mouth. He threw the phone on the couch, disconnecting it. He'd have to go find her. Walk across the Brooklyn Bridge. Now. He clutched his slept-in suit jacket, stared down at his boxers. Find your pants. Your pants.

The sound of the key in the door made his heart stop, and for a brief moment he didn't grasp its significance. The door opened, and relief flooded through him. Giselle padded into the room in her pajamas, carrying a laundry basket with a *Vogue* magazine stuffed under her arm: "I didn't feel well, but couldn't sleep. I was downstairs in the laundry room. I'm going back to bed." She passed her hand across her tummy clearly uncomfortable. Her hair matted in a sleepy-head rat's nest. "Can you call Mitch at the office for me?" She was in her poodle jammies, elegant women walking high-nosed poodles. They always made him laugh. Now it made him cry again.

"Dad, what's wrong?"

He led her to the window, to the terrible sight. They stood there, and she clung to his shoulder, and he let her cling. Then wrapped his arms about her and desperately pressed her to him with every fiber of his being. The second Tower collapsed into itself, and a great plume stood in its stead, reaching to the sky.

"I don't understand." Giselle said.

Johnson's relief gave way to horror again. Johnson realized there might not be an office to telephone anymore. And something worse. No more Mitch. God, he'd never even met the man. Just heard the gracious timbre of his voice, the occasional work-related call, asking kindly for Giselle. He really seemed to like his daughter. What else did he know about him? Lived in Jersey. Married. Wife with early signs of Parkinson's.

The clean white toilet in his bathroom beckoned him, and he offered up his guts to the holy sewers of New York. But nothing came, a poor offering, just retching and a little blood.

After a while he caught his breath, and the bathroom mirror gazed at him. That magnificent specimen of British-American manhood: the sodden eyes, the belly pouch, the stringy legs of a fifty-year-old who sat on his ass too long, the rumpled but expensive Brooks Brothers' suit jacket and once-starched white shirt. He wiped his mouth on the sleeve. Let the dry cleaners have it. Then he remembered: he used the same one as Giselle, Fleur de Lys French Dry Cleaners on Liberty Street right by Tower Two.

He should really take a shower and get dressed—get it together. People would be trying to reach him. When he emptied his pockets and tossed his apartment keys on the washbasin shelf, a business card came out with them. Ah, yes, the Boy Scout with the sober gray eyes:

Banquo & Duncan
Robert Wallets, Vice President
30 Rockefeller Plaza

After the shower, a shave, and three aspirin, he came out of the bathroom in his robe and slippers. The TV droned. Giselle was standing at the window looking at the blotted city. Without turning she spoke to the window.

"Why did they do this? *Why?*"

He didn't trust himself to speak out loud. The answer too ugly for words. Then they did what so many other people did that day. They watched it up close. They watched it on the news.

The rest of the day proceeded in a blur. The best thing about it—besides Giselle feeling under the weather—the hangover vanished before noon. Jo von H, chipper and crystalline as always, finally reached him. The woman's voice dripped honey.

"I want 750 words from you for the website. 'Why We Are So Hate-able.'"

"All right. Tell me again, Jo. Why *are* we so hate-able?"

"Peter," she replied with a touch of impatience in her voice. He knew that tone from way back, as though speaking to a simpleton. "The rampant commercialism. Santa Claus before Halloween. The arrogance and self-delusional imperialism. Teeth-whitening for the middle class. Disposable diapers manufactured on the burnt ruins of rain forests. The parasitic hegemony masked as do-goodism. You've written it a hundred times, and the chickens have come home to roost. We practically learned it from you," her voice rising, angry at the end.

He felt very quiet inside. Everything had changed. Couldn't she see that? God, if she'd only ask him to write something *new*. Fat chance.

"Don't go all flag-wavy on me, Peter," she continued. "And listen carefully . . . I *want* this piece from you. And I want it posted before the day is out."

He paused and thought, what Jo von H wants, Jo von H gets. . . .

"I'm on it."

His practiced fingers found the laptop keys; while a knot grew in his stomach, growing worse all day as he watched replays of people flinging themselves out of buildings on TV. Soon he'd be watching firefighters pulling body parts, a leg, a femur out of dusty rubble. Still, he typed on, *what Jo von H wants . . .*

Evening came, and the glow outside the window cast light inside the apartment; an island of smoke drifted over Brooklyn. Giselle and he hadn't moved from the couch all day. They'd ordered Indian takeout, but for some reason everything tasted sandy, bitter. The Styrofoam platters lay on the coffee table, lamb vindaloo growing cold. Johnson felt claustrophobic and went to the window and with a sudden impulse opened it; ugly streaks lashed the glass. He wanted to feel what the air was like.

"Dad, don't open it," Giselle warned him. "I can smell the outside from here already."

And indeed, it did smell, a sour reek. The odor of gas and metals and chemicals and probably something worse.

What people smelled like when you cooked them. Mutton.

He was going to close the window as Giselle wanted—when he stopped. The sill, the *outside* sill. He looked closer and closer and closer, leaning over. It looked like a piece of . . . He didn't know what it looked like. And then it hit him—it was a finger. A woman's finger with a manicured fingernail and a wedding ring attached. How? *Fallen* from the sky?

Without thinking he flicked the thing from the sill with a jerk of his hand, and it fell off into invisible depths. *No!* That was the absolute *wrong* thing to do. He should have taken it. He should have gotten a plastic ziplock baggie from the kitchen. My God, somebody would want to know! He grabbed the phone again, dialed 911 to tell them there was *a finger on my sill, on the sidewalk, below the window,* a finger in the bushes on Hicks Street between Montague and Fuck Me Street! A finger. But of course 911 was busy-busy-busy, and who was going to rush out for a reported finger? Was he crazy?

Johnson slowly slid the window shut.

He was going to scream, not a human word, but some primal howl without any conscious thought. Yes, he was going to scream right now, but he could feel the finger that belonged to that poor woman, the burnt finger going down his throat, going down his throat making him gag and bring up vindaloo.

<hr />

Azadi Grand Hotel, Tehran.

Nothing grand about it. A cramped couple of rooms with a view.

The call of the dawn muezzin out the slightly open window drifted across the city. *Somewhere in this country someone was always praying.* He should have closed the stupid thing and let the air conditioning do its work. He had fallen asleep with his clothes on again, his clothes damp from his sweat. A soft knock came to the suite door. Room service. Breakfast. The usual, surely. Yogurt, fresh figs. Black coffee. Even sober, the thought of eating anything right now wasn't enticing. Maybe if he closed the window, took a shower, let the air-conditioning do its work, he might get his appetite back.

The near-empty bottle on the table looked like he'd made a significant dent in the Tanqueray, but he knew the truth. If they thought
he'd drunk himself stupid, all the better. The soft, insistent knock
came again. Johnson knew he'd have to clean up good today. It was
back with Jazril the Jazz Man and maybe even the Big Mullah—
maybe this time the Big Mullah would deign to speak to him directly.
The Jazz Man, the Sheik, the Big Mullah, and finally Dr. Proton. The
object of all his desire.

"Hold on. Be right there."

CHAPTER FIVE

The Irreducible Facts of Life

Robert Wallets of Banquo & Duncan found him again in late 2002, over a year after the towers fell, after the invasion of Afghanistan but before the invasion of Iraq. Johnson was sitting on a panel at NYU law school devoted to the unpleasantness in Afghanistan and the unpleasantness still to come in Mesopotamia. It was called "Preemptive War: Crime Against Humanity or Legitimate National Interest?" Talking to a room with about a hundred snot-nosed kids. The panelists: himself as Lefty Writer, Eli Pariser as Executive Director of MoveOn.org from the Lefty netroots, Lance Evers of the Society Against War/USA as Lefty Peacenik, facing off against Bruce Meyer from The Patriot Project (simply Pee-Pee to its detractors) as Fascist Neo-Con Journalist. A three-to-one advantage constituted fair-and-balanced NYU Law–style. Whenever Meyer talked, a kid stood up and shouted some asinine question, "Can you *prove* there weren't controlled explosions in the Second Tower?" prompting derisive cheers and hisses aimed at Meyer, until the moderator settled things down enough for the discussion to keep going. Meyer was getting hot, too hot for his own good, and sputtering, "Look, where you people *live*. They want to kill *you*. If they didn't already kill you or someone you love, it wasn't for lack of trying. And they're going to try again, don't you get it?" Unbidden, Giselle standing in the hallway in her pajamas at the door that morning came back to Johnson, and he felt a twinge of horror, then the relief all over again. "I forgot to text Mitch at the office. Can you call?" Correction, Mitch's *widow*. Showing signs of Parkinson's.

Boos from the audience: "Fuck *yoo!*" "Shut up!" "Nazi!" And Johnson felt that surge headed up his throat again as he had on the night of Jo von H's party listening to the two pointy-headed profs nattering on about the Jews. "The numbers . . . 5 million Jews—yet we dance along to their every whim." And here were three more pointy-heads—himself included—dancing along to the ugly faces in the crowd slathering spittle toward the stage. He found himself staring at his hands, then at his clean manicured fingernails. Fingers . . . that did it.

He stood up and addressed the room without the mike, his voice shaking, "Please, please just sit down and listen. Listen. Mr. Meyer has come here, and he has a right to be heard. Surely you understand this?" He stumbled for a moment, uncharacteristically. Then noticed the faces in the crowd. No, they didn't think Mr. Fascist Neo-Con Journalist had a right to be heard. The faces thought the only right he possessed was to take a good thrashing. Take it and like it. But Johnson wouldn't stop. "Look, you don't have to be a fan of this administration or The Patriot Project to acknowledge there are Muslim fanatics, millions of them, both in foreign countries and here in the West, who want you dead. I'd have thought a couple of buildings burned off the face of the earth not too far from here would have made this point to any honest person's satisfaction. And if you can't acknowledge this simple fact, then you are an intellectual coward of the first order." With that he sat down, feeling the flush on his face.

A hush fell over the room. Then the rumbles from the crowd began again. Eli Pariser of MoveOn leaned toward him and whispered in Johnson's ear, brow knit and lips curling downward, "Whose side are you on, Peter?"

Meyer leaned over at another point, looking puzzled, "Thanks, but why don't you ever write that?" Johnson just shrugged; it was the best he could do.

At the end, everyone avoided him. Usually he was mobbed after such events, but not this time. He felt embarrassed and so eager to get out of there, he didn't even bother to chat up the cute brunette with the shiny coal-black eyes in the second row. He walked down the stairs, avoiding the crowded elevator—no point in talking to *these* students—and failed to notice the guy from Jo von H's party at his elbow. The man who had given him his business card that fateful September 10.

⸗∞⸗

Fact was—that fellow Meyer had a point—why *didn't* he write that way? Was he afraid of losing his perch at *The Crusader*? That his ex-wife boss would dump him again? That he'd lose his audience? He'd chosen his tin drum, beating it morning, noon, and night—finally reaching the point where he could write or say anything he wanted.

At the NYU building entrance, Meyer caught up with him, then invited Johnson for a drink, and they headed to a neighborhood Irish dive. "I've been following your stuff," Meyer told him.

He should have felt flattered, but he didn't.

He'd been writing his pickled little heart out, in fluid 80-proof prose. Damning himself at every click of the keys. He knew what *The Crusader* needed to feed the beast: "Why They Hate Us"; "Why They Hate Us More"; "Why There's Nothing Else to Do but Hate Us"; "If You *Don't* Hate Us, What's Wrong with You?"—anything Jo von H wanted. She had rewarded him handsomely, giving him the use of one of her cars and drivers. Not that he needed much more positive reinforcement. The TV shows kept lapping it up. Dan Rather over at CBS offered him a guest commentator spot, but he decided to keep his independence—better to be able to provoke on any network, any time. He'd bypassed *The Crusader*'s little publishing imprint, left his agent of eighteen years, found a new agent, and taken $500,000 for a two-book deal with a big house. So hell yeah, he took the first half of his advance, spent the whole wad, and hadn't written line one. Seizing every opportunity to rail against the sins of his adopted hateful country for the price of a drink at any party, in any apartment overlooking Central Park with floor-to-ceiling windows.

In the dark, empty, sticky-floored bar, he and Meyer fell into a deep discussion of the war, ignoring a bar-top video game flickering luridly at the end of the bar—the game, *Poke' Her*, your hand of cards dealt by a cute showgirl in a black brassiere and not much else. A finely crafted stained-glass FDNY 9/11 commemoration sat on a shelf by the hard liquor. Poker, girls, booze, and dead firemen.

Right, We'll Never Forget. Sure.

Johnson watched the barmaid make each of his black-and-tans, pouring the Guinness over an upside-down spoon—so thick, so milky, and seemingly miraculously floating on top of the Bass Pale Ale. He couldn't help drawing doodles with his pinky in the top of the Guinness foam, a habit of his for as long as he'd been drinking them.

They talked point by point and pint by pint: about the veil, the Saudis, the death of Arab pan-nationalism, Taliban teenage head-choppers, the insane cult of suicide bombings in Palestine. By 2 AM, they couldn't agree on much, except this: that the Islamo-Nazis belonged on the short list of Johnson's honest-to-God enemies.

Not a radical thought, but one Johnson had never let climb entirely to the surface of his mind. So obvious. So undeniable. Maybe he'd never wanted to deal with the regret over everything he'd done through the years to turn attention away from these honest-to-God bastards. Men who would do anything. Cut off people's heads on video. Blow up a chunk of Manhattan, scattering human remains into neighborhoods miles away. Johnson left the Irish dive sensing how much he had given away to his companion. An intellectual fault line had shifted under-ground somewhere in his mental world, and he headed home feeling he had committed some ill-defined indiscretion. A single honest thought that hurt.

As the wee hours began to get bigger, the pints of black-and-tan had their way with him. Staggering in the street before his apartment door, he fumbled with his keys. Somehow there were too many keys on the ring, and he couldn't decide which one fit. That's why he didn't notice when a pack of kids in hooded sweatshirts scoped him out to play a favorite New York game: roll-the-drunk. What these kids might have known about Paki weasels or Middle Eastern suicide cults was anybody's guess. Not much likely. What they did know were the rules of the street, and in fifteen short seconds Johnson was surrounded at his doorstep, his trousers belt sliced with a knife, his pockets ripped, and his billfold gone. The sound of their running steps echoed off the buildings.

A nearby taxicab parked by the curb turned on its headlights, and the window rolled down.

"Mr. Johnson?" He turned and tried to focus on the man inside, holding up his pants with one hand. He squinted, puzzled. "We met at a Josephine von Hildebrand affair," the man said. Johnson's memory wasn't at its sharpest. "I kept you from slugging some professors." A light bulb in Johnson's head flickered, but that's all.

"Then called the next morning. About a year ago."

The bulb flashed to life, a low forty watts.

"Ahhh," Johnson said. "Yes, yes. You're the guy who called me on 9/11. Robert Wallets. Vice President. We meet again. I lost your card."

"I've got another." The assured voice of the man named Wallets annoyed him in all its quiet self-control. "Why don't you hop in, Peter? Let's see if we can recover your plastic before it goes radioactive."

Johnson climbed in back, and suddenly Wallets' voice wasn't so quiet. "They went that way," he barked at the cab driver. "Let's get on it."

"Are we chasing them?" Johnson asked to the crew-cut back of Wallets' head, slouching in his seat to get his pants hitched up.

Wallets looked back at him with a curl of a knowing smile. "The predators have become the prey. Any objections?"

"I really, that's . . . it's not necessary," Johnson fumbled out. But it was the smile that scared him.

Wallets forgot him and talked to the driver in a quieter voice. "Take a right here. They usually don't run any more than a block or two before strolling again, congratulating themselves on finding an easy—" He never finished.

Three hooded figures walked together in a clump on the sidewalk to their right, waving their arms and laughing. "And here they are," Wallets said. "Take it slow."

The cab doused its headlights and crawled to a halt about thirty feet behind the lads. The cab door unlatched, and Wallets eased himself out onto the sidewalk like a cat, leaving the door open so it wouldn't slam. And what Johnson saw then was everything he'd ever imagined a human weapon might be. Even in the dark. In fact the dark seemed like Wallets' friend. Flitting quietly from shadow to shadow, in six steps he stood right behind the kids. One of them sensed something coming up behind, glancing over his shoulder, too late, "Oh, snap!"

Wallets dropped Snappy with a punch in the kidneys. It must have been a punch, because Johnson heard a *woof*, and the kid just folded, falling to his knees. Then started the hard business of trying to breathe. The second Snappy turned, surprised, his mouth agape. Wallets hit him next.

So fast, Johnson missed the punch, but what he did hear was a kind of *crack*. And two white teeth skittered across the pavement. The hood held his face, crying now and huddled beside the street lamp. "Oh man, oh man . . ." was all he said.

Snappy Number Three just stood there, hands at his sides, waiting to die. There was nowhere to go. It was as if he'd been corralled by the sheer force of Wallets' will. Even if he was packing heat, he didn't have the nuts to pull it. Wallets frisked him with practiced hands and led him gently back to the car where the driver rolled down Johnson's window. Johnson peered at his assailant, a sixteen-year-old black kid with fear in his eyes. Snappy One was still working on that breathing thing. Snappy Two, still huddled by the lamppost, covered his mouth as blood seeped between the fingers and looked around for his teeth. Bloody gums, but no guns.

"Apologize to Mr. Johnson," Wallets instructed the last of the Snaps. "I think you have something you want to return to him."

The hood looked at the ground. He wasn't such a bad kid, just a violent opportunist who didn't know any better. Whom nobody'd bothered to teach the golden rule or common decency, show him the straight and narrow. Now with a sudden knowledge of instant retribution. But that didn't make it any better; without looking up again the kid said, "Sorry, Mister."

Wallets looked at the others. Snappy One was breathing a little better but still couldn't stand. Snappy Two had found his teeth and put them in his shirt pocket for the ER dentist. Thinking ahead.

The kid in front of Johnson pulled a wad of credit cards out of the front pocket of his jeans, which were nearly as low-riding as Johnson's after they had cut them up. He handed the plastic cards through the window; yeah, Johnson's were there, along with a dozen others. Astonished, Johnson muttered, "Thank you. I'll see the others get back to their owners."

"Dexter got the cash," the kid said. The two other boys began to stick their fingers in their pockets, searching.

"You two, don't move," Wallets ordered. They went very still.

Then to Johnson, "You want to press charges?" A flat question. The man didn't care either way.

"Well, I . . . "

"Well, *what?* Make a decision," Wallets demanded.

"No." Johnson shook his head, ready for the whole business to be done. The other two opportunists held out their hands. Johnson's cash. Maybe fifty bucks. The cash in the kid's hand by the street lamp was smeared with blood.

Wallets measured Johnson for a moment. No, the scribbler didn't want his money back.

"You can keep the cash," Wallets said quietly. Then fished a business card out of his jacket pocket, and held it up in the street light for the kid at the car to see.

"Take it." The kid just stared with a look of fear and puzzlement, as if it might bite him. "Take it!" He reached gingerly, cautiously. Peered hard, reading.

"If you ever decide to give up smash and grab, if you ever decide to do something in life that doesn't disappoint your mothers, come see me. Call and tell the secretary where we met. She'll make an appointment." The kid didn't know what to make of all this, but the gears were working, and suddenly he knew *quite clearly* this was no bullshit.

"And wear your best Sunday go-to-meeting clothes. I work in an office."

Over eggs and bacon and toast and black coffee, Johnson glanced through the Acropolis Diner window at the cab parked outside by the curb. The coffee went right into his veins. He nodded at the Middle Eastern cabbie waiting patiently for them, before looking back at Wallets in the booth across from him.

"So you squire me home from a Jo von H party but call me the next morning. Vanish like a ghost. A year later you appear out of nowhere to rescue this damsel in distress, then take her to breakfast. So you're a full-service banker?"

Wallets glanced at him askance, then said gravely, "Actually, I'm curious whether you'd like to stand like a drunk in the street for the rest of your life holding up your pants—intellectual or otherwise—or attempt to have some effect in the real world." Johnson recognized the reference to a *New York Review of Books* essay he wrote last year, "Sartre vs. Camus: Collaborator and Freedom Fighter—Being with Nothingness?" on a biography of Sartre and one of Camus published at the same time. The line went, "Sartre held up his intellectual pants with the Gestapo's Death's Head belt buckle of approval. Camus actually fought them."

"As I recall," Wallets went on, "you gave Sartre of WWII the worst of it because his most famous work, *Being and Nothingness*, bore the official Nazi Occupation Authority's stamp of orthodoxy on the copyright page."

"He deserved it. He didn't resist." Johnson looked at his toast, growing cold, leathery.

"Funny you should mention it." Wallets gazed off along the empty stools in the diner. "Resistance is exactly what we'd like to discuss with you."

"We?" But Johnson could feel where this was headed. The big *They*. Was he being recruited? He'd read about such things in spy novels, but like something in a *Penthouse* letter, never thought it happened to real people. And now the opportunity—the call to *résistance*—appeared out of nowhere, a man in the night, a caped crusader without the cape. Now sitting across from him in a lonely diner booth at 3 AM.

Intrigued, amused, and even a little flattered, Peter Johnson agreed to meet Wallets later in the weekend. At first, in a flush of drunken ambition, Johnson insisted he could meet him the next day. Wallets said they'd make it Sunday, 10 AM, at his office in Rockefeller Center. Which was fortuitous—because after his dive into the stout earlier in the night, the next day Johnson could barely rouse himself to open his apartment door and pick up the *Times* sitting in the hallway.

Walking into the empty lobby of 30 Rock, Johnson already didn't like this place, or these people. The echoing imperial lobby, the huge twisted torsos in the Diego Rivera murals, made him feel very small. Who in Manhattan besides custodial staff and lackeys worked at 10 AM on a Sunday? So he thought he was doing well to have on dark trousers and a dress shirt with no tie.

He immediately felt underdressed and unprepared. When he met Banquo for the first time, the man looked as if he had already come from making a PowerPoint presentation at Bank of America—dark blue, pin-striped, cuff-linked, and polished to a precise, spare formality. He sat at the end of a long conference table and neither offered his hand nor rose to greet him, seemingly absorbed in a thin file in front of him, with a capped fountain pen sitting nearby. He looked at Johnson over tortoiseshell granny glasses.

"Thank you for coming."

And with no further pleasantries Johnson took a chair, then glanced at Wallets. The fellow was dressed likewise, in a dark charcoal gray, giving him a sharp prosecutorial edge, but said nothing, content, it seemed, to let the older man take charge.

"Mr. Johnson, if you are going to be any use to us, it's best if we come to some mutual understanding. And such understandings are best when stipulated up front. Your presence here indicates you wish to be of use. We wish it also." Banquo cleared his throat once. "Very well. Let us understand each other."

And for the next few minutes the older man gravely explained how things would go:

"You have to keep writing, no matter what. And you are going to have to fulfill that book contract. The publishing house has been nice to you so far, but the cancellation of your contract for," Banquo looked down his reading glasses, glanced at a paper on his desk, and magisterially quoted from it, "ah-hem, 'an untitled work of nonfiction,' is around the corner. And Banquo & Duncan will not allow your journalistic credibility to be compromised—at least not any more than you've compromised it already."

"You afraid I'm a dead-beat?" Johnson snorted. "What—have you been reading my agent's emails?"

Banquo pointedly didn't answer. He turned from Johnson, addressing his next remarks to Wallets. "Explain to Mr. Johnson the facts of life."

And the irreducible facts of life were pretty simple. He would come into their offices to meet with them whenever requested. He'd keep his literary bona fides impeccable, do everything he promised to do. Hurt the war effort every chance he could. Keep his drinking within reasonable bounds so he wasn't a target for punks. And more importantly make himself available to any graft that might come his way. This last bit to endear him to those whose only measure of mankind was their insatiable potential for corruption. The unsolvable riddle of men:

If you couldn't be bought, you weren't worth having. And couldn't be trusted.

Actually, he wasn't anywhere close to sure he "wished to be of use." He made no commitments, not in his own mind at least. Hell, conversations were harmless, no? A little chitchat about how he could help the "resistance"? It could make a piece: "Why They *Should* Hate Us: The Inside Story from a Would-Be CIA Operative." Frankly, he was curious, and though he didn't want to admit it, he also liked the taste of betrayal, of double-crossing his ideological soul mates whose entire intellectual construct was a kind of national betrayal. How twisted was that?

Anyway, he could back out at any time. Just as he told himself many times, back when he was married, in the wee hours of a bar crawl with some lonely, available, easy-to-amuse woman ready to be plucked: The first drink never meant anything. *Just one drink—of course he was going to be faithful.* Two drinks? *She seemed to be having a good time.* The third?

A very good time. The fourth drink—*still telling himself it was nothing,* as she snuggled her ass up to him at the bar; then back at her flat . . .

Only to wake up with a stranger, having of course cheated on his wife, regrets buzzing around his head, getting entangled in the cobwebs of his hangover. Could this be like that? Minus the drinking and the woman? And except that this time he really could, and would, stop? That's what Johnson told himself.

While another part of him secretly loved being worth having. The only question: What would it take to get there?

The answer: more than he ever imagined.

Years and years of talk. Just talk. The calm and sober voice of Wallets poked and prodded him at every turn. And it seemed to fill his head with cinders; even in his dreams, the unrelenting voice binding him to the chair in that dreadful office one rope at a time, making him squirm. Beginning with every squalid detail of his life:

"Peter Johnson. Born 1955, Wickham, England. Father, Colonel in the 8ᵗʰ Light Infantry, ret. Mother, librarian, Wickham Public Library. Both deceased. Graduated Magdalen College, Oxford, 1977, taking a first in modern European history. Married Josephine von Hildebrand 1976, amicable divorce 1978. No children. Immediately took a job with the *Guardian* newspaper. Then *Newsweek*, immigrating to the United States 1980. Married again, Françoise Ducat, amicable divorce 1987," Wallets coughed, quietly clearing his throat, "more or less. Daughter Giselle, offspring of your second wife Ms. Ducat—now living in Paris. Third wife, Elizabeth Richards, forty-five, assistant curator for the ancient Middle East, Metropolitan Museum of Art, NYC. Amicable divorce in—"

"All true as it goes," Johnson interrupted.

"No one asked you a question, Mr. Johnson. Would you like to tell me something that isn't 'true as it goes'?"

Johnson shut his trap. Wallets wanted to impress on him, if you have nothing to say, don't say it. Harder to learn than you'd think.

"Reported on the first Iraq Gulf War for *Newsweek*, was assigned to the Third Infantry Division—Rock of the Marne, of course— during Operation Iraqi Freedom for *The Crusader* magazine. Managed to file viciously antiwar pieces about the most popular American military engagement since World War II. Wrote 'The Myth of the "Rape" of Kuwait,' expanded into a small book. *Crusader* cover piece, 'Dresden for Our Times: Fear and Loathing on the Highway of Death,' won a National Magazine Award." He paused, then sarcastically, "Nice work, Peter."

This time he kept his tongue between his teeth.

Not only did they play *This Is Your Life*, but they showed him the world from many new angles. Over the course of time the men at Banquo & Duncan gave him a tutorial on matters related to the Middle East worthy of a PhD. It might have been easier to memorize Jane's *Defense Weekly*'s rundown for every country in the region, given the military details they poured into his ear. The number of divisions, the chain-of-command, the weaponry, where purchased, and even the uniforms—with a special emphasis on Iran. He could have earned a minor degree in physics and engineering, in learning how a nuclear reaction worked and how a bomb was built. By the end, he could rattle off the specifications of the Iranian reactor at Bushar. They marinated him in Middle Eastern culture, which tribes were which and the social niceties that made them go—an overflowing tea cup meant you were welcome; if not filled to the brim, not so much. The details of Sharia law, down to how it mandated that you respond to a sneeze. *Yarhamukallah!* May God bestow His Mercy on You.

He learned to listen—and at the same time absorbed almost word for word Banquo's discourse. The man always had a telling little detail or an appropriate quotation. "Did you know King Farouk in Egypt owned two hundred red cars—and banned anyone else from owning a red car in the country?" "When the Saudis first did a census and found out just how sparsely populated the country was, they immediately doubled the figure. A touching belief in the power of the convenient lie." When they first discussed the Iranian revolution, Banquo urged him, "Always remember your Orwell, Peter: *One does not establish the dictatorship in*

*order to safeguard the revolution; one makes the revolution in order to estab-
lish the dictatorship.*" And on and on.

Through it all Johnson grew truly weary of the conference room. It
amazed him how much you could hate a simple room in a stupid high-
rise office building in stupid Manhattan. It was like being in the principal's office after school, only worse. And he'd learned to despise
Banquo's factotum for the West Point, Parris Island, super-trained,
smart asshole jarhead he was. Soldier boy had smooth-talked the
soused scribbler that night in the diner. Brought him into the fraternity. But now he had him by the scruff of the neck. Every day was
pledge night, the hazing going on for years. And Johnson was sick of
the paddle.

Three sessions a week after work, then one more on Saturday morn-
ings at Wallets' club, The New York Athletic Club. Another thing Wallets taught him—how to behave. Friday nights, no longer a debauch, as
he had an appointment at the club in the morning. Five laps in the pool,
then ten, then twenty. He built up slowly. Oddly, the perfect place to
talk, as this was the Bankers' and Brokers' Saturday morning hangover
cure: The Big Apple's manly swells lay semi-naked about the poolside in
lounge chairs, pots of coffee or pitchers of orange juice at their elbows,
with towels about their sodden carcasses and over their heads—dead to
the world. The high marble atrium softly echoed with their grumbles
and moans, but mostly snoring. Later, the poor dears would retire to the
steam room to sweat out the remnants of Friday night, but not before
Johnson and his host had gone over the week's particulars in every
detail. When the first sot sadly shuffled through the steam room door
at the stroke of ten, Wallets and Johnson got up to leave.

Over time, Johnson could swim thirty laps, had become somewhat
richer, and had published a lot of inflammatory copy against the Catastrophe of Iraq. The Second Gulf War was very good to him and *The
Crusader*, whose circulation spiked so high that even Jo von H's busi-
ness-savvy late hubby might have considered it a worthy investment.
Johnson reported exclusively on the men and women of the Iraq prison
scandal, "Dumb and Infamous: Guards of Abu Ghraib." And was asked
to leave his embedded position with the 26th Marine Expeditionary

Unit after dubiously reporting the Tikrit Massacre of ten men, women, and children in the Salah ad Din Province by Marines of that unit. The controversy only gave him more publicity and enhanced his standing on the yowling Left.

———

Yet another session around the dismal conference table.

"All right, Peter, let's start again." Wallets' flat, self-assured tone wouldn't let him go. A steady drip-drip-drip. "A little ancient history of the personal kind. Can we go over it one more time?" Johnson rolled his eyes in exasperation.

Sitting quietly a few feet away, Banquo glanced up from the Johnson file, nearly three inches thick and growing. A withering stare that never failed to chill him. The message: *behave yourself.* In this session Wallets was playing the role of the erudite, infinitely polite grand inquisitor, going over ground they had covered again and again.

Wallets went on:

"During the 1990s, extensive reporting on the ravages of sanctions in Iraq, and a *Foreign Affairs* piece, 'The Dual Folly of Dual Containment: The Case for Engaging Iraq and Iran.' After Clinton's Operation Desert Fox in 1998, your private account in the Cantonal Bank of Switzerland received a payment in the amount of $75,000, in Swiss francs. What did you do with this money?"

"This *again?*" He squirmed in his seat. "I told you I pissed it away."

"No, don't lie. That's *not* what you did with the money. Stop confusing reality with the kind of tall tales you tell yourself after you've had three too many."

Johnson shifted in his seat and said, "All right. It went to Giselle's college bills. And as I've said before, it seemed to be the going rate for someone of my particular qualifications. I wrote and was widely read. Let's call it a 'thank you' paid in advance."

"No one had to ensure your loyalty?" Wallets asked.

"I would have done it for free. Like Mirabeau said, 'I am paid, but not bought.'"

"Who contacted you first? And where?"

"Late 1998. At a cocktail party at a private residence in Westchester County, New York. A Maharaja's estate. Then we all were ferried down in limos to a United Nations dinner at the Waldorf-Astoria for an African children's fund, called *Hands for Peace*. They build schools, give vaccinations, adopt and foster children out of war zones. A perfectly legitimate charity. The man's name was Breuer, a Dutch national with Dutch Shell, attached to that guy Brown's office at the United Nations. But with a very vague-sounding job description. I remember his business card: Jan Breuer, United Nations Office of Oil Producing Countries— North American Relations."

"Mark Malloch Brown, the number two man in Boutros-Boutros Ghali's/Kofi Annan's New York office?"

"That's right. But Breuer isn't with their office any more. Back to Dutch Shell. The first contact was merely to glad-hand me. It turned out we were both in Belgium three weeks later. I was covering The Hague and Breuer was on his way to Saudi Arabia, via the UAE and thence to Indonesia. He asked me if I'd care to relax in Dubai, on his nickel."

"So you went?"

"And partied like it was 1999." Johnson looked to see if either was amused. No.

Wallets kept on: "Between 1999 and 2002, while several millions of Breuer's money went into the Cantonal Bank of Zurich from which you took a measly cut, you wrote articles denigrating the United States containment effort against Saddam."

"Correct."

"If you were to guess at Jan Breuer's secondary motive for contacting you, what would it be?"

"You want me to guess?"

"That's what I asked. Would a man of your 'particular qualifications' have anything to offer besides the kind of press they want?"

Johnson looked across the wide conference table. He couldn't be sure what Wallets was driving at.

"Well, if I had to guess, I'd say giving me a $75,000 bribe I didn't really need was his way of drawing me closer to Mama's teat. You see, they get all the glowing press they want; they don't need me just for that. My buddy at *Newsweek* writes this crap all the time, and no one pays him . . . "

Johnson noticed Banquo and Wallets' eyes locking, and Johnson began to wonder about the provenance of his *Newsweek* buddy's new Jaguar. "But I *am* an honest John Q Citizen, and that's valuable in and of itself. Because getting money from point A to point B is slightly more difficult than most people realize. Say you have a group of men in a London suburb who want to accomplish certain tasks. This requires money. But how do you get it to them? I think Jan Breuer had the notion this drunken scribbler Peter Johnson might eventually do some banking for him and some of his closest friends. But that raises the stakes considerably. A bribe can hurt my reputation and get me a letter from the IRS. So what. But transferring funds from Saudi Arabia to Indonesia on its way to Amsterdam or Wycombe, that could get you jail. Or dead."

The cool, sober eyes of Wallets seemed hooded for a moment, and he nodded silently, seemingly pleased with the answer. Silence fell around the table. And suddenly Johnson sensed all their talk had finally come to an end. Confirmed a moment later when Banquo closed the cover on his file with a soft slap, and Wallets calmly asked:

"What are your plans for the next two weeks? Whatever they are, you'll have to change them. We've been together six years creating your legend, going over your pedigree. It's time you learned some fieldwork."

"I'm fifty, for crying out loud—"

Wallets held up a stern hand. Then sarcastically, "We never mention a *lady's* age." He glanced at his watch. "I'd say that's enough for today. Thank you, Peter. You can show yourself out."

—◦◦◦—

As the skyscraper shadows darkened the streets of Manhattan, Banquo poured Wallets a large slug from the decanter of Armagnac he kept on a lower bookshelf right between *Darkness at Noon* by Arthur Koestler and *The Painted Bird* by Jerzy Kosinski.

The magisterial voice had come down a few notches. It was the truth that mattered now.

"Well, what do you think?"

Wallets looked into his Armagnac and took the first taste.

"I think I'm going to love torturing this guy to death in North Carolina for two weeks."

Banquo harrumphed. "That goes without saying. Have you decided who you're going to bring along?"

"No, not yet."

"Marjorie wrote me today. Says she's getting *fat*. And doesn't like it."

"She *wrote* you?"

"Of course, she always writes me." Banquo inhaled the fragrance. "For all its flaws, the United States Postal Service is the single best way to keep a secret. If you've learned nothing all these years with me, learn that!" The man contemplated his drink for a moment, then took a draught. "And if you've learned nothing about women, learn this. Their weight—good, bad, or indifferent—is *always* a secret." He took another deep satisfying drink.

"Now stop twiddling and answer me," he said. "What do you think? Is Johnson really with us? Can he do it?"

Wallets took his glass to the clean office window and looked out onto Fifth Avenue. So many people swooshing by who had no idea these sorts of conversations took place—let alone so close to the imperial windows of Saks Fifth Avenue. He frowned and shrugged. Murder was always a nasty business. Assassination, executive action, termination—call it what you like. But call it unpredictable.

"It's always the same, Banquo. Unless you want to hire a sniper or shoot a commercial airliner out of the sky . . . you never know."

All that time to prepare the patsy. Now the only truth: you never know.

CHAPTER SIX

The Patrician

A few hundred miles south of New York City in the Commonwealth of Virginia, the highway lights were coming on along Old Dominion Road—the broad artery that passed before the entrance to Langley Air Force Base and many other military and intelligence operations on the southern corner of the Chesapeake Bay. In a seventh-floor office nearly identical to the one in Rockefeller Center the double wooden doors were marked:

DEDCI: Deputy Executive Director Central Intelligence

The office of Trevor Andover. Nicknamed by friends and foes alike "DEADKEY," as if this were a real codename. It wasn't. His codename was a random series of letters and numbers.

Director Andover was a pale, trim man with something of a bloodless undertaker about him. The aptly named DEADKEY stared out a window at the passing suburban traffic. Behind him an ever-present plasma flat screen flickered with images. He turned from the passing evening traffic to catch the latest offering on his Eye Spy global scope. The satellite's name: Long Eye; longitude and latitude: 33° 54' N 35° 28' E; time: 15:45Z; place: LEBANON Beirut. A city square as seen from space. Caption: "Hezbollah 'Celebration' South Beirut: 15:45Z."

The scene showed a hundred thousand people in a Beirut city square, a sea of yellow flags. The crowd chanted: "*Allah Akbarh*, God is Great." But what they were celebrating was anybody's guess—no elaboration on Long Eye, no explanation.

Climbing onto a stage draped over with a giant yellow cloth, Sheik Nasrallah, the Hezbollah warlord, appeared in his usual black turban, followed by his retinue and security men. Three of his retinue's turbans flashed yellow "here we are!" as they headed onto the stage, then disappeared against the bright yellow cloth. Yellow on yellow didn't show up, a glitch—the color of the marker should automatically change. He'd have to talk to Bryce about that. Another *damn* glitch. But what troubled Deputy Director Andover was the great man himself. Nasrallah's turban was *not* yellow. The carefully marked turbans were getting spread around to the *wrong* heads. And Nasrallah's headgear wasn't blinking.

Andover went back to the window, disgusted. He'd have to talk to Bryce about that too. See if they could plant a blinking turban on the great man's head. What was the bloody point if the turban didn't blink? Ahhh—the young lad himself knocked and entered without waiting.

"You wished to see me, sir?"

"Yes, Bryce, take a chair." His assistant sat. Bryce was of slender build. He wore wire-rimmed glasses under short curly hair that he tried to keep under control with a prodigious amount of mousse making the top of his head shiny and seemingly impregnable. Andover looked back out his window.

"You know, Bryce, I brought you over, and *up*, I might add, from the State Department's backwater Bureau of Intelligence and Research, the office of nobodies, because I know your father. The Attorney General of the United States. And your father, the Attorney General of the United States, told me you were a smart kid and a fast learner. Smart and fast. Smart and fast. I'd like you to be one of those things. Either will do."

Bryce sat back in his chair prepared to listen, staring calmly at Deputy Director Andover's back. The patrician always started out this way. First came the tongue-lashing, then came the lecture in which DEADKEY showed how impressively learned he was, then came the requests for action. Nothing new here.

The deputy director took a deep breath, "I've directed the Action Center to unplug our assets in Turdistan at the request of State. The striped-pants know-it-alls think they're going to referee the spoiled brats at Turtle Bay to force the turbans to lift their nuclear skirts for us. Okay, so we'll play nice for a month or two."

Bryce blinked at all the name-calling, but Trevor Andover always had an adder's tongue.

Translation: The State Department has requested any pathetic vestiges of our human intelligence personnel in Iran to lay low or withdraw to Kurdistan, while they took their bloody good time dancing a minuet at the United Nations with the president of Iran, he of the nuclear skirts, in hopes of forcing him to do something stupid, either show us his hand, castrate himself into a political eunuch, or bluff himself into a war. Any of the above would do. But it would probably turn out to be Russian roulette, with neither set of diplomats knowing which way the gun really pointed.

Andover turned and picked up a paper on his desk. "Now I've got a red flag from DOS that they've processed *three*—get that? three— Green Books, plus visas, and confirmed plane tickets for Tehran International, and sent the blank Green Books to Banquo & Duncan in New York. Photos TBS."

Translation: The Directorate of Support notified the Deputy Executive Director that they processed three Green Books, i.e., Passports— color green for the Middle East—in this case Iranian Passports, with photos TBS—To Be Supplied later by Banquo & Duncan. Therefore Banquo's gang in New York was planning on sending three of their people into Iran, on some sort of look-see, cloak-and-dagger op. Despite the Deputy Executive Director's direct orders, orders from DEADKEY stating to all departments and agencies: Stand Down.

Andover sat behind the desk, flipping the red flag notification into the wastebasket.

"I want you to go to New York. Tonight."

"All right. But why didn't we simply email the old fart and request his presence for dressing down?"

"On what pretext, pray tell?"

"Cut off his funds. He'll come down."

Andover's mild blue eyes grew exasperated. He rose from his place, went to a bookshelf, and took out a bound folder the size of the Manhattan yellow pages, then tossed it into Bryce's lap. His aide jumped as it hit his thighs.

"Young man, sitting on your prep-school pecker is the *$30 billion* Central Intelligence Agency Budget for the year 2006, several years out of date. In it you may indeed find the $5 million our Agency spends on our old friend Banquo. Actually it's only $2.5 million, as we share it with some clowns with the White House's NSA guys, or the National Intelligence Director's office. I can't remember which, and they don't even know."

What came next was a rebuke:

"Banquo's shop actually runs on about $35 million a year. He has four expert Exchange Traders working the street 24/7/365 who last year alone beat the S&P by seven points. You think our crummy $2 million is going to get him down to this office? Have a Pimm's Cup on me. That 'old fart' as you call him is actually 'old school.' He pays his way. A government operation that turns a profit every year, even in down markets—*imagine* that. Just because the director doesn't take him seriously doesn't mean he doesn't rightly take *himself* seriously."

Without a touch of embarrassment Bryce reversed himself completely. "What should I do in New York?"

"Thank you for asking. I want you to dig up the son of Banquo's old associate—Fanon, O'Bannon—"

"*O'Hanlon*. Deputy U.S. Attorney, Southern District. His *dad* was Banquo's partner?"

"I'd stick to 'associate.' And you march right into that cheap Mick's office and get us wiretaps. Brain whatever judge you have to. Home and office."

"You want it official then?"

"Clearly. I want a record."

"So you want Banquo & Duncan's phone and personal computers tapped? Do you also want surveillance to include the physical office space too?"

"No, no point. That boy scout of his sweeps the suite twice a week. But I do want roving taps on street-side conversations."

"If he's old school like you say, he's very careful."

"True enough," Andover admitted. "But everyone slips up once in a while."

Without saying farewell, Bryce rose and left DEADKEY's office. The plasma screen had frozen in pixilated fragments, how nice . . . electronic modern art. Put it in a museum. Director Andover realized he'd forgotten to tell Bryce about the turbans and the software color glitch. The screen cleared, but only to a pleasant blue field this time with the caption: *sorry, temporarily out of service . . .*

———

The United States Attorney for the Southern District of New York kept his offices at 86 Chambers Street in lower Manhattan. But Bryce didn't go there; instead he went to O'Hanlon's house in the Westchester suburb of Hastings-on-Hudson just as the commuters were leaving for the city. What used to be called a "bedroom" community was really Manhattan North, with houses starting at $600,000 up from $200,000 not ten years ago, three- and four-bedroom Tudors with a half an acre's lawn and swell backyards, on roads named Maple Street, Oak Lane, and Shady Dell. Places the lower-middle class clawed their way to from ugly Bronx streets, way back in the dark ages of the 1950s and 1960s, and thought themselves damn lucky. Now the sons and daughters of those early Westchester pioneers clung on with their fingernails, Mom taking that extra job just to pay the property taxes.

Bryce watched from the sedan's window, as O'Hanlon's family got ready for the day. First the two girls came out the front door, hovered over by the Missus and packed into the school bus with their Pokemon knapsacks. Then O'Hanlon himself, carrying a briefcase and large stainless steel coffee mug. The Missus would drive him to the Hudson branch of Metro-North in the white Ford minivan. Bryce got out of the sedan, leaving the door open.

He walked toward the couple: "Mr. O'Hanlon? Can I give you a lift?" And then drifted back toward the other side of the street again.

The Deputy U.S. Attorney looked up sharply, then at the sedan under the shade of the trees. A worried look crossed the Missus' face, but he reassured her. "It's okay." Getting her to focus on Bryce standing across the suburban street. "He's got 'DC' written all over him. Get a load of that paisley bow tie for Chrissakes. Look up the word 'Poindexter' in Webster's, and his friggin' picture's there."

The Missus laughed hard. She was a handsome woman, and you could see she liked her husband. "Hey, watch your mouth, mister. I got some soap inside," she chastised him. "Or you'll be talking to Father Meeks through the little screen."

O'Hanlon chuckled and walked across the street.

"See ya later, Angel."

Somewhere on the Henry Hudson Parkway southbound, below the George Washington Bridge's bumper-to-bumper ramp traffic, O'Hanlon was still holding Bryce's government ID. The cute picture, the Eagle Shield Badge with the red compass star. He had glanced at the Coach leather ID case when Bryce handed it to him and kept glancing at the thing without returning it. Clearly it annoyed Bryce, but he didn't own the onions to ask for his property back. And the geek had pissed O'Hanlon off. Instead of just saying what he needed from the Department of Justice, he was doing some smart-aleck routine, either just to show off or because he thought he was being intimidating. From the wheel, Bryce repeated facts he had remembered on the flight up, adding his commentary as he went:

"Patrick O'Hanlon, forty-seven, U.S. Attorney, Criminal Division, Southern District of New York. Married, Angela Sandolini, Italian, two daughters, nine and twelve. Votes Democratic—"

Then as an aside, "We have to fix that, eh?" When O'Hanlon didn't respond, the dossier went on: "Grew up on Grand Avenue in the Bronx, then Riverdale, Fordham Law, top of your class. So you moved out of the neighborhood, north a little, into your late father- and mother-in-law's split-level colonial—but Angela still gets you to buy mozzarella and homemade cannelloni on Arthur Avenue, just like her folks did, right? You both go to that little pastry shop, Il Dolce, where you used to take Angela way back when her name was Italian, when you were courting, when the two little girls were but a gleam in your—"

Which is when O'Hanlon pressed the window button and nonchalantly tossed Bryce's Very Important CIA identification card and badge in its chichi Coach leather holder out the window. The thing landed in a grimy puddle with a black splash, and the sedan was a quarter mile away before Bryce could even get his breath. The cheap Mick had given him a wedgy, and there was nothing he could do about it. Thank you, sir, may I have another?

"Sorry," O'Hanlon said softly. "It slipped out of my hand. I'm sure they'll replace the Coach case too, if you kept a receipt and promise not to lose it again." Bryce, clearly overmatched, looked over at the Irish lawyer with a mixture of loathing and now respect.

Fear.

"I'll come directly to the point, then."

<hr />

Bryce followed O'Hanlon into the lobby at 86 Chambers Street, but without his fancy CIA identification. Bryce pulled out his wallet and went digging for his Maryland driver's license. The DOJ lawyer merely said to the guard at the desk, "It's okay—he's with me. He'll sign in on the way out."

In the elevator on the way up, O'Hanlon told his guest, "If we decide to pass on your little proposal, I'm not sure I even *want* you signing in on the way out. I think I'd like you better if you were never here."

The elevator doors opened, and they both exited, through more double glass. The lawyer waved at the sharp girl at the receptionist desk, who said, "Fix your tie, Paddy." Then as they walked past open cubicle doors, O'Hanlon stuck his head into two offices in succession, saying, "Hey, got a minute? Hey, got a minute?"

The two men arrived at a door that said:

Patrick O'Hanlon
Deputy U.S. Attorney

Bryce followed the lawyer into the office, watched him throw his suit jacket over the back of his chair, pick up his mail, and put his feet on a wastebasket beside his desk. He waved a vague hand in no particular direction. "Have a seat."

Which is when the two invitees from the two cubicles joined them. Two women in their thirties who could have been the living sisters of Veronica and Betty from the *Archie* cartoons. Only all grown up, in business suits, serious as heart attacks and not smiling or gossiping. They wore their FBI badges in the breast pockets of their suit jackets, and photo IDs hung around their necks. That was because they had firearms in a federal building, custom .32 Berettas, not much stopping power, but they did fit in the waistband of an F. Tripler skirt. They stared at Bryce as though examining a rare species of insect.

Without looking up from yesterday's unopened mail, O'Hanlon introduced the two women, "Agent Barbara Smith and Agent Darcy Wesson. No relation to the Hasbro Corporation or the firearms manufacturer. Can you *believe* that? And they didn't pick their office assignments either, so you *know* this had to be a government accident. We call their presence 'The Holy Order of Saint Beatrice of the Babes.' And that wasn't in your frickin' briefing book was it?"

Bryce made no remark. Accustomed to his place at the spanking pole.

Disgusted at the state of the world, O'Hanlon threw a couple of pieces of unopened mail into the wastebasket, then looked up at the two FBI agents assigned to his office.

"Let me introduce Mr. Bryce here. His Central Intelligence Agency boss down in Virginia sent him up. The Agency man is a big wheel, or thinks he is. He has an interest in my old man's 'Rabbi,' back when my old man was alive, God rest his soul. Back in the 1970s, the Rabbi showed my old man the ins and outs. The two guys came up together, y'know, a chunk of Vietnam. My dad an infantryman, his friend—well, it was never discussed. When they both left public service, they started a little investment firm together, my dad as junior something-or-other. At least one of them made a fortune. But as everybody knows, my dad lost his cut, spent it on wine, women, and song. Broke my mother's heart, and I don't remember the words to the song, so don't ask."

Here O'Hanlon gave them the important stuff, raising a single finger to the ceiling as though indicating their own dingy government suites. "Well . . . Dad's Rabbi never *really* left public service. He still works out of an office in Rockefeller Center. And Mr. Bryce here thinks maybe this guy—his name's Banquo—has wandered off the reservation. So a three-piece suit in Virginia wants us to spy on one of our *own* guys, who my old man knew once upon a midnight dreary . . . Open a criminal investigation, which gives me hives all by itself. Like we don't have enough to do, right?"

The two women, mildly more interested now, began to cock their heads one way, then the other like curious cats—as if gradually more intrigued in this species of insect named Bryce.

"Go on," O'Hanlon told Bryce. "Explain to Barbara and Darcy. Start over from the point I threw your damn ID out the window."

CHAPTER SEVEN

Fieldwork

"It's time you learned some fieldwork." Those had been Robert Wallets' exact words in the offices of Banquo & Duncan. Up till now it was merely laps in the pool and some treadmill at the New York Athletic Club. Later, a little Tae Bo Boxing with a handsome trainer so he didn't trip over his feet. Neither boxing nor walking came naturally to him. But what Wallets had in mind now was of a different order entirely, and nothing in the man's eyes betrayed the struggle to come.

He'd shown up at the Rockefeller Center building as appointed, first thing in the morning, meeting his soon-to-be tormentor downstairs. Surprised to find Wallets standing there not in his regulation gray flannel suit but wearing an expensive, weathered field jacket and Gander Mountain hiking boots. Johnson looked down at his own clothes, his swell city duds: Brooks Brothers' $1,500 navy blue special, pinstriped and cuffed. Watch fob across the vest, $200 starched white shirt open at the collar, and diamond cuff links. His cordovan wingtips were brand spanking new. He looked down at himself and then at Wallets, realizing he was overdressed and for the wrong occasion. He assumed of course he could just show up as usual, assumed there'd be some preliminaries, some orientation, and then B & D would provide any necessary outdoor wear.

"I think Orvis is about to open. They have two stores, one just off Madison—"

But Banquo's man cut him off.

"Never mind, Peter. You go to war with the wardrobe you have."

And Johnson didn't like the sound of this at all. "Where are we going?"

Morning rush hour at the New York Port Authority Bus Terminal on the west side of Manhattan. Yeah, another kind of fraternity hazing ritual. *I'll follow you anywhere, Sir.* The exterior of the place looked like a parking garage made of blue Erector Set pieces. Inside, your skin crawled every step you took. The grime on the ticket counter, the strange crunchiness underfoot, as throngs of grumpy commuters from across the river streamed into the city for their slave wages. Wallets advised him he'd "better eat something," and so he did, from a Nathan's counter. A cockroach peeked at him from behind the mustard spigot. And that was after he'd doused his $3.50 frankfurter. For a moment he considered throwing it away, but commonsense intervened, and he ate it anyway. The smartest thing he ever did. That frank lasted him what seemed a long, long time. And before too long it became the Über Dream Wiener, the best he'd ever tasted.

The grimy concrete bus bay was poorly lit. Hurrying to keep up, he never saw their posted destination, but he did notice spilled mustard on his vest. Oh, for Goodness' Sakes, he'd stained his own pretty blue party dress. Well, you go to war with the wardrobe you have. So it was with a queasy feeling Johnson slumped next to Wallets on the Greyhound to ride the dog. The Lincoln tunnel stench filled the bus and didn't leave; it lingered across the meadowlands past the refineries and most of the way through New Jersey. They were heading south.

A little after midnight they crawled off the bus, stiff and limp at the same time. A tin sign said "Bus Stop—Danbury, NC," hammered beside the screen door of a rural diner. Johnson peered hopefully up and down the empty street for a motel or car park, something. A couple of streetlights, the place shut for the night. No Holiday Inn, no McDonald's, no KFC, only local shops: the Danbury General Store, a couple of small restaurants. Welcome to Nowhereville, North Carolina.

They promptly walked out of town, down the paved streets, past the lit entrance to an army base, to where the pavement gave up. The base sign read:

Fort Blue Ridge/10ᵗʰ Mountain Division/ Special Tactics Unit

Past the main gate the road turned to dirt and rose. They climbed.

Below them, Johnson could see the lit fort fencing, Quonset huts, array of buildings, and guard posts. And Johnson got the idea that Wallets had been here before. That he must have been with the 10ᵗʰ Mountain once upon a time.

"Hey, you know that place, Mr. Eagle Scout?" Johnson asked.

"Won my merit badges there," came the reply.

They marched from around midnight to 3 AM, Johnson's watch told him, with no idea where Daniel Boone here was headed. Growing more and more winded, straining his casual smoker's lung capacities. He had never taken to the outdoors and had never spent one night out camping, even as a lad. Out here, there were crickets and the sound of wind in the trees, the air sweet and clean. But he was hungry and worn out. One of his wingtips was rubbing one ankle raw.

With every step, the pain grew a tiny bit worse. So what was all this crap about—the Flat Foot Test? Did they expect him to wander out of the wilderness in Jesus boots? Such a small thing stinging down on his ankle, a toothache kind of pain. Why did a mild discomfort make you want to worry it? The annoying in-between state, neither here nor there. He toyed with the idea of taking off his shoes; no, dumb idea. His feet were softer than butter. Best to leave the shoes to rub.

It occurred to Johnson that he had lived his whole life in a buttery in-between state. For he never chose to take a stand, never confronted some difficult issue with one of his wives so they could press through the pain together to something better. Never committed himself to a dangerous point of view unless there were some compensating benefit that outweighed the personal jeopardy by several orders of magnitude. Never saw any authority higher than himself. And never really knew what a bad place that was to be, except for now.

So would he press through this time? He thought he heard something in the crickets' song—the lonely sound of an abandonment of everything including himself, to this cause, to the *resistance*. He felt himself gripped by a kind of vertigo; while the crickets spoke to him, taunting him with every step, mocking his pain, his self-pity and fear. Words for each step as his wingtip rubbed his ankle raw:

Manhattan Scribbler! *reek-creek* What no Starbucks? *reek-creek* Call a Taxi! *reek-creek*

Would he give himself to this cause? No. No, he wouldn't. Suddenly he stopped. That's all he had to do. Just stop. And stand in the dark, to stop the madness. Making the decision to save his dignity right there and then from the inevitable humiliation he was sure to endure from some cockamamie scheme authored by those he'd spent his entire life hating—in particular that polished CIA Methuselah and Uncle Banquo's spit-and-shine Jarhead. He would go no farther.

His ankle no longer spoke to him. It had made its point, and he waited for Wallets to stop and turn around so he could make his case to the martinet bastard. He began to form the words in his mind, a rebuke that would make Daniel Boone feel every bit the laughable excuse of a caricature he was. And he waited.

But the man wasn't stopping for some Manhattan Swank missing his latte; he just kept crunching ahead. Wallets' steps began to get a little fainter. Johnson wanted to yell out, "Hey!" But that felt just too pathetic. He lifted his arms, palms upturned in confounded futility. No one there to see it. And soon he was alone, alone with the crickets and his sore ankle, alone in the dark, alone on a path where he didn't know how to go ahead or go back, all alone, Peter Johnson.

Hours later, close to daybreak, almost too tired and distraught to care if he ever made it out of these black woods, Johnson came to a large clearing. He had followed Wallets the best he could but with no idea whether his feet had tramped off somewhere on their own. He made out the clearing as some sort of abandoned service station for heavy machinery, cranes, bulldozers, backhoes, and such, their hulking forms like petrified dinosaurs in a dark museum. The broken bits of rusting metal were everywhere. He picked his way through them but felt something slice sharply across the side of his wingtip. Pretty sure the sharp refuse hadn't cut his foot, but he felt damn sure the thing cut his $30 sock, exposing his right big toe to the air. Oh, for Chrissakes. A final indignity. He fought back tears and wanted to kick something, but then he might really hurt himself. If this were a test of endurance, he was losing. If a test of manhood, he'd already failed.

A little ahead, the ghost of a service station garage stared at him. He made out a human figure. Someone sitting. Wallets—naturally—propped up on an upside-down plastic five-gallon empty joint compound bucket. His white teeth smiled broadly. "Thought I lost you," he chuckled.

Johnson thought of a hundred things to yell at the man, from "F— you" right down the line to "Your Mother Wears Army Boots and Swims after Troop Ships" (a distinct possibility), but finally gathered himself and said as deadpan as possible, "I once was lost, but now I'm found. Hallelujah." The pain from his ankle nagged him again, and he stared down his trousers leg, all the way down to his exposed, cold naked hobo toe.

"Now that you've deigned to join me," his wilderness guide said, "I get the office; you get the garage."

The station was in two parts like any service station: a cavelike workbay area, with concrete floor slab, work pits, and broken garage doors. Then off to the side, an "office" with its counter, a couple of plastic chairs, old Snap-on Tool calendars, and the faded poster of Miss Liquid Wrench 1991—"When You Need a Good Yank"—curling at the edges. A rather lithesome blonde dish with admirable assets. She wore only her panties, a blaze-orange thong that seemed to light up the dank office all on its own. The office stood intact, the large plate-glass window informing all the world they'd reached that pinnacle of rustbelt Southern industry: Dobbs Machine & Diesel.

In less than four minutes, Wallets rummaged a tall steel locker with a combination lock on the latch and took out a large waterproof freezer tote sack, from which he drew out a sleeping bag in a large sealed baggie, a folded hammock, a length of mosquito netting and a few other items. Before the four minutes elapsed the hammock hung in the office from two cleverly placed hooks, the sleeping bag lay on the hammock, the man lay in the sleeping bag, with each of his boots on either side of his head to give him some air space, and the mosquito netting over all.

"I'm going to knock off for a couple of hours. In the meantime, make yourself comfortable."

Johnson stared, aghast. In another thirty seconds, gentle snores filled the dingy office. Johnson went to drag one of the office chairs out into the garage. No luck: bolted to the floor. So was the other. He took the bucket Wallets had occupied and sat on it, staring out the open bay into the darkness.

Johnson guessed the temperature up here in the foothills of North Carolina in early September hovered around forty-eight to sixty degrees at night. It felt like thirty. His feet were numb. The sweat from the climb chilled along his spine. His hands began to shake. And out of nowhere hungry mosquitoes found his face.

A breeze blew in at the open bay and suddenly the heavens opened up, dark splattering rain soaking the edge of the concrete apron. He shoved his bucket back half a foot. It caught on something and toppled him onto the wet concrete. More insulted than injured he managed to right his seat. Waves of mosquitoes sought shelter from the rain.

Finally he spoke a couple of sober, judicious words to the slowly lifting darkness, the sum total of everything he'd learned so far about fieldwork:

"This . . . *sucks*."

Late morning found him nodding on the bucket and twitching only when a very large mosquito sank its needle into his neck. He'd fed the hordes. The rain kept on. Thirst woke him, then its old comrade hunger. At the last Greyhound rest stop he'd bought two things. A pack of Marlboros and a package of peanut butter cheese crackers. A pack of matches came with the cigarettes, now very damp. He dared not open the salty crackers—they were just too dry for him to choke down at this moment. He looked at the rain sluicing down an open gutter.

"Here's the rule." Wallets stood in the open office door looking for all the world fresh as a daisy. "Water you find in puddles or even flowing down a stream can make you sick. You have to boil it. Rain from the roof is good."

Johnson hastily stuck his bucket under the open gutter. He was frozen through and through. He began to stamp his feet and slap his sides. The man kept talking:

"In other places survival may depend on seizing an opportunity, keeping out of trouble or just dumb luck. But here, survival depends on three things: Food. Fire. Shelter. I've given you one. You're responsible for the rest." And so began the hardest and possibly the most rewarding two weeks of Johnson's life.

That first day, fire was going to be a problem. Johnson found some dirty plastic, which he made into a poncho, and a dirty baseball cap in the broken toilet. Soon a pile of soaked twigs and kindling and some larger deadfall was stacked against one wall to drip dry, along with his pack of Marlboros and the pack of matches that he left in the hopeful light of a window to salvage them. The weather cleared about 10 AM with a brisk breeze coming out of the north. After the deluge, ten or twenty bullfrogs began hopping between puddles and rusty machinery. One look at his companion's cocked eyebrow and Johnson knew what he had to do.

"*Bien Sûr, Mon Général*," Johnson said. "*Grenouille à la Provençal tout de suit!*"

Wallets cocked an eyebrow at the French for Frog Legs Provence style, and Johnson heard him mutter, "*Ça va.*"

Right after "this *sucks*" . . . the second thing fieldwork taught him: food seemed to be everywhere, if you could find it. The third thing: every night was take-out, but not delivered. Though half-drowned frogs came close.

Seventeen frogs in the bucket later, Johnson's wingtips were soaked, his suit trousers ripped, and he was sweating again. At least they'd eat. "Sorry we don't have a Cajun cornmeal coating," Wallets remarked, "but there *is* a war on, *garçon*."

In a fit of divine inspiration, the two men dragged a padded damp backseat couch from a dead Chevy into the garage bay. In the process Johnson found an abandoned case of baked beans in quart tins, and a rusty jackknife with a broken can opener. It took him twenty minutes to open the first can, with the hole punch and another slip of rusty metal to jerk around the rim. But he got better as he went along. Empty cans made good pots and pans.

Johnson couldn't feel his hands or feet. The whole first day it didn't get warmer than sixty-two degrees. "I'm going to try for a fire."

Which he did in one of the work pits, laying a huge metal oil pan from a bulldozer crosswise. Having read the story *To Build a Fire* by the immortal Jack in public school, the first thing he remembered was to make sure nothing wet would fall on his effort. Nope. No holes in the ceiling. Then he went about finding accelerants in the dark recesses of the garage, old oil for the twigs and dirty rags to get the thing going. Once started burning, with the damp Chevy couch in front of the beautiful flames, the fire caressed him better than any woman.

The fire burned brightly, the frog legs cooked to a turn in a crust of crushed cheese peanut butter crackers, the old beans bubbled in their own tins—and nothing had ever tasted that good to Johnson *ever*. They sat on the couch while his wingtips and trousers hung nearby on an old hand truck to dry. The soggy scribbler feeling better about himself than he had in twenty-five years. When the bottle of Jack Daniel's mysteriously appeared out of Wallets' marvelous locker in his "bedroom," the first pull sang to him like the heavenly host, warming his limbs right down to his skivvies. He hoisted the magic bottle in a toast.

"I vote you a capital fellow," he told his host.

"So you don't think this is all bullshit?"

The question jarred Johnson. He'd stopped pondering such matters long ago. Every hour out here felt like days. He pursed his lips, bottom lip curling over the top in a vaguely primate way, as it often did when he lacked a ready answer.

"Well, I hope you're not planning on sending me camping in the woods to stick a knife into the heart of Johnny Mohammed."

Wallets smiled and shook his head no. "The reason we put you through this is something you'll hear a lot from us: we don't know."

"Exactly what don't you know?" Johnson repeated, amused.

"What may happen to you. What skills you're going to need. *Doubt is the only certainty*, Peter. So learn what you can here and now. You might find it useful later."

Fair enough, Johnson thought. He nodded to himself, wondering if he would truly remember the lesson if the time ever came. He glanced at Wallets, ready to acknowledge his own doubt, when he realized the man wasn't staring into the fire anymore but to the gaping garage bay. A figure stood out in the darkness silently watching them. The figure took a step closer, staring at Johnson in his u-trou. Slowly, the figure took a pack of cigarettes from a chest pocket in a checked shirt, undid the cellophane wrapper, and lit one from the pack, inhaling deeply. Johnson glanced to the shelf under the window where he'd put his Marlboros hours ago. They were gone. Now he stared across the concrete apron and watched the stranger smoke his cigarettes.

"Mind if I bum a smoke?" the stranger asked. Less a question than a challenge.

"Keep the pack."

His companion chuckled. "Peter, allow me to introduce a colleague. Marjorie Morningstar—not her real name—Peter Johnson."

The figure strode into the light: a woman about forty-five, short hair, clean complexion, but clearly strong, wearing a lumberjack outfit, slouch hat. She placed a .22 caliber pump-action Remington with a scope carefully against the wall. Then slung a large bedraggled thing onto the concrete.

"But you can call me Large Marge."

The thing on the concrete was a wild turkey, sans head. She'd shot the thing with a spitball and blown its head off. Annie Oakley. At the time Johnson didn't know enough to appreciate what skill that took, but Wallets sure did, murmuring "Hmmmmm" with great admiration.

"If you want breakfast, pluck it." She eyed Johnson in his skivvies somewhat dubiously. "Hard day at the office there, Sport?"

Johnson lost all words. He handed her the whiskey with a shrug of shared admiration. "The commute is hell," he finally replied. "But when I get home . . ." Johnson looked around him, at the fire, the garage, the coil-sprung car seat, "I'm in the country."

Large Marge showed him many things. How to catch fish in a stream and how to trap a rabbit. How to heal his raw ankle with some leaves in the forest. How to wash and shave, and even how to make a hood of burlap to keep the mosquitoes at bay so he could sleep. As the days passed, Wallets seemed to fade into the background, watching from afar yet occasionally offering a suggestion: "How about trout tonight?" Or a test: "There's a firearm stashed in an abandoned shed two hundred yards off the base perimeter. See if you can get it without being spotted."

From that task, he returned at dusk to find both Large Marge and Wallets missing from their base camp and the reason perfectly obvious. A boom box was blasting ZZ Top into the trees surrounding Dobbs Diesel. Inside the garage bay two large Bikers and their pretty Bitchslut—who looked and acted about fourteen years old—had moved in for the evening, finding the accommodations Johnson struggled to build much to their liking. Large Marge and Wallets found him in the dark some hours later quietly sitting in the woods near the camp. The Bikers had partied and sexed up their bitch all night and now lay snoring on the hammock and couch.

"Could be The Outlaws," Marge whispered. "Bikers who run crystal meth from Florida to Maine. Model citizens."

Wallets gave Johnson a handful of fallen leaves, saying, "This should do it."

Johnson wrapped his shoes in rags to keep them quiet and managed to put a fistful of crushed dried leaves in one of the Harleys' gas tanks. Never mind the other—it needed a key. Damage done, he retired to the trees. If Wallets was impressed, he never showed it.

"They'll get down the hill all right and konk out somewhere around the gate to the Base," he explained. "Then the Sheriff will come for a look-see, as these two studs seem to be boning their own sister. They won't be back. Did you find the gun in the shed?"

It had been concealed under some broken clay pots and spilled potting soil, sealed in a plastic ziplock bag. Johnson showed it to them. "Good. Let's do some plinking."

The first thing he learned was that anybody could shoot a gun. The second thing was not everybody could hit something. The gun itself, a

.32 caliber snub-nose revolver looked like something Dick Tracy might carry—small, short, silver, ugly. It fit well in the palm of Johnson's hand. Marge showed him how to load it: pull the hammer back halfway, flip the portal, drop in the cartridges, keep the first chamber empty. Five shots in a six-shot gun.

"That way if it drops, it won't go off."

No safety. You pulled the hammer back all the way, heard the click, squeezed the trigger—*bang*. Simple.

Wallets had taken the poster of Miss Liquid Wrench outside and nailed her to the side of a rotting truck. Now at about ten yards Johnson tried to hit the poor girl. *Bang* again. Nope. Not even a bullet hole in the driver's side door. Where the hell were the bullets going?

"Try a little closer," Wallets suggested. Five yards. *Bang, bang*. Nope. "Closer." Seven feet. Johnson pointed at her head. The last bullet, *bang*—a hole appeared in her forehead.

"Now you know," Wallets remarked dryly, "with a gun like that, that's how close you have to be. Maybe closer. With a hollow-point bullet it'll come out the back in a chunk the size of your fist. When we're through, you'll be able to take the thing apart in the dark and load it with your eyes closed."

Johnson stared at the coy poster of Miss Liquid Wrench still smiling. She didn't seem to mind too much.

"Stand aside!" This from Large Marge, seventy-five yards back in the trees. Wallets and Johnson moved out of the line of fire. Three quick bangs from her .22 caliber pump rifle. Two holes appeared in each of Miss Liquid Wrench's breasts and one in her navel.

"Show off," Wallets exclaimed.

CHAPTER EIGHT

Within the Range of Plausibility

The fieldwork came to an end as suddenly as it started. Johnson woke up alone one morning; first thing he noticed: Wallets' hammock and other gear were stowed back in the locker. Realizing shrewdly that Large Marge and Wallets had departed for good, he took it on himself to walk his way back to town. A passing glance at his reflection in the Dobbs Machine & Diesel glass window showed his suit jacket split at the shoulders, his white shirt a lovely shade of gray. Pants open at both knees, rags about his feet. A few days of scruff and uncombed hair. The wild man of Borneo. Then as if to add pedantry to abandonment, he found a note scribbled on a scrap of paper in the office.

> *All you have to do is walk back to town during daylight hours, purchase a bus ticket and get on a bus. We'll be waiting for you in New York.*

Another test.

———— ∞ ————

Shortly before leaving for the Middle East, Johnson headed again to Rockefeller Center. Instead of the usual routine, Banquo and Wallets brought him to a room in a different part of the Banquo & Duncan suite, adjoining the conference area by another set of double doors.

"We sometimes use this as a stage set," Wallets explained to him. "It helps us get a feel for how things can turn out." Johnson followed the two men through the doors and stopped dead cold.

A little bearded middle-aged fellow sat at a desk, behind him a bookshelf with what appeared to be mathematics and physics journals, a blackboard along one wall with formulas chalked in long incomprehensible rows. He was paunchy and wore glasses. Johnson recalled him at once as the "taxi driver" the night Banquo & Duncan made their move on him. The little fellow glanced incuriously at the three intruders, then went back to his work, some notes and figures on a legal pad. Banquo and Wallets each took chairs, the double doors closed. An armed guard locked the door from inside and went back to his post, leaving Johnson standing in the center of the Persian rug looking lost.

The guard made an impression.

The man looked like one of those Turkish wrestlers you saw in the summer Olympics when they're broadcasting at 3 AM: coffee complexion, broad, balding, about 220 pounds, height five foot eight, and 100 percent solid beef. He wore his sidearm on a web belt. The rest of his outfit was like a hospital's physical therapist—white sneakers, white pants, white T-shirt. Puffs of black hair from his back sprouted about his neck, melding into the smooth skin of the densest, closely shaved five o'clock shadow in the world.

"He's right out of central casting in *Midnight Express*," Johnson quipped. No one responded. The Guard stared at him; Wallets stared at him. While Banquo elegantly crossed his legs and flicked some invisible lint from his trouser leg.

"Actually, his name is Yossi, and he says he's an Iranian Jew, but it would probably take an army of spooks and genealogists to determine his true origins," Banquo explained. "We found him working in a Yemeni prison, masquerading as a common guard under an assumed name. He was pretending to conspire with some Al Qaeda lads who were plotting a breakout, hoping to eventually blow up something or other when they got over the wall. Typical Yemeni/Israeli security service pony express operation. Send someone in, make nice through the bars, then after the breakout ride hell for leather to cut them off at the pass. At our request the Israelis urged the Yemenis to behead him in public, which they faked on TV, and we spirited him out. Now he's ostensibly dead and can pass under the radar. For various common professional courtesies, I allow him to operate as Mossad's mole in my house. He speaks Hebrew, Arabic, Berber, and Farsi. His English is so-so. He's a very useful man to have around. Banquo & Duncan never opposes hiring men of dual loyalties; it's dual results we abhor. Which brings us to the object of our lesson."

Here he directed Johnson's attention to the little man at the desk, still writing away, as if he were alone.

"Allow me to introduce Dr. Ramses Pahlevi Yahdzi of the University of Isfahan. Physicist and nuclear scientist." The little man didn't look up from his papers. Johnson repressed the urge to say, "How do you do?" to the little bent head. He was one of Banquo's ghosts, an unobtrusive man willing to perform the mundane tasks without which the grandest operation couldn't come off, from driving a car to playacting. Banquo's silk-stocking voice kept on, to Johnson's ear a rich blend of Boston Brahmin and Jean Pierre Robie in Hitchcock's *To Catch a Thief*.

"Pahlevi Yahdzi, born April 23, 1945. Graduated Harvard, Massachusetts Institute of Technology, Vienna Mathematics Institute. Married, father of two. The Persian Robert Oppenheimer, the mullahs' greatest living hope to acquire nuclear weapons, the single most important man in Iran. Not the imams, not the president who sees holy auras around himself—this gentleman. The man you're going to interview, your nuclear tour guide on the Al Jazeera Fairytale Express. Peter, do you know what happens when Iran succeeds in testing its first atomic bomb?"

Without waiting for a reply, Banquo answered his own question:

"Here's one scenario. Extreme, I admit, but within the range of plausibility. Oil goes to $500 a barrel. Iran becomes the hegemonic power in the Middle East region, using the Straits of Hormuz like the tollbooths on the Tri-Boro Bridge. The Mahdi Army of the shitty Shiite Sheik al Sadr reconstitutes itself and takes over most of Iraq. The U.S. forces in the entire region are 'redeployed' to Okinawa by an act of Congress.

Afghanistan returns to its natural troglodyte state. A long period of retreat sets in. Across Europe, the socialist democracies that presently suffer 14 to 18 percent unemployment, reach 20 to 25 percent unemployment in a single month, with spikes of 80 percent in their Muslim ghettos, and default on their national financial obligations. The nice parts of Paris are burned to the ground. The London Tube stops operating. Anonymous gangs murder a thousand Pakistanis in Berlin. Switzerland expels all nonwhites from its Cantons. Italy tries the same thing and fails. Vatican City is beset by immigrant riots. Nobody bothers noticing anymore the millions who perish in the pestilent sewer that is Africa, the Indian subcontinent, or other Southeast Asian cesspools.

"Closer to home, unemployment in the United States goes from 5 percent, close to statistical 'full employment,' to 19 percent overnight. Current officeholders are impeached or thrown out on their asses. People in the northern half of the Republic have trouble heating their homes in winter or getting fresh produce, while a new strain of pneumonia infects 25 to 35 percent of the population between October and May in the Rust Belt cities. Below the Mason Dixon line air conditioning becomes a luxury, is rationed, and for the first time in seventy years cities such as Atlanta and Houston, Vicksburg and Charleston, get a taste of what it was really like living in a Margaret Mitchell novel. Needless to say no one goes to the mall anymore. The only place you stop sweating is in a hospital emergency room and next to your Food Lion's frozen food case. Death from heat stroke brought on by obesity becomes commonplace. Rats within city limits multiply. When Mr. Rat crawls out of his sewer into the sun to die in places like Orlando and Los Angeles, Disney World and Disneyland close their doors during the summer. Americans' average life expectancy drops from seventy-nine years of age to sixty-five in five years. There are 10 million more deaths than expected; life insurance companies pay off on their policies, but rates skyrocket. Only millionaires can afford health insurance now, and they don't need it. Predictably, the Social Security system and Medicare system *do* fail. Many U.S. cities are effectively governed by the National Guard. Or worse, semi-organized crime."

Banquo took a breath. "That's what happens if we're lucky. If we're not so lucky things could be much, much worse. President Ahmadinejad ushers in The End of Days. His promise to 'wipe Israel off the map' is kept. Several technologically enhanced dirty bombs are detonated in the cities of Tel Aviv, Jerusalem, and Haifa, their population centers poisoned. No one claims responsibility, but Arab populations across the Middle East erupt in spontaneous celebration. The United Nations in New York issues a strongly worded statement condemning the violence and asks Israel to refrain from 'disproportionate' retaliation."

Banquo paused again. "Contrary to expectations due to internal miscommunications and a strong peace contingent in the Knesset—the IDF does not immediately retaliate against any Arab or Persian country. Casualties, dead and wounded, in the Jewish cities reach a hundred thousand. First five thousand initial deaths, then lingering radiation sickness from a contaminated water supply. As the country staggers toward collapse, rogue elements of the Israeli Air Force execute their own action, code named Down from Sinai—simultaneously bombing Qom, Tehran, Riyadh, Mecca, Cairo, and Damascus with thermonuclear weapons. Arab and Persian casualties are estimated at 60 to 70 million—"

Banquo's refined and assured voice floated across the room. The little man at the desk did not look up. Peter Johnson found his hands sweating despite himself, and he rubbed them on his trousers.

"At this moment, various Jihadi sleeper cells in the United States are activated. Even as a resolution in the United Nations is unanimously passed by all countries—and quietly supported by a Democratic administration—which demands that the surviving Jews in the United States pay 'reparations' to the afflicted countries. To no one's surprise and to little avail, many of America's richest Jews willingly offer to comply. One of the few who doesn't is George Soros—who emigrates to New Zealand, and just in the nick of time."

Banquo wasn't even looking at Johnson but examining his trimmed and clean fingernails. "You see, the five steamer-trunk sized 'suitcase' nukes placed here by the KGB during the Cold War, and which we've been looking high and low for, lo these many years, are suddenly discovered in various storage facilities and locked water closets in the subterranean basements of various urban skyscrapers. *But not by us.* By guys named Vronksy and Karenin and Karamazov, who want to kick us while we're down. Four of them don't go off, given that they are Soviet engineering at its most reliable—but one *does*. Along with a few of those dirty bombs that proved so useful in Israel. Well, they're useful here too. Miami, Chicago, New York, Seattle, almost every major city gets one. Casualties of more than one million U.S. citizens. And no one claims responsibility. All property and casualty insurance of any nature whatsoever defaults. The United Nations relocates to parts of Westchester County in order to issue another strongly worded statement. Five million people attempt to flee the tri-state New York City area. Later generations will call it, 'The Great March to Nowhere.'"

Banquo stared at nothing in particular for a moment or two, then snapped back and looked at Johnson with a little smile.

"How did Cyril Connolly put it, Peter, although prematurely?"

"'Closing time in the gardens of the West.'"

"Precisely. Call me an alarmist; argue with some of it. Fill in your own details if you like. They don't matter; the trajectory on which we are headed matters. Nothing else."

"There are ways to stop this," Banquo continued, after a breath. "The United States can for the second time—the Iraq war of course being the first—launch a pre-emptive war based on shaky intelligence. Intelligence that is not going to be accepted by the collective tyrants, crooks, bed wetters, and pantywaists of the so-called 'international community.' But take it from me—we will *never* do it. Even if we did, we wouldn't be able to destroy Iran's physical assets, short of using bunker-busters or mini-nukes. What American president wants to have a couple little Nagasakis to his name? Eh, Peter? You're the political writer."

Banquo kept driving nails into the coffin of current delusions:

"So we continue to squeeze the Iranians with economic sanctions and hope something comes from it. The triumph of hope over experience, right, Peter? You've been married how many times? We will never be able to levy enough sanctions to convince the Iranians to abandon dreams of the strategic doomsday weapon they nearly have within their grasp. Never. The Russians and Chinese have opened the toy soldier store seven days a week, selling on credit. Did you notice any dirty bombs going off in Moscow or Beijing in my scenario?

"They know which side looks like a winner. And it's not us. Oil at a couple hundred dollars a barrel means Mr. Putin or his nearest henchman can dream of endless Soviet Summers. Can shut down the press at will by friendly persuasion, hostile takeover, or murder most foul in London Sushi bars, leaving them free to slaughter whomever they like in any former Soviet so-called republics. As for the Celestials, Beijing has been cushioning itself against this kind of oil shock for years: employing side deals with grubby Third World greaseballs the world over. Pardon my French. When the shock hits, China will likely move in to directly administer these areas, finally securing its share of colonial spoils a mere century late, with names like The Caribbean Kowloon Oil Company or Hong Kong Energy—and again, who is going to stop them from walking into Taiwan or even Indochina? Beg your pardon, I mean Vietnam. A nuclear-free *Japan*? We'll all be the Castratos of the Straits of Hormuz."

Banquo looked right at him. The always glib Johnson had nothing to say, feeling slightly stupid standing in the middle of the room on that fine Persian rug in front of everyone. He didn't even shrug or meet the sophisticated man's eyes. He looked down.

"There is one way out," Banquo continued at length, "that could avert all these terrible consequences." He paused, weighing his words. "But such a way out would take a very unusual fellow. A loose cannon. Someone flagrantly on record opposing the U.S. government. Someone so unreliable that no one in their right mind could possibly think we'd entrust him with even the simplest of errands. An amateur, a simpleton, a naïf, a cad with a history of heavy drinking and erratic behavior. A corrupt letch so utterly unaccountable he'd go off half-cocked at the first opportunity like the jack-in-the-box *everyone knows* he is."

Banquo stopped again. Wallets, hunched over in his chair with his elbows on his knees, looked up from the carpet, arched his eyebrows at Johnson.

Banquo picked up his thread again. "Human capital matters more than anything else in this world. There are such things as indispensable men, Peter. The Dr. Yahdzi whose simulacrum you see here is one. All those centrifuges, all the nuclear infrastructure, the countless millions spent—none of it matters without the man who knows the physics and the engineering: the one man capable of bringing a 7th century Islamic tyranny into the nuclear 21st century, without the slightest moderating influence of the Renaissance, the Reformation, or the Age of Reason. That single man is on the verge of delivering to crazed monkeys high on Apocalyptic crack a supply of radioactive handguns, matches, and gasoline—then sending them into a kindergarten with unsupervised children and hoping for the best. That's why I introduced you two just now. You see, you could be an indispensable man too."

Now Banquo leaned toward Johnson, almost in a posture of pleading: "You can stop all of this, Peter, perhaps delay it enough that other events will intervene. Cooler heads. The tectonic plates of world politics will eventually pause, adjust, *relax*. Then we can avoid the earthquakes, the next tsunami, the next volcanic eruption. We just need a little time."

For all this elaborate Greatest Game gumbo, most of which made Johnson want to sneer, he knew enough not to laugh this time. Laid starkly in front of him was a real bit of derring-do: the place where all the jokes came to die in the face of a single mission. *His* mission. Not some document drop, shady banking, or some cheesy bribe. But something much darker. Something irrevocable.

For the first time since his arrival into the little romper room, the man playing Dr. Yahdzi stopped his deskwork and looked up. Measuring Johnson with a stare.

Wallets nodded an unspoken command in the armed guard's direction. The Turk un-holstered his .40 caliber Beretta, yanked the slide chambering a round, and left the cocked firearm on the desk in front of "Dr. Yahdzi." The little man glanced at the weapon, then went back to his papers. The Turk returned to his place by the door.

Johnson sucked a breath in disbelief, contemplating the gun. This monster was ugly: big and black, heart-attack serious with death written on it from butt to muzzle. Big enough to give any Metrosexual the vapors. Nothing like the little Dick Tracy popgun back at Dobbs Diesel.

Everyone seemed to be waiting for him to do something. At last Wallets' sober voice filled the room. "Peter, you have a chance to save the world. The little rat lives; millions die. The little rat dies; peace really does get a chance. Well?"

Johnson didn't move, didn't blink an eyelash, didn't even trust himself to shrug his shoulders. He knew what they wanted. And for an instant he swore he'd swoon. Hit his chin on the desk, go out cold. But the feeling passed, and he stood there on the Persian rug with the terrible question staring him in the face. What to do?

Wallets took a deep, quiet breath. "Show us."

"I'm not comfortable pointing—"

"*Show us.*"

He gave Wallets a long doubtful look. Then tried to reach for the Beretta but his hand trembled from wrist to fingers with palsy. Like a hundred-year-old man. He stared at the shaking thing. How *embarrassing*.

"It's only adrenalin, Peter," Wallets said. "Nothing to be ashamed of."

He felt stripped bare. He had walked into this room expecting a visit to Banquo & Duncan like any other. Some pointed conversation, maybe a few awkward questions, but he had long ago stopped letting that bother him and even felt warmly now toward Wallets after their roughing it together in North Carolina.

In other words, he had felt comfortable, in control. Which meant never being in a situation where anything fundamental was at stake.

And now they wanted him to pick up that instrument of death and enact a murder, an act that might not change history as they said, but would certainly change his life—perhaps end it. Confronting him was a choice more momentous than he'd ever faced. He looked at the black gun, and it loomed so large he imagined it being too heavy to lift, that he could yank at it with both hands and it wouldn't budge. He looked at his trembling hand again and took two steps toward the desk. But suddenly the weakness in his hands spread to his knees, sapping the strength from the rest of his body. Slowly, he turned his back on the little man and slid gingerly to the floor.

He propped himself up against the desk with his back to Yahdzi and put his elbows on his knees and his hands on his head. "I think we need to talk," he said to the dead silence of the room.

⤬

And they talked. Banquo pulled up a chair for his journalist, while he, Banquo, and Wallets all scooted together in a semicircle and talked it through. Johnson noticed something different in their tone. They weren't talking to him like a recalcitrant outsider or someone who needed to be coaxed or cajoled into anything. But as equals, as an insider. Johnson liked the feeling, if not what he was hearing.

The "scientist" stayed at his desk, working at figures and reading physics books as the hours passed. He deserved some sort of prize for staying in character, Johnson thought. Yossi stood at the door, then leaned against it, and finally pulled up a stool at his post. They talked over the method (uncertain), the legality (none), and the ethics (dubious but defensible)—then went over it again and again and again.

The facts really weren't in dispute. Iran declared war on the United States at the time of the Khomeini Revolution, thirty years ago. Spreading a reign of terror from Tehran to Buenos Aires. That made Dr. Yahdzi a kind of soldier, a combatant.

"No one who is serious about these matters—a category, alas, that excludes nearly all your journalistic colleagues—could regret a nuclear-neutered Iran. Only the pathologically deluded believe in nuclear moral equivalence. The rest of us live in dread, dread at a horizon of burned cities and millions dead. Bombing in retaliation for any Iranian reckless-ness would be indiscriminate, killing countless innocents whose only offense is living in the wrong Iranian city. But *one* shot. One precisely targeted shot could delay the reckoning for years."

Johnson couldn't argue. He wanted to, but he couldn't. And as far as he could see there was only one upside to the deal. In a strange way this was *for the children*, as the cliché went. His child especially. One single act to give them a world where Giselle would never have to ask again, "Why did they do this? Tell me, *why?*"

Banquo explained how his legal and personal exposure would be total. Should Johnson complete the act successfully, he would be a hired assassin in the eyes of Iranian law—and everyone else. Red Queen Justice: "Sentence first, verdict afterwards."

And here Banquo opened the door a little wider.

"We have someone on the inside," he explained. "You'll have to allow the situation to mature, ripen. There will be a signal for you to act, but we can't tell you what it is because, frankly, we don't know yet. But when you're on the ground, it will become manifest to you. An obvious opportunity. I wish I could tell you more. I wish I knew more. But our man inside—a great Iranian patriot in my mind—is putting it all on the line. Everything. In the most difficult of circumstances."

Johnson sensed a kind of challenge in Banquo's eye: *Could the same be said of him?*

Everyone went quiet, and Johnson was about to pipe up with, "Okay, even if I grant all this . . . " when Dr. Pahlevi Yahdzi's voice startled them all:

"It's a terrible burden for anyone, a terrible burden." He shook his head, and bent his eyes again toward his papers.

Something about that simple declaration struck Johnson as a powerful act of empathy. Dr. Yahdzi had stated just what Johnson himself felt but didn't want to admit—how scared, worried, and confused he was. How burdened. And the phrase "even unto death" came to Johnson's mind and floated around in his head, signifying he knew not what. But his eyes misted, and he couldn't meet anyone's gaze.

"He's right," Banquo said, filling the silence. "From the moment you start to move against Yahdzi, your life is forfeit. We would understand if you prefer to decline." Would they even attempt to rescue him?

"What happens if I say no?" Johnson asked.

Banquo gestured to Yossi the Turk, whose chin was nearly on his chest but who roused himself to stand up and unlock and open the door: "There's the door."

Johnson ignored the gesture, found it almost insulting, and changed the topic. "So assuming I seize the opportunity, and assuming I'm not eager to have a close encounter with the Iranian cattle prods, how do I get out?"

"Ah," said Banquo. Then simply left it at that. Wallets looked down at the carpet, with an elbow on a knee, his chin in his hand, and audibly expelled some air through his nostrils. "There *will* be a way out. We'll never be very far from you," Banquo said at last. "But the first thing you can do is to help yourself. From the minute you start, every move you make counts. Do what makes sense. But don't wait for the cavalry, Peter."

Johnson suddenly wondered how much they'd care if he got dead, so long as he took the pride of Persian Physics with him. The answer was obvious and not particularly reassuring.

"And when I get caught?"

Again, that awkward silence.

"What am I supposed to say? What am I supposed to tell them?" Johnson asked again.

"It doesn't matter really," Banquo replied, without acknowledging his discomfort. "For any number of reasons. They'll most likely put you through the ringer, perhaps use sodium pentothal or something like it. But that never works like in the movies, and you'll probably just babble on about Camus or your last girl. Moreover, as far as our connection with you is concerned, first, you're a provable liar, Peter. *Provable.* And second, no matter what you say, *we've never heard of you.*" Johnson's mind flitted over the tape recorder he had slipped in and out of some of their sessions, and he smiled to himself. Home Insurance, he called it. For just this eventuality.

"So the U.S. government . . . ?" he asked, letting the question hang, unstated.

"A little history," Banquo replied. "When the Soviets invaded Afghanistan, invaded *a whole country,* the Politburo decision memo was entitled 'Concerning the Matter of A.' And you're not even the invasion of a country, Peter. You're just a journalist."

"Uh-huh," Johnson said.

Wallets tapped Johnson's forearm. "But if you say no, none of this happened. We have been operating on the basis of trust. If you breathe a word, I'm sure the IRS will discover a keen interest in those questionable cash payments from abroad on which you paid no taxes."

Johnson didn't have anything to say to that, but Wallets wasn't finished. "So, please, whatever you do, don't try to be clever with us." He pointed to Dr. Yahdzi.

The faux scientist fished around inside his suit jacket pockets, found something, and placed it on top of his paperwork. Johnson's cute Sanyo miniature tape recorder and the half dozen mini tapes he'd made. He'd hid a couple of the tapes in the offices of *The Crusader*, Jo von Hildebrand's desk, for Chrissakes, and the rest in an envelope addressed to his literary agent in his *own* Citibank safe deposit box.

Johnson started to mumble an apology, but Banquo waved him off. "Consider your options, Peter. If you want to move forward, we need to come back in here for a long session and go over specific scenarios. I don't envy you. There are no good choices. But I would argue doing nothing has far worse consequences, ones that you won't be able to drink away. You are implicated now, one way or another. You represent a unique opportunity to secure victory at the price of one bullet. Fellows like you don't come around very often, Peter Johnson. But when they do, I simply cannot resist demanding of them what they *say* they want."

"My ceremony of innocence is drowned?" Johnson mused, almost to himself.

"You know your Yeats," Wallets said.

Johnson pursed his lips. What was there left for him to say? Nothing. Just a decision. To go or not to go. A million years ago, it seemed, he'd asked to join *la résistance*. But that was before anyone asked him to pick up a gun and point it at another man. It still sat, with all its black metallic solidity, in the same spot on Yahdzi's desk.

Banquo stood up. "Let us know your decision today or tomorrow."

Later, alone in Banquo's office, once more Wallets looked at his boss. "Do you really believe all that crap you fed him?"

Banquo stared at the huge plasma TV screen; CIA-SPAN showed mobs from the Religion of Peace burning effigies of the Pope for baptizing a prominent Muslim writer. He forgot the screen and pondered the thick file on Johnson before him. Slowly, he opened it and began turning the pages; then paused—a page caught his eye. It had come from very early on in the process, when Banquo read everything

Johnson had ever written. Examining the man like a bug under a glass. Combing his past for anything that might give Banquo & Duncan a clue to the man and his character. Even going back to a tiny screed in a defunct Oxford magazine called *Scrivener*. The article about the old nursery rhyme in Orwell's *1984*:

> *"Oranges and lemons," say the bells of St. Clement's.*
> *"You owe me five farthings," say the bells of St. Martin's.*

Ending with the dark lines:

> *Here comes a candle to light you to bed*
> *And here comes a chopper to chop off your head!*

But something in those bells spoke of a long buried, long ignored deep care for the past and regret at a great civilization slipping into oblivion. It spoke well of the student Johnson, that he could see as much. They'd paid the scribbler five measly pounds.

"It's not important what I believe," Banquo murmured softly, finally answering Wallets' question. "It's only important what *he* believes."

—— ✖ ——

Giselle came home for dinner that night. Mexican takeout, enchilada Suisse, and lots of beans and red rice. They ate at the big kitchen table under the shiny racks of pots and pans, shoving the white Styrofoam platters back and forth, trying not to make a mess of things. Then digging in the Sub-Zero fridge for cool glasses of milk when the salsa kicked in. Giselle turned the pages of a recent *Vogue*, occasionally showing Johnson the latest must-have and asking, "What do you think?" But answering herself before he could, with a simple "Blech." The spread showed a red John Galliano gown strung with loopy threads from bust to ankles like a flapper's dress, the whole thing a quivering mess of fringe.

"Maybe for my *funeral*," she said. "If I'd died during Prohibition."

She kept on, turning pages and making remarks; Johnson watched her. He stopped hearing the actual words and nodded silently at each new silly picture. Quietly enchanted that she was with him that night and talking about things that didn't matter. There was something safe and normal about it all. The young lady perusing the latest goofy fashion, her father simply watching.

When they were finally done and stuffing the remnants of Paco's Tacos into the compactor, Johnson managed to say, "I'm going to be away for a week. An assignment. Want me to bring you anything back from Iran?"

Nothing unusual in Daddy going to strange places. Giselle didn't raise an eyebrow. "No, just you."

CHAPTER NINE

What to Do with a Lemon

A very sober Peter Johnson looked up from his hospital bed. The taste of gin and tonics in his hotel room at the Azadi Grand long since faded from his tongue. Compared to this bare hospital room the hotel seemed Shangri-La, a far distant place of ease and comfort. That crap in North Carolina had never prepared him for this. Or had it? He wasn't sure.

Over the course of several days the patient had lost count of the procedures. The barium enema. The catheter up his urethra. No solid food, just a vitamin-protein drip. Stomach pumped twice. An anal probe worthy of an alien abduction. He remembered a series of X-rays, including his testicles, squeezed between photo plates. A full CAT scan. The hospital's new name translated roughly as The Hospital Center for the Promotion of Health and the Celebration of Virtue, but before the Revolution known simply as Vanak Hospital. His "doctor" was a lovely, gentle man named Ali Ebtekar. Every day he came in to look at Johnson's chart, and every day he said the same thing, "We're very close now; thank you for your patience."

Johnson knew the score. First, the authorities were looking for an implanted global positioning chip stuck in his body somewhere. As the technology got smaller and smaller, the procedures got longer and longer. Soon, they'd shred you to find the thing. He didn't have one, so he wasn't worried. And secondly . . . obviously . . . Sheik Kutmar intended to soften him up like butter, then squeeze him through a sieve before the mullah deigned to meet him. God, if he ever got to Dr. Proton, what would be left? Today his polite physician came in with a broader smile than usual. Ahhh, Johnson knew: the day of release.

With many a tut-tut-tut and some pleasant clucking, a fey male nurse wheeled him in a wheelchair to the front desk and glass doors of the hospital. The nice lad smiled sweetly at him, and Johnson knew that if the mullahs were ever overthrown, this guy wouldn't lose a minute applying for a visa and moving to Massachusetts to settle down and get married to a guy named Hansel.

"I'll be your best man," Johnson confided, but the kid didn't speak English.

Releases and forms in Farsi were handed to him. At least he assumed they were releases, but he signed them anyway. The clerk processed the bill for his stay on his Visa card, liberated on the day of his arrival and now returned to him. The whole business cost about $6,000. He signed the charge slip without comment and wondered what other mysterious charges would appear on the next bill cycle. After all, the plastic had been out of his possession some three days. That's a lot of charge time. Right now, he'd bet it was refrigerators, air conditioners, and satellite dishes. Maybe some personal computers or software they'd copy and pirate. Trademarks, intellectual property, and copyright protections didn't mean squat in this corner of the world. Never had.

What's mine is mine, and what's yours is mine. He'd square it with Visa later. Let Banquo do it, for that matter.

Kahleed from the Information Ministry and his driver from MahdiCab were waiting for him at the curb. Both men took each of his hands in welcome, almost petting them, grinning, one after the other as though delighted at the outcome of some long arranged plan.

"Auspicious day!" Kahleed exclaimed, opening the taxi door. "Sheik Kutmar and Jazril Mahout say to meet them at the Ministry. His Excellency wishes to meet you. Yes. *Him.*"

Kahleed gave Johnson a large beautiful poppy flower, bright red, in a clear plastic stem vial to keep it fresh. "Give this to His Excellency. He is a man of many sympathies, among them the most fleeting symbols of life. He will look kindly upon you."

As they drove, they left the windows in the cab open. The driver apologized—the air conditioning wouldn't work today, but maybe tomorrow. Johnson knew where the Information Ministry was, straight across town from the hotel, but they seemed to be taking a roundabout route. First, through a crowded bazaar. It was an open market, with saffron and yellow awnings, stalls of fresh produce, melons, grapes, olives, open-air butchers hanging skinned upside-down goats with deathly grins straight out of *Guernica* and booths selling everything from Cabbage Patch dolls, to DVDs and cosmetics. Among the stalls were the inevitable heroic posters of Mahmoud Ahmadinejad in open-collared shirt and even larger posters of His Excellency Mohammed Gul, former president, spiritual leader, "reformer," and lover of pretty poppies.

The man's full name ran like a babbling muezzin: Hojat al-Islam wa al Moslemeen Sayyed Mohammed Gul. Rendered in English the tongue twister: Proof-of-Islam-and-of-Muslims-Master *Mohammed*—a name used only by those who claimed direct descent from the Prophet himself. *See?* his name said, *I come right from the Prophet, so don't think, just obey. Islam. Submit. Or else.*

Thousands of his fellow Iranians, journalists, doctors, poets, and professors rotted away in his jails. Many were beaten to death or died of starvation, while others were rendered back to their families for a night or two, then whisked off to jail again as a lesson to others. His Eminence had just returned from a victory tour of Harvard University, where no one mentioned the trail of blood dragged along the floor by his flowing robes, where nary a soul mentioned the stink of corruption and death that followed him like a dank cloud. Giving truth to the old Persian saying, "When a mullah calls, an undertaker is sure to follow."

Inside the cab, Johnson could smell the street, miles of dusty roadway, beneath which shallow sewers trucked their filth off somewhere else without really enough water to flush them clean. The whole Middle East smelled like that—never enough water. The odor of too many people living over too few drains. Where dried dung was still used for fuel in rural towns and kerosene cookstoves were more common in apartment buildings than Magic Chef ranges, even right here in the heart of oil country. Dung, burnt oil, human waste.

The noisy bazaar gave way to an open boulevard of apartment complexes, and the cab speeded up. Johnson saw dozens of mini satellite dishes sprouting from every other window and rooftop like a forest of gray mushrooms. The religious police couldn't keep up with demand. Every time they cracked down on privately owned satellite receivers, smashing them or cutting the cables, they sprouted up again overnight. The great window on planet Earth, the eyes and ears to the forbidden outside world with its endless temptations and earthly delights. No matter how hard you tried, no one could keep the Home Shopping Network from your door.

They were coming up to the Ministry building, still several hundred yards away, when Johnson saw something was wrong. The cross streets on either side of Mosaddeq Boulevard were blocked off with barricaded police lines, and behind barricades were the Thuggees of Ansar-e-Hezbollah, the "unofficial" religious vigilantes all in black, black kaffiyehs with clubs and machetes. The cab passed three cross streets, each one blocked off with several dozen Hezbo toughs behind the police lines. The Tehran Metropolitan Police stood in front of the vigilantes in their blue uniforms, as though to hold them back, but they seemed bored, as if they knew the outcome of this job all too well.

"What's going on?" Johnson asked Kahleed. But the Information Ministry man said nothing, and the driver pulled over, a block away from their destination. The cabbie turned around in his seat and threw a panicked look at Kahleed, rattling out something in Farsi. And Kahleed rattled back, waving his hands about in frustration.

Then it became clear. Fifty yards off, a huge body of protesters turned a corner and came into view marching right before the Information Ministry Building, several thousand strong, holding banners and chanting. Three or four local "news crews" were dancing ahead of the crowd, videotaping the scene.

"Who the hell are they?" Johnson demanded.

The cabbie and Kahleed shouted back and forth at each other for a second, arguing about whether to pull up in front of the Ministry building or stay put. The cabbie wanted to stay put, Kahleed wanted to go for it.

"Kahleed, answer me," Johnson said.

Kahleed left off his argument. "These are nobody! Apes and pigs. Can't you see?"

But what Johnson saw were Iranians of all manner and age, young and old, man and woman. "What do the banners say, Kahleed?"

At first the man sputtered, "I can't read. I don't know—" Then read off what he could: "We have not been paid—workers of the Kashan Weaving Company. Father has no water; Father has no bread. Iranian Labor Laws is the blood money of the martyrs—students of the scientific center for management of the province of Kashan." Kahleed took a breath. "This is nothing, Effendi. Nothing. Unhappy people, that's all. Nothing better to do than watch *Dynasty* and *Bay Watch* on pirate TV and make noise."

Then a sharp scraping sound. The uniformed local metropolitan policemen pulled aside the barricades on either side of the boulevard and let loose the Hezbo vigilantes. They came out of their cross streets with a roar of "*Allah Akbar!*" and swarmed about the cab like locusts, then ran straight for the protesters. The first ones to go down were the video guys, one cracked on the skull from behind as he filmed the banners, another as he turned to film the black-clad assault. When the Hezbos reached him they slashed his leg and arm, and blood flashed over the camera as it hit the ground.

The women in the crowd of marchers began to scream, pleading for their lives; many were beaten about their bodies. As the number of wounded mounted, the crowd began to disperse, then scatter as the banners fell. Suddenly, elements of Hezbos turned from the melee and rushed the cab. Clubs smashed the taxi's window glass, and all the doors of the cab were yanked open. Kahleed, Johnson, and the cabbie were bodily dragged out and thrown to the pavement. The thugs were yelling, and Kahleed was begging, trying to explain and ward off batons all at the same time.

Johnson kept shouting, "We're here to see His Excellency Moslemeen Sayyed! Moslemeen Sayyed! His Ex—" when he was clubbed on the elbow, and a ribbon of white pain flashed across his body, shutting his mouth.

Kahleed pointed frantically at the Information Ministry and cursed the fanatics when Tehran's Finest in their blue uniforms intervened, sensing something amiss. They shooed off the vigilantes and helped the three from the ground. The cabbie had a cut over his eye that dripped blood, and Kahleed limped. Johnson moved his elbow a little, and the ribbon of pain talked to him again, but nothing was broken. The Tehran local police grunted noises of annoyance and helped them toward the Ministry building. In a phalanx they walked the three men the last few yards to the granite entranceway steps, holding the glass doors open for them and ushering them inside. Johnson looked at his clenched fist. Somehow through all of this he'd clutched the pretty red poppy. The plastic vial was cracked, leaking a little water. The flower stem was bent at a peculiar angle, but not completely ruined.

Civil servants from the Ministry's reception desk came forward bearing antiseptic nappies for the cab driver and cooing at Kahleed in soft tongues. Suddenly the Ministry's glass doors were flung open once more, and a man in blue from the Tehran Police flung Kahleed's briefcase and Johnson's work satchel across the marble floor. The two items skidded to a stop at their feet as the doors swung closed, and civil servants from the Ministry graciously picked them up, clucking apologies. Johnson brushed himself off.

The more elegant of them gave a smile of welcome. "Please don't be distressed. It is very kind of you to come." At the bank of elevators Johnson noticed the wiry Sheik Kutmar looking like an enormous praying mantis in his flowing robes. He bowed once, directing him to an open elevator.

"You go now," Kahleed told Johnson. "The Ministry men take care of us."

––––––∞∞∞––––––

Sheik Kutmar joined Johnson in the elevator for the ride up. He glanced once at the bent flower, but his face betrayed nothing. The elevator doors swooshed open, and Sheik Kutmar led him outside. Through another set of glass doors and into a bright, luxurious sitting room. His Eminence sat on a gold brocade couch and stood up when they came in. Two security men in suits and sunglasses flanked the couch a step and a half behind the mullah. Another security man covered Johnson from the corner of the room, never taking his eyes off him for a second.

Sheik Kutmar stopped Johnson a few paces away from His Eminence and motioned for the bent red poppy in the cracked vial.

"Please, may I?"

Johnson gave it to him. Sheik Kutmar brought it to show the former president, kissing the fat man's outstretched hand before presenting the gift. Moslemeen Sayyed nodded, gazing at it mildly, looking for all the world like a plump happy turnip in his purple robes. Then smiled as if the flower pleased him. He murmured a few words as if to bless it. Then his eyes strayed to a large vase on a table. It contained nothing but poppies—and not just red ones but yellow and black and blue and orange ones. In fact, Johnson didn't think he'd ever seen a more wonderful display. Sheik Kutmar took the blessed flower stem and placed it carefully in the large bouquet, where the other stems kept it upright.

Moslemeen Sayyed spoke a few words clearly to the room, staring directly at Johnson. But it was Sheik Kutmar's voice that told him what it meant:

"His Eminence says, 'The strong stems uphold the weak ones.' Would you care to sit?" He motioned to a chair by the great man's side. Johnson approached and, as the mullah did not present his hand to be kissed, just paused for a moment. As the holy man bent to sit, Johnson followed suit, and so they reached the cushions together.

"Thank you for seeing me, Your Eminence."

Every time His Eminence spoke, Sheik Kutmar translated directly, and every time Johnson replied, the Sheik did the same for him, his cold, calm voice precise and startlingly clear. The former president was nothing like his emissary, not aloof, but familiar and genuine. Like talking to an old family friend.

"It is our pleasure, Mr. Johnson. I apologize for your reception, but Persians are a passionate people. Especially when we feel we are in a new world. But the truth is, the new world is really just the old world we know so well. Yet occasionally some event or realization is so strange and awful it breaks through our everydayness, and people don't know how to behave. And then disagreements occur." He waved vaguely to the windows, acknowledging the events outside. The turnip sighed.

"In the end, all passion fades; we get old and tired." Here he pointed to himself and touched his white beard. "But you're still young, like our people, and we must try to turn our sour days to . . . sour cream?" He indulged a smile, "Do you not have a similar saying?"

Johnson grinned and moved his elbow. "Indeed, we say, turning lemons into lemonade."

At which point His Eminence Moslemeen Sayyed laughed and clapped his hands.

"Precisely!"

A tray of lemonade was brought as if from nowhere. The security men filled glasses. At an un-translated word from His Eminence, the security men poured themselves glasses as well, and everyone drank. Johnson savored it, as sweet and tart as life itself. Then His Eminence began to speak in earnest.

"I am very glad you didn't give up or change your words as so many did when these larger troubles began. So many lost their bearings with regret and confusion, but not you. It was as though the terror in our world made you see clearer, and the truth of this rose up from your heart and soul for everyone to see."

"You're very kind, Eminence."

The graybeard dismissed the remark with an easy shrug.

"Hardly. Kindness is not one of my vices. I leave that to women and the children of the West. Let them bathe in kindness. It is obvious to many people that you have obeyed the stirrings of your heart. I'm here to ask you whether you are prepared to respect our total individuality. And by that I mean Persia. By that I mean Iran. I'm here to ask you whether you are fighting for ethical norms, the relativism of civilizations, the complex mosaic of the world that can never be resolved. I'm here to ask you whether you intend to use your gift once more."

Peter Johnson put down his half glass of lemonade.

"It's what I do, Eminence. That's what I do."

The blue eyes of the turbaned man stared into him, with the hidden question of *Really?* shimmering below the surface. And so Johnson drove the nail home.

"I'm not here to uphold norms of any kind. I'm not here to answer questions or resolve problems. I'm here to raise questions that can't be answered, pose problems that beg no easy solution. And demand answers only from those who have the power to push a button and end the world."

This last bit seemed to finally satisfy the graybeard turnip in the turban; he glanced silently at Sheik Kutmar, an unspoken command.

"Well, then you should start right now, Mr. Johnson," the Sheik told him. "Jazril Mahout and his crew were asked to stand by, and so the Al Jazeera people are here now. It's high time he took you out into the field. That is why you're here, after all."

Yep, Johnson thought. That's *exactly* why I'm here. But instead he merely said, "What of my luggage and laptop and so on?"

Sheik Kutmar waved off his concern.

"The hotel will be notified. We'll send everything along."

Johnson's heart leapt. And now he knew for certain they were going to give him all the lemons he could handle.

CHAPTER TEN

Kodak Moments

The road to Lake Kavir-o-Namak in the province of Khorasan ran some four hundred miles due east and then south of the capital across a salt desert, a whitish crystalline pan that passed for a "lake" maybe a millennium ago. Some two hundred miles east of Tehran the highway was wide, blindingly sunny, and, at noon, nearly empty. Dun-colored hills stretched off into the horizon; a grove of fig trees stood near a rocky stream that ran by the highway. A shepherd led his goats to the water's edge. The Jazz Man and the cab driver stopped for midday prayer on the road's shoulder. The minivan carrying the camera crew pulled up behind. Then all the men got out, put down prayer mats, and faced southwest.

When Johnson balked at joining them on a prayer rug, the Al Jazeera man, Jazril, gave him a withering look. For some long moments the men knelt in prayer bowing and speaking as one. At last, they finished with a final "*Akbar.*" They stood and rolled up their mats, and everyone got back in their respective cars. When the taxi was rolling along the road once more, Jazril turned to him and said mildly, "Mr. Johnson, be warned. This behavior will not be acceptable when we reach the facility at Gonabad. Dr. Yahdzi is a very pious man."

The facility at Gonabad! Would that they had reached it already! Johnson's irritation faded to amazement the deeper they drove east and then finally when they turned south toward the great lake. Fields of saffron flowers surrounded the road on either side, a magical carpet of pale violet petals stretching mile after mile, lazily nodding their heads in the hot breeze. The scent of saffron filled the air, making Johnson think of grilled shrimp or chicken turning that beautiful shade of yellow as the silken threads melted into the meat.

They reached the facility at about four in the afternoon. The guards at the checkpoint looked at the papers Jazril handed over and then got on the guardhouse telephone for a few moments. Regular Army? Johnson didn't recognize the regimental chevrons. A soldier waved them through, and they drove slowly past the open water cisterns toward a cluster of buildings. The place was a fortress. Barracks, guard towers, anti-aircraft emplacements with flak guns. Johnson saw camouflage netting on the side of a low hill, a surface-to-air missile battery. With what looked like a Chinese crew.

But the four gorilla-faced guards at the facility entrance were pure Persian. In an adjoining room he was strip-searched. He'd expected this. Then the body cavities, and not by anybody half as nice as his Tehran doctor. No one spoke a word. Finally, they marched him down a flight of utility stairs and round long hallways. Down more sets of stairs into the subbasement. Around more corners until he was thoroughly lost. The guards opened a pair of double doors and left them open throughout the interview.

Beyond lay Yahdzi's office. Dr. Ramses Pahlevi Yahdzi of the University of Isfahan. The office looked nothing like the one in Banquo and Wallets' charade. The place was filled top to bottom with servers and computer towers. The physicist glanced from his desk, circles under his eyes beneath his spectacles. With his lab coat rumpled, he looked as if he'd slept down there for a month.

"They say you've come to kill me," he remarked, nodding in the direction of the guards. Johnson started despite himself. "That you have photos of me on the walls of your study at home." The doctor shrugged to himself sadly. "How anyone could discover that, I wouldn't know." The only objects on the professor's desk besides a PC monitor were family photos. "Here, come see my pictures," he said to Johnson, motioning to him to come behind his desk.

One of the murder scenarios from Banquo's office came to Johnson, and he wondered in a panic: Was this *it*? This his chance? Why so fast? How about the gun? Or was there some other weapon he hadn't noticed? Was this the occasion for him to use his bare hands? The thought nauseated him. Worst of all, the two guards had retreated back down the hall and now sat at a metal desk drinking tea and reading magazines. The signal?

And then time slowed down as in a car crash, an adrenalin-fueled moment-by-moment slide show, as if he were inhabiting one of those picture flipbooks that kids fan through with slightly different pictures to create the illusion of motion: he saw the tiny wiry hairs on the tip of Yahdzi's nose and the squiggly red lines across the whites of his eyes.

When he blinked, the back of his eyelids flashed blood red. A rush of overwhelming failure washed over him: he didn't know what to do. Didn't have a clue. After all he'd been through, he was just going to exchange pleasantries, admire the man's photos, and studiously ignore the man himself, the engine of radical Islam's greatest leap forward since—when? Since Mohammed conquered Mecca? Since the Muslims took Spain? Since the Ikhwan rampaged through Saudi Arabia, creating the predicate for a Wahhabi petro-state? So Johnson stood on the precipice, staring into irrelevancy, perfectly useless to all and sundry. His grand plan? Sit on his thumb, admire the snaps, and have a cup of tea.

He followed Yahdzi's hand, dark creases across the pink-mocha palm, directing him toward the pictures. Each one leapt at him in a different way, telling a slightly different story, each adding to the previous:

First a black-and-white: Yahdzi and wife as a young couple. Yahdzi in a suit jacket, no tie. Smiling broadly in more carefree times. A tall slender woman stood beside him. She had an alluring, self-possessed gaze, elegant and pretty—a woman, indeed. Husband and wife, their eyes full of hope and anticipation at the wonderful future that lay ahead of them: those magical plans people make when all they see is clear skies to the horizon.

Next: Yahdzi and wife at the seaside with a new addition—a three-year-old girl holding one of her parents' hands on either side, this picture in the stilted colors of 1970s-era photography. Mama held a baby in her free arm, her eyes a little surprised at how things turned out. Not disappointed but not overjoyed either.

Another: everyone older now, a glossy group portrait. The two daughters, seven and four, rapscallions. The older daughter looking like her mom, everyone sitting close together in a photography studio smiling aggressively for the camera. Happy, prosperous, even blessed.

Still another: A group shot again, everyone about five years older. Standing outside. The background showed a Spartan trailer in a bleak landscape, a house that looked like it was hauled over miles of desert, streaked with dust. Yahdzi's wife leaned into his shoulder. One of her fingers gripped his forearm. But all those blue skies were long gone over the horizon of her life, hopes and dreams that never seemed to materialize. And you could see as much in the lines around her eyes.

Last of all: just his wife. Standing. Her arms hanging by her sides, hands empty. Inside some sort of scientific facility: concrete walls, cold neon lighting making her olive complexion slightly green. Horror show. She looked unnatural, forced and strained. Johnson was drawn to her eyes again. Gleaming dark brown eyes that faded seamlessly into her pupils. He saw something new there. He saw what he thought was alarm. The road of life had taken an unexpected, irrevocable turn and not for the better. Yes, *fear.*

⸙

Why include this picture of all pictures? Unless it had some point. Unless—in a flash Johnson understood. This man was no fanatic. Jazril the Al Jazeera man was full of it. The professor was a hostage. And *terrified.* You could see it in the gray pallor of his face. The way he tapped his fingers on the desk. A facial tic blinked at Johnson, and what was really frightening—Yahdzi knew about it. Each time the spasm jerked his face, his fingers as if by instinct began to rise to calm the tic down, knowing all the while it wouldn't help.

Johnson's brow furrowed, and his eyes met the professor's, showing he understood his dilemma. And Professor Yahdzi nodded, acknowledging the fact. Then said matter-of-factly, "They tell me that if my work is not completed on time, my wife and daughters will be terribly disappointed."

All of Johnson's panic evaporated. Something in him knew he owed it to this nervous wreck of a man to betray no surprise. Pretending everything was normal would be their bond. Their secret in this strange and awful place. The pretense of strength, almost as good as strength itself. Betray nothing, and you betray no one. Keep my secrets, and I'll keep yours.

"Thank you for seeing me, Dr. Yahdzi," Johnson said. "The last thing I'd want is to distract you in any way. Can we make it easier if an assistant showed me around, and I reserved my most important questions for you?"

"I think it's only proper if I start you off on the right foot. Begin with me. End with me. What happens in between we can let God decide." Johnson could tell the man meant what he said. But just then he glanced over Johnson's head, a brief smile crossing his face; someone had come into the office. "Ah, our Between is here already!"

Yahdzi's assistant was a young woman of about twenty-five, with a sharp nose and cheekbones that couldn't possibly go any higher, her face complicated, even lovely. Sober and polite, she was the professor's finest student at the University of Isfahan. Now assigned to him exclusively. Johnson took to her immediately, as she was called, deliciously enough, Yasmine. She followed silently beside him as Professor Yahdzi explained the various features at the Gonabad facility. The Jazz Man's Al Jazeera film crew stumbled along behind taking some standard setups. In this building, that meant the double row of silver centrifuges under the banks of lights—the whirligigs that spun yellow cake into fissionable gold—as Dr. Yahdzi explained how this particular enrichment would never be pure enough for weapons, but energy and medicine instead. Johnson took notes, while the goons, ever present, hovered nearby. The Revolutionary Guards seemed more concerned about this woman doing a man's job in the presence of strange men than the physicist showing state secrets or a scribbler taking it all down. And Johnson wondered whether it was always like this for her—in class, in the street, every time she came to work?

When the whole group took a break in the facility's cafeteria, the goons sat at a table to themselves, while Dr. Yahdzi, one table over, explained how much he had been instructed to show the Western journalist and where they were headed.

"We will be driving west, stops at Yazd, Zarrin Shahr, and north to Zanjan and Tabriz. In this way you can see a good sampling of our facilities—five out of twenty-five sites in a ten-day period. Some, of course, are not as remote as Gonabad, so I can guarantee you better dining," he said with a wan smile.

He glanced at Yasmine, silently cueing her. "This is a rare privilege for a Westerner," she said. "Even the IAEA hasn't inspected the last two sites." She handed him a glossy folder bulging with paper. "Here are briefing materials about the facilities we will be visiting. I think they will repay careful study."

Then, from out of a manila folder, Yasmine slid some photos with Farsi captions, the English printed below on taped slips of paper. These were the facilities in question. Johnson flipped the photos over and saw a longer paragraph in Farsi typed on the back.

"Can we get these translated?" he asked Yasmine.

"I will for you," she replied. "That one says, 'Tabriz Number 3, built 1998. *Fabriqué en France.*' Made in France."

Johnson glanced at another photo, then flipped it over. But instead of an explanatory paragraph, another photo was taped to the back. Yasmine didn't want to meet his eye. Nor did Dr. Yahdzi. He fidgeted, staring down at his lap. The second smaller photo showed a New York street scene in fuzzy black-and-white. He recognized it immediately. Abdul's Delicatessen near his apartment in Brooklyn. The photo showed Giselle leaving through the glass door plastered with stickers advertising the *New York Post*, Boar's Head Smoked Turkey, Marlboros, and Copenhagen Mint Snuff. She was beginning to unwrap a pack of cigarettes. It could have been taken yesterday. Johnson recognized the new Prada black techno suit jacket she had just bought. And her haircut was up to date, a short bob. It seemed his two guides felt personally dirtied by all this. While from the goons' table, one of the men met his eye boldly. A tiny smile crossed his eyes.

Johnson wanted to get up and throw a chair at him. He had never minded people assuming that he had his price—since he did—but he hated threats. They were insulting, premised on his essential cowardice. Although this was a new one. No one had ever threatened Giselle before. And that they would stoop to it—against a supposedly friendly, in-their-back-pocket journalist—told him more than he wanted to know about the medievalists, the supremacists and hacks who ran the show here.

He used to think evil was subtle, alluring even. He had come to realize that, more often than not, it was dumb and ham-handed. Its instrument not some silver-tongued Deceiver but a fanatic whose head was stuffed with idiocies and lies barely controlling his snickers over a threat to an innocent young woman. What was it that Bruce Meyer the lone Righty at that NYU panel said those years ago? "If they didn't kill you or someone you love, it wasn't for lack of trying."

He had another urge to throw that chair. But they'd simply beat him and send him home empty-handed. He wasn't going to betray any fluster right now, despite a flutter of panic in his chest. He even forced a smile. "You've given me a rare privilege, Dr. Yahdzi. And I'm going to take advantage of it the best way I can."

CHAPTER ELEVEN

One of a Thousand Iranian Nights

The whole caravan left late that afternoon. Dr. Yahdzi and Yasmine returned to the lower office to collect some papers and books, but the Professor curiously avoided overloading his briefcase with printed materials, choosing instead to take his family photos off his desk, all of them. An odd gesture, as if he couldn't bear to be without them.

At the entrance to the facility, the cab was nowhere in sight, and three small vans waited for them. They seemed to be trading up. The Al Jazeera news crew took one van. Jazril, Johnson, Dr. Yahdzi, and Yasmine the second. And six goons from the facility took the third, outfitting themselves from a fourth, large panel van nearby, unloading tents, sleeping bags, kerosene stoves, water, and food lockers. Then arming themselves: AK-47s, flak jackets, sidearms, wireless headsets, and what appeared to be night-vision goggles. What they needed all this hardware for Johnson couldn't imagine, until Yasmine explained:

"Some nights we will not be staying in houses with beds or in villages with policemen. We want to keep Dr. Yahdzi safe. Their van has the big radio and cell phones." And then he noticed that yes, their van was outfitted with a satellite dish. Not even the Al Jazeera news crew had that.

"What did you think of our briefing materials, Mr. Johnson?" Yasmine asked, pulling his attention back away from the preparations.

"Call me Peter. And sorry—I took a nap instead." He hoped to elicit some warmth from her. Instead he got something chillier. She wasn't impressed with him, and he read her eye, which said, *Lazy* man.

"I didn't prepare them for my benefit, Mr. Johnson, but for yours. I *know* what's in them. If your trip is going to be of any use to us, Mr. Johnson, you should too." She put a particular emphasis on the honorific 'Mr.,' almost scolding him. And it made him squirm. So maybe his time would have been better spent during that stolen hour trying to snooze on the couch in Yahdzi's office.

In true Peter Johnson style he'd taken the Professor's offer to lie down for a spell like a duck to water. But his racing mind didn't let him sleep; the snapshot of Giselle was as real with his eyes closed as it had been when he had been holding it in his hands. He thought of Yahdzi and what they had in common—a picture to remind them both of the insidiousness of a regime willing to turn a man's most intimate ties of blood and marriage against him, to make what should be a refuge from this world an instrument of coercion.

∞

They piled into the van under the watchful eyes of their minders, the facility's goons. The driver and Al Jazeera's Jazz Man up front. Yahdzi and Yasmine in the next row of seats. Johnson behind them. And another empty row behind. But what struck him were the evil looks he and Professor Yahdzi received when Yasmine entered the van with them. Something visceral from the eyes of the guards, as though the three adults committed some mortal sin that no absolution could possibly put right. And Johnson could guess exactly what. Yasmine covered her body with a chador and behaved, compliant and submissive, but neither Jazril the Jazz Man, Professor Yahdzi, Johnson, nor their driver was one of her relatives. Though higher authorities, like Sheik Kutmar or Gul, might tolerate it in the cause of Johnson producing a favorable story, for the local goons the presence of Yasmine was in itself enough to make her obscene and profane.

One of the guards shouted something in their direction. An insult, or a warning, sounding like, "*Asanzan, bahdzan, sagzan.*" Spitting the words out in contempt. If Yasmine thought anything, she kept it to herself.

The three vans pulled out of the facility about dusk, as the sun showed them its final red eye and the shadows crawled from building to building. Johnson looked again for the surface-to-air missile batteries. He spotted two more this time. One was off a roadway cut into a hill, where the large green tubes sat on their tractor-trailer launching pads. The whole array carefully camouflaged to be invisible from the air and protected by overhanging rock. The other battery sat on its tractor-trailer backed into a cave. Unless you had your own eyes inside this fortress, you'd never know they were there. And that was the idea.

Johnson, the Professor, Yasmine, and the Jazz Man rode in silence for some time.

"What does *sagzan* mean?" Johnson finally asked. No one in the van seemed to want to answer him. The driver blew on an opal ring on his left hand, to fog it up with the moisture of his hot breath, then rubbed it against his thigh as if to polish it—clearly some sort of nervous habit. Jazril, the Al Jazeera man, pretended to read something in the failing light. Professor Yahdzi looked down and opened the briefcase on his lap searching for something without any real intention of finding it.

When Yasmine realized none of the men would speak, she answered for them. She turned back toward him. Coldly and calmly:

"*Sagzan* means 'dog-woman,' Mr. Johnson. *Bahdzan* means 'bad woman.' *Asanzan* means 'easy woman.'" She paused to take a breath, to glance at the two other men in the car with her, then back at Johnson. "The Revolutionary Guards were calling me a whore."

He suppressed the urge to look into his lap like the others. Instead, he met her eyes and saw in them a brave defiance. A deep reserve of nerve.

"I'm sorry. I should have guessed."

"That's all right," she said. "We can't all be Scheherazade talking sense into those who have none."

At this, Jazril rebuked her, and she gave him a rapid-fire response with a few darts of her own. Finally the driver shouted at everyone.

Unholstered his pistol and banged it on the steering wheel with one hand. That needed no translation: Shut up! This wasn't just a driver, but another enforcer.

They all lapsed again into silence.

After a spell, she translated: "I told him, 'Shut up, Pig-Boy.' He said—"

But Johnson waved her off, "I get his drift."

And Professor Yahdzi grunted at the Jazz Man in contempt, clearly siding with Yasmine. Al Jazeera's Jazril was a pig-boy from a long line of pig-boys. They rode the rest of the way that night in silence.

———

Sometime during the night, all the vans pulled to the side of the road and shut down so everyone could catch a few hours of sleep. The Revolutionary Guards pitched a single tent some ways off the road, in the desert. One of the goons came forward, hammered on the window, and started shouting. Then furiously pointed at Yasmine. Apparently they wanted her to seclude herself out in the tent for the remainder of the night for decency's sake. At first Dr. Yahdzi shouted at the man, telling him to go to the devil, but after a few moments as the goon's face twisted in a gargoyle of rage, Yasmine put the issue to rest, touching the Professor lightly on the forearm.

"It's all right. I'll be fine." And with that she exited the van into the custody of the religious police.

The three hours of sleep passed slowly. Johnson dozed off and on, curled up on his seat, his mind occupied with Yasmine and the insults hurled at her. What must it take to bear such contempt, not to suffer a catastrophic internal loss of confidence? Then, his imagination took over as he drowsed.

Despite himself, he suddenly saw Yasmine's dark lips speaking words to him, words he couldn't make out but knew were meant for him alone, enticing him to some delicious moment, shrouded and veiled—but more satisfying than any he ever knew. What Jo von H said of him once in pure admiration, "Peter, you're a dog through and through." So true.

A quality considerably more plausible before three wives, the downward slope of middle age, and the alcoholic's inability to focus on the task required even when a young woman was available to focus his mind.

∽

When the vans started their engines at dawn, they caught Johnson in mid-snore with Yasmine sitting beside Yahdzi as she had before.

She looked back at him. Over the back of the seat she held out the briefing materials once more. Thirty solid pages, single spaced in a manila folder. "Please don't forget about this." Reality banished his reveries. There were few things Johnson hated more than a nag. He sat there, slowly coming to his senses, rubbed the rheumy white gunk in the corners of his eyes, worked a tongue around a cottony mouth. His joints groaned from being cramped all night. God, how he hated being told what to do. First thing in the morning, or any time. When he took the damn materials from her, the whole bundle fanned into his lap, falling to the car floor with a rush and a slap.

"Christ."

Yasmine turned away in disgust. The man was hopeless. Johnson sighed in defeat. A nagging harpy lurked somewhere in the heart of womankind; it queered the romance every time. Cheat on him, rob him blind, ignore him—anything but tell him what to do. Over decades, he slowly came to realize you couldn't achieve real intimacy without give-and-take that included—tragically—being told what to do. Realized too late. Too late for his first marriage, to Jo von H when they were kids. For his second, marrying a classical dancer he thought he would dominate by virtue of his worldliness and a preponderance of knowledge. Giselle's mother. Françoise turned out to be the worst of all, and he couldn't help smiling. What a bobcat. Like Mother like Daughter. And even for his third, to the mature and sensible Elizabeth Richards, art curator, who had always told him that, when he died, she—not the others—would be the widow.

Briefing materials, Mr. Peter. Remember? He retrieved the splayed folder from the floor. Then sat with them in his lap, staring stupidly out the windows. He hated reading in a moving car. Presently they left the desert, and the vans climbed into mountains. Very slow going, as the roads were single lane, barely wide enough for a tractor-trailer with its long turn radius. The air cooled as they followed the road ever upwards, a thousand feet, then two thousand, then three. Pear orchards clinging to the steep hills showed their fruit in the September sun, then thick copses of trees and patches of bare rock, a running mountain stream. A doe and her Bambi gingerly stepped across the rushing water.

The papers in his lap seemed as dull and worthless as pretty much any briefing materials ever stuck under his nose on any junket anywhere in the world. Perhaps man didn't feel a universal hunger for freedom, liberty, and "All-the-Shrimp-You-Can-Eat Night" at Red Lobster, but he sure as hell felt the all-consuming urge to disseminate propagandistic, barely readable briefing materials. It united every government in the world—liberal capitalist, Afro-kleptocratic, Communist, Islamist, Euro-socialist. The one true God.

Johnson's eyes began to glaze over—the poorly produced cheap grainy pages, dense Courier type all running together—when he noticed something unusual. A single letter bracketed in faint green ink. He thought he had seen that before, and sure enough, flipping back three pages, he saw another. He flipped ahead and found yet another, then another. He was wide awake now. He stared at the back of Yasmine's neck, at the all-covering folds of her green chador. Coincidence? The same color green as the pen. She was looking resolutely ahead.

He began to piece the letters together. Flipping ahead frantically now. More letters faintly bracketed. N-O. N-O-*C-H*. N-O-C-H-*O*.

NO CHOICE.

Another series spelled out: KILL HIM.

And then another, simply: DO IT.

Johnson's breath came fast. He thought he was going to have an asthma attack. *I-T-S-W*.

IT'S WHAT HE W.

Wants?

He was through one side of the folder. There was more; several paper-clipped sections. He moved to the next. P-T-O-Y-O-U. He flipped to the next. Nothing. What the? IT'S WHAT HPTO YOU? IT'S WHAT HE PTYO U? He worked it over and over but could make no sense of it. When he dropped the damn thing earlier did he lose something? Or maybe mixed up the order? He flipped through all the pages, his eyes searching for the faint green ink. Maybe on the backs of the pages? He turned them upside down. He went through from the beginning, making sure he had everything. But there were no other marks. He wanted to reach up and shake Yasmine, demanding, "What about—?"

But what did he want? The message was obvious.

YOU MUST.

NO CHOICE.

KILL HIM.

IT'S WHAT HE WANTS.

Last of all picking up with the text P TO YOU.

UP TO YOU.

—∞—

He sat bolt upright in his seat, as though the message had frozen him in an electric current. Dr. Yahdzi was absorbed in the contents of his briefcase, flipping from one family photo, one Kodak moment to another. Touching the framed pictures as though they were flesh and blood. Yasmine clearly heard him going through the papers—how could you miss it? But she didn't turn, said nothing. And he interpreted her silence as a confirmation, a kind of command.

Banquo had said, "You'll have to allow the situation to mature, ripen." Is this what he meant? What the hell was Johnson supposed to do with this rotten peach? Attack the physicist bare-handed and hope the driver shot one of them in the struggle? Wait for another sign from heaven?

Johnson barely noticed the distance they had traveled. As they entered the tiled and stucco town of Natanz, a single peak loomed over their heads. "Vulture Mountain," Dr. Yahdzi explained, looking back at Johnson. "It's told the troops of Alexander the Great killed Darius III somewhere close by." And Johnson strained for some hint in that seemingly innocuous historical observation. Was he supposed to play Alexander to Yahdzi's Darius? To keep the vultures at bay? Nothing seemed innocuous now.

He began to pay attention again to the passing scene. The caravan rumbled through an almost empty town, a ghost town of closed shops and no real street life. A few women head to toe in black, faces covered, walking along the cobblestone streets. They passed a number of walled mosques, then left the town behind; ten or fifteen miles onward they reached a plateau and the long straight road to the Nantanz Enrichment Facility.

The road broadened out, fully two-lane now so as to accommodate opposing traffic. A cluster of concrete buildings to the left, flat like square pancakes.

"The original uranium separation pilot plant," Yahdzi said. "No point in going through there—it's an antique. They've cannibalized most of the equipment for other projects."

Their van reached a traffic circle, a large one enclosing the everpresent concrete open water pond, common to nearly every nuclear or industrial facility. Johnson smelled a stink coming up from the water—sulfur, rotten eggs—was some of it sewage? Run-off waste product? Somehow they'd missed that at the Banquo briefings.

Coming up on the right, another six buildings, pancake-style again, but the interesting area lay behind it on a raised berm, maybe a quarter mile square, like a huge, flat, fortified hill. There a small army of men busily toiled away, steam shovels and huge Kubota bulldozers moving earth, cranes dropping scrap into huge dump trucks to be carted away. Even at the distance of a thousand yards Johnson could tell the earthmovers were enormous, with fifteen-foot tires and many cubic yards of hauling space. They would make quite the impression at even the most well-appointed Monster Truck Show. They roved about the top of the mound like intent yellow construction robots, back and forth, belching exhaust.

And yet nothing much to see at ground level. Clearly, the workers were in the finishing stages of some large underground installation and now packing earth over the top.

"That's where we're going," Yahdzi told Johnson, pointing straight ahead. The entrance was a huge tin-roofed affair like a long airplane hangar. It sloped down, the roadway vanishing into the ground. The concrete mouth larger than the double barrels of New York's Holland Tunnel, but it was traffic-controlled in a similar way, red light/green light. With a fortified checkpoint and a heavy-gated barrier with yellow and black warning slashes.

The first two vans pulled up to the guardhouse. The van with the goons stayed behind in the hangar. For a few moments, Jazril the Jazz Man dickered with the security personnel, while the open concrete tunnel mouth waited to swallow them all. Then the gated barrier slid sideways, and the two vans were cleared to descend.

What Johnson saw that day was what many people since have come to see only in photographs, video pictures, and blueprints, which convey little but curious technological stainless-steel forms, like sci-fi art. The high-capacity, high-purification centrifuges. Much more elaborate than the ones at Gonabad. A forest of tubes stretching down one side and up the other, all humming at once. Twenty-four hours a day. Three hundred sixty-five days a year. Taking radioactive material, whether in rough cake form or slightly processed, breaking it up, spinning it 'round and 'round, separating the heaviest elements, making it purer and purer. Until at last it could be packed into a nice little baseball and put to God's divine purpose.

What you felt when you walked down one side was the raw power of spinning cycles, a steel whirling dervish of scientific ecstasy: not in the peaceful Sufi staves of devotion, but in the Mahdi's righteous anger at all things not-of-Islam, *not-of-submission*. A throbbing wrath ready to rip the heart from the very earth and show it still alive and pumping to the stars.

One of Shakespeare's sonnets came to mind, driven into Johnson's head eons ago by a master at Bradford Grammar Public School. The teacher's excruciating exertions lasting him a lifetime. He closed his eyes and repeated it to himself:

> *They that have power to hurt, and will do none,*
> *That do not do the thing they most do show,*
> *Who, moving others, are themselves as stone,*
> *Unmoved, cold, and to temptation slow;*
> *They rightly do inherit heaven's graces*
> *And husband nature's riches from expense;*
> *They are the lords and owners of their faces . . .*

What disturbed him most about what these men were doing here was that they did it all in a country where many women never showed their faces. Keeping their heads, ears, and mouths hidden in some obscene mockery of chastity. Those who strayed were called a dog-whore. Or forced to sleep in a tent. While these men who toiled down below were not people "to temptation slow" but still and every day subject to every temptation known to man. The first and foremost—to "inherit heaven's graces"—actively lusting after the "power to hurt."

And no one here, in this place—above ground or below—grasped the consequences of husbanding "nature's riches," what it meant to manufacture this madness on their own.

Except for Yahdzi, of course. He was the indispensable Iranian indigenous contribution—evilly coerced—thus a testament to force and intimidation as much as to native skill and know-how. Take him out, and all that was left in the equation was the will to power, a bunch of pious morlocks tending their hardware, praying to machines with murder on their minds. Leaving one last hope: if you could take out this one little cog, the whole juggernaut might grind to a halt.

The green ink was never far from his mind, but as Yasmine and her Professor chattered innocently, Johnson took dutiful notes, a good little monkey scribbling like the very embodiment of Hear No Evil, See No Evil, Speak No Evil, writing down everything they said about "peaceful uses" and "medical applications" and "civilian electrical power" and other imbecilities. Johnson left the facility saying, "Thank you." Jazril's Al Jazeera crew got their video, and everyone got in their proper van, going up the great dragon's throat, and thence out the tunnel mouth, under the eyes of the guards. Thankful they had looked at Medusa through Athena's mirrored shield and lived to tell the tale.

⊗⊗⊗

As the caravan left Nantanz at midday, the centrifuges pumped away in Johnson's mind, jumbled up with the words on those pages. *IT'S UP TO YOU* . . . They retraced their trail from the great plateau on the planet of the construction robots. The sky above turned a sickly shade of yellow ochre. And the wind spun dust dervishes along the roadside. They didn't make it as far as they wanted. Down through the tiled ghost town of Natanz, with its similar-sounding name to the Nantanz facility's, and back down out of the mountains and into the desert. Only as far as the outskirts of a nameless village. A dozen concrete huts, no café, no Holiday Inn, and no heated swimming pool. The three vans pulled up just outside the town in a circle on the sand like a wagon train. They could clearly see the unpaved town square.

The Jazz Man said, "These are a very *pure* people."

While Dr. Yahdzi warned, "Here, we must really behave ourselves."

They wandered outside the van and thought about scrounging firewood for a campfire, but abandoned the idea as the wind picked up, streaming across the sandy ground, blowing yellow dust. They settled for ransacking the coolers for food, bringing bread and olives and hummus into the van to eat.

The goons went off to pray with the imam, whose ancient ancestor, one of them told Jazril, "converted Alexander the Great to Islam." This, of course, absurd on the face of it, as Alexander and Darius preceded the Prophet by millennia. Still, many in this part of the world believed the Prophet's influence reached back into the depths of time as well as forward.

The storm came like a great ochre wave, blinding any view of the cool, green mountains in the distance. The travelers felt the sun go down in the changing shades outside the car window, the ochre light slowly turning gray, then finally black. They could see houses in the village lit up, blurry lights barely showing through the storm, and hear under the sighing of the wind the chanting and the praying of many voices answering the imam.

But the voices faded as the wind moaned about the metal panels of the van. They ate a little and drank a little water by the light of a Coleman lantern. When it came time for Yasmine to cloister herself for the night in a tent that the Revolutionary Guards had set up, Johnson wondered out loud. "Is it really necessary? The storm—"

"Yes, it's necessary," she told him. "Especially here, in this village." But even as she reached for the van door handle, the wind lowed to a near shriek shaking the van. Only a few yards off, Yasmine's tent tore at its mooring, yanked its stakes from the ground, and took off, first hitting the side of the van with a thunderous clap and then sailing off into oblivion.

God seemed to have taken a hand. And silent glances were exchanged between Dr. Yahdzi and his assistant. A resignation to fate—she would stay. The storm erased those lights of the village, leaving blackness all around, even though the houses were only fifty yards distant.

The driver barked something out in Farsi, pointing at Johnson. Now what? Yahdzi translated, smiling: "He says you are a lazy bastard and you got to stretch out last night. He says you should take the front seat so Yasmine gets to be secluded in back." They didn't dare open the doors, so Johnson clambered up to the front seat and watched with some amazement as Dr. Yahdzi and the Jazz Man hung a prayer mat from the van's safety handgrips, using the large paper clips from the briefing material as their hooks. Yasmine vanished behind the hiding cloth.

Johnson noticed the driver making what he guessed—so hard to see—was his ring-blowing motion. Johnson tried to ignore him, slumping, the van black inside with its lights out and the Coleman turned off. He could hear the others breathing. Over time, even as the temperature dropped outside, inside the air grew stuffy. You could smell the acrid body sweat of the men.

Johnson's mind swirled in a riot of conflicting thoughts. It seemed he could feel them pressing against his head, or maybe the storm affected the barometric pressure. In any event, he wasn't going to sleep. What he would give for a few hours of blessed forgetfulness, a few hours without those green ink letters looming in his mind. Although for all he knew, they would disturb his sleep in grotesque porn-shop neon, flashing, taunting, glaring.

He stared ahead at the black windshield, listening to the millions of sand particles bouncing off it, faint tic-tacs, like they were in an insistent sleet storm. How precarious he felt inside the swaying van, with the tumult pounding him from without—and from within. Who was he to decide whether to kill a perfectly decent human being, on the slim basis of some inked up words?

Then, it came to him very clearly, a wave of relief washing over him: sure, he was imagining the whole thing! Why was he worrying himself? He could be here, as he had been so often in his life, literally just along for the ride. Learn something no one else knew, get a guided tour of exotic locales, and dine out on it for months back in Manhattan. Why was he ruining all that? There was even a cute bird along that he could try to charm out of her chador. *Relax, Peter,* he told himself. *Relax, and the whole predicament goes away.*

The very next moment he pondered Banquo's within-the-range-of-plausibility scenario and how one act could change the world. A Serb assassin. An archduke named Franz Ferdinand. Millions dead. Didn't the Professor *want* him to do it? He recalled Banquo's spiel that if he failed to act, he wouldn't be able to drink away the consequences.

But he could try, he gamely thought. *He sure as hell could try.* He shifted in his seat to turn on his side, facing the driver, and the words loomed again, DO IT.

As Johnson wrestled with himself, the driver stirred, as if uncomfortable. He reached to his hip, pulled off his holster, and methodically placed it on the dashboard. Johnson stared in horror at what he could barely see. He sat straight up in his seat and pressed against it as hard as he could, trying to get as much distance from himself and that weapon in the dark, away from that talon of fate.

He imagined he knew what Belshazzar must have felt when those words appeared on the wall during his feast, damning his worship of false gods:

MENE, MENE, TEKEL, PARSIN

A half dollar, a half dollar, a penny, and two bits. Except Johnson didn't need a Daniel to interpret this sign for him.

He wrapped his arms around his queasy belly and sat buffeted in the night, the recesses of his mind calling up somehow that in Aramaic *parsin* had been a pun on Persian.

He closed his eyes tight for a long time, like he was in pain. He tried to picture what kind of gun sat in the holster. A small revolver of some kind. Yeah, the Dick Tracy gun straight from the Prop Master back in North Carolina. You pulled back the hammer and squeezed the trigger. Simple as *bye-bye bang. Now you know how close you have to be . . .*

He wanted to evade it but couldn't: This was his sign. The debate over. He wasn't imagining things. What they told him at Banquo & Duncan had been borne out. And now—and now the only question was *tekel*, the word for "weight," interpreted by Daniel as "you have been weighed on the scales and found wanting." Would he be found wanting?

And he knew he had decided. He tried to tell himself he hadn't. He told himself, sure, he could back out any time. But those felt like fake reassurances, like when he was about to go on a bender or cheat and tried to argue himself out of it, knowing all along he'd succumb to temptation. And this too was a temptation, more delicious than he ever imagined. To finally commit an act that *mattered*. Now only the question of courage remained. Of will. Of somehow arriving at the sticking point.

For a fleeting moment he worried about Giselle, but he trusted Banquo or Wallets would go to her. Help her through the aftermath. He felt that little twitch of fate, banishing all the doubts and inhibitions. The final rightness of his act. Slowly he reached out from his sitting position, achingly slowly. His fingers touched the dashboard.

Beside him the driver gently snored.

He waited a while, no idea how long in the murmuring dark, listening to the driver's breathing. Finally he leaned forward and reached the holster on the dash, feeling the smooth molded leather. The holster was a snug grip, no safety clasp. The gun came away into his hand without any fuss. He held the gun up in front of himself, in a kind of homage. What had Banquo said about being in jeopardy the moment he arrived in this awful place? Everything he had always been was about to vanish. Say good-bye, Peter Johnson. And he thought to himself, "See you at the other end."

"They're all dead," said a soft voice. "That's why I keep their pictures." Johnson shifted in his seat, looking aghast at the scientist behind him. Yahdzi looked right back, as if he knew everything passing in Johnson's mind. "You'd be doing me a favor."

Johnson felt an asthma clutching at his windpipe. The muzzle pointed, tremblingly, toward Yahdzi's chest. The physicist looked passively back at him. Maybe he'd have done it himself long ago, given the chance. Suddenly Johnson was aware that the driver was staring at him too. Wide awake. Daring him to finish.

For a moment he wished he hadn't picked up the gun but left it alone on the dash. Like in Banquo's office. But he was adamant. Nothing personal, Professor. His finger curled around the trigger, surprisingly tight, just a little more pressure, just a little more, one last tug—

The van rocked, and there was more noise than simply the wind. The goons were back, heads wrapped in keffiyahs, violently slapping the van windows. A sharp crack, and window glass sprayed across Johnson's face. The sticking point arrived. Now or never. He pulled the trigger and shot. Pulled it again and shot, emptying the chamber, round after round. Until a dozen hands came for him, dragging him into the screaming maelstrom of the night, punched, kicked, face in the dirt, the only way to know if he was facing down or up, gasping for air, shouts, and he went limp, giving in to the chaos.

As his body hoisted in the air, his mind drifted to Yasmine. Did he hit her by accident? He didn't know, but he hoped she was okay.

CHAPTER TWELVE

A Peter Johnson Solution

Banquo appeared in Trevor Andover's office in Langley, Virginia, without a summons from DEADKEY to account for his actions. The inevitable plasma CIA-SPAN showed a news conference with the execrable Sheik Kutmar. He stood before the marble front of Parliament, the Majiles, his narrow face over a small microphone. This time the man wore a suit jacket and open collar, no robes. He was making his statement in Farsi for NITV, National Iranian Television, and a single Persian reporter translated immediately into Arabic on a Teletype line, and above the first type line, another real-time translation into English courtesy of CIA-SPAN. The Sheik knew he had somebody in the U.S. Intelligence Community by the balls, so he squeezed them softly and without malice in the smallest venue possible. You couldn't hear the questions, just his answers:

"As I said before, this man, this American journalist, was present at the incident. We're checking his credentials. I have no information on the condition of the professor, Dr. Ramses Pahlevi Yahdzi, at this time."

Pause, while taking a question.

"Assassination? Attempted assassination? I don't use such words."

Again he paused, while taking a question.

"A spy? Of course, he's a spy. We let many spies into our country; we have nothing to hide. He may well be tried; he may well be executed, but that decision is not up to me."

Again, another pause, while he listened to the next question.

"Retaliation?" And here Sheik Kutmar stroked his finely chiseled beard. "If a trust is broken between one nation and another, if legitimate journalism and the free exchange of information are sabotaged by one power at the expense of another, there are . . . there are always consequences."

Deputy Director Andover used a small, thin remote to lower the sound on the picture. He turned his gimlet eyes on Banquo, who seemed to have ignored the whole thing. Infuriating. His old colleague steadily thrummed his fingers *one-two-three-one-two-three* on his chair's armrest as though annoyed at having to wait. DEADKEY's voice came out pure acid:

"Pleased with yourself?"

Calmly, Banquo measured the man across the desk. "Are you accusing me of something?"

Deputy Executive Director Andover at first bristled, then with every ounce of self-control managed: "Do I have to? You've brought disrespect to the U.S. government, made a mess of our position, and put innocent lives at risk. Deny it."

Banquo sighed, then spoke quietly and methodically, as if explaining to an adolescent, "First of all, Deputy Director, no one respects the U.S. government, not the one you represent anyway. Secondly, our position is already a mess; you and others put us there. And thirdly, outside of your mother's belly there's no such thing as an innocent life.

"Let's be frank," Banquo continued. "You and I are in the business of betting lives, occasionally saving them, but generally spending them on an infinite board, with an infinite number of moves, in an endless game. If you can't bet those lives, then don't you dare sit in that chair and lecture me. I'd bet *yours*, if I thought it would help."

"Oh, spare me the Cooper Union lecture," Andover said. "You've handed the Iranians a tremendous propaganda victory. I can't imagine a bigger one. You might as well have the president of the United States announce that we've discovered, yes, the mullahs *are* in communication with Twelfth Imam after all, down in the well—just like the little Turbans say. Besides the fact, you've violated the law. It's worse than a blunder; it's a crime."

"Trevor, please tell me you have a copy of *Bartlett's* somewhere in here." Banquo had decided if they were to have a sarcastic bitch-fest, why not go all the way?

"What?" Andover asked, incredulous.

"You mangled the phrase. The Talleyrand remark goes, 'It's *worse* than a crime, it's a *blunder.*' The phrase doesn't work turned around. You robbed Talleyrand of all his surprise and cleverness." Banquo wagged his head, amazed that a man such as DEADKEY could arrive at such an exalted position under the nose of the gods. "Trevor, you've got the mind of a cutpurse with the blade of a butter knife."

"Sneer at me all you want, Stewart," Andover said, calling him by the name he knew him by when they both got their start decades ago. "You still have to answer to Executive Order 12333. Just like everyone else."

"Ah ... the prohibition against assassination. Issued when the country scraped bottom in its prestige and power in the world? The one you cheered on as we staffed the upper echelons of our intelligence services with geldings and their attorneys at law?"

Banquo paused for a moment, thinking, then remarked, "I imagine you think all that legalese somehow protects *you.* Well, line your pants with national archives if you think it helps. But you'll wet yourself when they slap on the handcuffs like everyone else."

There was nothing about Banquo DEADKEY didn't hate. Where could he even start with him?

"Look, Stewart. This office is not the Harvard Debate Society. One of your clowns, in effect, an agent of the U.S. government, was captured in an assassination scheme. The London Litvinenko sushi hit played big in the international press, but this could be bigger, and we're not even Russians, not yet anyway. You own this fool, Peter Johnson, and now you're going to have to pay for the privilege."

"Make me."

DEADKEY was flustered for a second. He expected at least a shimmer of regret and instead he got 110-proof insolence.

"Just for the record," Banquo continued, "Banquo & Duncan believes the Litvinenko assassination was a *warning*. To all and sundry that the Russians will do anything they want, anywhere they want, and we'll just say, 'Such a pity Mr. So-and-So ate bad sushi.' However, if you think B & D had a hand in this Yahdzi nonsense, *prove* it."

Trevor Andover sighed. Now it was his turn to explain matters to the village idiot:

"Prove it? I don't have to. That's a U.S. attorney's job. You met with Peter Johnson. You sent him to Iran. I have copies of passport requests for your team. Airline tickets. There's no coincidence here. Johnson will last about forty-five minutes under mildly stressful interrogation. Tomorrow they'll have him in front of cameras confessing he was put up by *you*. Every Donkey in this capital will be braying for your head, as soon as my friends in the press tell them who to bray for. And every Elephant will be hiding under his bed, pretending they've never heard of you before. You're a pathetic relic, Stewart."

DEADKEY paused to let that sink in. Then finally, "I pilot this ship. So when I see a drunken sailor, the Director doesn't get involved. It's slap the drunk in irons, throw him in the longboat, or man *overboard*. Able Seaman, you're walking the plank at dawn. Every news account is going to start with the words 'rogue operation.' Remember this number: 202 371 7000. The law firm of Skadden, Arps. Ask for Bob Bennett's assistant. And pray for a pardon when the legal bills approach twenty-five mil."

Banquo looked at Andover for a beat, with his brow raised, as if to say, *Are you quite done?*

"Consider the following, Trevor. I didn't think I'd actually have to explain:

"One. Peter Johnson is a well-known crank, a toiler with a long history of attacking the U.S. government. Nobody's going to believe him when he suddenly claims he's *my spy*.

"Two. Johnson has a string of felonious financial transactions, documented by Banquo & Duncan and certainly worth the time of the IRS.

"Three. The one name he knows to cough up under mild interrogation is Trevor Andover."

At that, Andover blanched, and Banquo suddenly wished that one of his people thought of it before the scribbler left for Iran, that the bluff was true.

"Deputy Director, not only are you going to run interference for Banquo & Duncan, keep the bats out of my hair, but, actively help me."

"Why, in heaven's name?"

Banquo thrummed the armrest again, but went on, his assured voice seeming to enclose DEADKEY's head in a vice. "Because you've been sloppy and foolish. Your predilection for certain 'art,' and your ongoing nonsecure and . . . ah-hem," he paused for a moment, "prurient instant messaging with a nice young lad in Chevy Chase, one of your school chum's sons, just fresh from his bar mitzvah. Lovely gift by the way. So I come to present you some options. Take them, or not. If not, you know the number of Skadden, Arps as well as anyone."

Trevor Andover's face went red, then deadly white as it sank in how thoroughly his colleague had bided his time and laid each chit in his secret strongbox, only to produce the bill when he needed it most.

"*Robert Wallets* helped you with this, didn't he? That goose-stepping brown shirt. And that fat, sloppy dyke you always use."

"Of course. Both very reliable. I believe in long-term relationships. Also two of my traders. They get bored. So I set them to tasks. Opposition research, mostly." Banquo dropped the thrumming and took a cigar from a leather case from inside his jacket. He removed it from the wrapper and inhaled the fragrance.

"There's no smoking in the building."

"Wouldn't dream of it." Banquo held the cigar between his two first fingers; content to feel it there, then clipped the end, letting the nub drop to the carpet. "First of all, I may require your assistant, Bryce, for a while. It never hurts to have the son of an attorney general on your staff, if only for insurance purposes. I commend you on your choice of aide-de-camp. Also, control of the O'Hanlon investigation, which we have to change from a fishing expedition to a whale hunt."

The CIA-SPAN plasma screen showed a scene that Banquo paused to watch: a balding Muslim intellectual talking to an interviewer in Arabic. He wore a suit and one of those shiny ties so popular right now with talk show talking heads. The Teletype read: "Interview with Sheik Safwat Higazi, Egyptian preacher, Al-Nas TV, "I Have a Dream" speech, clarifying religious matters and fatwas where Muslims are free to kill Jews . . . ." Underneath the scholar's smiling talking head the translation: "When I said what I said, I was dreaming a beautiful dream . . . that we were one country called the Arab Islamic States . . . This is the dream I dreamt . . . that the Israeli Jew, not just any Jew . . . in order to kill an Israeli, one must make sure that he is a Jew . . . that he is between twenty-one and fifty-four, the age of the reserves, and if she is a woman, she must be between twenty-one and thirty-four, which is the age of the reserves [for women], and even then [the killer] must be sure that she has no children . . . "

Banquo turned away from the screen in disgust. "Well, I'm glad he cleared that up. But the point is, I think, that I *do* believe him, and without reservation. Don't you?" Here, he glanced at Deputy Executive Director Andover. "I see not. Well, that's why we're having this discussion. This man we just saw happens to be an Egyptian, but his views are commonly held not only by tens of millions of his countrymen, but also by hundreds of millions across the Islamic world. From country to country, capital to capital, mosque to mosque from Mauritania to Mongolia."

DEADKEY cleared his throat. "Is there a point?"

Unperturbed, Banquo went on as before, "In a way I admire him. He wants the Jew dead, and he's honest enough to say it. Which leaves people like us in a rather awkward position. Should we stand aside? Or stop him? And if we're going to stop him, perhaps things have to change—so that it's no longer simply reformers, moderates, and pro-Western politicians in the Middle East who wind up shot in the head or blown to pieces in their cars along with their wives and children. Ponder the question at your leisure.

"Anyway, I will need from you real-time updated Long Eye satellite information over Iran and elsewhere in the Middle East *on demand*. We are going to turn our Peter Johnson problem into a Peter Johnson solution. Congratulations, Trevor, you've been promoted. You are now part of the big Us. That being: *us versus them*. As such you will string the Director along and maintain the story that this is a rogue operation— your favorite phrase—by a *rogue journalist*. You will feed that line to your friend Walter Pincus of the *Post*, among others. Meantime, I think the Iranians will want to know what they've really got in Johnson, and even if he starts implicating us immediately, it will take them a while to believe him. We have some time to play with."

"So we are going to lie to everyone we know," Andover said. "Cover up an assassination scheme. And then what? Send in the Marines to rescue your clown? Or better yet, suicide him? And remind me, what do we—sorry, *Us*—get out of all this?"

Banquo looked gravely at the pale slice of white bread across the desk. "We're going to get him out, and if we don't get him out, we're going to minimize the damage of not getting him out," and here Banquo dropped his voice, "one way or the other."

"Just so I'm perfectly clear. What's stopping them from squeezing your newest employee like a lemon?"

"Nothing. Let them. What's he got to say? Not much. The twenty-four-hour hold-out rule doesn't even apply to him."

Andover looked away and shook his head, muttering to himself in horror at the entire business, "The *risk*."

"There's a word!" Banquo responded, as if Andover had been addressing him. "I have another for you: 'Prevail.' You know that one, right? Look it up on the thesaurus feature on your computer if you don't. We're going to try to disrupt the Iranian program again and again, until it's clear that other means are necessary. We're playing to win, Trevor. Add the word 'victory' to your vocabulary."

DEADKEY snorted in contempt. "OK, let's see where your man is." He turned to the laptop on his desk and hit a few keys. The image on the CIA-SPAN plasma screen shuddered for a second, then crystallized to clarity. A satellite shot of the earth from a hundred miles up. In one corner of the screen the word "Asset" appeared, then a blinking cursor, awaiting an answer.

"You have a code name for your drunken scribbler?" Andover asked. "Save me the trouble of looking it up."

"Bartleby. Case sensitive." Banquo paused. "And now you know."

DEDCI Andover smirked. "I'd prefer not to." He struck a few more keys, then typed in "B a r t l e b y," which appeared dutifully from the cursor on the large flat screen. He hit Enter, and the Long Eye satellite image found its target, zooming downwards toward earth in huge jumps: Forty miles. Twenty miles. One mile. One thousand feet. Thirty feet. Longitude and Latitude. It wasn't Tehran but another city. Maha%#!*—something—the letter field space couldn't quite get a grasp on the proper name. Then finally straightened itself out. Mahabad. Local time. Name of the street, number of the building. But buildings in this part of town didn't have numbers, so that space was left blinking N/A. First you saw a visual of the structure's roof, the common layer-cake type, flat squares. As the view came closer, the words—signature mode—came up on the screen as the satellite system switched from visual to the software filtering program that detected what lay below. The image of the structure dissolved into mist as Long Eye found what it was looking for. A radiation signature.

Finally, fifteen feet. What you saw was a living suit of clothes, pants and jacket, filled out in human form. Just like Claude Rains in *The Invisible Man*. The cursor space now read: Bartleby, Peter Johnson.

When offered the low-grade uranium-dioxide dye by Langley, lately used on turbans, Banquo had decided to give it a try. Nothing to lose. So his team impregnated every shirt and jacket, pants, skivvies, and socks they could find in Johnson's wardrobe. At least a hundred articles in all—spiriting them out of his closet and back again during his two-week camping trip. Chances were he'd pack some, and pack some he had. Unless his captors stripped him naked, Long Eye could find him. So far, so good.

"Operations wants to call our special fabric tagging 'After-glow.' But the Director thinks it's too effeminate," DEADKEY remarked. Clearly, he didn't think so.

Banquo shrugged. "I think by the time this organization decides on a name for your fancy dry cleaning our opponents will have figured it out.

Then we'll have a dozen naked men on payroll with no clothes, and we can go back to the occasional suppository or rice-chip."

Oh, how Andover hated him. But even if he despised the guts encasing Banquo's cold heart, the man deserved credit. After *all this time*, still in the game, surviving every attempt to castrate the last hard men of secret war, perfectly capable of doing things out of necessity that quailed fainter hearts. Shocking the geldings and their attorneys at law.

Andover held his tongue. In every sense, Banquo had him, *check and mate*. Still a last kernel inside DEADKEY wouldn't relent, like a spoiled child arguing with deserved punishment. "Even if I'm sent to a federal country club for an *entirely platonic* friendship with a bar mitzvah boy, what makes you think I could ever agree to this?"

Banquo stood before the desk and sighed. Sometimes repetition helped:

"Three simple reasons. First, because you're not going to get away with cutting me loose on this—I've been playing this game as long as you have, Trevor. Second, because we've got a man down in Iran, and even a coward like you has to realize it's best to salvage the situation, turn it to our advantage, before feasting on our own. And third, because you're a bloodless worm. Have I missed anything?"

CHAPTER THIRTEEN

Attack of the Green Slime Body-Snatching Triffids

Inside the U.S. Attorney's office at 86 Chambers Street, O'Hanlon showed Agent Wesson, Agent Smith, and Bryce a book he had been reading. It was an old book, a paperback. He fanned the pages and then showed them the cover, a yellowish-green image of vines entangling fleeing people. "I went on Amazon and found Banquo's last book purchase. So I bought it too: *The Day of the Triffids* by John Wyndham. I'm a bit of a sci-fi buff but had never read it. It's a 1950s novel about a genetically altered species of mutant walking killer plants that take over the earth."

The two agents stared at him blankly. Bryce looked first at his shoes, then at the ceiling as if embarrassed to be in the presence of a man losing his senses. O'Hanlon kept on: "The plants were farmed for their seed oil, you know, like corn oil or safflower. They could walk on their three stalky legs, so they planted roots where the ground was best, then ranged at will. Men kept them in herds. But the mutant walking plants possessed one serious hazard, a whipping tendril with poisonous sacs. Unless properly neutered, very dangerous. But controllable. Until a doomsday device concocted by some Evil Government, in the form of a spectacular green meteor shower, blinded nearly every living soul on earth. The lucky few who either slept through the deadly spectacle or worked underground awoke to find themselves owners of the world.

With only one competitor: the mutant plants, now escaped off their reservation, who would soon overrun the stinking remains of civilization, a collective intelligence, hunting down every warm body—Triffids—and the leeks shall inherit the earth."

Again blank stares greeted O'Hanlon, and so he explained. "If we're going to investigate the man, we should investigate his mind as well. What kind of fellow reads a book like this?" He tossed the paperback across his desk for them to examine. "Who knows, maybe between you three potted plants you can make me one good Triffid. Banquo's blind to us. Go hunt him."

U.S. Attorney O'Hanlon's investigation started out like every other investigation: court-ordered wiretaps, lists of probable cause, in this case possible securities fraud, put to a pliant judge, under investigation himself and willing to do any favor offered. Moreover the operation had no name, just a file number: NYDOJ 228: Agents Smith and Wesson; subject: Banquo & Duncan; complainant: A. Bryce, redacted.

The two agents allowed the redacted Bryce a small desk outside their offices. A desk with no telephone, no PC, but at least a chair, making him sit there like the class dunce in detention, waiting for them to include him in their Girl Scouts ritual campfire. Which they eventually did, letting him do scut work of every description—for which he was thoroughly grateful, if only to break the monotony of staring at taupe-colored walls. And eventually he even got to use his own laptop.

Every day or so at 6 PM the two women and their boy gathered in O'Hanlon's office to review the day's results, going something like this:

O'Hanlon: "Well?"

Agent Wesson: "Standard trading. Volume about $10 million on a couple dozen trades. The rest of the portfolio lost a few points. Nothing serious. No communication whatsoever between the B & D computers and any suspicious entity, including Langley. It's all bank-to-bank, account-to-account. Banquo is on the phone constantly. He orders lunch delivered to the office from one of the delis on the concourse. Chicken salad on white, lettuce, mayo. Dr. Pepper. His traders go upstairs to the Rainbow Room; B & D has a reserved table—the two swells live it up. Clams casino. Steak. Two martinis. Later, the first night shift trader comes in and starts to follow the dateline around the globe, L.A., Tokyo, Seoul, Hong Kong, Sydney, and so on. He's relieved by the Late Late shift, same thing, Berlin, The Bourse, Paris, London. The night guys play a lot of online chess and poker and cruise porn. One of them is seeing a gal he met on a site called Cheating Wives. We can follow her around if you want. Another is planning a trip to Vegas for a miniature modelers' convention, where he's going to receive an award for constructing a realistic WWII Panzer diorama named Counter-attack Below Monte Casino in 3:40 scale. I saw a picture of it online; it's really nice. Then the whole shebang starts all over again. These guys are the most boring people in the world."

O'Hanlon to Bryce: "Okay, what about you?"

Bryce: "Around 6ish, I join Agent Smith on roving stakeout. It's sort of an overlap thing—Banquo goes to dinner, generally a top-end restaurant, Le Cirque, the 21 Club. Then he goes home. Three times a week his Chinese cook makes dinner. Sometimes a lady friend visits, the widow Mrs. Dorothy Faneuil Farmer-Madison, Park Avenue socialite, and mother of celebutant Tiffany Farmer-Madison." An item from the *New York Post*'s Page Six—about the Farmer-Madisons' renting out the Fifth Avenue Jimmy Choo's boutique for Tiffany's seventeenth birthday party and letting all the girls take home a pair of $500 shoes—slid across O'Hanlon's desk and thence directly into a file.

"Sometimes he reads, sometimes he rents DVDs from Netflix. The last three delivered were *The Thing from Another World, Invasion of the Body Snatchers,* and *The Green Slime.*"

Here Bryce paused as the U.S. attorney mused out loud: "First he's reading about killer plants. Now he's watching 1950s sci-fi. *The Thing* is about soldiers and scientists in an arctic research facility finding a frozen creature from a flying saucer. The creature can't be killed and has a cellular structure similar to vegetable matter." Bryce snorted. O'Hanlon ignored him and continued, "As everyone knows, *Invasion of the Body Snatchers* is about killer man-mutating pods. And *The Green Slime* speaks for itself. A killer mould on our space station."

"Maybe he's worried about a fungus among us," Agent Wesson volunteered dryly. Agent Smith looked at her askance as if saying, *You just had to, didn't you?*

Bryce picked up again. "Other than Mrs. Madison, he's a monk, except the three drinks a night before bed. I know this because I've counted his bottles in the trash. Armagnac. $200 and a smile to the doorman let me scrounge to my heart's content. I go back to my hotel about 1 AM, after Agent Smith returns from a couple hours sleep or that other agent relieves me—I didn't catch his name."

The first time Bryce gave his report, O'Hanlon said nothing. Merely glanced in Wesson's direction. And she seemed to acknowledge his eyes. The second time the Irishman glanced even more pointedly in Smith's direction, and the second agent squirmed, gritting her teeth in frustration. The third time, Bryce finally added, "Once again I got back to the hotel after the other guy relieved me. The Grand Hyatt is really nice; I meant to thank you."

O'Hanlon finally growled, "Glad you like the Hyatt. They built it special for you. What *other* agent?"

Wesson put her head in her hands in dismay.

While Smith countered, "We *tried* to tail him. To nail him down. He's practically a *ghost.*"

❦

Then came the proverbial knock on the door.

"Come in," O'Hanlon grumbled. He seemed to know what was coming. The door opened. A gray-eyed man stood there, suit and tie, plenty of poise, no nonsense and all business.

"Mr. O'Hanlon, my name is—"

But the lawyer held up a hand, interrupting, "I *know* you from somewhere. Wait a minute; lemme think."

"Can I come in?" And there was something else about the newcomer; he seemed to bring a chill with him into the room. The kind of presence that made people catch their breath, take a step back. You could see it in the faces of agents Smith and Wesson, a touch of flush, a touch of fluster; Smith fussed with her hair; Wesson smoothed down her skirt. Tiny little gestures, but very uncharacteristic for both of them. And O'Hanlon didn't like it. "Oh, for Chrissakes have a seat." The newcomer found a chair and sat. Finally it dawned on the lawyer.

"I got it!" O'Hanlon exclaimed. "Wallets." Then to the others, "A couple of years ago we got a tip from your firm about a guy named Hammoud, a Lebanese Al Qaeda creep who had it in for the Holland Tunnel. God, how could I have forgotten *that!*" He shook his head in dismay at his own lapse. Then sighed, "I never made the connection. Too many cases come through here . . . "

With his memory returned to him O'Hanlon didn't need any further introduction. He said to Bryce, "Is *this* the agent who relieved you?" Bryce's ears turned red. Wesson harrumphed. Agent Smith made no remark, a wry smile on her face.

"So how did you know where to find me?" Bryce asked, chagrined.

Wallets didn't deign to look at him, gazing straight ahead as he settled in and folded his arms. "From your little bread crumbs."

Bryce looked devastated. To the silence of the room, Wallets added, "Don't beat yourself up. Banquo & Duncan has followed your operation with interest. I kept my distance and my head down while you did your initial snooping. I watched the watchers." Still looking straight ahead, head cocked at an angle. "Agent Wesson here is partial to the salad bar at the Fantublau's across from Rockefeller Center. No croutons, low-fat dressing, and a diet Cherry Coke. Agent Smith—"

"All right, all right, you've embarrassed us enough," O'Hanlon waved his hand to him, the new man in the room. "Just know I reserve the right to do the same to you some day."

Wallets nodded slightly, as if to say, *Yeah, right,* but instead said coldly, "Let's talk about how I can help Department of Justice, for the Southern District of New York Case 228 known as: NYDOJ 228: Agents Smith and Wesson; subject: Banquo & Duncan; complainant: A. Bryce, redacted. Can we talk about that?"

O'Hanlon took his feet off his wastepaper basket. For Chrissakes. What *didn't* he know? Investigation, redacted or not, totally blown. Mildly, he said, "I don't know, Mr. Wallets. Can we?"

Wallets put his feet up on the other side of O'Hanlon's wastepaper basket. "Your case has taken an unexpected turn. You're working for us now."

With superhuman effort, O'Hanlon kept the steam from rising into his head. Was it possible? Nobody at DOJ had bothered to give him a heads up, nobody at Langley. Was he to take the word of this grim messenger boy? "Let's slow down a minute," he said.

As if on cue the fax machine on a corner file cabinet whirred to life, spitting out a communication. From DOJ. Smith handed it to him. The official redirection. "Please show every accommodation and professional courtesy to—"

At this point O'Hanlon wished he'd sent Bryce away when he showed up at his doorstep that morning: *Did he need this?* On the other hand, he hadn't been psyched by the pointless original investigation anyway. Say what you will, Banquo & Duncan at least appeared to be on the ball.

Cooperating with them would be unusual, but in his years in New York, O'Hanlon had gotten used to the CIA mucking around where it wasn't supposed to. A playground for foreign diplomats and spies, the city always had provided the CIA leeway for working on domestic matters where it didn't belong.

O'Hanlon let the fax drop to his desk. "Okay, I guess we're working *with* you."

Wallets took his feet off the wastebasket and uncrossed his arms. For the first time he looked like he didn't want to drive his broad shoulders through someone or something until he got his way. "Should be advantageous to us both," he said. "Now, you want to look across the river. There's a girl who's picked up some questionable friends."

O'Hanlon glanced dourly at his two agents, Smith and Wesson, including Bryce.

"What kind of friends?"

"You tell me," Wallets said. "Let's find out."

"Well, ladies, what do you say?" O'Hanlon said. "Shall we move our Federal Clown Show to Brooklyn?"

Which they promptly did, picking up their girl as she went to work that very next morning from the Brooklyn apartment and covering her 24/7 until they got somewhere. The minute the apartment door closed, a quick toss of Johnson's pad. Nothing much.

Then traveling to work with her to the Metropolitan Museum of Art. On 83rd Street east of Fifth, the Publications Department occupied a four-story annex. The department created the Metropolitan's swank gift catalogue four times a year. Giselle proofed advertising copy, a job she took after leaving the 9/11 ruins of Salomon Smith Barney. It had been wangled by Johnson's third ex-wife, Elizabeth Richards, Assistant Curator, because she liked the girl, still friends even after the divorce. It wasn't Giselle's fault if StepMama and Papa couldn't get their act straight. So they tapped into the stepmom's phone and PC too.

The surveillance was a combination of low tech and high, the old fashioned and the new. Agents Smith and Wesson followed Giselle on foot or by cab or subway, cell phones plastered to their heads and yapping like everyone else in New York. Bryce displayed an unexpected talent for picking locks and jimmying open doors. A talent learned from panty raids at Choate, no doubt.

They also had at their disposal one of the city of New York's four spanking brand new federally funded microwave surveillance trucks; something the Department of Homeland Security finally did right. The mobile unit was concealed in a slightly beat-up panel van stenciled on the outside with red Chinese pictograms and in English, "Hung Fat Oriental Food Distributors—Long Island City," like a purveyor truck for Chinatown restaurants. Inside, packed to the shock-absorbers with the latest listening and watching gear. So much of it had been miniaturized since 9/11, the Hung Fat van was actually roomy enough for the whole crew, including a technician. All manner of homing devices to track people, shotgun microphones, digital recorders, uplink to Langley, and, most importantly, microwave itself.

Here, the technician, Jordan, a young, shiny-faced black guy who always wore a flat-brimmed classic tan-and-brown San Diego Padres cap and operated with quiet, deliberate movements, occasionally pausing to unwrap Bonomo taffy or tear into a bag of Lay's potato chips.

Jordan could monitor multiple groups of targets on multiple screens or even split monitors, plus sound, if you could drop a mini-mike close enough to the action. And not just out in the open either—around corners, behind doors, and even walls; through twenty feet of concrete into a subbasement; through the steel of a bank's safe on ground level; or fifty stories up in a high-rise apartment building. The targets looked like the images from the movie *Predator*, but you could still distinguish facial features, as preprogrammed templates.

With staggering effort a faceless team of code-writing drones had reduced the whole city to a global positioning grid, street by street and room by room, not quite down to the last closet or stairwell, but damn close enough. In this way, when Wesson, Smith, or Bryce spotted a promising mark, they could swoop in. All under the gray eyes of Robert Wallets.

O'Hanlon's leggy agents scored that first evening as if they'd been working the case for weeks. Giselle's date picked her up from work on 83rd Street and took her to dinner. He was a good-looking boy, with the kind of handsome, manicured appearance only a sophisticated city dweller can manage. The sporty, casual open shirt, the loafers, the managed scruff, and the $300 slacks didn't hurt either.

Smith and Wesson followed the couple south on the Downtown IRT subway line to Astor Place in the village. Using their cell phone cameras, enhanced imaging and passport photo database, they soon pegged the lad as Anton Anjou, twenty-seven, associate account representative in the local Banque Luxembourg. The French kid oozed beaucoup euros, flashing a gold Rolex and a gold link bracelet as if he didn't mind losing either or both to a mugger or a bet.

All of this was meticulously gone over and analyzed the following day at the B & D offices, where they'd regularly gather since their "redirection."

"Where'd she meet him?" Banquo wanted to know.

"We think a gallery opening," Bryce told him. "The Caselli Gallery doing Art Spiegelman for a *New Yorker* spread back in June. Frenchie bought her a Spiegelman original from the *Maus* book. $25,000 on his AmEx."

"How do we know he gave it to her?"

"She's got it hanging in the apartment. We checked."

"Does he stay there?"

"He did last night," Wallets told him. "But I'll bet she stays over with him a lot—he's got quite the townhouse on Grove Street; all four floors renovated. This kid is *loaded*. Nephew of some sort of duke."

"*Mais oui. That* Anjou. His uncle has been investing with us since '73. Only a fraction of the family fortune, you understand. About four million, high-risk stuff. Now about the girl. Is our gal seeing anyone else?"

"Not a chance." This from Agent Wesson. Then Agent Smith, pointing to a picture, "Look at her. She's a good girl."

Giselle was not a leggy beauty with sky-high cheekbones and a perfectly dimpled chin. She had been named prior to anyone knowing about *that* Giselle. Tom Brady probably wouldn't have given her a second look. Still plenty pretty with a $250 color-tint blonde 'do. Sure, a little thick in the middle, a round face, and yet to lose all her baby fat. Maybe never would. But most of the men in Manhattan who'd never date world-famous supermodels would be happy to be with her. It didn't look like Anton thought he was slumming.

The second night she was decked out, in knee-high shiny black boots and a silver shimmering blouse with the top three buttons undone. Smith and Wesson with Bryce along traipsed after the lovebirds to a place across town on 14th Street, Dirty Disco. Either a small club or a large lounge, depending on how you looked at it. Groups of people sat on the low-to-the-ground leather. The 100K sound system pumping out house and 1980s hip-hop ensured everyone would go home with their ears ringing. A small dance floor was crowded with dancers, seemingly jerked this way and that by the bass beat that made your feet vibrate if you stood still on the floor. No pictures possible in the barely lit club, and forget about recording anything.

The two G-Women and Bryce stood on the sidewalk watching the passing traffic and tried to decide which of them would least stand out. Bambi, Thumper, or the Preppie? Finally it was decided that Smith and Bryce would go. In case someone went to the rest room, they'd have both the men's and women's covered. Bryce loosened his tie and rolled his French cuffs on the outside of his suit jacket Wall Street trader–style, while Smith opened her tailored shirt another notch, and passed her sidearm to her partner. "There's no way I'm packing in this zoo. Too crowded."

Braced for the worst, the two shouldered their way into the midst of the dancing, drinking, grinding bodies. As arranged, Bryce hung back, and Smith got hit on within thirty seconds, letting various gentlemen buy her drinks that she managed somehow to avoid actually drinking. She flitted from gentleman to gentleman with a butterfly's grace, pretending to be offended by something or other they said and telling them, with a pouting smile, "See you later."

Until she had the one she wanted. He came from a group of three, him and two buddies, not at all fitting in. What would you call them? Swarthy foreigners? Middle Eastern *types*? Hell, they could have been Greeks or Cypriots just off the boat. But they weren't.

They were what you'd call Queens Boulevard *haute couture* from the cheap stores that lined the immigrant avenue. Cheesy knockoffs that would have seemed the sultan's robes in their country-of-origin, but downtown made them stand out as never-gonna-bes waiting for an imminent arrest by the Fashion Police. All three had sat, staring hard at Anton and Giselle, as though to cement the two in their collective minds. Anton seemed oblivious to their staring as he paraded his conquest in front of them. But there was something about his manner that implied yes, he knew them, yet acknowledged nothing. Giselle, for her part, like many women who loved the attention paid to them by one man, seemed oblivious to all others.

Smith noticed the table-lurkers watching. When she caught one fellow's eye, the others reproached their pal for taking the bait. But the eager one snapped something at his friends that in any language translated to "Why don't you have another glass of shut-the-fuck-up?"

His conversation with Smith was rudimentary and bordering on crude. His name was Abu Bakr ibn Tahlal. Student visa, economics, New York University. Did she know where Jordan was? Did she have many boyfriends? When the liquor began to work on him, his hands began to stray, and she excused herself to the Ladies' Room. Abu Bakr exchanged a few "I'm scoring" looks with his friends and eagerly awaited her return.

Which never came. And after fifteen minutes of lounging, his buddies laughed Abu back to their table for being such a sap. He sat, occasionally looking in the direction of the Ladies' Room, hoping against hope there had just been some misunderstanding. They all still kept an eye on Giselle and Anton. And when those two left, Moe, Larry, and Curly waited a few moments and left behind them.

The French nobleman took his princess back home to Brooklyn but didn't join her for the night, begging off with some excuse, which she took quite well—giving him a long smacker and him giving her some squeeze before she tripped upstairs. In another ten minutes he was sitting in the Acropolis Diner with the three musketeers, speaking a fluent mixture of French and Arabic. Where the three got very angry at Monsieur Anjou and where he told them to *"Calmez-vous. Maintenant et toujours!"* with a long extended finger in their faces like he was scolding children.

The DOJ Clown Show got it all in the Hung Fat van.

Wallets decided they should follow Abu Bakr and his two pals back to their own lodging, where they hit pay dirt. The three "students" lived together in a cramped smelly Brooklyn walk-up. Here, they did a fair bit of cursing, mostly at the unfairness of the world and how could a woman see anything in that French fairy. It's always the money, the money. But his time was coming too, when his money wouldn't count shit. Then some more arguments whether to fire up the DVR to watch "Jeck Bow" on *24* or *Disparate Housewives*, and fuk yeh, always pay the cable bill.

Back in the van, the whole gang was wedged in, watching the monitors. The technician quietly informed everyone, "You guys can knock off for the night. I'll get a Sniffer in there under the door and take a reading. But I can tell you right now—we're gonna get traces." Wallets knew what he meant: a sensor probe on a wire that registered explosives.

"You mean because of that?" Wesson said, pointing to a corner of the cheap flat.

"Yeah, exactly. Look at it. Soldering iron, wire spools, cell phones, chargers, magnifier with fluorescent bulb, top of the line Dell tower and wide flat screen . . . "

"A work bench."

—⊗⊗⊗—

First thing the next morning O'Hanlon himself rode in the Hung Fat van, more than pleased with their score, dubbing Abu Bakr and his two buds the Workbench Boys. Wallets failed to join them this time, giving them all a little more elbow room inside the cramped interior. They parked the Hung Fat van on 83rd and watched Giselle go into the Metropolitan Museum's Publications Department Annex.

"It's a long shot," O'Hanlon told Wesson, "but let's see if they've rented some storage unit out in Queens or Staten Island, a bill or something. If they have, we'll toss it."

Suddenly Jordan the Technician became uncharacteristically agitated as he listened to something. "Shut up, shut up! Get a news program. Turn on a news program."

"Whaddya got?" O'Hanlon demanded. They flipped on a regular TV, found a cable channel. "Who you listening to?"

"It's Elizabeth Richards. The Curator's office, somebody named . . ." he glanced at his PC monitor, "Josephine Parker von Hildebrand, *Crusader* magazine, Irving Place. She's calling the stepmom about the girl's dad. Very upset. Want me to put it on speaker?"

"Go ahead," O'Hanlon said, as he watched the TV screen. Sheik Kutmar's interview with the little-known NITV had finally broken through to Al Jazeera and thence to cable as the "credentials" of the American journalist had been confirmed. Now "under arrest" by elements of the Revolutionary Guards on charges of spying. The Fox News split screen showed the Sheik talking into that small microphone on the steps of the Majiles, while an insert showed a grainy photo of Peter Johnson.

High up on the entranceway of the Metropolitan Museum of Art, a well-dressed woman ran out the main doors—Elizabeth Richards,

Stepmom–Third Wife, Assistant Curator—nearly tripping in her heels as she went tic-tac-tic-tac down the broad stone stairs, her elbows clamped to her sides, hands keeping balance. The distress in her body and face plain from thirty yards away. She ran across the staggered traffic of Fifth Avenue, up the curb, and into Publications Annex, crying now. In a few moments Giselle would know.

"Apparently," O'Hanlon said, registering Wallets' absence once more, "something's come up."

CHAPTER FOURTEEN

Give Us Everything

Somehow Johnson had slept a few hours after being dragged from a vehicle, and—his hood finally removed—thrown in a heap on a sandy floor. Pure exhaustion. He awoke with sand gritting across his teeth, up his nostrils. Light entered the bare concrete cell from a small window high up a wall, the only light. And the first thing he realized was that he couldn't rise. Get up even to his knees. He felt like the condemned Man in the Iron Mask, condemned to the Bastille to rot in obscurity with a metal head. All alone—well, not quite.

In a corner of the cell, in a mound of yellow sand, lay a bat. The tiny brown creature—its flimsy, veined wings curled about it—lay there as though in the cone of a miniature volcano. It looked at him without fear, as if to say, *This is where I live, do you live here too?* Johnson stared at it a long time. What else was there to do? Musing on its extraordinary intricacy. So fragile yet indomitable. Sandstorm outside, not to worry—I'll sit it out in my little volcano. When it yawned with a tiny squeak, it seemed to smile at him.

He steadily grew more awake, his nerve endings working again. *Pain.* From a welt on his cheek. From both shoulders, where he'd been kicked and dragged hither and yon. Bruised tailbone; he'd smacked it against the van's door frame. When he tried to crawl to his knees, his groin shrieked *no!* But he needed to take a leak, worse than he could ever remember. He managed to crawl to the wall, unzip his pants. His knees would have to do. He tried to let go, really tried, but only razor blades came out. Like acid. Afraid even to look, afraid there'd be blood. All that effort yielded a few miserly squirts.

He looked. No blood. But the razor blades didn't go away—they just receded into the background. Shaking, he clung to the wall for support.

Then, when he just began to think of lying down again, of finding some comfortable position, curled up like the bat, the goons slammed the door open. Light from outside blinded him, and he covered his eyes. The hood came back, the inside of it covered in grit and dirt. Dragged out of the cell and then tossed into a different vehicle. It felt to him like the back of an empty U-Haul truck. Hard metal floor. There was a lurch forward and then a bumpy ride. The fuel exhaust wafted through the floor, making him nauseous. He concentrated mostly on his spinning head and the effort not to throw up, or gag on a bout of dry heaves.

Yet through it all, snatches of shocking clarity came to him. First, he was sober and didn't mind. Second, he felt *no self-pity. No guilt.*

Self-pity and the guilt had been like the rumbling background noise of the saloon where he had lived much of his life. A philanderer and a drunk. Staggering from one lost moment to the next. Dreading more than most what Coleridge called the dread watch-tower of the absolute self.

And now both were gone. Vanished under the darkness of this shitty, sweaty, smelly hood. He was free of them. Shanghaied, beaten, pissing razor blades—yet free, free at last.

He had done something of consequence for once, something from which only others, not himself, had stood to benefit. The mullahs had to be very unhappy today, *inshallah.*

People always fantasized, Johnson mused, *if they'd only killed Hitler*—never really knowing who the mysterious, faceless "they" were. *They* would do it, that's all people knew. Wishing *they* would take a hand. Well, now he'd taken a hand. Not the anonymous *they.* Peter Johnson. For good or ill, forever and ever. Amen.

The van lurched, and he fought the feeling of a fist gripping his guts and shoving them back up his throat.

Two miserable hours later, Johnson sat on a wooden chair, hood still over his head. Hands and feet tied. He heard the sound of traffic somewhere outside the room. The sound of footsteps reached his chair, coming from behind. Once more the sack came off. Johnson blinked, even though the room was darkened. The air tasted stale but a thousand times better than breathing inside the sack. He saw the outlines of shuttered windows. A table with a lamp, chairs around the table. No one sitting there yet, the lamp switched off. Beside the table a video camera for recording purposes and a TV monitor, switched off.

A familiar voice came to his ears. "Let's be clear about one thing, Mr. Johnson."

A pause. The figure came around to where Johnson could see him. Sheik Kutmar in his familiar robes floated into his line of vision. The trim, clipped beard, the dark and knowing eyes. He approached the table, swept his robes behind him, and sat in a chair.

"You are a bandit with no one to claim you. We can take you outside, cut off your head, and sell the video on the web. Who's to stop us? Unless you're prepared to be completely frank with me, you will never get out of here alive. Because no one has an interest in a failed assassin."

The Sheik scooted back in his chair. The metal legs made a teeth-on-edge scraping sound on the concrete floor. He turned on the light, more so he could make notes than shine it into Johnson's face, like when the Movie Nazis gave the brave prisoner the "Treatment." Johnson's bladder was hurting him again. The words "failed assassin" echoed in his ears.

He heard the door open behind him and footsteps. Then a figure in his view.

Johnson blinked. He thought he was hallucinating. It was the sweet girl of his napping reveries, the proto-feminist of his imagined Iranian future—Yasmine.

She was glowing and more striking than ever, the effect sharpened by her green headscarf and the harder set of her mouth. Johnson struggled to look behind him, as if there were some sort of joke that he could understand if only he could see back to who was stage-managing it.

He began to sweat, as he did as a child in school when he didn't have the answer to a problem or he had said something embarrassingly wrong—a flop-sweat breaking out on his forehead at the sight of Yasmine and at the word "failed."

"I'm sure Sheik Kutmar told you of the consequences of resisting us," Yasmine began, her voice expressionless. At this point, resistance was the furthest thing from his mind.

"But you . . . ," he said.

"I was assigned long ago by the Ministry of Intelligence and Security to watch Dr. Yahdzi. We're not as childish as you think, Mr. Johnson."

"But why?"

"Because he is," and here she paused weighing her words. "Unreliable. An unreliable member of our team. But useful nonetheless."

Our team. So she *was* a rocket scientist after all. Something about his doubting eyes made her cut him to the quick.

"Professor Yahdzi hasn't seen his wife in seven years," Sheik Kutmar added. "Didn't even know what his children looked like anymore. They died in a car crash last year. A simple accident. A pity."

Johnson obsessed over the tense: "*Is? Is* unreliable?"

"Present tense," Yasmine said. "You failed to kill him, Mr. Johnson."

Johnson contorted his body to one side and that fist gripped his guts again, this time sending acid burning up his throat. His nose began to run. He tried to spit the bile out of his mouth, blowing as hard as he could, but it hung on his lips and chin. He tried to wipe his nose and mouth on his shoulder, but couldn't do it, too constrained.

"Are you finished?" the pretty olive face in the scrap of green cloth asked him, flatly.

He tried to say, "But—but," but not much came out.

"But what, Mr. Johnson? Shouldn't a 'famous' journalist ask better questions?"

He managed.

"But why—who? Why the gun on the dashboard?"

"The driver was your contact on the inside. He did everything the Americans wanted him to do—except . . ." She trailed off, and the revolver from the dashboard appeared in her hand. She shook a couple of empty shells from the wheel. Then showed him the box where they came from, brass casings, powder cartridges. Hollywood blanks.

"*That* he did for us," she continued, "because we found him out and paid him a visit in front of his parents, wife, and son." No point elaborating the threat. "He performed admirably, but still paid a price."

She removed something from her pocket and, with a curl of contempt on her lips, tossed it casually across the table at Johnson. It tumbled awkwardly, like an eight-sided die from a game of Dungeons & Dragons, and came to rest. Johnson saw it clearly. An opal ring. Smudged with a stain that looked like blood.

"Such amateurs," Yasmine practically spit out. "You Americans aren't very good at this. At least not since overthrowing Mosaddeq, and even there you bumbled and fumbled and got lucky. Your masterly manipulations then were a concoction of our fevered national imagination. Sending a sodden journalist to do a man's job. A sad joke."

So the whole thing had just been a fantasy of his own self-importance. No guilt this time, but shame overcame him in a rush. His body contorted; the razor blades were coming back.

"You . . . I thought you . . ." But she cut him off.

"I'm a patriot, Mr. Johnson. I believe it is our national right to possess a nuclear weapon. We are a great nation. Israel has one. India, Pakistan. Do you know what our country was like at the beginning of the twentieth century? A backwater. Take the village we were in the other day, a dung heap: multiply it the nation-over. Now we are close to taking our place in the sun. If you had killed Yahdzi, it would have hurt us badly. Set us back years. But we would have ended up in the same place. Kill the mullahs; topple the regime; we'll still be in the same place. Kill me. There are millions more like me. We will still be in the same place."

Silence settled on the room, and she stared at him hard, seeming to feel her nation's ascendance in her youth and her dominance at that table. Her adversary was crumpled and puke-flecked, pathetic. Looking at him seemed to make up for decades, for centuries of backwardness and decline. She could see he felt the humiliation sinking into every bit of him and that he couldn't say anything, couldn't think anything, couldn't even think of thinking something without the hot influence of a perverse, person-twisting pang of shame. Good.

"The green ink?" Johnson asked faintly.

"Bait."

"If you knew I was a spy, why did—"

"Because the ideal result was to have you incriminate yourself. The truth is the most powerful propaganda. Mr. Peter Johnson, *clumsy assassin.* Can you deny it?"

He couldn't.

"We discovered your mission when we turned the driver. But not with 100 percent accuracy. So we couldn't arrest you without risking an embarrassing incident: *Mad Mullahs Arrest Daring Journalist.* Of course, the BBC or CNN International would never run with that story, but other outlets might. Now we know with certainty." Her face seemed to shine at him, with an eagerness he'd forgotten since childhood. This scrap of a man wasn't worth speaking to anymore, and she sat in a chair across from him in silence.

Sheik Kutmar completed the thought for her. "Your foolish act has provided us with a great opportunity, Peter. This war will not be won with bullets and tanks, but on the pages of newspapers and on the flat plasma TV screens shining over every soft, overstuffed American couch. And you're going to help us win it."

He didn't look up. The razor blades were coming. And with a sick pit of recognition in his stomach, Johnson suddenly realized, she *knew* all about the razor blades. And didn't care. Wanted him to piss himself. Cry and beg. And yes, in front of the predatory Sheik Kutmar. And suddenly *he* knew—yes, he would cry and beg. And there was nothing he could do about it.

She wriggled forward in her chair and leaned toward him, her pretty olive finger pointing at him like a weapon: "Now tell me exactly who sent you. Give us everything."

And Peter Johnson, *clumsy assassin*, tried his best.

Josephine Parker von Hildebrand ran the media operation, working with Giselle and her fellow Johnson exes, Françoise Ducat and Elizabeth Richards. She knew all the cable news producers and made a point of doing them favors that made them beholden to her at times like these—not that they all weren't eager to get a piece of the story anyway. Jo von H flew the second of the Mrs. Johnsons, Françoise Ducat, Giselle's mother, in from Paris that very morning. There were statements that had to be made, pleas if you will, and Peter's family gathered in one city to make them the following day.

For the 8 AM group news conference, Josephine used her own apartment—nowhere better. The four women sat together on one couch, expanding on their collective statement: "We appeal to the government of Iran, and the president of Iran, to please let us have him home safe. To all who know Peter, who know his passion for the truth and for international understanding, keep him in your prayers for a safe return home."

Then Jo von H covered her bases, sending each of the three women to three different outlets and reserving the evening news—should the networks get interested—for herself. First Giselle to Fox with hostess Megyn Kelly at the top of the 9 AM hour. Quick-witted, likable, and loved with a passion by the camera, if Kelly couldn't make Giselle look smart and sympathetic, nobody could.

"You look like you're handling this pretty well. If it was my father, my husband, I'm not sure I'd be able to cope."

Giselle looked like she was dealing, just barely. "I'd be lying if I told you I'm not terrified. If he can hear me, just know I love you, Dad. And we're doing everything we can to bring you home. Everything. I swear."

Then Giselle's mom, Françoise Ducat, over at *The View*, where Joy Behar pounced on what she considered the most consequential aspect of the story:

"So do you think that this administration is going to try to make use of this . . . ?"

Elisabeth Hasselbeck began to try to interrupt. Behar didn't relent: "Please, please. Now do you think this administration is going to try to exploit this tragedy to say that there's something *wrong* with the Iranians?"

Applause and appreciative nods from the audience.

"Deeze Government *Americain* is the most arrogant in the world," Françoise said, perched on the couch between Behar and Barbara Walters. "At war wiz everyone, lying to everyone, acting bad bully every chance. And when ze world become mad at *les États Unis*, misunderstandings are made to happen. Made, do you understand? Not accident."

"What do you say to the Iranians?" Walters asked.

"I can say, you make mistake. Peter is good man. He love Iran; he love the people and always wanted to tell their story. It's better if your story comes to us by him."

"And to the administration here?"

"Peter's life in your hands. What you do and what you do not do. If ze world, if Iran know it have nossing to fear from ze U.S., Peter will come home. Every day he stay, we know who to blame."

That night, the urbane Elizabeth Richards headed to CNN so Anderson Cooper could give her the furrowed-brow treatment.

"Welcome, Beth. Now even though you're divorced, both of you are close, you especially with his daughter, Giselle. As you know, we had him on CNN not ten days ago. I'm going to play a clip of that interview on *Larry King Live*, where Peter Johnson says the Iranian nuke is nowhere near complete, or even planned for that matter. But first, is there anything you'd like to say to the president, to the administration, to the secretary of state?"

And here the smart Metropolitan Curator got her whammy in: "Of course, I'd like to know why the United States can't have diplomatic relations with Iran? Not one office in Tehran, not one desk, not one telephone? Why not? What's wrong with talking? Can someone tell me that?"

Giving Cooper the chance to smack the ball back over the net:

"Which makes me want to ask, has anyone from the administration, anyone at all been in contact with you?"

Scandalized, "*This* administration? First they promise to talk. Then when something comes up, something real, they do nothing. Nothing's changed—nothing!"

Cooper looked very, very concerned.

Days later. Two? Three? Johnson lost track. The interrogation room had become his world. He heard the sound of traffic beyond the blinded window, now much dimmer with long spaces between batches of cars. He wasn't sure of the time, but it felt like night.

While time divided into long periods—first endless spells before the light, the table, the video, question after question; then much shorter periods of sleep on a mattress in a windowless empty holding cell. A little plate of unmentionable food, plastic bottles of water that tasted of copper and chlorine, a shallow pot to relieve himself. The razors passed, leaving him weak and shaky but not yelling every time he pissed. And two out of the four intervals between interrogations, they beat him. Mostly about the soles of his naked feet with a sharp reed that bloodied them. Then the hood came back on, and they marched him to the interrogation room with the sound of traffic beyond—on the fifth day shuffling slower and slower as his feet refused to hold him.

He answered every question the Sheik and Yasmine put to him, so the beatings couldn't be about that. Just something to amuse the guards. From what he could tell none of them spoke English, but it didn't matter. When the door cracked open, he'd jump from the mattress as if stung, then huddle in the corner. And when the first hand touched him, he yelled—without even the first blow. Sometimes one of them would just flick his ear with a thumb and forefinger.

Then their laughter, mocking his cowardice. Yes, they did beat him for fun.

Now in the interrogation room the sound of footsteps reached his chair, coming from behind. And the sack came off. They didn't bother tying him any more. What would be the point?

Sheik Kutmar sat behind the table with the video recording light shining into his face. *Thanks for having me on, Larry.*

"Let's talk about Robert Wallets, again." This, from Sheik Kutmar.

"He works for Banquo, late thirties, some kind of soldier, maybe Special Forces. Took me into the field for extra training. He was my primary interrogator at the firm."

"What kind of training?"

"Survival camping and some small arms. But not in a desert—in the mountains of North Carolina, the woods. About a mile or two from a supplemental training area for the 10ᵗʰ Mountain Division. He might have been part of them, but I can't say for sure."

Yasmine rose from the desk and thrust some photos into Johnson's lap. "Which one?" she demanded thickly.

He flipped quickly through them, but none of them looked like Wallets.

"Sorry."

"And the woman?" Kutmar asked.

"Marjorie Morningstar. An assumed name. Again late thirties, sort of butch."

"Butch?" Kutmar asked.

"Not feminine," Yasmine explained.

"Strong, like a peasant woman." Johnson added.

"Any of these?"

Kutmar showed him more photos. A femme French masseuse. A stolid Spanish factory worker with meaty hands. A tough-looking prison guard from some Eastern European bastion with her hair in a severe bun. Johnson shook his head.

"No, sorry. She was American, raised in the area. Some kind of local mountain girl—but with education, college, master's, maybe even a PhD."

"Can you identify the Jew?" Yasmine loved the word Jew; you could see how well it tasted on her tongue.

"Nobody's quite sure about his pedigree." Johnson said dryly. More photos in his lap. Johnson flipped through them, discarding the thin faces, concentrating on the heavy-set balding ones. There were three possibles that looked like the Turk; then he narrowed them down to two. He showed those two.

"Could be one of these. Can't say for sure. These men have beards. He didn't have a beard when I saw him. Maybe. Hard to tell—"

Yasmine took the photos back. Discarded one as irrelevant; the other man in the second photo she knew. From his place in the chair Johnson couldn't see which photo was discarded.

"And the fourth man in the little play they put on for you?" Yasmine asked.

Johnson shrugged. "Might be one of their office workers, one of their stock traders."

More questions that fell under the capacious penumbra of his ignorance: Who were his contacts in Iran? He had none. Who did Robert Wallets know in Iran? He had no idea. What was his plan for escape? None that he knew of. What was he supposed to do upon capture? Never really been told. Johnson now realized the brilliant foresight of these lacunae in his training. The Iranian couldn't believe he was so ill-informed about his own circumstances and said they'd come back to it. Not a pleasant prospect.

———

Sheik Kutmar lit a cigarette and poured some coffee from a stainless-steel thermos into two matching chrome cups. No cup for Johnson.

"We checked your account in the Cantonal Bank of Zurich with the number you gave us. You were initially bribed for $75,000 many years ago. Now you say it stands roughly at $250,000."

The Sheik took a drag on the cigarette, letting out a long serpent of smoke. "The man, Jan Breuer, who paid you the bribe to write about the Gulf War—where did you meet him?"

"At a party in Westchester County, north of Manhattan, at the Horse Estate of the Maharaja—"

Kutmar cut him off with a wave of the hand, as if that's what he expected of such a profligate. "Yes, we know who he is. A harmless playboy who likes women and horses. Preferably together."

Yasmine leaned over the desk again in a strange eager way. "How would you describe your relation to Jan Breuer?"

"I was his pass-along. His front man. I put the signatures on the checks or drafts to be deposited. I was the face at the teller's cage. My prints on the pen. Nothing more. The balance floated at about that $250,000 figure. Though the bank statements came to me, they may have gone to a dozen others as well. I suppose I could have taken a cut every time, but I didn't. Originally I used some of it to pay my daughter's college bills. But as the years passed, I decided it was probably best if I never touched the money again."

Johnson paused; his mouth dry, his eyes grainy. Even sitting in the chair his heart throbbed in his ears without making a sound, but he felt himself recovering his equilibrium with them.

"You might not recognize Jan Breuer if you met him again." This from Kutmar.

"I'd recognize him," Johnson grumbled. "He's a large, florid Dutchman with bright blond hair and drinker's veins in his face." Johnson paused, looked lovingly at the coffee and the pack of cigarettes on the table. "Men like Jan Breuer, Dutch Shell oil executive, and people like me, Western journalist, appreciate your problem."

"You do?" the Sheik asked. "Please explain."

"Your *Sukuk* and *Zakat* look too much alike." Johnson let the strange words hang. He was insulting their banking system. *Sukuk* were low-interest–bearing bonds and *Zakat*, alms for the poor.

Suddenly the DVD recorder's red light died. Without the DVD, they were off the record. Yasmine removed the disc. This day's interrogation would never exist. For the first time Yasmine reevaluated her measure of the man. "You wish to expound on the principles of Islamic banking?"

"Not without coffee and a cigarette."

Johnson got his coffee; he got his cigarette.

"What principles? You possess no modern banking," Johnson said flatly, daring them to challenge the fact. "Mohammed condemns usury. Allowing only 'Gold for Gold, Silver for Silver, Wheat for Wheat' . . . " Here Johnson sipped his coffee, lit a cigarette, and a look of scorn came across his face. Muslim Mickey Mouse Banks offered *Sukuk*, worthless bonds that looked a lot like *Zakat*, alms for the poor. In other words, *thrown* away. The point not lost on his gracious hosts.

"The mullahs do handsprings over medieval fatwas so you can offer lousy 3 percent bonds. A return on investment far below what's commonly available to the average American housewife." Yasmine sat back in her chair, wary now at the man's knowledge, an unexpected quality. Kutmar's face was stone. Johnson twisted the knife.

"What any modern *woman* can do, you cannot. Instead, they cut off your head."

Johnson came back to his coffee and his cigarette again. It amazed him how those two simple delicacies made the throbbing in his cut and crusted feet somehow shrink to a manageable proportion. Johnson chuckled, the first smile since he'd come to this awful place.

"Sheik, you're not worried about losing your head as much as losing your country's money. Jan Breuer and I deposited a few million, but you're looking at *billions*. You can buy a lot of Jihad for that, now can't you?" And here Johnson's face twisted from scorn to a sneer. "That's a ton of *self-discovery*, a heap of *personal struggle*."

Sheik Kutmar's face remained behind the veil of his mind. "I didn't know you were such an expert," the Sheik finally said.

The cigarette and the coffee were gone. Johnson shrugged. "I try to keep up."

Johnson awoke on the damp, lumpy mattress to the throbbing from the soles of his feet. For some reason the goons hadn't beaten him before putting him to bed that night. And now, this morning something crucial had changed. The door to his windowless room was cracked open, a sliver of light falling across his face, the hallway beyond dead silent. Coming somewhere beyond the door ajar the sound of traffic floated through the open crack. What the hell was going on? An open door? Were they letting him go?

Johnson rose and tried to stand—an act that took a little more than mere balance. Both feet had swollen from the beatings, crusted with scabs. His bloody torn socks lay in a filthy corner of the room, his shoes beside them. The socks useless, and the shoes? There's no way they'd fit. Holding on to the walls he edged toward them, then stooped for the shoes. Tying the laces together he threw them over his shoulder and made his way to the door. He suddenly remembered that silly woman at Josephine's cocktail party, a million years ago, it seemed—the one with the wooden boxes for footwear—where the hell· was she when he needed her now? He could use her shoes.

A dirty, flyspecked hallway greeted him, layered with peeling paint and powdering plaster. Still holding onto the wall for support he shuffled to the sound of the traffic. That door was open too, the sound of traffic stronger. He recognized the interrogation room at once by the sickly color of the walls. He pushed open the door and staggered inside. No Sheik, no Yasmine, no goons. Just the empty table. They'd even taken the lamp with them.

Against one wall stood a large, old-fashioned tape recorder with sixteen-inch spools, something out of the 1970s that could play ten hours of tape at a time or record as much. By the way they placed Johnson's chair and yanked off his hood there'd be no way he could have seen the bulky device without twisting his head off his shoulders. Besides, most of the time he was simply too beaten down to care much about his surroundings. The tape recorder was still playing its endless tape. The sounds of street traffic, cars, and muffled honks dribbled from the little speakers. For a long moment he marveled at these cheap theatrics, driving home the dagger that whatever lay beyond these dirty walls was nothing like he imagined. Even as he watched, the endless spool ran out, the sound of recorded traffic ending abruptly and the tail end of the tape going *flap-flap-flap* . . .

Johnson managed to find his way downstairs, wedging himself through a heavy front door that stuck, emerging at last not onto a busy thoroughfare but some sort of warren, a Kasbah with shuttered windows high up on whitewashed walls, no sound of people in an unknown city as the noon sun blazed down. And each way he looked the same view presented itself, like a white stucco maze, doors and high windows; the windows shuttered and all the doors made of the same heavy wood with paint flaking off.

Over the warren's rooftops he spied a more modern building, a kind of apartment complex. There, try there. So, in his bare feet with shoes thrown over his shoulder, in dirty shirt and pants, Johnson picked that direction, west, and started to stagger.

At the first intersection of the Kasbah he paused to get his breath. Beyond, he saw the colorful and noisy corner of a marketplace, a bazaar. A beggar sat at his feet. A man in loincloth and twisted feet, curled into a strange hooked shape next to a wooden bowl and prayer mat. The wizened and toothless old man grinned at him, offering the bowl for alms. But beside the cripple stood his crutches, leaning against the plaster wall.

Johnson saw a spark in the old man's eye as he glanced at his swollen bloody feet. Then a flash of lust as he dwelled on the expensive shoes dangling from the white man's neck. For a moment Johnson was tempted to barter his wingtips for the crutches, but immediately abandoned the fantasy. Better just keep moving. Find a way out.

As he stumbled into the colorful bazaar, the noise and throngs assailed him. Each way he looked, another row of stalls, merchants hawking, dozens of narrow colorful pathways, leading everywhere and nowhere.

CHAPTER FIFTEEN

The All-Iran Burka Company

Johnson's heart sank, his eyes flashing from one useless direction to the next. Each lane led off blindly; bright awnings in every direction covered mountains of goods, spilling over trestle tables. Crowds of shoppers milled in the narrow confines of the bazaar. Women covered head-to-toe in red and blue and yellow cloth followed their men, who haggled with the shopkeepers, leaving the women to fetch and tote. The throbbing in his feet welled up to overwhelm him. *Damn*, he thought, *shoulda just swiped the cripple's frigging crutches*. He glanced back down the whitewashed alley. The beggar was gone.

He tried to form a plan. First, find out what city he was in. Second, find a consulate, maybe Swiss or British. Throw himself through the gate. Who knows? Al Jazeera might even have an office somewhere. Looking past the overlapping awnings, he kept moving toward the hard modern edge of concrete buildings. *That* way. But first his feet—the wingtips were worthless. He found a few thousand crumpled Rials in his pants pocket. As he staggered toward the silhouettes of the modern buildings, he stopped at the first stall he saw to buy a pair of cheap rubber sandals. A few hundred Rials bought him some CrocsRX knock-offs, a size too large. Bright blue. And two pairs of white cotton socks.

In four minutes, the $1,000 Brooks Brothers wingtips sat in the shoe seller's stall, and Johnson was hobbling along on more comfy feet, bleeding into his socks. He could see the concrete buildings quite clearly now at the far end of the bazaar: apartment complexes. Normal streets, cars, and traffic. Sure, find a taxi, and say "Al Jazeera" over and over again. That might work.

But Johnson suddenly noticed shooflies, dogging his steps, seeming to appear from nowhere out of the crowd. The first one with his back turned, choosing olives from a stall of barrels—at a word from the olive merchant he turned, forgetting his purchase, glanced at Johnson, and then followed quietly in his footsteps.

Another squatted on a low stool by a colorful rack of scarves. Abandoning his post, he stood and joined the Olive Man, walking as a pair. Johnson slid into the most tangled parts of the crowd, hunching behind a stall hoping to be overlooked. Then scurried on again into another noisy swirl of buyers and sellers.

Yet even as he ducked awkwardly behind a large butcher's counter— hidden for the moment behind a rack of lamb carcasses on meat hooks and thinking he'd given them the slip—another man joined the hunt. Then another turned, a barber cutting hair by his barber chair, handing off comb and scissors to his assistant to finish off the job. And another who loafed against a wall simply threw down his cigarette and fell neatly in step.

Johnson counted five, slowly trailing him, not letting him get too far ahead, but not coming within clutch distance either, a game of cat and mouse. Or were they driving him? He couldn't tell.

And what was worse: now he recognized two of the men, the brutes from his windowless room. The goons who beat him. A terrible sweat broke out all over his body. He wanted to run, but where? And how, given the state of his feet?

It occurred to him that the Iranians hadn't let him go idly. Now officially *escaped*. Could he deny it—as Yasmine might have asked? For the first time since he picked the gun off the dashboard, he felt sure that right now he was going to die.

He resisted the urge to sink into the dust, cowering. A rush of fear they'd drag him back to the beating room. Finish him off for good this time. Instead, he stumbled his way toward the edge of the marketplace.

He saw a crowded open plaza with kiosks selling ice cream and falafel, then the flow of busy traffic along a broad boulevard, while a line of white Yugo taxis idled by the curb. He paused at the edge of the bazaar at the nearest kiosk selling bottled water and meat kabobs. He was dying of thirst, but the smell of the burnt lamb nauseated him. Paralyzed, he stood there, frozen in place.

A knot of military policemen had gathered along the edge of the plaza, not loitering but tensely waiting, as if uncertain what they were really looking for. Could he make it to a taxi without being pinched? What was the Farsi word for "drive"? The colorful crowds flowed around him, while the goons lurked in the shadows of the awnings, not twenty feet away. In some animal way, he knew if he moved so much as a muscle they'd pounce.

Two women in full chador rudely jostled him. Niqabs covered them from head to toe with only a slit to see. Dutifully he shuffled aside. The stockier one touched his wrist. Something about the eyes, but it was the soft voice that spoke English, which made his heart leap.

"Nice shoes."

And to Peter Johnson's everlasting shock, Miss Morningstar's bright eyes shone out from between the slash in her burka. "Marjorie! Please! Get me the hell out of here!"

"*Walk* toward the taxi stand." This from the other woman, who was a little tall for a dame, Robert Wallets in his own chador, covered from head to toe, his voice urgent and his words clipped. "When you see Yossi's taxi, bolt for it."

They turned their backs on him, facing the goons in the shadows of the awnings. Johnson began to weave his way across the crowded plaza. Thirty steps from the line of taxis, twenty-five, twenty. He peeked briefly over his shoulder, only to see the goons from the bazaar moving out from under the shadows. Johnson froze again like an idiot.

Then gunfire erupted all around him. Marjorie's and Wallets' guns spat fire from the folds in their robes, hosing down the five goons dogging them, some spun around from the force of the rounds, others doubled over. And Johnson didn't stay to watch more. *Time to die? This moment?* Hell no. Run!

And he did—in an absurd hunched-over way, like the guy who stumbles out to the driveway for the morning paper in his slippers and bathrobe only to find that he's walked into an NRA shooting range.

People and cab drivers were screaming, diving for cover—where was Yossi? Then he saw him. The short, dark man emerged from the driver's seat of his cab with a stripped, stockless AK-47, firing toward the military police, who scattered like a herd of cats. Johnson dived into the backseat of the cab, his nose flat against the vinyl seat, feet still sticking out the door.

A lull in the gunfire and Yossi shouted at him, guttural, indecipherable yelps, and yanked at his legs. He was trying to pull him out of the car's backseat. Johnson started to fight and kick. Then it dawned on him. He'd jumped into the wrong cab.

He no sooner stood up than Wallets descended on him and tackled him into the back seat of the right taxi, lying on top with his elbow in his back. Johnson tried to stick his head up, but Wallets yelled, "Stay down!" Doors slammed, and the cab lurched forward, gunfire crackling again. The back window shattered, showering them in cubes of glass, like costume jewelry baubles. Otherwise they benefited from *Inshallah* marksmanship, one of the region's great contradictions in terms. *God Willing, we'll hit something.* Wallets let fly a farewell burst of suppressing fire through the empty back window.

Then they were moving, hurtling into traffic. The taxi barreled through the streets, past dun-colored buildings and storefronts. Wallets in the back scanned for anything coming up behind. Yossi twisted the rearview mirror so he could get a good look at their important passenger. He seemed to be laughing.

"Nice rubber shoes. You buy in Mahabad bazaar?"

"Yes," Johnson croaked, his voice parched. "You can tell everyone I got my nice blue shoes right here in . . . . in Mahabad." During four minutes of wild driving it seemed they'd given everyone the slip. For the moment, at least. Wallets began to methodically squeeze and knead Johnson's neck, running his fingers wherever the skin was exposed. Johnson, now sitting upright, objected, "Hey—what the . . . ?"

"Don't argue. Take off your shirt," Marjorie told him from the front seat.

The searching, merciless hands ran up and down his body when suddenly Wallets found something in the soft roll around his middle.

"Okay, got it," he said to Marjorie.

The car slowed, then pulled up to the curb. They seemed to be in an abandoned part of town, with empty stores and weedy rubble-strewn vacant lots. "Stick your belly over the seat," Wallets commanded.

"What?"

"Just do it."

Johnson bellied up to the bar. Marjorie wrenched around in her seat, and her arm clutched him close. A knife appeared in her free hand and went straight for Johnson's gut.

"Wait!" Johnson pleaded.

"Don't move," Marjorie told him.

Wallets pressed the weight of his body against Peter's back, jamming him in tight. Marjorie leaned on Johnson's gut with her other arm, just working with her wrist—one quick cut into Johnson's love handle, then going back for another.

"Got it," she said. She showed Peter: a sliver of metal about the size of a grain of rice, slimed with blood. A chrome seed. And Johnson grasped at once, some sort of tracking device. A solid week of foot beating had proved to be more than enough distraction. Kutmar and Yasmine could've given him a suppository, and he'd never have noticed. But then it occurred to him maybe Wallets' team picked up its frequency and tracked him too. "Is that how you found me?"

"We hef ahr vayz," Marjorie said, in a comic German accent. "Let's just say, we're very happy you didn't lose your pants." She glanced at the slimy chrome seed as if wondering what to do with it, and then scanned the vacant weedy lot. Three bone-thin dogs were scavenging the rubble for rats and garbage. Her eyes flitted about the glass shattered inside of the cab. A bottle of water and two greasy kabobs still on their crushed paper napkins lay on the dashboard, crammed up against the vents and cracked windshield. Yossi's abandoned lunch.

She grabbed for the kabobs, stripping them off their sticks. Then stuck the chrome seed in one lamb chunk and tossed the lot out her window. The dogs looked up and smelled it at once. They ran as a pack to the fallen meat.

"Time to go."

And Yossi drove with even more abandon this time.

"Helicopters and roadblocks," Wallets kept saying. "Choppers and blocks, that's what's going to get us." He kept craning his head out the window to look for aircraft overhead. And they all strained to see as far as they could into the distance, where a shimmering heat distorted the horizon, to look for a telltale checkpoint.

They drove among buildings again, the outskirts of another populated area. Suddenly they pulled up to a locked garage with ancient gas pumps. Another car waited on the concrete apron, newer, a fast Audi, no broken rear window.

"Time to switch," Wallets ordered. "Though we shoulda changed the profile. We're still four people. Minus one chrome chip."

Four hours later they pulled down an alley in a new town and quietly stopped. The long shadows of afternoon stretched across the buildings. They hustled Johnson out, and he hobbled through a metal door. It clanged shut behind as they climbed metal stairs—fire stairs, lit occasionally by naked bulbs. The place felt like some sort of factory. The sound of whirring from the landing above grew louder as they approached.

"Here, put this on so we can get across the floor to the office without drawing too much attention."

Marjorie handed him his own burka, and Johnson cloaked himself in a woman's robes, even his head with the niqab, covering his face except for the eye slit. He labored his way up, barely able to see, to the third

landing, where they paused. They stood before a back door, the fire exit
to some kind of assembly line. They could hear the sound of machines
whirring on the other side, like the thrum of a thousand bees all humming at once. The door was marked, first in Farsi script,

شـرکت چـا د ری ایـران

then below in French,

La Toute-Persane Burqa compagnie, Kermanshah

and finally English,

The All-Iran Burka Company, Kermanshah

The name of this town, Johnson realized. Farewell, Mahabad.
"Ready?"

Johnson nodded. The Turk pulled open the door and led them inside.
A triple row of long tables ran before them in sweatshop fashion. At each
station a sewing machine and a woman, clad head-to-toe, doing piece
work. The work was simple: sewing labels onto garments, burkas, the
noise of a hundred sewing machines deafening. Huge stacks of burkas
waiting for the labels stood in one corner, in scarlet and yellow and aqua-
marine. When one or two women looked up from their butterfly stitches,
the Turk glowered and pointed harshly at them over the noise. Their eyes
fell, and they went back to work. In seven long seconds, the Turk led
them through the sweatshop to the overseer's office, a few steps up on a
raised platform, a long glass window overlooking the floor.

Once inside the office, Johnson found a chair by a desk furthest from
the long windowpane, feeling totally exposed. When the door shut, the
thrumming diminished by half. But he didn't feel any safer. The Turk
ignored everyone and immediately opened a Dell laptop, which began
its power-up dance. Wallets slumped in one corner, as far from the
window as possible. Marjorie found a first-aid kit under another desk
and came over to look at Johnson's feet.

"What the hell is this place?" Johnson asked.

"You mean besides our safe house?" Wallets remarked, then muttering, "to the extent anyplace here is *safe*."

"It's the All-Iran Burka Company," Marjorie's voice came through her hood, "just like it says on the door."

"Except Iran no make burkas," spat Yossi without looking up from his computer. "Just steal them from Label Makers."

"Huh?" Johnson was totally lost.

Marjorie dabbed the cuts in Johnson's feet with a cotton swab. "They can't make enough burkas here to satisfy demand or the mullah's edicts, never have. Just like soap or toilet paper. They buy and import the burkas from Pakistan, Indonesia, Egypt, and a few hundred thousand from a factory in northern Israel. But they don't want to admit they can't do it, so they sew on fake labels. 'Made in Iran.' Then everyone feels better."

Johnson digested this. It seemed nearly incomprehensible to him that the country couldn't produce the one thing pious men made their women wear. But then again, who'd invest in an Iranian company if it weren't selling oil? Nobody. No return.

"What are we doing here?"

"Right now you're going to heal up," Wallets told him.

"What about them?" Johnson nodded in the direction of the work floor. He hated the thought of so many seamstresses a few feet away, any of whom could pop their heads in the door. Uncover their ruse. With only a single closed door and the cloth of a burka between them and discovery.

"Tomorrow's Saturday. Nobody works. The place is empty."

As if on cue, the whirring of the sewing machines stopped almost as one. The seamstresses rose, filing out the front door of the sweatshop, punching out their timecards as they went. When all were gone, the burkas came off with one big *whew!* and Wallets lit a cigarette. Yossi picked up the phone on the desk and began what immediately became a contentious conversation, his voice becoming more and more heated the more he talked.

"I assume you realize the Iranians let me go," Johnson said at length.

"A gamble," Wallets blew smoke up toward the ceiling in a long column. "They could have made a big deal of your capture, but they risked catching hell from the international press for holding a journalist.

Sure, they'd called you a spy, but they call *everyone* U.S. spies. So they rolled the dice. Played you back into our hands."

He threw the cigarette to the floor and crushed it decisively under the heel of his boot. Even with the seamstresses gone, Johnson didn't like their refuge any better. He worried that anyone from the street could wander in.

"So they knew you were coming for me?"

Wallets didn't answer. Instead, Marjorie began to minister to him in earnest after rummaging through her backpack. She softened some of the crusts from his soles, and washed his feet thoroughly with peroxide. The skin bubbled.

Drawing two liquids into one hypo: "An antibiotic and an anti-inflammatory full of steroids. I've got a vitamin shot for you too. And keep off your feet for now. There's a mattress here you can lie on."

Yeah right, like he could sleep.

"When are we getting out of here?"

Marjorie shrugged. Apparently not immediately. Wallets pulled a bottle of Maker's Mark out of a desk drawer. "Let me look for some glasses."

He handed glasses around, but Johnson didn't want to take his first sip, because he knew it would taste better than any Maker's Mark he ever had tasted or ever would taste. He wanted that experience to be ahead of him instead of behind. Finally, he closed his eyes and took his draught and let out an almost erotic sigh.

"Easy boy," Marjorie frowned.

Yossi's conversation with the mystery jerk on the phone rose to the level of a shouting match. Johnson winced at the man's harsh voice, his eyes flitting about in alarm. Didn't he know they were in hiding?

"What gives?"

Marjorie dropped her voice to a whisper. "This is Yossi's territory. He knows the ground. And actually runs this business—otherwise it wouldn't be a viable safe house. We're dependent on him, even if—" she glanced over at his swollen neck, veins standing out in wrath—"he's a little volatile."

How reassuring.

"Easier to just leave me back there." The thought made him sick. What did Aristotle say? It's harder to be free than not to be free? Now it made a kind of sense.

Marjorie snorted. "True. But after all, we said we'd try to get you out. And a promise is a promise. You held up your end."

Yossi argued even harder on the phone, and Johnson's urge to drink evaporated. He set the glass carefully on the desk when their host suddenly snarled something in Farsi and slammed the headset into the cradle. The glass of bourbon slid an inch. Yossi began to curse in English. "*Pig* Mullah. I give him forty free burka for his fuck family, and he still not let my girls work Monday. He says they must make pilgrimage outside town to shrine of old dead imam who make miracles. So, factory closed. I lose $1,500 in sales in one day! Mullah wants more bribe. But give nothing in return—he makes no hand wash, girls still go put flowers shrine. Before we leave, I crap his turban and tell him it monkey shit."

Part of Johnson thought he should remember these piquant profanities for use later. But instantly forgot about that when he finally grasped the crux of their precarious situation. "*They let me go to get to you.*"

The three spies looked at him. Marjorie's and Wallets' eyes calm and sober, while Yossi dismissed him with a grunt. Wallets poured himself another slug and patiently explained: "Right, Peter. They wanted us. Real spies. Better than Brit sailors even. They catch us in Iran, put us on trial, and sell tickets to the circus. If we're lucky, they'd eventually swap us for some of their own guys we picked up in Iraq. They know how the system works. Like I said, they took a gamble."

The light began to soften outside, the first phase of twilight coming on in the long, slow fade toward night, Johnson's favorite time of the day, when everything seemed softer and quieter and more peaceful. But not this time. Not in here.

"We lucky," the Turk explained. "But others come looking soon."

Wallets took a deep pull on his drink and lit another cigarette.

"Now tell us what you saw in Gonabad. Russian missile batteries, right? And south of the Nantanz facility, there's a big underground operation, right?"

Marjorie put away her first-aid kit. "Give us everything."

CHAPTER SIXTEEN

Four Blind Mice

He found it harder than he would have imagined to recall the events. You'd think the memories would be there on demand, just like the replay button on a DVR. But no, the mind picked and chose what it deemed important. So over and over again Yossi or Large Marge or Wallets returned him to some point, all over again.

"You said you saw two surface-to-air missile batteries at the Gonabad facility?"

"Chinese or Russian crews?"

"How many to each battery?"

"Any other camouflage emplacements?"

"Maybe another missile battery? Only two? You sure?"

"Can you show us on the map?"

Now it became clear why Yossi had a laptop. In addition to helping him run the All-Iran Burka Company's inventory, shipments, accounts payable, and so on, it also linked to fresh satellite images from Long Eye: first the Gonabad facility where he met Dr. Yahdzi, then the monstrous Nantanz refining operation.

"How many guards inside the hangar at the underground entrance?"

Johnson fought his exasperation over the repetition. "Like I told you. A fortified checkpoint, combination pill box with machine gunners, two of them; one pointing into the hangar, the other pointing down the

Holland Tunnel, as if they could mow down anyone trying to escape. A large traffic light—red-green—beside a metal sliding gate barrier with black and yellow warning slashes."

"Sturdy? Could it take an impact?"

"No, it's just for show, traffic control. The tunnel has steel hydraulic sliding doors at either end."

"Railroad tracks?"

"What?"

"Did you notice railroad tracks? They might be concealed under metal plates flush with the concrete floor."

"I'm not sure. Maybe. I . . . *yes*. They weren't covered by plates, just silver rails, European gauge, and flush with the floor. Shiny silver, like they'd almost never been used."

His questioners exchanged dark glances.

"Did I say something wrong? Wouldn't any industrial facility use a rail line to ship heavy equipment in?"

"Or out."

Johnson's feet were sore, his mouth sticky and his eyes grainy. "Bombs?"

Wallets explained. "They don't make bombs here; they refine fissionable material."

"Right. Yellow cake to fuel rods. Why the hell use a railcar for a hundred pounds of Strontium 90? Use a truck."

"Unless they want to transport more than a hundred pounds. And something more deadly than Strontium 90. And they'd need it encased in lead so there was no heat bloom. No signature that we could see from space."

Johnson needed a bracer. He reached for the Maker's Mark and his third drink, but the booze disappeared into the magic drawer under Wallets' steady hand. He felt a flash of wrath, which he chalked up to Drinker's Thinking. It passed quickly.

Down in the work area, Yossi rummaged through an old Whirlpool refrigerator, taking out large colorful plastic shopping bags filled with what looked like somebody's takeout leftovers. The worker girls' food? Then he pawed through the shopping bags themselves, sniffing cartons and takeout trays, keeping the good, tossing out whatever was ripe. Finally lugging the remainders up to the overseer's office. The bright orange and green takeout bags were labeled in Farsi, English, then French: Jabba's Kabob Hut. The giant Tatooine Star Wars gangster slathering over a delicious scented skewer. Johnson's appetite was returning, but wolfing down cold gristle that others picked over turned his stomach. Not quite hungry enough for that. The shopping bags also yielded coffee in "Jabba" bottles, and green liters of flat Vichy water.

"If you want to drink the water, you'll need this," Marjorie handed him a tiny white pill.

"What is it?"

"A combo Lomitil/all-purpose parasite killer. Drink either the water or the coffee, not both. And don't take it on an empty stomach." Marjorie warned him, "or you'll crap yourself right down the toilet."

Johnson looked dismally at the cold takeout trays wondering how much he could choke down. Suddenly realizing that up till now in Iran, he'd only drunk boiled tea or bottled water. During his days in captivity, he quenched his thirst out of liters of stale Evian provided by his hosts. If Sheik Kutmar had really wanted him dead, he would have let him brush his teeth out of a tap. He ate a few mouthfuls, then a few more. He gave up on a whiff of one rotten scrap Yossi overlooked. Johnson's eyes felt heavy, very heavy, and a part of him knew he was snoring.

"Well, let's try to find out before it's too late."

Johnson awoke with a snuffle and didn't catch who said what. Sounded like Wallets.

They were both staring over Yossi's shoulder at the laptop.

The screen showed another nuclear facility from the Long Eye satellite, a collection of roads, bunkers, and buildings, but this time the caption read "Esfahan Nuclear Technology Center."

"What's that place?" Johnson wanted to know.

"Near the city of Isfahan," Yossi told him. Esfahan. Isfahan. Everything sounded alike in this crazy place. Like modern and Middle English, Shop and Shoppe, Public and Publick.

"It's where we make the bombs," Yossi told him. Johnson blinked at the use of "we," then remembered, *yes*, this man was Persian, Iranian.

And they called him the Turk out of sheer laziness. But still, you couldn't miss the unmistakable note of pride in the use of "We."

We make . . . Us. It gave him something of a shudder.

Each time the mouse-pointer clicked on a structure in the satellite image, that structure's name and use appeared in a little dialogue box. Click on one concrete bunker building: MNSR—Miniature Neutron Source Reactor. Click another: LWSCR—Light Water Sub-Critical Reactor. Click again: HWZPR—Heavy Water Zero Power Reactor. This complex was half a mile on either side, a bewildering number of buildings and structures: Graphite Sub-Critical Reactor, Fuel Fabrication Laboratory, Uranium Chemistry Laboratory, Uranium Conversion Facility, Fuel Manufacturing Plant—

"They didn't take me here," Peter Johnson remarked naively.

"They wouldn't have, darling," Marjorie replied.

Wallets lit another Marlboro. "Nobody has. Nobody we know, anyway. Maybe your guys, Yossi?" This was about Wallets' tenth cigarette for the evening. Johnson glowed with secret satisfaction. So the man *wasn't* perfect.

The Turk grunted, shaking his head. Then took one of Wallets' Marlboros. He pointed to the topography surrounding the Esfahan Nuclear Technology Center. "Three thousand Revolutionary Guards patrol. Night vision goggles. Bobby traps. Motion detractors. Hopeless." No one smiled at his mangling of English. "Yemen Security told me Mossad try back in 1999. Five guys in cleaning service for business office. All Iranian. No Jews. Three dead. Never made it inside. Two sent home still alive, tongues cut out."

Johnson interjected with a firm grasp of the obvious: "They were betrayed."

Yossi gave the journalist a long searching look that said, *Really, you figured that out all by yourself?*

"Who, do you think?" Wallets asked.

Yossi shrugged. "Why not you? Why not Frenchies? They built damn place."

Wallets didn't answer, just stared at the screen lost in thought. "I wish the Frenchies could get us in now." He propped his chin on his hand

and kept looking wistfully at the screen, like a kid who'd dropped his lollipop on the sidewalk.

"Darling, remember, we're trying to get *out*, not in," Marge said.

"Right, I know. Get over the border. Get home. Let daring journalist do a news conference. A teary reunion. Another book deal. Maybe do some business with Anton Anjou. That could have been what Sheik Kutmar wanted, right? Get a few zillions out-country via our eminently corruptible American scribbler? Buy some Jihad?" Wallets' eyes came for him.

"He didn't say in so many words."

"He wouldn't have."

Johnson came back to the strange name: "*Anton* who?"

"Anjou. A Frenchie banker Giselle is dating. A recent interest. We've been keeping an eye on her."

"So those were *your* photos of Giselle that Professor Yahdzi showed me."

"Don't be an ass," Marjorie told him. "They were theirs. Did you really think they'd squire you around without taking a few pictures just to put a mousetrap in your trough? As for the Frenchie, we lucked into Anton Anjou of Banque Luxembourg by accident. Assume he helped some of *them* take the pictures. Then stayed on to sample the goods."

"I'll kill him," Johnson said with some honest red-blooded bravado.

"You're not going to have *time* to kill anyone when you get back," Wallets smiled thinly at him.

"You'll be the media's go-to guy on the whole Peter Johnson captivity," Marge said. "Lawrence of Irania."

Johnson almost started to gush, *Think so?* But knew enough to hide his tingle of anticipation at being the object of desire at a media orgy. He hoped the feeling passed quickly too, like his anger about the booze. If only Jo von H knew. She'd be proud of him keeping his eye on the PR angle in the most trying of circumstances. But this was no place to think about his bookings.

"The Sheik made statements, accusations," Wallets elaborated. "Hordes of lemmings in New York ran to the mikes. They're waiting breathlessly for you."

Yossi clicked the laptop; Giselle's appearance on Fox News sprang to life. He clicked again; it was Jo von H before a forest of microphones. Again, Elizabeth, talking to Anderson Cooper. Clicked again, Giselle's mom, Françoise, on *The View*.

"Sheesh," Johnson said, failing to cover his admiration—then, with a touch of disappointment: "No *Larry King*?"

Wallets and Marjorie made eye contact with one another, almost hiding their mirth. "We ran out of disc space," Wallets said. "Anyway, pretty soon Sheik Kutmar will go on Farsi TV and tell the world you've been released. 'On your own recognizance.' And no, he *won't* know where you went. Or words to that effect."

Yossi clicked away the news stuff, and the Esfahan Manufacturing Facility came back. This time the image was real time—dark, as it was night outside. They saw no real shapes, just a sprinkling of lights. Wallets kept an eye on it. "So the Sheik gets to keep building his bomb, and we get to cover our backsides," he sighed. Then found his eleventh cigarette, shaking it out of the soft pack and sticking it in his mouth. It bounced in his lips as he finally said, "Not what we hoped for." A shrug. He paused to light up.

Suddenly Yossi became agitated. "Wait! Wait!" He began pointing at the screen. Wallets leaned over his shoulder, squinting at the screen. "There!" Faintly, they could see movement on an arterial road leading from the Esfahan complex. A convoy of trucks, four in all.

"East? West?"

"Looks west. Yes, west."

Wallets, Marjorie, and Yossi huddled and clicked and pointed at the screen. Huddled and clicked and pointed some more. It went on for a long time with their backs to Johnson, and he started to feel left out. He tried to follow their discussion, the "what ifs" and the "yeah, buts"— eventually giving up and resisting the impulse to ask, *Well??*

Bits of their conversation mingled with his thoughts of Yasmine, and his eyelids drooped, and he fell into a half-reverie. He saw her in a white lab coat standing over a stainless-steel drum at the Gonabad Complex, stirring methodically, incanting "Double, double, toil and trouble . . ." Then Marge directed five dark words at him, awakening him again:

"Something wicked this way comes."

Wallets confirmed. "I agree," he said boldly. "Right friggin' here to Kermanshah." He paced away from the laptop, then back.

"How long would you say?" he asked Yossi.

"Tomorrow night, maybe day after tomorrow, in the morning." Then, guessing: "To Piranshahr, right on the frontier."

"Where's Piranha?" Johnson asked meekly.

Wallets and Yossi the Turk ignored Johnson. They began busily hammering emails into the laptop. Wallets rattled off a list of contacts. "And don't forget to cc Centcom; the way shit's going, some martinet Major on staff in Florida will start playing 'Red Light/Green Light' with us, if they're not in the loop."

Marjorie came over to Johnson, seeing the questions on his bleary-eyed face:

"We think whatever's in those trucks is heading right for us, from the Esfahan complex where they make the triggers. What we can't see is the train from the Nantanz facility with mountains of gunk. Might have shipped already. Trucks meet trains." She paused, when she saw the look of confusion on Johnson's face. "Two separate sites, understand? The one you saw where the nuclear material is produced—which everyone says doesn't exist. Then the second site, which you didn't see. Some sort of trigger device from the most secure fabrication plant in Iran—which everyone says doesn't build triggers. They bring them together and pack 'em like hot sausage. Right here in Kermanshah, end of the railroad line. Fully mated and loaded, back in the trucks they go. Next comes *Piranshahr*, not Piranha, the very last city before Iraq. Then up the mountains and over the river to Grandmother's house we go."

"Iraq?" Johnson asked, still trying to grasp what he was hearing.

"Sure. Most porous border in the world; once over the mountains they could have those trucks in Marseille in a week. Then container-shipped God knows where."

"But . . ." he started slowly. "You don't even know what's in these trucks, right? Or if the train—if there's a train—is already here. I saw the trucks, show me the train."

Marjorie leveled him with a look. "You want to get a search warrant and go back to Dr. Evil's Persian lair? No, I didn't think so. Right now we're four blind mice tapping along with our tin cups and maybe bumped into something. What's *your* plan? Wait till we find out what's in those trucks on the streets of San Francisco?"

Johnson had no answer.

"What we *do* know is that if they are moving something, this is the closest we're ever going to get. With any luck we'll track the trucks into Iraq, head them off at the pass, and nail them cold."

"I see," Johnson said, still skeptical.

Wallets' voice broke through their argument. "No, Yossi, you tell that peckerhead *Loo*-tenant Colonel, I *want* that exact unit. 10th Mountain Division, Second Battalion, Delta Company. No fucking substitutes, 'cause I know every Ringknocker's résumé, every 201 there. And besides, the Hummers—a deuce-and-a-half. SITREP grids on site. If we get a target, we can bushwhack them down in the foothills. If it turns out they're just smuggling Tupperware, we'll let them know."

Yossi became agitated again, this time with a touch of panic. "Hey!" The laptop screen began to flash with a red glow and beep an alarm. After two clicks the glowing stopped; the alarm died. The screen showed a street grid from Long Eye. A troop of men moving door to door in infrared outline. Body heat. They stopped in front of one place.

Yossi pointed to the screen: "Right next door here. Syrian Take-Out, Jabba's," Yossi explained. "Revolutionary Guards. They checking. Block to block."

Long moments passed as everyone watched the view from space. The men were dragging patrons out of the restaurant. People being kicked, beaten. Interrogation. You could see the writhing bodies. Even without the sound, very ugly.

Abruptly, the screen went blank. Yossi jerked back and barked in frustration. Wallets hovered over him, really worried now. "Did we lose satellite feed?"

Yossi's voice came back, this time scared. "No, satellite signal strong. See?" A slim field on the PC showed a satellite icon, bold green.

For the first time ever, Johnson saw Wallets at a loss.

The satellite image on the laptop suddenly flashed back. This time just with a message: "Data Loss. Stand By. We Apologize For Any Inconvenience."

Yossi slammed his palm on the desk, disgusted. They'd been zonked. They all looked from face to face, silently, weighing their situation. Thinking the same thought. Leave now? Marjorie stole a cigarette.

A banging thump rang through the cavernous Burka Company. Someone pounding on the metal door. And not the downstairs door either. Everyone thought of the men outside Jabba's. They'd been compromised. Three large bangs. Then a loud voice. Everyone froze. Four blind mice. Yossi got up. "Stay."

Four terrible minutes. Johnson couldn't take his eyes off Wallets and Marjorie. They'd gone deathly still. Wallets sitting up on his cot. Marjorie watching her cigarette burn. Their eyes strayed to the automatic weapons leaning against the wall, but made no move to touch them. Johnson's feet throbbed as if to mock him. The sound of Yossi talking from the stairway door drifted back. Someone else talking. Then stopped. They heard the door clang shut; the bolt thrown. Yossi appeared in the glass-fronted office once again, mightily pleased with himself.

"Shit Mullah. I make *bigger* payoff. So he no go shrine. Forget holiday. He send girls back here Monday work. I lose no dollars."

"What about the men in the street?" Johnson blurted.

Yossi glanced at the laptop. In the interim, the image of the nearby street had returned—sorry for the inconvenience. A single man in infrared was waving, gesticulating wildly at the drumhead justice gang. Yossi's Mullah. The gang broke up. Yossi shrugged. "I ask Mullah what noise in street? I trying to work. Then give him more bribe. So he send assholes to make Shabbat, yell at them, 'Go to Mosque! It way past sunset!'" And Yossi winked, "People here. *Very* holy."

CHAPTER SEVENTEEN

Injun' Country

They left the All-Iran Burka Company at dawn. In a curious way, Johnson felt sorry to leave. The place had been strangely comfortable, an unexpected refuge in a dangerous land. The cruddy food, the whiskey, watching Yossi's laptop magic lantern show, the camaraderie—and what comrades. Wallets could simply reach out and demand the cavalry come and get them. The 10th Mountain Division, Second Battalion, Delta Company. It made Johnson feel important to be with them, like he had made it past the velvet rope line of U.S. national security. Even the wormer didn't seem to bother him.

He balked for a moment before descending the steel stairs on his swollen feet. But he managed to hobble along, gripping the railing for support. Marjorie promised this day's travel would be easy, and he had no reason to doubt her. Tomorrow, she warned him, would be harder.

Wallets, Marjorie, and Johnson donned their head-to-toe burkas before passing through the metal door to the alley. Yossi waited for them in the car, the engine running. They all piled in. Back out the alley and into the streets of Kermanshah. Here on the outskirts of the city in the industrial district, the town was just coming awake. Buses belched black exhaust and paused for passengers, sitting by the curb at the start of their routes. Small street-corner cafés were already open, waiters or shop owners wiping off tables and setting up chairs, Saturday till sundown, still Sabbath, a big coffee day. As they drove east toward a line of hills, the two-way street broadened to a four-lane highway, split by a concrete median. The Turk gunned the accelerator, and the car hurtled forward.

Inside his stifling black hood, Johnson tried to watch the passing scene. He had the impression of low stucco walls, satellite dishes, the occasional storied public housing project of poured concrete. But as his breath blew back in his face, the sights fled across his vision, and all he could think of was tearing off this ugly hood. How could anyone live like this? Why would anyone want to? Only out of fear, subservience, shame—all safe under a cloak of anonymity.

They sailed along for a bit, then pitched forward as the car squealed to a halt. Johnson tried to peer through the little slit, but Marjorie hissed at him, "Be still!" They had stopped at some kind of checkpoint, a traffic barrier across the road. Armed men barred the car from moving front and back. Marjorie's voice again in a loud whisper, "Be ready to get out of the car."

Sure enough, one of the armed guards at the driver's side window began barking orders at Yossi, and before ten words were exchanged, the Turk grunted something in Farsi: "*Baleh! Baleh!*" like *Okay, okay, no problem!* Then turned to them in the back, ordering, "*Moshkeli nist!*" meaning, "Get out!" Clearly, the armed guards didn't want to touch the "women," holding the car door open for them and allowing them to stand in a small group beside the car while they searched it. Johnson saw Wallets shrink his height by bending his knees, and he tried to do likewise, wondering whether any of the men would notice it under the robes. So far none did, treating the women as if they didn't exist.

A long stream of excuses came out of Yossi's mouth. As the chief checkpoint guard ordered him around the vehicle, Yossi waved his hands plaintively, shuffling to the car's trunk. Johnson had never seen the man so abject, but he understood the ruse: absolutely no point in trying to bully or shoot your way out of this. Better the goons take him for some grubby peddler.

Yossi popped the trunk, and the checkpoint guards clustered around it. Several made appreciative grunts, oohs and aahs. A half-dozen Fujitsu laptops sat in the trunk, still in their shiny factory boxes. And a hundred or so DVDs, the latest Hollywood movies. Baksheesh: bribery goods.

The checkpoint guards began to reach inside the trunk without waiting for an invitation, exclaiming their approval, impressed at the quality of the merchandise.

Yossi's voice rose an octave as he haggled with the chief guard, begging him to spare a few laptops. But his pleading failed. In the end, they took every one. The Turk looked every bit the dejected, ruined merchant and barked the girls back into the car with a curt wave of the hand. Then slammed himself into the driver's seat, placing his head on the steering wheel in despair.

The chief checkpoint thug slapped the roof of the car, telling them to stop wasting his time: *All right, already! Get a move on!* The Turk turned the key, the engine purred, and as if by magic, the traffic barrier opened before them as the other guards dragged it aside.

⟡

Two hundred yards up the road, free and clear, Yossi began to grin, first a chuckle, then stuttering hoots—*heh-heh-heh.*

"All right, what's so bloody funny?" Johnson said behind his veil, his breath puffing back in his face.

"Our friend programs those laptops special," Marjorie explained. "Once they're in use for twenty-four hours, an irreversible sixty-second PowerPoint media show appears. Hormel Bacon advertisements, a gay male porn clip from a flick called *Harem Guards*, a couple of Danish Mohammed Cartoons, a Photoshopped pic of Ayatollah Gul in a yarmulke praying before the Wailing Wall, and the climax, a Windows Media Player File video of President Ahmadinejad being spanked by Dominatrix Madonna while she sings 'Like a Virgin.' The PCs work just fine, once you've watched the floor show."

Johnson sat back in his seat aghast. "Yossi, you're a sick man."

At which the Turk laughed again: "I sold program to RUK Kurdish rebels for $5,000 cash. They beam it into Iran from Kurd pirate TV station every day. Pretty soon YouTube get it."

Johnson reached for his face to slip off the hood. "Can we get out of—?"

But everyone in the car shouted, *"No!"* at the same time, and he desisted, sitting back in discomfort for the remainder of the ride. Well, at least he didn't have to walk. The swelling had receded, and Marjorie gave him another two shots of the steroid cocktail before the day was over.

"Don't get used to it," she cautioned him. "Once we're back in the world, it'll be bourbon and bon-bons but no boom-boom."

The wonderful stuff made him feel like The Hulk: invincible, powerful, and alive. But like every drug when it's ripped away, a part of you is ripped away with it, an ounce of flesh you sacrificed to the anabolic Demon, leaving you weaker.

But that was for later.

Not now. No, sitting in the back of the car watching as they left town—the unexpected, wondrous green and wooded hills of Iran sliding past the slit in his veil—Johnson felt like a god. Somehow he was going to wrest the best book of his life out of this, the best novel ever written. The hood over his head no longer stifled him but became a dark movie theater of the mind where he saw how it would all come out. Him, safe at home in safe Manhattan, working, with Giselle helping—reading every page in the swell Brooklyn condo. The markups, the polish, the page—warm to the touch—printing from his PC printer. Every wild scene, torture, confession, the gunfight—now in black-and-white, sharp as tacks, sent to a dozen publishers, who all bid more and more and more. The phone rang, and he heard his agent's voice telling him of the advance . . .

"Hey, wake up. We're here."

"Piranha?" The hood was choking him. His mouth like cotton, worse than any hangover he could remember.

"That's right, the outskirts of Piranshahr. You can take off your burka now."

Johnson breathed a sigh of relief and pulled the thing off in a great whoosh. His face was sticky with sweat, the cool air like some heavenly blessing. Marjorie now wore a crimson babushka but no face covering. Little Red Riding Hood.

He took some time to look around. The late afternoon sun illuminated all before them. They had stopped on the curve of a road, an overlook. In the distance, a haze of smog hung over a small city in the lap of low wooded hills, maybe a mile off. You'd think Iran was all scrub and desert, and you'd be wrong. This part was green and forested.

Below their road lay what looked like an abandoned quarry. The place filled with fifty-gallon drums. Some stacked in pyramids. Yossi stared into his laptop. He had managed to track the trucks from the previous night from the Esfahan complex to the railhead in Kermanshah, then right here.

"Don't understand," Yossi said. "They side track, make detour. Make unexpected stop. Why?"

Wallets considered for a moment, thinking it through out loud: "We were just thinking a two-part plan, mating triggers from Esfahan to nuclear fuel from Nantanz. But this is a *three-part* plan. Like you said, a detour." Wallets traced the route and, yes, pure speculation: "So maybe they railed some lead boxes packed with radioactive product from Nantanz, so we couldn't see it from space. Whatever they've got refined. Twenty pounds, a hundred? Didn't have a signature. Just a moving train, provided we even had satellite cover. Then trucks from Esfahan with some kind of trigger mechanism met the train in Kermanshah, where they mated the mechanism to the payload—as we surmised. But now what?"

They watched the vehicles roll into the quarry, through the gate in a chain-link fence, which opened automatically and closed behind them. Men got out and began to wrestle with the nearest pile of drums, opening them up. The men wore military-grade protective radiation suits, hoods, and gas masks, thick booties on their feet. They moved slowly in their gear, wrestling four drums open and carefully placing the drumheads on the ground. Besides the automatic gate, the place was surrounded by a high fence, twenty feet at least, topped with razor wire and capped with klieg lights pointing both inside and out. The first thing Johnson noticed: "No guards."

"Don't need them. No one would want to go there," Wallets told him.

"Looks like landfill. A waste dump?"

Wallets was impressed. "TRU waste. Transuranic. Meaning 'between Uraniums.' Neither here nor there, get it?"

"Not really."

"There's a lot of waste when you process fissionable material. You can't use it, but you can't flush it down the toilet either. You can put it in a New Jersey landfill or stick it in asphalt-lined drums out in the middle of—"

"I get it," Johnson said. "So those are asphalt-lined disposal drums. With waste inside."

Like slow-moving robots, the men moved stiffly in their protective suits, hoods, and filter-masks. The Iranians shoveled some of the contents from each drum, about half into a wheelbarrow, and then dumped the contents in a nearby pit, until all four were half empty. Then the top robot motioned to one of the others leading him back to the truck. He lifted up the flap in the back, and the two men lugged out what looked like a yard-long tube wrapped in some kind of protective metallic covering. Three other tubes inside. The protective covering fell away from the tube for a moment, and there was a glimpse of titanium—the tube shiny silver metal. Then the protective covering was wrapped back in place.

Laboriously, they slid yet another bag around the tube, but this one was thick canvas, with handles so they could carry it. A kind of cradle. You could tell the object or device was heavy, eighty or a hundred pounds. Other robotic drones came to assist.

"What in the world?" Marjorie wondered out loud.

"Those tubes are bombs," Wallets said softly. "What kind of bombs I don't rightly know." He thought for a moment. "Something we haven't seen before. My guess is some kind of mini-bomb. There's a trigger assembly and detonation device at one end, igniting a payload."

Now the men placed one titanium tube into an open waste drum to see if it would go in smoothly—like they wanted to see how well the tubes slid into the drums. And how much waste to remove from the drum to get a snug fit.

The slow-moving men hefted one titanium canister in its cradle from the truck. At the first drum, they paused, lowered the covered tube into the half-empty drum. The cylinder vertical, sizing the hole. Did they take out too much waste? Too little? No, just right. Thence onto the next drum. Carefully they lowered the tube into its new cocoon—making sure the hole would comfortably accommodate the canister. Then took it out again. As each titanium cylinder was the same size, they only used one for their "fitting."

Satisfied that the poisonous drums would accommodate each of the tubes at last, they slid the now contaminated canvas cradle free of the last tube and dumped the cradle unceremoniously into the pit. The sizing tube they returned to the truck.

Marjorie nodded. "Say it's something simple. Say the trigger at the top of the canister has fifty pounds of C-4—enough common explosive to take out a bridge or a building. But they've added a little bullet of highly purified plutonium—this they manufactured at the trigger place, Esfahan, the *really* guarded place. Say the remainder of the tube is filled with semi-refined material from Nantanz, an even larger radioactive wad. The tic-toc tube goes boom, driving an ounce of plutonium into a hundred pounds of hot, semi-refined uranium. 70 percent or 80 percent pure."

Wallets nodded. "Pure enough to get . . . what would we call it? A *semi*-reaction? So when the C-4 nuke tube goes off, not only will it level a building but will drive the little bullet into the larger wad inside the canister and blow the cocoon of the waste drum for a mile in every direction. A radioactive cloud. Fallout. The ultimate dirty bomb."

Already the other slow-moving handlers set about sealing the half-empty drums, pounding the tops back, then crimping the lids tight with heavy pincers. Finally, they hefted them on hand-trucks, wheeling them up an aluminum portable ramp into another truck. Soon all four drums were inside. The men wriggled out of their protective gear, leaving them on the ground, then climbed into their vehicles. The trucks' engines gunned, belching exhaust, and they rolled out the automatic gate.

Marjorie completed the circle. "So they came here right on the border to insert the device in a drum. Step three: make it fit. Sink your tic-toc tube in Transuranic waste, all inside a fifty-gallon asphalt-lined waste drum. Take it out again. Ship it in pieces. Reassemble and arm it near the intended target."

"And . . . *hide it?*" She glanced at the Turk, with a touch of doubt. "What do you think?"

Yossi stared into his laptop. A satellite shot. The quarry glowed, but the trucks didn't. "Asphalt-lined drums, no signature. Silver tubes, no signature either. Shielded."

Wallets nodded his head. "Right. When you're back in civilization, match it up again. Deliver it by panel van. Take out a building? A city block? Leaving twenty blocks in every direction poisoned. Fallout for twenty miles. People exposed would take from two months to two years to die. Forty thousand casualties?"

He looked from Marjorie to Yossi. Plausible?

"Pick your city," the Turk growled. He turned the key in the ignition, and the car crawled off the overlook as the sun sank into the hills. They drove the rest of the way to the border, a mere few miles into the mountains, in silence. And somehow the last twenty minutes of their trip seemed longer than any that went before.

Dusk came on fast. But Johnson could still see quite a bit as a three-quarter moon rose in the east. They had finally come to some kind of plateau at the end of a paved road in a tragic state of disrepair. Of all things, an abandoned drive-in movie theater nestled into a forest of trees, the kind of outdoor entertainment that went out of date forty years ago, even before the Shah's time. The projection booth sat in ruins. The high billboard screen had been shot through with gaping holes and plastered over with a huge banner of the Ayatollah Khomeini—now so faint and faded he'd be unrecognizable if it wasn't for his power-mad eyes, his bitter beard, and the cruel twist of his mouth. A large black bird sat on the billboard screen and cawed once as if to mark them.

So this was where civilization's road ended. Beginning as a shiny bauble of Western decadence, mutating in anger to an outdoor stadium where the faithful chanted "Death to America, Death to Israel," then dying in obscurity, only to be born again as a smugglers' camp. The Crow of history's last harsh laugh.

Teams of horses and pack mules stood tethered to a few of the metal poles that once held the window speakers. Now most of the poles were gone, metal and wire too valuable to simply lie around to rot. Groups of men stood by their horses, quietly talking, waiting for the night to close in. But no lit cigarettes, no camp fires. Below them and across a shallow valley lay the small city of Piranshahr, blazing and lit up like a toy town with far more bright lights than Johnson ever imagined in such a remote place. The hills behind the city were strung with lights as well and reminded him of the favelas, the slums of Rio perched on their clay-chiseled hillsides overlooking the swank hotels and beach at Ipanema. But here there was no beach, just a rundown drive-in movie theater from the Shah's 1950s heyday, sitting on the edge of a forest below the mountains. He could see Yossi and Wallets haggling with some men.

"Seeing a man about a horse?" Johnson wondered.

Marjorie nodded, "A mule more like it. But you get the idea. It's for you. We'll walk. See their packs?"

"No."

"That's the whole point. They don't have any. They're vice merchants. They smuggle in liquor and cigarettes by horseback, but not much goes the other way, except guns and bombs. Iran has nothing worth exporting that doesn't go bang. And that's what they'll think we are too, just another gang of cigarette smugglers."

Just as she finished speaking, engine noise from the broken-down road rose into the air. The trucks from the waste dump site, lights blazing, entered the concrete apron of the drive-in. They pulled up side-by-side some ways off and killed their engines. But kept their lights on. The headlights blazed into the crowd of horses and mules. The haggling men turned to face the trucks, and Yossi, Wallets, and the smugglers all shouted and waved at the drivers to kill the lights. But the truck lights didn't die. These guys weren't afraid of making their presence known.

Instead, four armed men got out. They pointed their guns at everyone, barking orders, taking over the scene, as though used to being in charge. You could see how disgusted the muleteers were, making apologetic gestures to Wallets and the Turk, who shrugged, turning away without an argument.

"That's it then," Marjorie whispered to Johnson. "We lost your mules to the top lad there and his three lackeys."

"The same truck guys." They weren't moving robotically anymore, free of their protective gear.

"So it would seem. Mujahadeen. Direct from the Esfahan Trigger complex, lately from the Kermanshah railhead, fresh from the quarry and with more juice than us. Unless you want to go over and tell them you're the daring Peter Johnson and you're late filing a story for *The Crusader*, so gimme your cruddy mule, you sissy Raghead. Or words to that effect."

Johnson measured the men with the guns and thought about how poorly the damn magazine's name would resonate with these thugs. They'd been fighting crusaders for a thousand years. Then thought about having a drink for the first time since his head popped out of the burka. His feet were still somewhat swollen, and he looked at them forlornly. Then with a little pluck, "Well I am kind of over deadline . . . "

Yep. All the horses and mules were spoken for. The armed Mujahadeen from the trucks expropriated what they wanted—four mules and two horses. That left another four horses for the vice merchants to ride, so Wallets' people were hoofing it out.

"I'm not worried about losing them, even in the dark," Wallets explained, "and I didn't expect to go faster than walking, but I did want to spare your feet. Sorry."

Johnson shrugged. "If I faint, Marjorie will carry me."

"Here, have a shot," she offered. The steroid boom-boom cocktail went into his arm.

The caravan left after dusk. Johnson noticed everyone was dressed so much alike. Khakis, combat boots, and checked kaffiyeh head scarves. In the dark, nobody'd even notice Marjorie was a girl—a reverse of the gender ruse of the last few days. And Johnson and Wallets looked scruffy enough to vanish into any bazaar.

The four mules were laden with two fifty-gallon drums each. You could tell the drums weren't totally full, as each was hefted into place by two men and sat lashed into a wooden X-cradle over the mule's back without making the beasts strain. Across the horses' rear ends hung two yard-long torpedo shapes, wrapped in thick padding, hung like clock weights. The titanium tubes. The men fussed with them to try to keep the things from knocking against one another against the horses' hind legs. Clearly, the Mujahadeen considered it something to be avoided.

Before long, they'd gotten it squared away, and the string of men and animals left the open apron of the drive-in movie theater for the darkness of the trees. Wallets let them get a ten-minute head start, not wanting to trail them too close. At first the four Blind Mice followed slowly, trying not to make any noise. There was something dangerous close at hand. Then Marjorie pointed it out, across a canyon: the dark outline of a pillbox, about four hundred yards away.

"Iranian border guards. They call them the Mullahs. In a country full of them, go figure. But they're more worried about stuff coming in than going out."

Everyone carried an AK-47, and pretty soon the sling on Johnson's rifle began to dig into his shoulder in awful ways. For several hours they climbed, the forest opening out, finally giving way to brush and rocks. The trail was clear enough, and when they reached a high ridge, Wallets stopped to let them rest. They could see the others still heading up, gaining distance. What looked from the abandoned drive-in like a final ridge was really just one in a series, and Johnson's heart sank, realizing they'd be at this all night, ridge after ridge—God knows how much longer. When he stopped to rest, that's when his feet really told him where he could get off.

Marjorie saw he wasn't doing so well but offered nothing but tepid tea from a canteen and sympathy. Her caring eyes illuminated for a moment when she lit him a cigarette.

"At least we're going by trails," she whispered. "If we weren't doggin' the Mujahadeen and their mules, we'd head west and stay off their tracks. Too easy here to meet a bad guy on the way up or down."

———

They pressed on; ridge after ridge, down some, but always higher on the climb. The stars hard and clear. Up about five thousand feet, Johnson began to pant hard.

"Here, it'll keep you breathing, but your feet won't like it."

"I don't care—I gotta breathe."

It was a little green leaf. "Chew it."

"Coca?" Johnson wondered with a touch of awe.

"Close. Khat. Another kind of stimulant. Works about the same."

Johnson didn't care. The bitter tang on his tongue went right to his head and heart, and the next two ridges blew by so fast he barely noticed. Somewhere in the back of his mind he knew he'd pay for this big time. But it didn't matter—the bright stars loved him; Marjorie loved him. And he loved her back. When they got out of this, they would marry, have many Mini Marge children who would all know how to shoot wild turkey in the woods. And live happily ever after. With an endless supply of Khat.

Out of nowhere a commotion erupted up the trail, and they could hear it all the way back. The lead mules and horses had met some kind of gang on their way down. A posse. Marge, Yossi, and Wallets surrounded him like clucking hens, shoving him off the path. They stumbled into the rocks, going further and further off the beaten track, while the noise of the altercation echoed off the mountain.

Thirty yards into a garden of stone pillars, they sat on him. Really sat on him, slipping the AK-47 off his shoulder without even a clink. Then split away, taking up firing positions a few yards on either side. Nobody needed to say "hush." Wallets stared back at the trail, a pair of night goggles at his eyes. Yossi and Marjorie cautiously locked and loaded their guns, quietly hugging their boulders for cover, the muzzles pointing toward the path.

Even without the night goggles, Johnson knew the score. Men were searching. Searching for them. The posse had gotten in ahead, up above, and figured they'd catch them on the way up. And Peter Johnson deeply understood why the Sheik and Yasmine let him free. The cripple fakir in the Kasbah, the goons in the bazaar, the military police waiting in the plaza—nobody gave a shit about Peter Johnson. They cared about the real spies, just like Wallets told him back at the Burka Company, but now he understood the lengths their pursuers were willing to go. Even hinder the smuggling of a great weapon, risk a firefight on a blind mountainside—*anything* to get the deceivers in their midst.

The sounds of arguments faded; the men on the mules with their radioactive burden were free to go, the posse headed down. Yossi's soft voice whispered, "Mule men say we just cigarette traders like them. No keep up. Must be down below. The posse gang say drum smugglers and vice merchants worthless Jew Monkeys. You just be quiet now."

Very quiet. The sound of men, a troop clattered down the slope. They went slowly, some splitting off the path to search either side. One paused at the entrance to their stone-pillar garden. He walked in a dozen steps. Then another dozen. From his huddle under a great stone, Johnson saw the man, his face right over an edge of rock. A semi-shaven face, now with a couple days of scruff, a face that needed regular shaving. Very odd for Iran, where every man was required to grow some kind of a beard. Obviously, this group received special dispensation from the authorities to shave, so they could blend in on both sides of the border. No long beards required. Just the ubiquitous Saddam moustache. The searcher looked this way and that, peering intently. He put on his own pair of night goggles. Then looked some more. No one breathed.

A shout from the Posse Boss turned him around. The night goggles dropped from his eyes, and his footsteps faded back out toward the trail. Johnson suddenly wanted to cry Hosannas or kiss the rock. Then he found he'd wet himself. *Hosanna*, no razor blades.

They weren't going up-up-up anymore but down-down-down. And he was sick and dizzy inside, and his feet throbbed. Up front, the Turk and Wallets were going slower so as not to trip and pitch themselves on their heads. A quarter mile down below, the vague outlines of the laden mules and awkward horses bobbed this way and that in the dark in and out of the rocks. They slowed to a crawl. Wallets didn't want to catch up with the drum smugglers and the vice merchants. The landscape had also changed. No longer woody, with trees and brush, these hills were bare rock with lichen and little twiggy shrubs.

"Iraq?" he asked Marjorie.

And she nodded. "Iraq. Strange, huh? One side green and lush, the other bare."

When suddenly the whole caravan stopped short in a bit of a narrow valley. The mules and horses huddled by a stony bank. A small stream splashed down from nowhere, alongside the rocky trail. Down below, the vice merchants gathered over by one shoulder of rock, the mule drivers crossed the stream to the opposite bank, all in sight of each other, but none too close, as if they didn't like each other's company. The animals went down to water; the men warily filled their canteens, hugging opposite sides of the bank.

Looking down from their own perch along the stream, Johnson could see them all quite clearly, even in the faint light of the setting moon. Not a hundred yards away. He splashed water on his face, feeling *wow*, then noticed one of the Mujahadeen mule drivers look up sharply in his direction. Could he see them up above? But no, the man went back to his canteen. "I think we're safe up here," Marjorie said. "With any luck we'll lasso the lot a mile or so on the way down."

Johnson splashed water on his face again and then stretched out on a flat rock by the stream. It began to dig into his flesh, but his feet hurt so bad he almost didn't notice. Marjorie tossed him a padded length of stiff Styrofoam padding not half an inch thick. He looked at the stiff, measly thing thinking, *I'll never be able to sleep on that cookie sheet—*

Dawn inside the narrow barren valley caught him full in the face. The sun over the high ridge beat down. Eight o'clock in the morning. No more than four hours' rest. Johnson didn't even remember passing out. He'd slept like a dead thing on that square pizza pan. What woke him was the bartender's bill for his feet and his head. He'd gone off on some benders before, but this one took the cake for pure pain. A splitting head. He felt like he'd swallowed a salt stick. Whole. He couldn't even manage to get Margie to toss him the canteen, trying to whisper, "Water . . . ," but nothing came out. And he couldn't walk either. Down below the four Mujahadeen were loading the drums on their mules again.

Quietly up the valley the cutting sound of choppers echoed into the rocks. Everyone froze, panicked, looking wildly around. It would be seconds now. Wallets ran to his pack and frantically tried to get inside it. A stream of profanity came out of his mouth, "Christcuntfuckshit!"

Taken completely by surprise, the vice merchants scattered and ran in every direction. The drum smugglers went for their guns and drove their mules across the stream, heading down. Yossi the Turk and Marjorie stumbled a few paces along the trail with their guns and, afraid the mules were going to get away, began to fire. The Mujahadeen ducked behind some rocks and let fly back. A ricochet caught Yossi full in the face, and he fell over swearing in Farsi. More bullets caromed around the rocks, and Marjorie ducked behind a boulder. Johnson saw her face. Very white. Despite the chaos, he crawled down to her. Twenty feet, then closer, ten. Then slumped against the same rock.

"Stay down!" she hollered at him. Yeah, he'd heard that before.

At the mouth of the valley, two Apache helicopters roared toward them in formation.

Wallets was hollering into his Centcom phone. "Get 'em off, get 'em off us!"

"Ours?" Johnson shouted at Marjorie. She'd pulled him safer behind a boulder as the Mujahadeen mule drivers lay down a long burst. And he cowered, pressed to her back. Rocks flew and skipped all around.

"Yeah ours. But not *ours*. A patrol. Scouting the border for Iranian IEDs. *Our guys* are a couple of miles ahead—" but she never finished.

An explosion went off somewhere very close by. An Apache rocket? The concussion drove the air from his lungs, and Johnson hit his head on the boulder. From then on all he heard was roaring, the loudest roaring he'd ever heard, going on and on.

He saw Marjorie bleeding from her ear, her face ashen. And suddenly Wallets was there. He cradled her in his arms talking seriously to her, as if he loved her—but she didn't seem to respond to him. Her head lolled around like a rag doll's while he stroked her face with stiff wooden hands. From the corner of his eye, Johnson caught a glimpse of the drum smugglers' mules laden with their deadly cargo. The mules heading off down the valley at a brisk trot through chest-high boulders, braying as they went. And yeah, at least two Mujahadeen close behind. The sound of choppers faded into the distance.

PART TWO

HOUSE OF WAR

Who is in charge of the clattering train?

The axles creak and the couplings strain,

And the pace is hot, and the points are near,

And Sleep has deadened the driver's ear;

And the signals flash through the night in vain,

For Death is in charge of the clattering train.

—Anonymous, quoted by Winston Churchill,

who recalled it from childhood,

in a volume of *Punch* cartoons

CHAPTER EIGHTEEN

Damage Control

Back up the stream, another copter had arrived to extract them, a large medivac Black Hawk. Before the oxygen mask came over his nose and mouth, Johnson saw Marjorie bleeding from the head. When they snapped the oxygen mask on the woman's face, he guessed still alive—but for how long? Soldiers called the instant medivac arrival the "magic hour": that single hour where prompt treatment saved those who otherwise died on the battlefield.

Wallets' face was as gray as his eyes. And Johnson knew why. Yet how angry could the man get at the wild-flying Apache that roamed these hills? Even after the surge, Iraq was no place for gentlemanliness—even if there were fewer IEDs, suicide belts, and chlorine truck bombs blowing up good soldiers and good people from Mosul to Kirkuk. Specially manufactured copper shape-charges coming off the Iranian defense industry production line could still burn through armored Humvees and shred the men inside. And nobody cared about stopping it as much as the wild Injuns of the U.S. Military. So many people to be angry at—where did you start? A needle slipped into Johnson's arm, making the flying sky and insistent whine of rotor-blades blur away to nothing.

The teary reunion show started first at Mannheim Air Force Base in Germany, where Johnson landed for a required "medical checkup," but quickly worked its way to Manhattan, where all the important people lived.

The checkup amounted to an Army doctor taking Johnson's blood pressure, examining the bump on his head and the soles of his feet. Telling him, "You may feel dizzy and nauseous, but there's nothing serious here. Whoever treated those abrasions on your feet really knew what they were doing. Somebody told me you bought some rubber shoes in Mahabad and *walked* up a mountain? Good for you."

Johnson started at the phrase "rubber shoes"; did that mean Yossi still lived? But Johnson was smart enough to keep his trap shut.

As Mannheim was the Army's center of military policing in Germany, no surprise that two MPs stood at the emergency room door with wooden faces. Their mission: make sure this wreck with the bandaged feet left Mannheim in one piece. And it went off without a hitch. They hustled him through a phalanx of reporters, mostly Germans shouting questions at him as a male nurse pushed his wheelchair to a New York–bound military flight, a darkened and nearly empty Boeing 727. He left the wheelchair on the tarmac and found a seat in First Class a few rows down from Robert Wallets, who glanced once at Johnson before pressing his face into a small flight pillow. Wrapped in a blanket, head covered, Johnson barely recognized him. He'd shaved and washed his face and looked like a ghost.

Once on board, Johnson found the ever-enterprising Ruth Lipsky from the *Washington Post* planted across the aisle, looking at him. As the woman who broke many of the CIA rendition stories, the reporter had a contact or two at Mannheim, and it was no surprise she could find her way onto a plane. She was a cute brunette, short, in her mid-thirties, with a solicitous, girlish manner that made you want to open up to her because she seemed to care about you so much. At least until she had her story. Then you would find out how much she really cared in the next day's paper.

"Have you called home?" Lipsky offered her Blackberry Pearl. "I won't eavesdrop. I promise." She winked, and it struck Johnson as flippant.

Johnson stared at the reporter's phone. "My daughter called me at the hospital. I'll see her in six hours." Then thought for a moment. It'd be advisable to get his spin on events out there so it could travel at least partway around the world before the truth—not that anyone would be telling *that*—got started. Whatever he told Lipsky would precede him to New York.

But what the hell should he tell her? They'd never practiced those things during his sessions at B & D—what to give the press in the event of a botched assassination? Capture, then release? An unforeseen Iranian plot to nail them all? Another narrow escape only to get hit by a U.S. helicopter? How could they have?

He looked over to Lipsky, who was staring at him with a look of tender concern. "Look," he told her, "I know you didn't go to all the trouble of getting on this plane just to let me borrow your phone."

She smiled. "You're right."

"So, I'll tell you this."

Her micro-digital recorder, thin as a credit card, pointed his way before he'd finished the sentence. He resolved to be as honest as possible without actually being truthful.

"I'm glad to be back. I know there were a lot of people pulling for me, and those were the angels in this story. My daughter, Giselle, especially. One of the good guys. I've lost track of the bad guys. But the very worst by far occupy offices in the District of Columbia and New York."

"What do you mean?"

"I got caught up in something bigger than myself. A game between two powers, with layers I'm not sure I understand."

"The Iranians have suggested you are a spy."

"Ruth, do I look like a spy? Besides, who *don't* the Iranians call a spy?"

She shrugged. "Were you rescued? The Iranians say you were released as a gesture of goodwill."

"Yes, I was released, and then Americans ushered me out of the country."

"Then you were never trained by the CIA? Say in . . . North Carolina?"

Johnson wondered if she detected any reaction from him. He searched her shiny brown eyes; someone was talking to her. "Ruth, I went to Iran on a reporting trip at the invitation of the Iranian Information Ministry, a trip that went bad very quickly. I am a journalist. I've always been a journalist. What U.S. spy agency in their right mind would recruit from *The Crusader*? Jo von H wouldn't hear of it."

Ruth smiled sympathetically. "You look tired. I have a couple of extra Ambien if you want them."

Johnson took the pills and her card and curled up in his seat, facing away from her. He thought about the questions he had still to answer, thought about them so much he barely dwelt on the alluring twinkle in the reporter's eye. It intrigued him for a moment—but only a moment. Which in and of itself was newsworthy. The pills and exhaustion did the rest; Johnson awoke when the plane arrived at the gate in New York, sleeping the whole way without waking up once. Ruth Lipsky shuffled toward the open cabin door. No sign of Wallets—the man had vanished.

The CIA-SPAN in Banquo's Rockefeller Center office carried the news conference, and the whole New York team gathered to watch it— O'Hanlon, his two FBI babes, and even the preppie Bryce. The old spymaster made no secret of his masterfully reserved delight at the prospect of DEADKEY down in Langley gnashing his teeth and pacing and fretting through the spectacle of this must-see TV. They held the mike show at the JFK International Arrivals gate, upstairs on the concourse.

First, the haggard Johnson emerged from the metal customs swing doors, embracing Giselle, who ducked under the barrier rope, closely followed by his harem of ex-wives, Mama Françoise Ducat, the elegant Elizabeth Richards, and the predatory Josephine von Hildebrand, who held a few steps back, looking down constantly at her Blackberry, from which she Twittered the whole thing for the *Crusader* blog. Beside her, Giselle's beau, Anton Anjou, Banker/Nobleman, seemed more than content to hold the women's coats, which he did with great poise.

In two and a half minutes, the teary reunion crowd stood upstairs on the concourse with the local and national media present to lap up every word. Alas, some of the cables were doing a split-screen with another hot story—the arraignment of Jennifer James, the twenty-five-year-old blonde wannabe Maxim model/teacher. Her tryst with a fifteen-year-old boy in a junior high locker room proved irresistible to producers and had made her one of this week's most popular Google image searches. So Johnson would have to share his time.

At JFK, the questions at the presser were dense or leading, meant to draw an obvious picture so the dumb newsies could paint by numbers: daring, put-upon journalist (one) caught in an unfortunate clash of civilizations (two) for which the U.S. bears most responsibility (three). Don't stray too far outside the lines!

"Was I scared? Sure, when the machinations of your own government put you in that kind of situation, of course you're scared—and, I don't have to tell you, angry."

"Of course, something happened when we were out with the scientist, Dr. Yahdzi. His life put in jeopardy. So I don't blame the Iranians for detaining me."

"You want me to name an agency? All right. I have reason to believe the Central Intelligence Agency was involved. No, not in Virginia, right here in New York."

"No, I'm not going to name their offices. Do your own work. Call around."

"Will I be publishing the story? Only if my editor, Josephine, wants it."

"Iran's nuclear program? No threat at all. Only fabulists believe such things."

"Did *I convert?* Do you see me kneeling in this airport shouting *Allah Akbar*, frightening benighted passengers?"

"Sheik Kutmar's statement? Didn't see it. I was being held."

"Yes, he's right as far as that goes. Again, I believe the United States government was after their scientist. I've met the Sheik. I don't blame him for being sensitive about it."

"No, I didn't kill anyone. Wouldn't know how."

"No, I don't think of myself as the new Joseph Wilson, no—I haven't the hair."

"A book? That's getting ahead of ourselves. But let me say"—and here he was improvising and could barely repress a smile, he was so pleased with himself—"I would donate any proceeds to the Red Crescent."

"Anything else to say? Yes, I'd like to go home with my daughter. I'm sure you understand. Thank you very much."

"Someone really needs to give that guy a good kick in the ass," said Agent Smith, as Banquo hit mute at the end of the presser.

"We volunteer," said Agent Wesson.

"I appreciate the sentiment, ladies," Banquo replied, tugging at the shirtsleeves beneath his suit jacket and folding his arms in front of him, "but save the kicking for a more worthy recipient. He did fine."

"What do you mean?" asked O'Hanlon. "He all but named you."

"*All but,*" said Banquo. "*All but,* and that's the key. It's not easy to dance around those bear traps without losing your foot. But that's exactly what he did. Didn't even blow any of his street cred with his fancy friends. Did I say 'fine'? I revise. Call it brilliant."

Everyone went quiet, absorbing Banquo's praise for that weaselly performance.

Banquo broke the silence, chuckling and shaking his head, still not over Johnson's answers. "This is no surprise, really, but that man is an exceptionally good liar. I don't think anything he said was technically untrue, except the bit about there being no Iranian nuke program and, oh yes, donating his book proceeds to the Red Crescent. Hah! Don't believe that for a minute."

O'Hanlon looked at Banquo quizzically. "Doesn't this mean you're going to feel a lot of heat?"

"That," Banquo said, waving his hand toward the mute screen, "is the least of our worries. Bryce, do you want to do the deed?" He nodded to the shelf where the Armagnac sat. Bryce rose to get it. There was plenty for everyone.

Banquo rolled the brandy about in the glass, not a snifter but a rocks glass with bold straight edges, no soft bulbous curves. He raised his glass and looked at each of them in turn. "Ladies, gentlemen, we have not yet begun to fight." And then, much softer, and graver, "It's abundantly clear what we have to do now."

O'Hanlon's FBI babes' doe eyes came back at him without comprehension. They let their boss speak for them: "I'm just a Fordham criminal attorney, and you're going to have to make yourself abundantly clearer."

Banquo stared at the liquor in his glass. "According to Wallets, nuclear material is moving westward. Toward where, we don't know. Could be Paris, could be L.A. We live in the target of choice, facing people who will never relent until they've hit us again. And it's clear that a top Iranian nuclear scientist was nearly killed, which might make the mullahs very restless. So I would think, Mr. Fordham law school—don't be so humble; you're in the top twenty-five—it's clear that if *you-we-us* have to toss every crappy apartment in Brooklyn or Brookline looking for our lost weapons, *we will*. The mules in the mountains went somewhere. Let's make sure their cargo isn't coming here to our Workbench Boys in Brooklyn. As for Johnson, leave him to me."

O'Hanlon shook his head in disbelief. "We don't have the resources for that. *Nobody* does."

Banquo placed the brandy glass on the desk, unfinished. "Better *find* them."

⸎

Wallets' car from JFK didn't take very long even at rush hour. He found Banquo alone at his computer and the bottle of Armagnac back on the shelf, the glasses rinsed and put away. The office was totally dark, except for the CIA-SPAN showing matters of no consequence. Assad of Syria marching along a red carpet with Ahmadinejad of Iran—the former six foot one at least, the other nearly a dwarf. Everyone now videotaped or photographed the Iranian president from below, making him look tall.

Robert Wallets didn't bother to acknowledge his boss's presence, who wheeled around in his chair to look at him. Just went to the special place on the shelf, found a glass, and uncorked the bottle. He sat on the other side of Banquo's desk and drank.

"Marjorie?" Banquo asked.

The grim soldier didn't say anything. Last Wallets saw her in the Critical Care Unit of Mannheim AFB Hospital, the woman looked more dead than alive. Her head shaved along one side, a two-inch finger of skull missing, bandages, blood seepage, and with a tube in her mouth. A plug of cotton stuck in her ear canal, but no other marks. The Colonel in charge of the hospital just looked at Wallets with blank eyes and shook his head. No prognosis.

"We can't tell anything now."

"What about Yossi?"

Again, Wallets did not reply. Banquo looked out over Fifth Avenue. His voice floated in the room. "We have to assume, of course, that the lucky mules caught their ship in Marseille or someplace and got through."

"What does Dubai Ports World say?" Wallets asked.

Banquo shook his head slowly from side to side. "Nothing. Your lost devices might not have gone through their hands at all."

Wallets' shoulders hunched, and he bent over his glass, staring at the desk right in front of it. Banquo knew how Wallets' brain must be going into overdrive, not in thought, but in pure replay—over and over again, the sight of the looming, implacable Apache attack chopper, every tiny choice sifted from every possible angle. What he did do and what he didn't. How it all turned out. Yossi clutching his face. The mules, their deadly drums and canisters braying off into the hills. Cradling Marjorie's head. Again. And again. The images and thoughts crowding out constructive thought.

Unless he shook free of such second-guessing one day, they'd become utterly intolerable, until the only recourse was drink, drugs, or madness. Banquo thought of what he could say, what words of sympathy or wisdom. But he knew he had none, and simply sat there in silent solidarity.

Wallets took another slug of brandy. "Then we have to assume the weapons are here," he said.

"Exactly."

CHAPTER NINETEEN

Loose Ends

Something told Giselle her father didn't like Anton. His eyes seemed like drawn curtains darkening the room of his mind. When she flat-out asked him, he denied it. But she sensed he had to make an effort to be nice to her beau. When she told him she was going out with Anton, he'd usually respond with a flat "Ah," and sometimes offered an alternate diversion: "I'm having dinner tonight with the Estimable Person du Jour. You're both welcome." As if wanting to keep her close. Or keep an eye on him. Or both.

And she noticed how since his return her dad seemed at loose ends. He didn't want to write but didn't want to be alone either. Anton obliged by forever telephoning, inviting her father to gallery openings, cocktail parties, and such, basking in his celebrity and even asking his advice on random matters. Almost as though Anton wanted to be around the Man from Iran as much as his daughter.

For his part, Peter Johnson kept his own counsel. And at times seemed to enjoy Giselle's beau; there was a lot to like about the boy. The kid was smart, polished, sophisticated, but even with all that, Johnson's skin crawled every time the young man held Giselle's hand, put his arm around her waist, kissed her hello or good-bye. The little shit had seduced his baby on false pretenses so someone could take pictures of her—duly relayed to Iranian intelligence.

First chance he could, he wanted to force the issue with Wallets.

Johnson had tried to get in touch several times since their return, but somehow Banquo's man never answered his phone, and speaking into the "leave a message" voice mail was wearing thin. In the end, Johnson stalked him, catching him in the lobby of 30 Rockefeller Plaza as Wallets got off the elevator around lunchtime.

"Don't you like me anymore?"

That brought Wallets up short. And he seemed annoyed at being caught off guard. It had been two weeks since that night on the frontier and the friendly fire "incident" in the mountains. Johnson immediately noticed a change in Wallets. There had always been an edge of menace to him, but it had broadened out, coloring his entire disposition. Johnson could tell: he had grown colder, colder even than Banquo. His soul filled with a terrible resolve. He glanced at Johnson, unsurprised and unimpressed. Without missing a beat, they fell into step together. "It's been *busy* since we got back. Having fun at the parties?" Before Johnson could answer he offered, "Eaten lunch yet?"

They found one of those glass-walled sandwich places on the lower concourse level, where they sat at a tiny table and watched the crowds of subterranean office dwellers stream by on a thousand private errands—none of which meant life or death, but all the same seemed to weigh like a burden on every worker bee. The tuna fish was a trifle sour, the lettuce limp, and rye bread an hour away from stale. The air down below, filtered, thick, and heavy.

"Can you tell me about Marjorie?"

Wallets stared gravely at him, with nothing forthcoming. He finally answered, "Nothing I'd care to say. You can imagine the worst yourself."

Johnson looked away.

"It's not that we don't love you anymore, Peter," Wallets continued. "It's just since the last time we were together, a couple of mules carrying god-knows-what vanished over the horizon, and it's everything we can do to find them again."

"Bad break."

Wallets took a deep draw on a Dr. Pepper, the straw gurgling.

"Yeah. Very." He sucked the rest of the soda dry.

"Not angry at the news conference?"

Wallets smiled for the first time. "Of course not. Meant to tell you Banquo said, 'Bravo,' 'encore.'"

Now Johnson prodded, not sure if he believed the man. "You shutting me out?"

Wallets became exasperated, tossing a greasy ten on their plastic plates.

"No, Peter—we're cooling you off. What do you want, your own desk at the office?"

Johnson bristled at the sarcasm. He'd put his ass on the line for Banquo & Duncan and Wallets in particular. He'd jumped into the shit and managed to crawl out. This was the first week he could actually put on his own shoes and socks and not hobble.

He snapped back. "I want to know who the hell Anton Anjou is—every little crummy thing. I want to know why he's still with Giselle, why you don't have him upside down hanging from a meat hook in a warehouse, asking him questions. Is that too much to want?"

"It's too early for that, Peter. Anton needs more rope. And wouldn't you rather be in play, right alongside him, looking available?" To that Johnson had no reply. So he kept his mouth shut.

Wallets looked down at their Styrofoam plates, with their stray pieces of lettuce or crust. "You know," he said, still looking down. "We're not his ghosts."

The back of Johnson's neck tingled with alarm. He'd never known Wallets to employ illusive allusions. Something was wrong.

If Wallets noticed the look of incomprehension, he didn't register it, now gazing past Johnson over his shoulder. "Banquo sometimes calls us his 'ghosts,' because we'd haunt people in places unseen and so much of what we do is never, *never* acknowledged—operating on another plain, between the normal world and one much darker."

Johnson's sense of alarm left him, but not his confusion. Now Wallets fixed him with his eyes. "But the real ghosts live in the Old Man's past, claiming him forever. It's what drives him and by extension, us. I understand that now. Finally. And in a way I wish I didn't."

Johnson didn't know what to say. Wallets got up, and Johnson threw some of his own cash on the plates, splitting the bill. They walked out together in silence, and when they stood outside the door, Wallets' reverie had passed. "We'll be in touch," he said. "You're not cashiered; you're just in the change drawer. Soon we may slide you onto the counter."

Johnson nodded. His impatience with Wallets had vanished. He watched the man exit through a revolving door and disappear into the street. Somehow, even with the coldest eyes he'd ever seen, Wallets could still turn the moment. Graveyard eyes, Johnson thought. Looking at his watch, he realized that he'd better get a move on or he'd be late for a gallery opening with Giselle and the Little Twerp. Mustn't miss that.

A Soho gallery—how original. The artist—one of those with a single name, Blaire—specialized in American flags. The stars and stripes plastered on every available wall and in every imaginable condition: some torn, some burned, some upside-down, one on the floor that everyone walked on as they entered, another over a casket, another choking a toilet as a constant flushing sound emanated from the tank.

The first thing Johnson heard as the three of them—Giselle, Anton, and he—entered was the gallery owner holding forth to a group of admirers about his foray into Scientology: "I took my first stress test. Buddhism just isn't doing it for me anymore."

Johnson glanced at the man: short, paunchy, in wealthy middle age, wearing $500 horn-rimmed spectacles; a guy who'd never missed a meal and knew the proper wine for every occasion. What was it, Peter wondered, that Buddhism was *supposed* to do for a gentleman like that?

Then he heard a familiar voice. "Peter, *dah*ling!" Jo von H emerged from the crowd like a queen from her courtiers in a little black strapless cocktail dress, a second skin that seemed to move without moving. She zeroed in on Giselle and linked arms, then glanced conspiratorially at the handsome Anton. "Well done, Ms. Johnson. So you've been holding out on me. Does Beau Brummell have brains too?"

Giselle patted her arm, woman to woman. "What can I say, Ms. von Hildebrand? A lady *never* tells. In any case, he's not British; he's a Gaul."

And the two women laughed. From what Johnson saw the smooth Frenchie Banker didn't mind the admiration. But something in his ex's eyes pinged in Johnson's brain. He'd seen that look before. Aw, c'mon, Mrs. Robinson. Naw—no *way*. Not with Giselle's boyfriend. But there were bigger fish in the room, Johnson himself being the biggest, at least for today.

Before the first glass of Chardonnay was half way down a crowd had gravitated to him and his brood in an elaborate magic circle. Johnson had been on TV a lot, and people wanted to talk to him. Touch the hem of his robe. Of course, he let them. He glanced across the room to the artist—Blaire standing nearly alone near his flag-choked flushing toilet—and if the jealous fellow could have poisoned this unwelcome guest right now, he would have done it in a Lucrezia Borgia heartbeat.

———

Jo von H left early for another event, and later Johnson waved Anton and Giselle away in a cab. They were off to the Frenchman's renovated townhouse on Grove Street. Silently he watched the cab bounce over the cobblestones of the Soho street, catching the first traffic light and turning a corner. Then, unhurriedly, he walked after the cab; the exercise would do him good. Fifteen minutes later found him across the Village on Grove Street standing opposite Frenchie's stoop. The lights were on in the top-floor bedroom, and Johnson tried not to think about it. Instead he looked up and down the street. From what he could tell, nothing unusual, just parked cars wedged in too tight for comfort. He methodically walked down one side of the street heading west. When he got to the corner, he turned around and walked back on the other side.

All the time keeping his eyes on the opposite rooftops, looking for any sign of something out of place. The line of townhouse balustrades—some in red stone, some in white, some in brown—were an almost unbroken line in the Manhattan sky. On one directly across the street from Anton's steps Johnson thought he saw something. No movement, but some sort of wire or pole hanging over the balustrade that didn't seem to belong. A shotgun mike? A very thin video lens? Impossible to tell. But it looked as if it was aimed directly at Anton's lit windows.

He walked across the street toward the suspicious building. The townhouse door was locked, of course; bolted, locked, alarmed, and a private residence to boot. No chance one of a dozen tenants might come home and open the vestibule. Nope. This was a very desirable Manhattan address, and somebody rich lived there, even if they weren't aware that a long, strange wire protruded from their balustrade.

He wondered: Was there a Robert Wallets guy at the other end of that wire? Johnson plopped his behind on the stairs of the stoop to think. "Can we help you?" A metallic voice from a speaker. "No loitering, please." Of course, a security camera and a voice box over the stone stoop. But it wasn't a real person, just an automatic recording. Relieved, Johnson got up and shuffled away. He didn't like spying on Giselle or looking up at the apartment; his action felt all Othello-Desdemona. Halfway back to Broadway, he felt a stroke of mild genius. At one of the last corner payphones in all of New York, he dialed 911 and, when the operator answered, said, "Man with gun, Grove Street." Then hung up.

A mere ten minutes later an NYPD squad car rolled down Grove with its bubble lights flashing, lighting up every building, but no siren. The squad car rolled the length of Grove and slowly turned the corner.

But Johnson wasn't interested in that flashy show. At the roof of the townhouse right by the strange wire, shotgun mike, or narrow video lens, a man's head cautiously peered over the balustrade at the flashing lights below. And Johnson whispered to himself, "I see you . . ." A Robert Wallets man, if ever there was one. Watching Anton's pad.

Comforting to know Banquo kept an eye on her, but what stung him was how neither Giselle nor Anton bothered to come to the window to stare at all the pretty flashing lights. His ears burned, yet he banished the thoughts from his mind. Stop, Othello. *Stop.* It's about him and his pals, not *him and her.*

A short block back toward Seventh Avenue. Johnson found a coffee shop on the corner of Grove and Bedford and went inside with half a mind to wait out the night. From a well-placed window booth he could

see Anton's stoop. The upper light in the bedroom windows was out. He
had bought a half-dozen newspapers from a newsstand and ordered a
club sandwich, wondering how long he'd have before crawling home.
Some unspoken hunch told Johnson the young man wasn't through for
the night. Gallery opening, bedding his baby—still there'd be some
extra job to do. And after an hour, he wasn't disappointed.

About midnight Anton came out his front door. The windows
upstairs still black. Was he the kind of guy who left a note? And if so,
what would it say? "Just restless, G, going for a walk . . . be back soon."
Yeah, the young smoothie wouldn't forget the luv-u-note-thing.

Anton walked past the window of the coffee shop without glancing
through the glass and descended into the Christopher Street subway station. Hurriedly, Johnson slapped some bills on the booth table and followed the young man underground. He chose the Redline Pelham 1-2-3,
Downtown to South Ferry or under the East River to New Lots Avenue.
At midnight, the Christopher Street station still bustled, people going
home to Brooklyn from a night in the Village or just arriving, their night
about to get underway. So Johnson could stand in a far corner of the
Downtown car, hanging on a strap with his back turned, surreptitiously
glancing over his upraised arm. Anton never saw him.

The train went five stops south, still in Manhattan—Houston Street,
Canal, Franklin, Chambers to City Hall. Next stop Brooklyn? Suddenly
Anton wasn't in the car anymore. He'd gotten off at City Hall, and Peter
pushed his way out of the subway car onto the platform. Moving bodies
scurried through the labyrinth of the City Hall station. By sheer luck,
Peter caught the back of Anton's head descending the stairs to the Blue
Line Trains. So they were going under the river—just the northern tip
of Brooklyn, then on to Queens. Down in the lower levels of the NYC
transit system, the platforms were more deserted. Anton appeared to be
casually waiting for someone. And Johnson was forced to find a stan-
chion for partial cover. Anton didn't seem particularly concerned, seemingly absorbed in his own thoughts, only looking up when an A Train
arrived at the station. That's when things started to get interesting.

The A Train disgorged, a few passengers wandered off in various
directions, and the platform was empty again—but now another man

stood a car-length away from Anton. Where he came from Johnson couldn't tell; he just suddenly appeared. Nothing very unusual about him. The guy wore cheap knockoff jeans and sneakers, hooded sweatshirt, a backpack for books and personals—the uniform of New York's young male students and lower working classes.

But what startled Johnson was how the hooded young man waved once to Anton in greeting, and Anton acknowledged him back. In an easy four steps, the two stood side by side, now both apparently waiting on the platform. And for no reason at all, somehow Johnson knew this was one of the guys who took pictures of Giselle.

The rest of the night was a long, deafening blur of trains and platforms. Of rocking in the cars hanging to a strap and waiting for the *whoosh* of the pneumatic doors. Johnson kept well enough back to keep from being spotted—often riding in an adjacent car—though once or twice he came damn near to bumping into them. They weren't sneaking around but open about their travels, acting naturally, even bold in their manner. Often pausing to calmly scan the subway platforms. Whatever they were doing, Johnson couldn't imagine.

They took the A Train on its long journey out to JFK International. Only to be met by another fellow in a hooded sweatshirt. Now the three headed back up the line. They ditched their ride at the Broadway Junction station. Switching trains again to the J Line on its way out to the distant Jamaica Center in Queens. Somewhere during the switch they picked up a fourth guy.

At the end of the line at the Jamaica Center station, they switched over to NYC Transit's second deep underground Blue Line, the E Train, and headed back toward Manhattan. In the process, they picked up a fifth and sixth, dressed the same as the first three, hooded sweatshirts, sneakers—and all looking Middle Eastern or Southeast Asian. Johnson's mind simmered as he watched them, but for the life of him he couldn't detect an objective; nobody pointed or discussed anything—they simply rode the train like everyone else. A plan, obviously, but to harm whom and how? Mass hijacking? Multiple train wrecks? No way to tell.

As they headed closer to Manhattan, the group began to thin out. The first to peel off did so at the Jackson Heights station: a confluence of four different lines all heading to or leading from the heart of the city. Johnson saw a stray kid scoot off to Flushing Meadows and Corona Park, toward the site of the 1964 World's Fair—heading out to an extremity of the system once more.

Back in Manhattan the group lost three more Hood Heads at the 51st Street and Lexington Avenue station—of course, the IRT. Johnson thought he had figured some of it out now. From the 51st Street station those three could travel uptown the length of the swank Upper East Side to the Bronx: Wakefield, Eastchester, and Pelham. More extremities.

By the time Johnson's train reached Columbus Circle in Manhattan on the corner of Central Park, only the first Hood Head and Anton were left. They clasped hands and did a slight chest bump, then went their separate ways. Anton back to the Red Line whence he'd started. Sure, that made sense. He could travel the tony Upper West Side, either way up to Van Courtland Park or downtown to South Ferry, hopping off at Christopher Street. Johnson didn't bother following him.

It was the other guy who counted. Right, of course, he made directly for the Orange B Line. Brooklyn, the only borough they'd avoided. By riding the subway this way, the men had traversed nearly the whole system, going out each arm of the starfish and returning to its heart. The only major line they missed served Brighton Beach and Coney Island. Brooklyn. Safe at home base? And that came last. But what it all meant, who the hell knew. Would the B & D snoops have seen something he missed? Doubtful.

Johnson rode in the far end of the car away from his mark, his mind spinning with all the possibilities and occasionally getting caught up in the cobwebs of fatigue. He noticed a kid sitting across from him and briefly worried about falling asleep and getting rolled again. The kid kept catching his eye, then looking away. He wore baggy jeans, workboots, a bandana, and a Sean John T-shirt.

Relieved to be off the train, a bleary-eyed Johnson emerged from the New Utrecht station with his target about 4 AM as the sky lightened the low buildings of central working-class Brooklyn and a few very early birds began to chirp. People were getting ready for the day—the city's dawn patrol. And in a surprisingly brief three and a half minutes

Johnson managed to lose his mark as the man walked along the sidewalk into the deeper regions of the neighborhood. Though he'd realized as much subconsciously throughout his long subway trip, this hammered the point home: *During rush hour, a guy like this was virtually invisible in the crush of thousands.*

In the end, he stood wanly in the middle of the block of a residential street. Yeah, the guy might have gone into *that* row house. Or was it that set of dumpy apartments? The one with the blind windows?

He heard a familiar city sound: the doors of a panel van opening. Turning to look, a few cars down a guy in a San Diego Padres cap had opened the door to his food service delivery wagon, Hung Fat Oriental Food Distributors—Long Island City. They were a long way from Long Island City.

Somebody waved at him from the dark of the van and hissed *pssssst!* Wallets. "Oh for Chrissakes, stop standing there like a jackass and get in."

Inside, the van was comfortably warm but a little stuffy. Johnson found a stool by a console. "Don't touch anything," someone said. Must have been the guy who opened the van doors. He couldn't really see the faces, people he hadn't met yet.

"Are you *trying* to be conspicuous?" Wallets growled. "Why don't you just sneak around in a trench coat and fedora? Like *Spy vs. Spy.*"

Then the door slid open once more, and the kid from the train hopped in. Johnson visibly started, and Wallets smiled, "I'd introduce Cedric, but you've already met."

Johnson looked confused, but something stirred in the deep mists of his memory.

Cedric laughed and said, "Brooklyn Heights."

Johnson let out a long, "Ohhh . . . "

"Cedric kindly returned your credit cards that night, remember?" Wallets said. "We kept in touch, and now he helps with odd tasks in the city. He was following your Workbench Boy, but might I add, *doing it with little risk of being noticed.*"

Cedric laughed again, and Johnson joined in, until an exasperated voice barked at him, "Don't lean on that!" The guy in the Padres cap.

CHAPTER TWENTY

The Dirty Polak

Bryce and Smith sat in a grey sedan parked across from a new place in Queens, occupied by another set of Workbench Boys. The entire team had been following the various Ibns, Sadrs, Walids, and so forth like scattering pigeons hither and yon. Now the two agents parked off Queens Boulevard down the street from one of those cheesy row houses with fake siding and chain-link fencing enclosing a postage-stamp patch of grass. Old-fashioned visual surveillance. Time-consuming and boring. They had the whole place wired for sound and a receiver in their car to pick up landline conversations. Heck, nobody could use the Hung Fat van for everything. Besides which, even the dullest marks would eventually notice something like a huge ice cream truck parked in their neighborhood everyday. *Ding-a-ling-a-ling*: suspected racketeers and money launderers and terrorists, come and get your orange Popsicles and sno-cones.

Bryce sat in the driver's seat with his two hands on the wheel, like he was still driving. He had always found it hard to be natural around attractive women, and spending hours alone with Smith taxed even his prodigious capacities for awkwardness. She was one of those girls who was always shocked when someone said she was beautiful, but shouldn't have been. She was a redhead, with freckled porcelain white skin that showed her emotions in hues from faint pink when she laughed to beet red when she was embarrassed—which wasn't very often, except when someone called her beautiful.

She was one of five children, the youngest and the only daughter. So she had tomboy informality to her, just one of the guys, notwithstanding her high cheekbones, nice jaw line, and delicate nose that made men want to get lost in her sparkling, light-blue eyes. Not to mention her slender in-shape figure of a dedicated jogger and kickboxer. Today was a pantsuit day, so she had her right foot up on the dashboard and played with the radio dial with her left hand, switching from one hip-hop station to another, softly singing along to songs she liked and expounding to Bryce about the relative merits of the artists and their work. "Sure, Jay-Z might still sell, but he's lost his edge. Then again, why does he need his edge when he's dating Beyoncé, every man's dream, eh, Bryce?"

Bryce knew as little about the hip-hop scene as he did about gumshoe detective work, so he compensated for his inability to make conversation by seeming as absorbed as possible in watching the front door of this row house, feeling more and more like a stiff, holding the steering wheel tighter and tighter.

"Jay-Z? Beyoncé?" Smith teased. "Come on! You don't follow them? You don't even read Page Six do you?"

"No, but I get the idea," he said. "Like the Federal Page in the *Washington Post*, right?"

She shook her head—"You're hopeless"—and turned the radio up.

At that, the little speaker between their seats crackled: a dial tone and then the sharp beeps of someone hitting the numbers of a phone. Smith turned the radio back down. Lil Wayne would have to wait. The sound of a phone ringing and then a woman answering in a foreign language. A male voice said, "Hello," in English, and she switched to English too.

It was Abdullah, the only Workbench Boy in the Queens house at the moment, making a call.

"The polak is ready," he said.

"Good," she said, and hung up.

Dial tone again.

Bryce and Smith looked at one another. "The *polak*?" Smith said. "That's odd," Bryce replied. Smith's cell phone rang. Bryce heard her end of the conversation: "Of course I heard that . . . Yeah . . . Mmm-hmmm . . . You got it." She flipped her clamshell phone shut. "It was O'Hanlon. He's got his buns in a bunch over that call. Said it's the kind of code that could mean the start of something. We're to stick on Abdullah tight, really tight, and if we get the wrong feeling, forget about the surveillance, and just bring him in. That 'polak' stuff makes him real nervous."

Just as she finished, Abdullah bounded down the steps and jumped into his car. Bryce's hands got even tighter around the steering wheel, and now he wasn't even thinking of Smith.

⦕⦖

Abdullah drove a used Volvo of the sort you'd expect a sociology professor at Bowdoin to drive. They followed him from a distance through Queens' back streets, lined with scraggly urban trees struggling to make their way in a world of concrete, exhaust, and dog crap. The rundown brownstones they passed were quiet, the kids at school and the adults, most of them at least, at work. They made their way to the inaptly named Utopia Parkway, a four-lane road with a concrete divider and trash-strewn brown shrubbery at its sides. One of New York's grimy thoroughfares, a nowhere everyone always forgot on their way to someplace else—Oakland with some white dashed lines down the middle.

The G-Babe's phone rang again. She unclamped it—"Smith"—not taking her eyes off the road. This time it was Wallets.

"Where are you headed?" he asked, without bothering to announce himself.

"North on Utopia, less than ten minutes away from the house," she said.

"Where you think he's going?"

"I don't know."

He hung up on her.

"Wallets?" Bryce ventured.

"Yeah," Smith said, clamping her phone shut again. "His panty hose are in a bunch too."

She included Bryce among the men with twisted hose, though his uptightness wasn't anything new, more congenital, a factor of over-breeding. And his driving reflected it, trying so hard to do the "perfect" tail job, hanging three or four cars back, easier now that there were fewer lights and the highway broadened out to accommodate more traffic. Abdullah got in the right lane, headed toward an exit underneath a big green highway sign with white lettering that flashed by too fast to read. Bryce was blocked from changing lanes, leaned on the horn, and swerved, muscling his way in front of a car with shiny hubcaps and tinted windows. "Take it easy," Smith said, craning her neck to look ahead. "We still got him."

They merged onto the LIE. For anyone west of Manhattan: the Long Island Expressway. The word "express" a total misnomer. The Volvo well ahead, but still in sight, as they headed toward LaGuardia, jumping from the expressway to the Cross Island Parkway with the oval of Citi Field, home of the Mets, visible in the distance. The G-Babe couldn't help musing, "Can you believe that before they tore it down, Shea was the third oldest stadium in the National League? Hard to believe, huh? Friggin' Shea had become a classic." As usual, Bryce had nothing to say to her, since he knew less about baseball than he did about hip-hop. He kept half an eye on the Volvo as he focused on the cars around him, trying to weave to a better position to catch up. Smith said soothingly, "You're all right. We still got him."

Then they heard distant sirens. Bryce looked in the rearview mirror and saw a bank of spinning cherry lights headed up behind him. "Damn, where's the fire?"

"Watch him—*watch* him!" Smith warned. Abdullah headed to an exit that led to either LaGuardia's cargo areas or the local service streets adjacent to the runways. As they approached the airport, Bryce saw a milling crowd congregating outside the US Air terminal. The mob seemed to be streaming out the main doors at the Arrivals curb. "Busy day?" Smith wondered. They followed Abdullah to the exit, when a white police sedan appeared and parked directly across the road leading off the highway, lights flashing. Abdullah in his Volvo cruised harm-lessly past just as the Airport Police decided to set up a checkpoint.

Now the cop car blocked their way; Bryce hit the brakes. No choice but to stop.

"Now what?" Smith jumped out of the car and slammed the door behind her. The cop hopped out of his vehicle at the same time and stood in the roadway. Smith approached and flashed her badge. "FBI. We need to get through." Then quickly sized up the copper—young, strong Italian features—the kind she could have sweet-talked out of a ticket or out of his pants. "Sorry, Ma'am, no one goes through," the cop said.

Ma'am? Ma'am? Don't mammie me, she thought. "What's the deal?"

"Incident at the terminal," he said, hitching one of his hands on his belt and talking into his walkie-talkie after it belched a burst of static talk. *Quack, quack. Didn't copy. Come on back?*

Smith walked back toward the car, and her phone rang. "Yeah?"

"Where is he?" Wallets asked, again with no introduction.

"I don't know," she said, wincing.

"*Really?*" Wallets grunted, incredulous. "Well, do you know where *you* are?"

Screw off, Smith thought, but told him where they'd been stopped. "There's something going on at Arrivals."

"I know. US Air," Wallets informed her. "I'll be there in about five," and hung up.

Back in the car with Bryce, Smith saw the preppie had turned the radio to the local news station—1010 WINS. A deep newscaster's voice: "We are now getting word of security incidents at all three metropolitan airports. LaGuardia Airport is being evacuated. There has been an unspecified breach at JFK, and we also understand that there is a disturbance at Newark International. Stay tuned to 1010 WINS for all the latest, weather, and traffic on the tens. And now let's go to 1010 WINS reporter Steve Marigold for the latest on this developing situation, live from LaGuardia Airport."

"*Live? Live?* How'd he get there so fast?" Smith asked. Bryce shrugged; as an out-of-towner he didn't quite grasp the immense feat of traveling the three miles from Midtown to Queens at midday in New York City. But slowly it came to him.

"Somebody tip him off?"

Smith bumped her head with her hand in a mock "I coulda had a V-8" gesture of revelation and snarked at Bryce, "Yah think?"

Against a cacophony of crowd noise and sirens, the reporter belted out his story: "The scene is chaos outside LaGuardia Airport this afternoon, a facility that takes in and handles nearly seventy thousand travelers a day is now disgorging them right back outside the terminal doors. Confusion and fear reigns, as alarms sounded ten minutes ago and security personnel ordered people to leave. One woman told me just minutes ago: 'I was at the ticket counter when they started shouting, "Everyone out, everyone out!" and I knew it was serious when the ticket agents started leaving too.' That is the story amid the throngs outside LaGuardia Airport. Steve Marigold, 1010 WINS."

Smith turned the radio back down. From the rearview mirror, a black Lincoln sedan approached around the single file of cars stuck behind him, two of its wheels running off into the grass of the shoulder. Who else? Wallets.

The man got out of his car and charged toward the cop. It took all of about twenty seconds for the cop to jump into his driver's seat and, without bothering to close the door, back it up enough for all of them to drive through. Open sesame, as if no obstacle could withstand the force of Wallets' will. The roadblock closed behind them.

For a moment, the two cars idled side by side, as Wallets spoke through his passenger window, his left hand on the wheel and his right thrown over the passenger seat. Since Bryce and Smith didn't know which way Abdullah had gone—into the airport or into the local streets—Wallets said they'd go toward the airport. "If he's not there," Wallets said, "at least we know he's not in the middle of whatever's happening here right now, and we can try to catch up to him later."

They drove down through the cargo area: chain-link fences, snout-nosed four-wheelers—almost like off-terrain vehicles—pulling square steel boxes on wheels behind them. More steel boxes stacked twelve feet high. Guys in baggy gray jumpsuits with the orange ear protectors. Away from the runways and jet wash, the Mickey Mouse ears hung around their necks. Nothing looked out of the ordinary. No sign of the

Volvo or Abdullah. Wallets signaled to Bryce to keep following him, and they headed by a single-lane one-way extension road toward the airport itself.

Another cop car blocked the way. Wallets got out, and once again, *presto*, they were through. They looped around and up a ramp to get to the Continental departure area, the outside of which was thronged with milling passengers, aimless and befuddled in the slanting sunshine of a fall afternoon. They stood with their roller-bag handles extended, exhibiting the world-weary nonchalance of New Yorkers who always expect the worst, especially when it comes to inconvenience. Wallets was anything but complacent. He slammed his car in a no-parking zone, waved off another cop, and marched up to Bryce's rolled-down window.

"You guys wait here in the car in case you have to jump somewhere quickly. I'm going inside." His crew cut weaved through the crowd, and then, after another instant cop conversation, he vanished round a wide revolving door and into the terminal.

Smith's phone rang again. "Smith," she said. This time, O'Hanlon. "So you guys lost Abdul the Tool?"

"Kind of you to notice."

"Anything blown up yet?"

"Not that we can tell from here. Just a lot of bumped passengers smoking cigarettes by the curb."

"I'm headed back to the Workbench Boys' house in Queens for a look-see."

O'Hanlon's impatient, Smith thought. Impatience caused mistakes—slipups like risking a search in broad daylight with the neighbors watching. Bad idea. Problem was, first time around when they'd tailed the lads to Brooklyn and the New Utrecht Avenue apartment walk-up, Jordan the Hung Fat Tech had never gone inside after their single sweep under the door. Their Sniffer showed no evidence of explosives. Or radiation. None. Nada. Then the surveillance had traipsed halfway across

Queens to stare at grimy row houses. But nobody'd gotten a Sniffer under there yet at all, just some wiretaps.

"All right," she told her boss. "But you do know Abdul could be headed back to you *right now?*"

"Relax. I've got a Con Ed guy with me." That meant an agent disguised as a guy from the gas and electric company Consolidated Edison. Most likely Wesson, as a Con Ed employee in a blue jumper, which would at least give them a plausible excuse to be snooping around the place. "We've a report of your neighbor smelling gas"—a great standby.

O'Hanlon watched Wesson, his Con Ed Girl disappear around the side of the crummy Queens row house. She unlatched the gate in the chain-link fence at the front yard. Nearly tripping over the uneven concrete driveway—some slabs higher than others, with grass growing in between the cracks. Then moved around to the back. The backyard was overgrown, with browned-out shrubs and tangled ankle-high weeds, tramped down around a few flat stepping stones. A weathered deck, gray and warped.

First she knocked loudly, calling out, "Con Ed." Then, as she waited, glanced around into the other backyards. An outdoor above-ground makeshift swimming pool was left over from summer next door. There were the rusted-out grills and rickety swing sets and garden hoses and the abandoned toys one would expect in the backyards of such a neighborhood. But no peering eyes that she could see, so she slipped a thin steel wedge, a jimmy, into the door jamb down near the knob and coaxed the doorknob till the door came free.

Agent Wesson stepped into the kitchen. Her skin crawled. Dirty dishes overflowed in the sink, and the smell of overripe Middle Eastern food filled her nostrils. Baba ghanoush gone wild. The linoleum floor curled up near the walls and looked like it would need a sandblaster to be anything near clean ever again. Ten old pizza boxes were stacked in one corner. Next, the dining room. She recalled seeing the ghostly outline microwave image in the Hung Fat van of a workbench in the

Brooklyn New Utrecht Avenue apartment. This time no workbench but a round dining room table piled high with bills, Arabic newspapers, and a *Windows for Dummies* book.

The workbench here amounted to no more than a corner of the dining room table: a soldering iron, a tiny hacksaw, razors, and—strangely—a sewing machine, next to it a Starbucks travel mug stuffed with large acrylic paint brushes. Underneath the dining room table a stackable plastic bin of the sort you bought at the Container Store. It was full of a couple of dozen tubes of artist's paint. Wesson picked them up to look more closely: titanium white, an oil color, lead-based. A couple of plastic shopping bags from Blick's Art Supply had been tossed in the bin too.

Next to the bin were some crumpled up and shredded . . . *what?* Mystery garments. Maybe vinyl vests? The shreds of vests? Wesson couldn't tell. And next to them a stack of about a dozen pairs of brand new Jordache blue jeans.

She moved into the living room and opened a side cabinet that was part of the TV console. A couple of Adam Sandler DVDs. Did they know he's Jewish? A Jenna Jameson video, *Hell on Heels.* She suspected the lads didn't care about Jenna's faith one way or another. And another unmarked DVD. Wesson picked up the radio on her belt and asked O'Hanlon how she was doing on time.

"How the hell should I know?" came the grumpy reply.

Wesson popped the DVD into the player, searched the cluttered coffee table for the remote, and hit play. Sure enough, Arabic chanting and someone in a white hood kneeling in front of masked AK-47–toting kidnappers. Yep, that's our boys: A Beheading Video.

But then suddenly the scene shifted, and she stared at a new scene. Neon lights overlooking a troika of bearded, turbaned men. The hooded prisoner sat in a chair. Some kind of trial or tribunal. The pale canvas hood was removed. The prisoner was a woman. An accuser stepped into the scene, pointing and shouting. The woman in the chair stared at him with doleful eyes. But did not speak. The accuser—a man—was clearly angry at the woman. Was she his wife, daughter, sister? Wesson didn't understand Farsi or Arabic, but clearly the accuser was enraged. And somehow the FBI agent knew the accused was being charged with the worst crime in the world. Worse than murder. Adultery? She'd heard that victims of rape were often charged with adultery, as if it were the victim's fault. Then justice was meted out. They called them honor killings.

The hood was slid over the woman's head once more, and the camera wrenched away. A new scene flashed onto the screen. Daytime, in a backward village square. Rude houses, blank staring eyes of dark windows. A ring of men circled something on the ground. Each man carried a rock; first one threw his rock at the thing on the ground; then another threw his; then another. More rocks were brought and passed around the circle of men; the camera moved in for a closer look. The object on the ground looked like a soccer ball. The men were throwing rocks at a soccer ball—no! The thing was the hood, the woman's canvas hood. She'd been buried up to her neck, and what Wesson was staring at was her *head*. The rocks began to fall again. The men were stoning her. Stoning the woman to death. The pale canvas hood changed from light to dark. Bleeding through the fabric as stone after stone found its mark. The image ended abruptly.

Shaken, Wesson slapped the video back into its case. Jesus, who *were* these people? What kind of ghouls watched something like that? She turned away from the TV, took a deep breath, and climbed the stairs on watery legs.

Three bedrooms, mattresses on the floors. Wesson walked into each room. They were stuffy and smelled of sweat and other bodily fluids she didn't want to think about. Clothes strewn everywhere. They wore briefs, tidy whities—apparently not realizing that they shouldn't be worn by any straight man over age thirteen. The closets mostly empty, with a stack of *Penthouses* and *Puritan* magazines below the hangers. A communal porn stash.

In the last bedroom, three brand new backpacks were piled on each other. Wesson picked one up. Surprisingly heavy. She patted it and noticed the pack was reinforced, with stiff leather seams sewn into the sides. Curious. Better keep moving.

The dingy bathroom had crumpled tissues in the corners and more than its share of shed pubic hairs. The mirror was speckled with toothpaste dreck. Fetid water struggled to drain down the stopped-up sink. The Hung Fat crew should all chip in to get the boys a maid. But the shower took her aback.

The gleaming new shower head could have been picked by the producers of *Extreme Make-Over: Home Edition.* And the tub sported the damnedest shower curtain she had ever seen. You could zip it up all around to totally enclose a bather—a shower for the Boy in the Bubble. She opened a small cabinet in one of the walls and saw a bunch of sanitary materials of the sort you might find in a hospital—gloves, plastic footsies, shower caps. *What in God's name were these grungy bastards thinking...*

O'Hanlon's barking voice interrupted her reverie from her belt: "You've got about thirty seconds to get the hell out of there."

Shit! That was advance warning? Wesson started running down the steps, getting her story straight if she was caught inside. Front or back door—make a decision. Front or back? She headed to the back. Through the kitchen window she saw some lady from the house next door hanging wet laundry on a line. A Rottweiler with a studded collar was doing his business in the other adjacent backyard. Dammit! They could catch her either way. This was supposed to be a sneak-and-peek search—praise be to the Patriot Act—but so much for the sneak.

Outside the house O'Hanlon saw Wesson wasn't going to make it, so he called an audible, a naked bootleg. Hakim-Abdul-Mohammed hadn't parked on the street. He'd parked around the block. So O'Hanlon never saw him coming; the guy simply appeared a couple of dozen yards away from the front door. O'Hanlon jumped out of the car and tried to angle his approach just enough so he wouldn't seem to be running up directly to Hakim.

"Hey, hey," he called. Hakim stopped. "Hey, buddy." Hakim waited for him to get closer, a look of dark suspicion on his face. "Can you tell me which way is Vine Street? Oh, there isn't a Vine Street? Maybe it's Wine Street?"

At that very moment Con Ed babe Wesson came out the front door. Yes, the front door, and O'Hanlon nearly fainted. Hakim-Abdul-Mohammed forgot about the strange Irishman in front of his nose and slammed through the metal gate.

"Hey! What you doing in my house? Who give you key?"

Wesson completely ignored him like the good bureaucrat she was pretending to be. She made a big show of getting out her radio, and with what little presence of mind O'Hanlon still possessed, he surreptitiously switched off his own so it wouldn't squawk. Wesson, the complete Con Ed factotum, talked into her little black box: "Yeah. Done over here. No odor. No traces." Then boldly to Hakim: "Are you the owner of this building?"

Taken aback, the guy merely muttered, "No, no, we only rent."

"Well, listen up. We got a report of a gas odor coming from your house. Mandatory inspection. Nobody home, we still check. False report. Sorry about the back door. If you wish to file a complaint you can contact the district office in Grand Army Plaza, nine to five Monday through Thursday. Do you understand what I'm saying to you?"

On the sidewalk, O'Hanlon stared at them with his mouth open.

If Hakim-Abdul-Mohammed missed Wesson's nonexistent Con Ed truck he didn't remark upon it. He went inside somewhat chastened and clearly impressed with Consolidated Edison of the greater New York area. O'Hanlon vanished back into his sedan and drove in one direction; Wesson walked purposefully in another, up to the next house, and knocked on the door. There was a gas odor reported, and gas she would find.

Later, her boss got her on the radio.

"Uh, assuming you haven't found any leaks, shall I pick you up somewhere?"

"No," she radioed back. "I'll meet you in the Hung Fat van later. You just square it with the two neighbors, a Hausfrau and the proud owner of a puppy dog. Also the Con Ed Brooklyn office, confirming the gas story in case Hakim really decides to file a complaint. Maybe they can send him some undecipherable paperwork, a quitclaim, confirming our inspection."

<hr>

They gathered around a table in a Banquo & Duncan conference room that evening to take stock of the day, Banquo presiding. Little six-ounce bottles of water sat in front of each chair, a muted TV turned to a cable channel up in a corner of the room.

He'd never been a shouter. Not because he didn't run across many people who needed shouting at, but because he knew what the shouting would do—unhinge within him a ghastly temper the control of which he'd made a habit of a lifetime, lest its thrashing wrath destroy everything around him.

He suppressed his irritation and bore in on the problem. Banquo leaned forward, both elbows on the table. "So do we know anything that's not being reported about the airport incidents?"

Wallets replied, "No, not really. At LaGuardia, a half dozen guys ostentatiously started praying at a security checkpoint at each terminal. Prayer rugs, the whole nine yards. People got nervous. Then some bizarre and confrontational behavior with the TSA personnel. In two cases, they managed to run through the checkpoints, which meant the concourse had to be evacuated. I got a look at one of these guys at US Air. Young, shaved, and well dressed, spouting legal mumbo jumbo as soon as he was outside with a camera or two on him before the cops got him in the car to take him away. Clearly designed to have the most sympathetic spokesman possible for racial insensitivity complaints. Same basic story at JFK, although they didn't get through security, and at Newark—because the LaGuardia action started a little sooner—the other airports were informed and shut them down as soon as they started praying."

"That'll play well," Agent Smith commented, while Wesson remarked, "Yeah, yanked the prayer rug right from under them."

Banquo wasn't amused. "But in the process you lost Abdul at LaGuardia, correct? And managed to get caught in the Queens workhouse."

O'Hanlon cleared his throat, somewhat chagrined. "Obviously we're running all these prayer guys down and will have more on them in the morning." This didn't seem to impress Banquo sufficiently, so he added: "I'm getting the sense, though, that these Prayer Rugs are absolutely clean, per Wallets' impression. This is a political stunt meant to portray TSA as proto-fascists, file a lawsuit or two, and maybe get some loosening of security."

"Speak of the devil," Wallets said and gestured toward the muted TV.

Josephine von Hildebrand gassing on Olbermann's *Countdown*.
Actually—as it became clear when Banquo un-muted the TV—she was
mostly just saying, "You're right, Keith."

"You're right, Keith—it's almost like Muslims can't pray in this
country anymore."

"You're right, Keith—there's nothing scary about Muslim piety."

"You're right, Keith—there's something suspicious about the timing
of this so-called security incident."

Showing his usual commitment to balanced debate, Olbermann then
turned to his other guest, who totally agreed with him—Ibrihim Mahdi
of the Council on Islamic Peace and Tolerance. O'Hanlon nodded
toward the screen and said, "He's a big Hezbollah symp. Just try to get
that guy to condemn suicide bombing. He'll talk circles round you."

"Mr. Olbermann," Ibrihim Mahdi said, "we want people to reject
ignorance and intolerance. Muslims aren't frightening. Muslim prayer is
not a crime. We wish we lived in a society that understood the basic pre-
cept of tolerance."

"Ibrihim," Olbermann asked, tight-lipped and intense, "do you think
the neocons are going to take advantage of these incidents?"

Banquo hit mute again and tossed the remote on the table. "So what
did you find at the other workbench place today?" he asked O'Hanlon.

"So far we've got some guys with a sewing machine and bizarre
habits. No explosives. Nothing illegal. But lots of paint, blue jeans, a few
reinforced, hardened backpacks, and a special shower setup." O'Hanlon
described them all in more detail.

"What are the backpacks hardened with?" Banquo asked.

"We couldn't tell."

"Backpacks make everyone nervous," Banquo mused. "You sure they
didn't have ball bearings sewn in the sides, something like that?"

"No, definitely flexible plates of something or other."

"And the shower—that kind of setup makes you think biohazard.
What about strange liquids, lab materials, powders? Anything of that
nature?"

"Nothing."

Banquo stared at the now muted TV. "Just lots of paint?"

"Yep."

"What do you think, Wallets?" Banquo asked.

"I'm sure the same thing you do. These are strange cats that give off a bad vibe. But maybe they're freelance amateurs, or just low-level guys leading somewhere else."

Banquo raised a hand. "Or maybe they're really smart. They know the heat's on, so they tied a can to your tail and dragged you right to LaGuardia for a prayer meeting."

Wallets sighed. He had no answer for that. "Then there's the—"

"Phone call," Banquo, Wallets, and O'Hanlon said in unison.

"Her name is Farah Nasir. New player," O'Hanlon began. "We'll get a tap up and running tonight and should know more about her tomorrow. Wesson, I want you to peel off Giselle for a while and stick to Farah. Where does she work, who does she see, what are her days and nights like? Everything."

"She's my girl lollipop," Wesson said.

The table went silent for a moment.

"Anyone care to take on the word 'polak'?" Bryce ventured.

Banquo raised a silent eyebrow.

"Maybe we're dealing with an Eastern European conspiracy," Smith cracked. Six pairs of eyes looked dimly at her. Banquo's lips curled upward, and then he looked at O'Hanlon. "Tell me about the paint."

"Oh, yeah. They apparently bought it at Blick's, a local art supply store on Bond Street."

"Someone should go by the store and see if there're any patterns, anything odd, whatever."

"Can you *hurt* anyone with paint?" Bryce asked.

"Ever see a Hitchcock movie?" Banquo grunted. "Or read a Roald Dahl story or eaten a leg of lamb? You can hurt someone with anything, given enough malice and imagination. We'll give these Workbench Boys some slack just as soon as we see them working at their easels next Saturday in Prospect Park." His eyes drifted to the bottle of Armagnac on the shelf, and Bryce knew what to do. When the glasses finally came round the table, Banquo quietly mused, "Isn't *anyone* slightly bothered how quickly the WINS Newsman got to LaGuardia? Or is it just me?"

CHAPTER TWENTY-ONE

Do Me a Favor

Johnson stared at his laptop screen. His new mail icon flashed at
him. The email address read "JanB@petroconsulting.org.nl" with
the subject line "Good to See You Safe." Johnson knew the sender: Jan
Breuer, bribe master, once of Dutch Shell, now apparently associated
with an oil consulting firm working out of the Netherlands. The body
of the message was simple: Glad you're back. Visiting New York for
several weeks, perhaps they could get together. Gather you know my
friend Anton Anjou of Banque Luxembourg. Small world. And a cell
phone number.

Johnson immediately forwarded the email to Wallets, who replied in
under fifteen seconds: "Meet him. Find out what he wants." Johnson
sensed Wallets reading everything going through his PC. It didn't really
bother him; the snooping over his shoulder had long since ceased to have
an impact. For the first time in his life, Peter felt clear as a glass of water.

The TV in his Brooklyn Heights apartment droned on in the background. Yet another "small world" moment. From London, MSNBC
was conducting an overseas interview with a new and influential face
on the international scene: Dr. Yasmine Farouk, PhD, of the Tehran
Polytechnic Institute, while behind her stood the insect-thin Sheik
Kutmar. She, in Western garb and demure blue hijab covering her hair;
he, in traditional robes and turban. Underneath her face ran the title

"Vice President, Atomic Energy Organization of Iran." Behind them, the Thames flowing before the long stretch of the Parliament building and Big Ben. "We oppose obtaining nuclear weapons," Yasmine had said, "and we will peacefully use nuclear technology under the framework and observation of the Nonproliferation Treaty and the United Nations International Atomic Energy Agency."

Johnson felt a pit in his stomach. He had ostensibly escaped Yasmine and Kutmar but was not rid of them truly, not if they were going to become international media darlings. He thought *he* was supposed to be the media whore. A mere four minutes earlier Jo von H had left a voice message on his answering machine. The UN was sponsoring the young Iranian physicist and her mentor, Dr. Yahdzi, on a trip to the United States. In a coup de théâtre she'd snagged the right to sponsor the first American press avail, beating out the big guys. Apparently the Iranians liked *The Crusader*'s coverage. Tomorrow 10 AM. The Josephine von Hildebrand apartment. Be there.

Perfect. Life imitates Marcel Duchamp's 1917 Dadaesque sculpture *Fountain*. An upside down urinal. Sure, he'd be there and try not to piss on himself.

Giselle came out of her bedroom, paused near the couch, and stared at him gazing stupidly into his laptop. Finally he noticed her.

"Hi. Sorry—dreaming."

"You've been doing a lot of that lately." That sounded harsh to his daughter's ears, and she softened it some: "I mean, after everything—"

There was nothing to forgive. "I understand."

Giselle seemed to fret over some decision. Something she wanted to ask him. "Feel like—feel like coming to dinner tonight?"

He knew what she meant.

◆◆◆

Il Monello on 2nd Avenue and 76th Street was one of those top-end neighborhood restaurants that make Manhattan the envy of the dining world. Seating fewer than sixty people, a troop of small tables along couched walls, under nine-foot flat matte ceilings. With a few more tables in the middle. But what the place lacked in elbow room, it made up for in the whiteness of its linen and the polish of its service. There wasn't much space to hang over tables and gossip. If you came to a place like this, you were seated to be served. The acoustics were unobtrusive, the voices of those at supper gently cascading over one another. Not like in those cavernous ugly modern places where you couldn't hear yourself think. Here you could say, "Pass the salt," and your dining companion would actually hear you.

Anton was already seated when Giselle and Johnson arrived, but rose like a gentleman and held the chair for the young lady. In twenty minutes they were most of the way through an excellent Chianti, the appetizers of grilled shrimp Fra Diavolo and carpaccio devoured while Johnson couldn't remember what pasta he'd ordered. Oh that's right, parpadelle, bow ties with pancetta, broccoli rabe, and pine nuts. A feast for a king. But he didn't feel like a king this evening. More of a hovering wasp, waiting for the chance to sting.

It took all Johnson's self-control not to sling his wineglass into Anton's face; the indulgence with which he treated Giselle and unctuous yet easy way he sucked up to Daddy Peter—knowing all the while the smooth shit was buddies with the Brooklyn train riders. Almost too much to tolerate.

Suddenly the mood was broken when a voice came at them from the bar. "Anton! Peter!" A buttery voice with a slight accent. Belgian. Nederlandisher. And for the first time in years Johnson saw his old bribe master; the blond head of Jan Breuer bobbed at them from across the restaurant. His cheeks slightly florid with drink. Johnson wondered just how much a man had to drink to get those veins in his face. God, he'd done his share, more than enough to get a spider web or two of varicose blood vessels that grew livid with every glass he knocked back. The scent of cigarettes preceded the Belgian oil man, the odor saturating him from suit to skin.

"Jan! Amazing!" Johnson reached across the table with his hand.

"Indeed, my friend." Then to the Frenchman, "Anton, I'd heard you were assigned to New York."

The three of them had an extra seat. "Care to join us?"

The mildly drunk Dutchman accepted. "For a moment or two—my clients are late." Anton seemed a little put out to see the man, as if some business between them hadn't turned out so well. Saying, "You're looking well, Jan."

The middle-aged Belgian Big Oil consultant rumbled in his throat. Then coughed softly, a grisly nicotine cough. "Nice of you to say so. But I'm not." Then Johnson noticed the gray pallor about his eyes, the deepening blue circles. "I'm afraid my Marlboros finally caught up with me," Jan Breuer said. "Then sort of traveled up," he pointed to his head. "It's gone to my brain now, and as everyone knows, I was never so smart that I could afford to lose much of it."

All at once Johnson felt terrible. "I'm sorry I didn't answer your email this afternoon. I was planning to; of course, if I'd known—" Babbling. But Jan Breuer laughed and waved his apology away.

"You didn't. Let's plan on something tomorrow. No time like the present, eh?"

"Indeed," Johnson agreed. Suddenly glad to do it. Never mind the preposterous coincidence of seeing Jan in the restaurant. Sure the fantastic appearance nagged him, but seeing the dead man walking changed everything. Maybe that was the point. Maybe Jan contacted him after all these years to show him how it all came to an end. The final outcome. The one-way ticket paid in cash, no baggage. Nothing to declare.

"Ah!" Jan Breuer's eyes flashed at the door. Some people waved through the windows of the restaurant. He downed his drink. "My guests. We're going somewhere else. Peter, see you tomorrow, anywhere you choose. Anton, perhaps you'll see me too if time permits. And when you do, allow me to make amends."

At this Anton merely nodded but neither rose nor extended his hand for a farewell handclasp.

Before the man had gone five steps, Anton grimaced into his endive salad. Then hissed, "Good riddance. Couldn't happen to a more deserving charlatan."

Giselle was scandalized at her beau's callousness. "Anton!"

"It's true!" Anton shot back with an ugly flash of the eyes.

Now Johnson was curious. "What did he do?"

Anton snorted. "It was so complicated I'm not sure I can even explain it to myself. Suffice it to say, he deposited some funds that weren't his to handle. And worse than that, of questionable origin. Before long EU bank inspectors of various nations were knocking on our doors. The bank will have nothing to do with him now. I mean Bank Luxembourg isn't exactly House of Rothschild."

Then with some clicking of gears and the tic-toc of his mind, Anton addressed Johnson as mildly as possible: "How did *you* know him, Peter?"

Peter Johnson sighed, found the rest of the Chianti, poured it into his glass. Knowing he had nothing to lose but truth itself said just as mildly back: "I let him bribe me once." Then thought better of it. "No, actually about four times."

There was something incredibly liberating about being beaten on the soles of your feet, tortured for days, pissing needles on a wall, and then crawling over bitter mountains under the specter of Apache gunships. Now Giselle's eyes pierced him, rotten angry at Daddy's admitting such a thing before her boyfriend. Though she held her tongue.

For his part, Anton couldn't. Somehow Johnson knew in his gut Frenchie's high dudgeon was pure dog 'n' pony, and tried not to sneer.

"Oh, come now, Peter—you didn't really?"

But the Euro-weenie Romeo's act was cut short. A honking horn from 2nd Avenue blasted through the restaurant, along with a flash of headlights through the high front windows of the establishment. The squeal of brakes, a grinding crash.

Half the customers leapt to their feet, the sound of women gasping, and a whole platter of hot antipasti fell from a waiter's hands to the carpeted floor with a steaming wet slap. Johnson found himself clawing his way to the door of the restaurant. He smelled Anton's cologne hard behind.

The east side of 2nd Avenue at 76th Street was a mess. A couple of car lengths from the restaurant, a yellow medallion taxicab had jumped the curb and hit a glass and stainless-steel bus shelter, cascading broken glass in every direction. The cabbie stood in the street by his taxi, waving his hands and holding his head at the same time. "Green light! Green light! My eyes! My eyes!" as though he'd been temporarily blinded. He was a Sikh with full beard and saffron-colored turban; as his sight quickly cleared, the sorrow poured from him as the man realized everything he'd ever worked for, now sacrificed to the Manhattan Traffic Jinn. The Jinn had destroyed a perfectly innocent MTA bus shelter, and he stumbled about the wreck in dazed confusion. The poor man had to be restrained by pedestrians from trying to drag the roof of the bus shelter from the roof of his cab. The whole thing threatening to collapse.

But Johnson saw two things. First was that the dead man walking who hailed from the Netherlands—no longer walking. Just dead. Lying a few steps from the restaurant door. His head leaked a thread of blood from a small hole near the temple. So they wouldn't get together after all. Jan's guests wrung their hands, one middle-aged woman in a lurid pink pashmina scarf cried, "He just fell down, fell down, fell down," over and over like some kind of mantra.

The second thing he saw was the dancing green dot of a laser light pointer. "Green light! My eyes!" It danced across the sidewalk for a moment near Jan's body. When Johnson traced the light out of the corner of his eye, scanning the street, he located the source on the sixth-story roof balustrade of a brownstone building across 2nd Avenue. Yet even as he looked, the bright green Tinker Bell fairy light vanished from the rooftop. But what struck Johnson was the flash of a man's head as it withdrew.

He couldn't see the face or make even the vaguest identification, but still it felt strangely familiar. A man's head he knew. Yossi the Turk? He banished the thought. The man had been left hooked up to a respirator in a German military hospital. Now sniping on 2nd Avenue? A flush of worry went through Johnson—about the state of his own mind.

A kind hand touched his sleeve. Giselle. "Dad, let's go home."

Anton, very pale faced, stood on the sidewalk staring at the late Belgian.

"Is that okay with you?" Johnson asked him.

A shaken Anton nodded. He'd never seen a man like that before. Probably never seen anyone die up close. But they couldn't just walk away. Police arrived and started taking statements, names and addresses for later. Like everyone else, Johnson had seen precious little from the restaurant. What he'd seen afterwards, on the other hand, he didn't want to try to explain. But he'd be damned if he wouldn't tell Wallets all about it.

Thirty minutes later the cops let them go. Ten blocks downtown the city flowed around them like nothing happened. Anton broke their pensive silence.

"Peter," he mumbled. "Peter—I'd like to ask you a favor. Is that all right?" Johnson stared at the Euro-weenie.

"Talk to me."

Anton seemed at a loss of manhood. He shoved his hands in his jacket pockets, eyes flitting from corner to corner as though afraid they were being watched; no, just normal New York traffic . . . then screwed up the courage. "I'd like you to make a deposit for me."

At which Johnson gave him a long, searching look, weighing his options. Then replied, "Let's talk tomorrow. I've got that press conference *The Crusader* is hosting, and need to prep."

Back in the Brooklyn apartment Johnson sat with his daughter as they watched the late-night news. Something about them sitting side by side on the couch watching TV always comforted Giselle. This last episode, the accident on the street, seemed to have filled her with dread, resurrecting all the chaotic feelings from the Iran time. As if those troubles followed Johnson all the way back home.

"It'll be all right," he tried to assure her.

"But you *knew* him." A reproach.

And Peter could only shrug in resigned admission. "Yes," he told her, "I did."

The last thing Johnson saw on TV that night was a little-noticed three-day-old story of bureaucratic bungling that was explained away and forgotten within a week. In Nogales, Arizona, some Mexican drug dealers overran an Arizona National Guard checkpoint somewhere out in the desert. Dozens of shots, even a Vietnam-era M-72 Light Anti-Tank Weapon fired and thrown in a ditch—the familiar hollow green tube a silent yet eloquent testament to United States border insanity. Rules of engagement clearly stated no Arizona National Guardsman could fire back, even when fired upon.

As the Arizona National Guard retreated behind their vehicles, the drug dealers proceeded merrily on their way into the heartland of America. What no one ascertained for certain was the identity of these Mexican drug runners or where they were headed. No matter. The next day politicians of every stripe continued to celebrate themselves in their particular ways. Some postured on the cable shows about the dangers of transfats in corn chips, while others called for safer kiddy-kar kid seats. In a fit of statesmanship, Bangor, Maine, banned smoking in privately owned cars with children in them. Finally: kids in Bangor, Maine, were safe from second-hand smoke.

⌾

That night, as Johnson tried to sleep a restless sleep, some eyes slept not at all. Wesson, Bryce, and Smith sat in their slightly chilly sedan in a parking lot. But not just any old parking lot—the nearly infinite Autostan at the King of Prussia Mall in eastern Pennsylvania.

Smith was at the wheel and Bryce in the passenger's seat this time around. Relegated to the backseat, Wesson didn't like her spot. Around 9:30 PM, Bryce had made the incredibly stupid mistake of repeatedly calling the backseat of the sedan the Ladies' Lounge, or the Kiddies' Section, and now Wesson ate from a pound bag of pistachio nuts, eating the nutmeat and periodically tossing the shells at the back of Bryce's head. At first he'd said, "Will you please cut that out?" But every few minutes, *ping!* another shell bounced off his neck. One even found its way down his collar. His misery knew no bounds. But he knew enough not to say a word when Smith casually remarked, "Y'know while we're here, we should really pick up some panty hose."

And Wesson popped her cell phone. "Yeah, lemme call to see if Ann Taylor's still open."

Bryce bit his tongue with the words, *Yeah, go ahead, so I can strangle you . . .*

"They're open. Hey, Bryce you want to go for us? Go on a panty run?" At the wheel Smith guffawed. "Make mine champagne nude."

Ping! went another pistachio shell on the back of his neck. "Anything I can do to help." But suddenly the whole bag of nuts hit the backseat, and Wesson had her night vision binoculars up to her eyes.

"Shut up, shut up—there she is!"

Smith and Bryce could see their mark with the naked eye. Farah Nasir. The mysterious female voice at the end of the "Polak" call back in New York. Junior service officer, Iranian Mission to the United Nations. "Little Miss Strange." She seemed to take a lot of phone calls from guys in Brooklyn and Queens. Very short phone calls that started with nonsense like, "Polak" or "Klimteh" and ended with "Right" or "Fine." Her BMW had pulled up door-to-door with a black Lincoln Continental, favorite of car services and one indistinguishable from the next.

"Call in Big Bird," Smith barked. "If they take off in different directions we're going to lose them."

And Wesson got on the phone to the Pennsylvania State Police. The traffic copter was on the way.

As it turned out, the Lincoln followed the Beemer out of the parking lot and headed north out Goddard Boulevard around the world headquarters of Lockheed Martin. The PA State Police chopper phoned in to inform them there was some confusion as to whether the airspace over the aerospace company was restricted.

Wesson hung up on them in disgust with the words, "All right, forget it!"

In a half mile they still hadn't lost either the Beemer or the Lincoln, as Goddard Boulevard finally ran out and the two cars turned north on Gulph Road, exiting almost as soon as they got on and parking in the Sheraton Park Ridge Hotel and Conference Center right across from the Valley Forge Golf Course.

Smith ran the Lincoln's plates. Arizona. "Nogales DMV has it registered to Pedro Livery of Nogales. And we've got a parking receipt from the golf course. It's been sitting here two days. They charged it to the livery service."

"Yeah, they would charge it. Avoid cash at all costs. Leaving a big black Lincoln sitting around in a parking garage might get you red-flagged from Homeland Security, like there's a bomb in it or something." This from Wesson.

"So what are they carrying?" Bryce wondered out loud.

A little more patience brought them the answer.

Nothing. Yet. But that changed.

After ten minutes of scanning the surrounding area, they saw the bobbing lights of a golf cart appear out from a band of trees. The shiny white cart was driving off the course. It cruised around a sand trap, then a water hazard. In the dark, the sound of its electric motor whirring grew closer and closer. Finally the cart bobbed onto a Valley Forge/Sheraton access path and crossed over into the parking lot. Then pulled in front of the Conference Center behind a row of ten golf carts.

Wesson's cell rang. "PA State Police want to know if we want a SWAT take down? They've got a SWAT chopper hovering out by the third hole." Apparently there wasn't any restriction over the golf course. Smith spat back one word. "No." Then thought better to add, "Thank you." The G-Gals and their Boy Toy were all staring at the same thing.

The Valley Forge golf cart: it carried six golf bags.

And in twenty seconds one man from the Lincoln Continental had stowed them in the Lincoln's trunk. In another twenty seconds the Beemer and Lincoln were headed north on Interstate 276—heading home to good old New York City.

———

Johnson woke up in plenty of time for Jo von Hildebrand's news conference. He had been especially careful around Jo von H since he had gotten back. He said all the same sort of things politically that he always had, but with more calculation than ever, and it wouldn't surprise him if she noticed. People liked to scoff behind her back that she was a mere social climber posing as a publisher-intellectual. He always thought in reply when he heard these comments, "Well, if you're so much smarter, why is she Jo von H, and you're not?"

Since his return she'd really laid on the pressure for him to write about the Iran business. She wanted a massive piece as the seed for a book, *I Know Why They Hate Us: Guest of Iran, American Hostage*, or something in that vein. He claimed it was too painful to write at the moment, that he needed to spend more time with Giselle, that he was blocked—anything to hold her off, and she did the courtesy of believing him, for the time being. He knew eventually she would sit him down and dictate the piece, if that's what it took: visions of cable appearances, newspaper coverage, and blog rantings dancing in her head.

So by way of placating her, he resolved to go to the presser and do his best to channel Jo von H, to ask the questions she would most want to hear. Though Yasmine Farouk and Dr. Pahlevi Yahdzi were the last people on earth he wanted to see. Dutifully, he packed his mini-digital tape recorder, his note pad, and a few Uniball pens, blue.

Once again he met Neville Poore, columnist for the *Times*, in Josephine von Hildebrand's elevator on the way up. This time, the man wasn't chatty as he'd been on the night of the party those years ago. In a foul mood. Clearly, the last thing he wanted was some gaseous Metropolitan light opera—or even worse—breaking news at Jo von H's press conference preempting his column topic for tomorrow. A planned hit piece on the American flag pin: "the McCarthyism of America's lapels, disgracing the country's jackets with a simulacrum of patriotism."

He pouted at Johnson with a mixture of jealousy, repellence, admiration, and respect. Wondering how a notorious drunken putz like Peter rated an Iranian kidnapping, a wild escape, and a mysterious repatriation, while he, Neville Poore, *New York Times* editorial-page columnist, was still just feeding his own publisher a laundry list of cherry-picked quotes and facts for his next clip-job bestseller. Now a cute Iranian physicist pops up as VIP du jour, and dammit Peter even *knew* her from back when. Life was so unfair.

"You're looking well, Peter."

And Johnson nodded his thanks, not trusting himself to speak. He didn't know how he'd react seeing Yasmine and Yahdzi, those frauds so thoroughgoing they made him seem like Mr. Transparency. The elevator cage doors opened, and they both walked down that long, endless hallway again, the sounds from the large oval foyer with those chalky voices fluttering back to meet them.

The grand foyer was packed shoulder to shoulder with the ducklings of the media summoned to bear witness. ABC, CBS, NBC, the major and even minor wire services were all represented at this cattle call. As was every newspaper in New York, Boston, Chicago, Los Angeles, and Miami. Neville Poore's face dropped like a stone. "Oh, Gawd . . ." And Johnson nodded in appreciation of his disdain at the sheer fuss over it all.

One consolation, though. In the press of the crowd, Johnson himself wouldn't stand out. But then he noticed the best-coiffed hair a *man's* money could buy: $187 (including tips) at John Frieda Salon, the gorgeous locks visible over the shoulder of a burly cameraman. Was it? Could it be? Johnson moved a step to his right to get a different angle, and sure enough—Anton. So Frenchie banker's been invited to the presser too? Johnson couldn't possibly get over to him with the crush of people and mentally put it in his WTF file until the show was over.

A battery of microphones attached to the official podium of *The Crusader* stood near one curved wall, the cables snaking off to a general Wi-Fi box on the floor. Josephine von Hildebrand only pulled out The Big Podium on the most important occasions. The magazine didn't boast a logo, just the name in **Georgia** font large enough to read across the room.

The Crusader

Planting the magazine's imprimatur like Excalibur, the sword in the stone over the whole proceedings for everyone to see.

At a silent signal, a pocket door near the battery of microphones opened, and Jo von H emerged, brimming with gravity and suppressed enthusiasm. Behind her followed Dr. Yasmine Farouk, PhD, of the Tehran Polytechnic Institute. And following her dutifully came Dr. Ramses Pahlevi Yahdzi of the University of Isfahan. He looked just the same as the day Johnson walked into his office in the basement of the Gonabad facility, only dressed more neatly.

The questions from the hysterical press ran the gamut from pointless to criminally stupid. As Josephine knew all the gathered ducklings, she picked and chose who got to make fools of themselves, telling the crowd in a schoolmarm's voice, "Let's keep things simple, ladies and gentlemen—no two- and three-part questions, all right?"

So naturally the first question asked by the reporter from *Le Monde* began with the words, "One question and a follow-up, Monsieur Doktaire Yahdzi—" Johnson caught Neville Poore rolling his eyes in contempt. What didn't that little French *canard* understand about no *two-parters*?

The question went something like this: "In your experience with international inspecting bodies have you ever had the opportunity to raise the question about nuclear inspections of United States facilities or Israeli facilities? And if so, when and with whom both in Washington and Jerusalem?" Obviously the fellow was searching for the headline: Iranian Physicist Blocked from Evidence of Planned Rogue Israeli Pre-emptive Nuclear Strike.

Dr. Ramses Pahlevi Yahdzi of the University of Isfahan cocked his head as though trying to listen very hard and dissect the meaning of the words aimed at him. He did it with an attitude of immense patience and amusement, as if wondering what manner of creature was clucking at him. Finally answering with a thick accent Johnson never heard before and the halting speech of a man unaccustomed to speaking English. A masterly performance.

"Yes, I—um—yes. Jews refuse inspections. Always do." Then bowing his head in Yasmine's direction, where she spoke sotto voce into his tilted ear. Him nodding sagely as she explained some detail. Then finally addressing the reporter from *Le Monde*:

"We ask repeatedly. First seven years ago, then three times a year for every year." Then speaking with some inspiration, "Iran never give up trying to find truth from United States and Zionists."

And on it went. One stupid question after another. And Yahdzi making a dumb show for a gullible press.

Finally it was Johnson's turn to join the charade. He raised his hand, Uniball pen between first and second fingers. Josephine recognized him immediately. "Peter, please."

Neither Yasmine nor Yahdzi acknowledged Johnson's extraordinary past with them. They stared blankly and receptively waited for Johnson to speak. After all, why bother acknowledging what never occurred? The only accusations came from the execrable Sheik Kutmar on NITV, National Iranian Television, that one time. Purposely vague. Later, the usual suspects and guilty powers Johnson named were all alphabet soup, CIA-FBI-NSA and so forth. But not Iranian. No harm, no foul.

"Dr. Farouk," he said to Yasmine. And here the smarm in Johnson slithered up like an old friend. Yasmine's eyes opened wide in total innocence as she listened intently. "The last time we talked"—a knowing twitter went through the crowd of reporters, thinking of Johnson's Iranian adventure—"you spoke movingly of how your country's development had been held back for so long by the West, and that now, finally, the Islamic Republic is coming into its own. What do you say to those who would stop it?"

Without missing a beat, Yasmine said, "It's good to see you again, Mr. Johnson. And I'm gratified your treatment by the United States government upon your return from the Middle East was less harsh than those now being held as illegal prisoners in the military prisons of your country . . . "

"You're not the only one!" Johnson interjected, provoking a gale of laughter as approving faces turned his way from around the room.

But Yasmine's didn't approve. She didn't appreciate being interrupted. In fact, she would probably only be truly happy if she could make him piss razors again.

She feigned a smile and continued, "We are a sovereign nation. One that represents the world's greatest civilization, although one that has been beset by Western colonialism and arrogance for too long. We are strong now and getting stronger, so strong that you will never be able to keep us from taking our place in the sun. So what I say is, we are the rising tide, and how do you say? 'Time and tide wait for no man'? Or in American: Get over it."

Charmed chuckles from the reporters.

Johnson nodded his head, gravely taking down everything the woman said. Then raising his hand: "And if I may ask the second half of my one-part question." The crowd lapped it up.

"Dr. Yahdzi," Johnson said, "I'm glad to see the reports of your death were greatly exaggerated," which got another general guffaw of approval. And it made Dr. Yahdzi smile, though he seemed unfamiliar with the reference to that greatest of all American raconteurs. "Once again, last time we spoke you seemed concerned—*worried* you would be denied the ability to finish your work either by American or Israeli aggression. Are you still concerned?"

Here, Yahdzi cocked his head once more to Yasmine's softly speaking lips for a faux Farsi translation. Johnson waited patiently. At last Dr. Ramses Pahlevi Yahdzi of the University of Isfahan spoke, simply:

"Americans and Zionists stand in way at own risk. Iran have every right. American Jews have no right stop us. We are peaceful people. But enemies beware."

"If I may speak for those at *The Crusader*, the sponsors of this gathering, Professor," Johnson said, "they wholeheartedly endorse that sentiment, and send their best wishes to your country's long-suffering people."

The physicist bowed slightly, and Jo von H mouthed over to him, "Nice, Peter."

The news conference broke up after an hour with no one more informed than when they went in, which was the unstated purpose of most news conferences. The endless repetition of political positions or outright falsehoods constructed to advance those positions. News conferences merely a means to an end. In the case of Iranian Nuclear Authorities their ability to put a smiley face on Armageddon.

Neville Poore sidled up to him afterwards with a one-word verdict, "Banal." But Johnson ignored him, trying to keep his eye on Anton, who headed straight to Jo von H. His relentless Ex was mingling in triumph near the front of the room. But Anton didn't introduce himself, didn't need to. She put her hand around the young man's neck and whispered something; then he headed straight to a bar that had magically appeared to service the assembled scribes and strutting TV talent. Johnson stood transfixed. His WTF file was bulging to the breaking point.

Anton pushed his way straight to the bar and hustled back with a drink that looked like bourbon and handed it to Josephine, who opened up her charmed circle to him and gave him pride of place close to her. Too close. Johnson felt as if he were going to gag but couldn't believe he was seeing what he thought he was seeing. And then in the midst of making a point that delighted everyone around her, Josephine's left hand drifted behind Anton and settled on the backside of his shimmery, tailored-to-the-nines suit.

Oh. No. She. Didn't. Yes, she did. She squeezed the Charmin. .

Johnson almost let out a little yelp as if it'd been his backside that was tweaked. He charged toward them, and the circle opened up with murmurs of "Ahh" and "Here's the man!" Anton's face lit up: "Peter!" And he gave him a big hug that Johnson wouldn't have reciprocated if the Iranians had tried to torture it out of him: "You were marvelous!" Jo von H looked at Peter admiringly and shook her head as if she were constantly astounded by his abilities, and then with softer eyes, doe eyes— to the extent her wizened peepers could make them—at Anton: "We both thought so, darling."

Right. We. Her and her new *Lancelot*.

Johnson raised a finger to make a point he couldn't even begin to formulate, when Anton interrupted him, "Peter, I'd still love to have a word with you afterwards." A word with *him*. Peter stumbled out, "Yeah, sure. I'll be waiting downstairs," and he hardly saw anything until he was out on the street, pacing and punching up his cell phone.

Trying Wallets. Voice mail. Tried it again. Voice mail. Tried it again—and an annoyed voice: "Peter, what the hell is it?"

"Is that French son of a bitch two-timing on my daughter with *my ex-wife?*"

A long pause. "Hold on," Wallets said. And he heard mumbling and then muffled sounds and finally a woman's voice: "Hello?"

"Who's this?" Johnson demanded, keeping an eye out behind him.

"Agent Smith. I've been working this case with Wallets. Is there something I can help you with?"

"Yeah. Tell me something. Has that Frenchie *salaud* been diddling my ex-wife *and* my daughter?"

A couple walking by looked at him a long time and then giggled when they were past him.

"Hold on."

More mumbling at the other end of the call, and he thought he heard the word "cougar," but it might have been his imagination; then another voice, a baffled-sounding male: "Hello???" Johnson knew the drill; he was getting passed down the food chain and didn't like it.

"Who's this?"

"My name's Bryce. What's yours again?"

"Oh, hell." Anton floated out the front door, looking both ways and tilting his head up in recognition and smiling when he saw him further up the sidewalk. Johnson clapped his phone shut. "Peter!" Just as delighted to see him as he had been upstairs. "I know just the place to go," and he hooked his arm in Johnson's playfully and yanked him up the sidewalk.

He prattled on, while Johnson fumed and tried to think rationally. He kept coming back to what Wallets would want him to do, and that was unquestionable: Play it cool, and play out the string. Anton led them into a dark wine bar off Broadway called Veivers, where the Frenchman was hailed as if he were Norm arriving at the bar in an episode from *Cheers*.

They were served glasses of Pinot noir without asking and a tiny bowl of olives. Anton was still in prattling mode, as he popped an olive in his mouth and delicately removed the pit: "I've so enjoyed getting to know your family. Josephine is exquisite." Johnson couldn't help a tiny grimace, which Anton didn't seem to notice. In any case the young man changed his tone and got down to business: "I've got myself into a spot of trouble. If you could help me, the debt would last my lifetime."

Johnson raised his eyebrows and opened his hands, *pray tell*. Concern dripped off him like sweet beads of honey. "Anton, anything," Johnson said, manfully trying to keep the sarcasm to himself. Right now the boy was all about tête-à-tête and the young fellow made every effort to seem sincere.

"There's a man in Japan, an industrialist who wants to bid on a large New York real estate property. But he doesn't want his name used for the simple reason that if this industrialist's name were known, the price of the property would go through the roof. Simply because he was interested. I made the foolish mistake of promising this industrialist I could handle the transaction for him. Now my reputation is at stake, as is the reputation of Banque Luxembourg. If I fail, he'll take all his business somewhere else. And that amount is far larger than the bidding money on this single transaction. Ordinarily I would have asked Jan Breuer to help me, despite everything, but . . ." And here he drifted off.

Johnson took a deep breath. "I think I understand," he said at last. "You want to have the industrialist's money wired to my account and have me transfer it in my name into Banque Luxembourg for him. Like the currency says, legal tender for all debts public and private. And it makes sense; he wants it private. There are power-of-attorney papers involved, but there's no law that says you can't give money to someone to deposit, as long as the taxes are eventually paid."

Anton sighed a huge breath of relief. "And they will be paid; I give you my word, Peter, and the word of Banque Luxembourg's lawyers. No one expects you to pay the tax on a transaction of $35 million."

Thirty-five million dollars. A real-estate buy for a wealthy anonymous Jap. Sure.

CHAPTER TWENTY-TWO

Banquo's Ghosts

anquo stood at his tenth-floor office window at 30 Rockefeller Plaza looking down the promenade to Fifth Avenue and Saks Department Store. A yellow Ryder delivery truck had pulled up in the middle of the block. For what, he didn't know, as deliveries never came in the front. It idled with its hazards flashing directly in front of the gold front doors, framed by an august stone entrance emblazoned at the top "SAKS & COMPANY."

The truck glowed at Banquo, like Nasrallah's turban on one of those satellite images, and it lit up the synapses down a well-worn path of Banquo's mind. He felt his throat catch, and he couldn't help what happened next, his imagination taking that Ryder truck parked outside the store, then leaping to a herky-jerky Zapruder 8mm film behind his eyes.

First, the exaggerated silence—then the sucking sensation. Finally the flash and boom as his office window shook. A cloud of concrete dust rolled down the Rockefeller Promenade, mixing with a thousand windows falling to the ground. Through the wafting smoke an awful clearing: the facade of the lower stories of the Saks building sheared away, metal rods drooping out of the front. The truck nonexistent and the passing traffic turned into twisted metal, unrecognizable except for an axle or chassis—right there on Fifth Avenue. Pools of blood. Limbs. Burned people, half naked and running heedlessly. Survivors

staring, their faces contorted in a kind of madness. The color of powdered concrete.

Unsteady on his feet, Banquo touched the window. He looked down
once more. The truck had its right turn signal on and was merging into
the stream of downtown traffic again. He reached for his desk chair and
sank into it. He knew what was going to happen next. He knew where
his mind was taking him. It always did.

Anyone who spent time in Beirut in the 1950s and '60s spoke of its
charm, its easy cosmopolitan sophistication—Paris on the Mediter-
ranean. Of never being able to shake the feeling that you lived on the
edge of the great Middle East, but with all the comfort and class of the
Champs-Elysées. Monte Carlo with couscous and kabobs. Banquo had
been there in another era, and he couldn't shake what he had taken away
from it, regret tinged with anger, an aching uncertainty about what
might have been or, more importantly, what he personally might have
prevented.

That regret filled every crevice of his soul, arising out of a time when
trusting the wrong person or a wrong gut instinct could mean disap-
pearing into the abyss of swirling hatreds and rival agendas, where the
only certainty was the barrel of a gun.

Banquo had been stationed in Beirut for nearly eight months. Then
came April 18, 1983, the day the U.S. Embassy was hit. As if to spit in
America's face, the bombers used a van stolen earlier from the Embassy
itself. Four hundred pounds of explosives. Sixty-three dead.

Among them: chief Middle East analyst Robert C. Ames, station
chief Kenneth Haas, and six other CIA employees. In the 1970s, Idaho
Senator Frank Church, along with Admiral Stansfield Turner, Jimmy
Carter's CIA chief, had degraded U.S. intelligence capabilities beyond
recognition. In a single blow, CIA Director Turner had eliminated over
eight hundred operational positions in what was called the Halloween
Massacre. As far as Banquo was concerned, what Senator Church and
Turner began back at home in 1977, Hezbollah finished off by killing

those men in Beirut. Their experience, their contacts, their expertise—all wiped out, and they weren't coming back.

Banquo could still recall his safe house, a few white painted rooms in an office building on the Muslim side of the Green Line. There he ran a cutout, what appeared to be an export-import business. The last remnant of Agency operatives on the ground.

It didn't take long to finger who had blown up the Embassy. Such terror operations weren't simple affairs. They require enough operational sophistication that many people know about them, and they needed a guiding spirit. A guiding hand—no such thing as spontaneous combustion. In this case, the organizer had a name and an address, and Banquo found them in the first twenty-four hours.

The address: the Sheik Abdullah Barracks in Baalbek, Lebanon, home of the Iranian Revolutionary Guard. The name: Ayman Husseini, the red-bearded, oddly fair-haired head of operations. A complicated man with a degree in sociology from La Sorbonne and some graduate work at the University of Tehran. His pedigree impeccable: Iranian-provided, Iranian-approved, the bomber-in-chief to a nascent Hezbollah.

Of course, there was a sheik in charge of public speaking. One Sheik Fadlallah, the "spiritual leader," of the just-forming Hezbollah talked a good enough game. "What martyrdom is greater than a human bomb detonated in the enemy's face? What spiritualism, what blessing greater than giving your body and life for the sake of Allah?"

Oh, the Hezbo fellows had plenty of martyrs lined up, but all the virgins would go wanting without Husseini's technical expertise. Fadlallah had the boys, but not the toys.

Ayman Husseini provided the toys, and he adored them. A born tinkerer, a kind of cut-rate Edison who never took the trouble to invent a better light bulb. His father was a Western-educated electrical engineer in Tehran, his career waylaid when the Shah fell. His son didn't seem to care or notice, so swept up had he been by love for Khomeini and the revolution. He had been part of the crowd of students that stormed the

U.S. Embassy in 1979, then disappeared into Iranian intelligence. Now emerging to mastermind the destruction—not just the storming—of another U.S. Embassy.

How did Banquo know about Husseini? The way he knew about so many other things: human frailty. Never be surprised by frailty, for without it you're out of the spy business. And when such frailty hit him by surprise—when he was let down or tricked—he never cursed human nature, but only his own naïveté.

Husseini's weakness was hookers. Not for himself. Husseini was perfectly content to sit in a windowless room all day breathing the toxic fumes of whatever explosive he was mixing, or sniffing solder, and had already lost three fingers to a mishap while pursuing this passion. No, the ladies were directed to a mid-level Hezbo with access to the security arrangements at the Sheik Abdullah Barracks. All the randy lad needed to betray the barrack's protocols was a safe hotel room and two hookers dressed devoutly on the outside but, underneath their burkas, clad with the sexiest frillies available in pre–Victoria's Secret Beirut. That and $500 walking-around money a month.

Banquo happily supplied both, but since his horny Hezbo never wanted any of the same women twice, there was some hustle involved to keep him adequately supplied. Even in Beirut, female companionship wasn't inexhaustible. But well worth trying to make it so. Thus, thanks to a lot of girls, a little dough, and human frailty, he knew Ayman Husseini, the bomb maker, owned a car: a rundown Chevy sedan from the 1970s. He knew where Husseini kept his car: in a fenced compound near the Abdullah Barracks with an unusually large number of panel trucks. And most importantly, Banquo knew who Ayman Husseini trusted. No one outside of another former Khomeini-worshipping student from Tehran, who acted as his driver and all-around sidekick. Banquo knew how long it took his sidekick to exit the parking lot, swing around the corner, and pick up the bomb maker from the Abdullah Barracks. Banquo had even clocked their trip times, hither and yon. Some trips were shorter, some longer.

Banquo's team could attach a wad of plastique—radio-detonated C-4—to the bottom of that car, timed to kill Ayman Husseini, his swell friends, indeed the whole Abdullah Barracks, in the first three minutes as the car pulled out of the lot and came around front. A magical mysterious explosion of questionable origin. But what if the targets knew the origin of the blast? Radio-detonated C-4 often bore Uncle Sam's signature. Even better. The Hezbos would know that the United States of America realized the import of Embassy bombings and that we could reach out and vaporize one of their top players, anyone we wanted. Even if the attacks didn't stop altogether, we'd disrupt them; perhaps even force Hezbollah to abandon the next big bang in the pipeline. But most importantly—destroy once and for all the illusion that attacking America was free of reprisal, free of consequences.

But such a job would have to be done by Americans. No turning to outside contractors. No trusting amateurs or conflicted locals. So Banquo ran it up the Langley flag pole. He knew it would go all the way to Bill Casey at the top, maybe beyond. And he waited. Each time the Hezbo got his hookers, Banquo worried one of the girls would displease the lad, ending their cozy relationship. Fretted that a word from the criminal underground running the prostitutes, Beirut's pimps, would slip across the street to the terror network and no one would ever hear from the horny Hezbo again. Or perhaps the Hezbo lad might suddenly grasp the risks he was running, then just as suddenly back out, changing all the security procedures, times and places Banquo knew so well.

Each day he waited for word from Langley seemed an age. Each day without a decision his stomach twisted up more and more; after five weeks, even if there were no outward signs, his guts were telling him a story. And he diagnosed what the knots meant. At first, he thought they were anger. But it slowly dawned on him, not anger—foreboding. Fear. For his own safety? No. At what gift the future might bring.

———⟨∞⟩———

Banquo never heard back from Langley. Eventually he dropped the plot. Even so, he kept stringing his Hezbo lad along just in case. More out of habit than anything else. And he waited again. This time for calamity.

Catastrophe came six months after the Embassy bombing that had gone unanswered—October 23, 1983. Twelve thousand pounds of TNT delivered to the Marine barracks at the Beirut International Airport in a yellow van. The explosion so large the plume of smoke formed a mushroom cloud above the four-story building, all in a moment reduced to rubble. Two hundred forty-one Americans dead. The worst day for the Semper Fidelis since Iwo Jima. The worst day for U.S. power projection since the Tet offensive. Banquo wasn't surprised.

Langley sent a team from the U.S. to gather intelligence in preparation for retaliatory strikes against the perpetrators. Yet the director of operations pulled Banquo out. Perhaps because Langley wanted to claim insufficient intelligence for any further action. Banquo knew too damn much. So the good soldier handed everything over to the U.S. team and quit Beirut.

Sure enough, the guys from the U.S. came back home without striking even the feeblest blow. But they did, apparently, subcontract out to the Lebanese military the job of killing Fadlallah, the Talking Sheik. The Lebanese Military tried to do it with a car bomb, missed Fadlallah, and killed eighty civilians at a mosque. The U.S. got just as much of a black reaming as if it had carried out the attempt itself. And Banquo was reminded of a line from an issue of *National Review* back in the 1960s: "The assassination attempt against Sukarno had all the hallmarks of a CIA operation. Everyone in the room was killed except Sukarno."

Back in the States, Banquo's aborted scheme of retribution for the Embassy bombing never surfaced. One day when he was ruminating over it, a terrible thought occurred to him: that Langley's non-answer hadn't been an implicit no but an implicit *yes*, and it was he—not the nameless "they," the chickenshit bureaucrats—who had left the predicate for the barracks bombing in place. As if he'd rammed the yellow suicide truck through the perimeter himself. The screams of those trapped under the rubble his alone to bear. And the mushroom cloud his too, a smoky apparition—Banquo's own ghost.

That's why he hated yellow trucks.

Wallets startled the boss when he came through Banquo's half-open office door, dragging him from a sorrowful memory. Wallets knew that expression on the man's face, long ago learning to let it go, bite his tongue, as if he'd interrupted someone indulging an embarrassing habit. Wallets looked at his shoes, and soon enough Banquo fixed his face and demanded, in his usual all-business tone, "What have you got?"

"We think we've got some other boys."

"What do you mean?"

"Farah Nasir, the U.N.'s Farah Nasir. Junior service officer, Iranian Mission. She took a call from another young man. He said something about Klimteh."

"Has anyone tossed their place?"

"It's in Brooklyn. Bed-Stuy, do or die. Three of them living there, same circumstances as the others basically—cheap apartment, except these boys are neater. But all the same accoutrements. Paint, jeans, reinforced backpacks . . . "

"Klimteh, eh?" Banquo tried the word out on his tongue: "Klimteh."

"We figured out what that torn-up stuff was in the Workbench Boys' place in Queens." Wallets let it hang there. He liked it when he knew something that Banquo really wanted to hear, but he didn't let it hang too long.

"Well?" Banquo said.

"X-ray vests from a dentist office. Taken apart at the seams. Flexible leaded cloth. And guess what?" There he went again. He couldn't help himself.

This time Banquo didn't rise to the bait but simply raised an eyebrow.

"There have been a couple of burglaries in dentist's offices. Brooklyn and Queens. All the same. Late at night, nothing taken except the vests. NYPD arrested two guys coming out of a Pakistani dentist's office three months ago. They made bail, overstayed their visas. Then skipped their court date. Now wanted on a bench warrant. The thing is . . ." and here Wallets put some colored printout on Banquo's desk. "I think they finally realized how stupid it was to burglarize Ahmed the local tooth puller when they could get everything they needed online with a stolen credit card."

The few colored pages were from Pearsondental.com. Vinyl Backed Lead Aprons. Corduroy Backed Lead Aprons. In Gray, Light Blue, Beige, Mauve, Wedgwood, or Jade Green. In Adult sizes. Child. Technician. Child size without collar. Technician with collar. "Multi-ply construction makes aprons flexible and comfortable. 3mm lead equivalency. In Vinyl, Corduroy, or Velour."

Banquo got the point. "For the flexible lead cloth."

"Yeah, it must be for the lead. Maybe even paid cash in a supply house."

"So you're telling me these are the dumbest Pudknockers on earth, stealing something they could have bought for cash?"

"Two were. And skipped bail. The others were quick learners."

Neither of them said anything, lost in their respective thoughts.

"As for Farah—" Wallets couldn't say it without thinking of the ubiquitous Farrah Fawcett poster of his youth. God, the actress had to be sixty now.

"Our Farah's very careful. Never says anything incriminating like she knows she's on a party line. Not about herself. Not about her superiors. But she's not your run-of-the-mill Iranian diplomatic soldier bee. Yossi says she's Al Quds, a major, with lots of field experience under her belt. He tried to get some pictures of her in Lebanon overseeing Hezbollah resupply during the border war. And several years ago in Argentina, our Farah was attached to the Iranian Embassy there during the Jewish cemetery desecration of 2004."

Desecration? Polite way of saying it.

"So there's no glass ceiling in Iranian intelligence. Farah Nasir. Yasmine Farouk. Who knew the Iranians were so broad minded."

"One more thing."

Banquo sighed, slightly impatient, but amused at the same time. Indulging Wallets. "We don't need *one more thing*, Robert. Yesterday our old friend Jan Breuer is dropped by a silenced .222 or .223 cal laser-sighted sniper rifle, and within minutes Anton Anjou of Banque Luxembourg asks Johnson to transfer $35 million through his account. And the gang that couldn't shoot straight is making fancy lead-lined backpacks and cruising the subways. How many dots do we need to connect?"

This time Wallets didn't hesitate. "What do you want to do about it?"

"Time for O'Hanlon to earn his pay."

Wallets nodded. And his boss softened, "What was the last thing you wanted to tell me, Robert?"

Wallets found a seat across from Banquo. This time he really did stretch the pause, stretched it right to breaking point.

"I think we have a mole."

Banquo put his elbows on the desk and leaned forward, turning his clasped hands into a steeple, severity flowing from him like a heavy weight. "So you've noticed."

O'Hanlon didn't feel as comfortable with his feet up on his trash bin in the presence of Banquo—it felt disrespectful somehow. "Sorry. Justice just doesn't rate the digs of Banquo & Duncan," he said, smiling and sweeping his eyes over his metal government-issued desk that could have been pulled from a public school principal's office twenty years ago, but actually came from felon labor in federal prison. Wallets found a seat.

"We're accustomed to all manner of working environments, Patrick," Banquo said. "Nothing to forgive about your office furniture." The man hadn't bothered to take off his black overcoat, still standing. He changed his tone of voice to indicate the end of pleasantries: "We've got to roll these guys up, before someone gets hurt." A flat demand. From his silent place in the chair Wallets' eyes made the same demand.

"Do you know something I don't?" O'Hanlon asked.

"No. Of course not. I'm just reacting to what we already know. You have the Klimteh and Polak boys, rootless young Muslim men, engaged in suspicious activity with a known agent of the Iranian government. That's all we need to know."

"Well, not quite all, but they've definitely got funny names."

Here, Banquo swept his overcoat under him and sat as well. "Patrick." He started to speak, not talking down to the Justice lawyer, just speaking with a kind of Olympian calm that washed over the whole dingy room. "Patrick. Mr. O'Hanlon . . . Klimteh. Polak. Clearly not pronounced or spelled correctly. Instead, I offer you Gustav Klimt, late 19th century painter. A favorite of mine, his *Athena* is a masterpiece. I offer you Jackson Pollock, 20th century painter, some say the founder of modern art. Not really a favorite, since his pictures remind me of mental dementia, but still quite noteworthy. Our rootless lads go to art stores in search of lead-based paint and speak these unlikely names."

From his quiet perch, Wallets' eyes grew colder, awaiting some adequate reply from the lawyer.

O'Hanlon rubbed his temple with a thumb. "Fascinating. I grant you the words Klimt, however poorly pronounced, and Pollock are some kind of code. As in, 'time to go to the art store and buy more paint,' or 'Shall we meet at the Atlantic Avenue subway station?' And as you know, I believe all of this bears the closest scrutiny. But I need a crime to arrest them, and we don't have spitting on a sidewalk right now. There's no crime buying tubes of artist oils at Blick's Art Supply. It's not a crime to ride the subway. Even at 2 in the morning. Even if I had a crime, in my judgment we'd need to string them along to see what more we can learn, since nothing seems—whatever it is—to be imminent." Wallets shifted in his seat, now clearly annoyed, but made no remark.

Banquo let the lawyer have his say. It was a say worth having. Then capped it off for him. "We think there's a dirty bomb involved. We're really not sure how. You've got them playing around with lead, presumably for protection. You've got firsthand knowledge of nuclear material coming over the Iranian border. And we have the Iranian connection in Farah Nasir. A supply officer for Hezbollah. A Quarter Master. What else do you need? Thirty thousand dead in a four-block radius?"

"Hey! Hey!" O'Hanlon raised his hands in protest. "I'm not from Hollywood. I'm Fordham law, y'know what I mean?"

"Fine, Fordham," Wallets grumbled, speaking for the first time, then fixed the DOJ lawyer with his gray eyes: "You've got possession of stolen goods. The ripped-up dentist vests."

O'Hanlon rolled his eyes. "Oh, please. And what? We'll break them under the torture of doing community service, assuming we get a conviction? Do we have any evidence they *stole* these particular lead vests, or did they just buy them and then deface them?" O'Hanlon immediately regretted his sarcasm; no fool, he knew what they were driving at. But kept going anyway. Nothing changed the facts as stated:

"You guys have to stay in the *here-and-now*. My business is about reality—about what we know and what we don't know. About never confusing the two. You're chasing phantoms."

Banquo took two of his fingers and smoothed one of his eyebrows: "Anticipation is priceless. When you have your crime, it's too late. No one should *need* to tell you this. So find something. Parking tickets. Material witness. Conspiracy. Perhaps you'll discover something more incriminating at the moment of arrest, if you catch my meaning."

O'Hanlon recoiled at the implication. He never liked preachifying or speechifying at someone, but after his dad vanished and broke his mother's heart, Mom had put him through school by working as a teacher by day, then clerked weekends at the local public library. Never once complaining, never once deviating from her gospel. No cheating, no corner cutting, no whining, no matter what temptations or obstacles life threw her way. O'Hanlon made her creed his own and intended to pass it on to his girls the way she passed it on to him, by living it every hour.

"Hold on now," O'Hanlon said. "Don't say another word, Mr. Banquo. I'll pretend I never heard that. See: I'm an officer of the law. The *law*. I take this threat as seriously as anybody in this room; I see the dots—but nobody's going to break the law as long as I'm sitting in this office."

The spymaster's eyes fell to his lap. Then quietly: "You're saving *people*, not the law. And if you make a mistake by moving now, you've only made a mistake, and everyone walks on. The Workbench Boys can go on innocently living their squalid outer borough existence."

"All right, let's forget probable cause for the moment," O'Hanlon countered. "I've got a question for you." O'Hanlon kicked the trash pail a little in frustration, making a hollow sound. "If it's a dirty bomb, where's the radioactive material?"

But Banquo countered fast. "Did you get a search warrant on the Texas Pedro Livery Service sedan, the six golf bags you tracked from King of Prussia Mall and the Valley Forge Golf Course?"

Here O'Hanlon stared at the ceiling for a moment. Admitting ruefully, "Judge Hamilfish wouldn't give it to me. A theory or a guess isn't probable cause. And all we've got is a couple of drums you saw on the back of a jackass six thousand miles from here."

Wallets flashed him a look of daggers, but O'Hanlon didn't care now. His mind boiled; to snoop or not to snoop, that was the question; everything eventually reached its limit. And the DOJ lawyer wasn't gonna budge.

"*Do . . . it . . . anyway,*" Banquo said, measured, slow, a command.

O'Hanlon propped his feet up on the wastebasket and folded his hands over his belly. He brought his hands up to his chin, pursed his lips, and put them back down again. "No," he answered at last.

"Do you read science fiction?" Banquo asked, from out of nowhere.

"I read those books you bought."

"Ah . . . " Banquo nodded to himself. "As you know, they're about alien threats, threats that transcended the bounds and categories of what anyone thought was possible. Threats that couldn't be defeated with conventional tools."

"Yeah," the Department of Justice lawyer said. "My problem is *here and now,*" O'Hanlon repeated, pointing to the floor. "I've got to stay in the here and now."

What was left to say?

So Banquo and Wallets left O'Hanlon's office without saying goodbye. From their cubicles, Bryce, Smith, and Wesson all watched them go without rising to greet them. O'Hanlon poked his head out the door and barked across the bull pen, "Hey!" He shouted to Smith, Wesson, and Bryce, "Anybody *work* here?"

⌾⌾⌾

Deputy Executive Director Andover usually arrived in his office by around 7:30 AM, before his secretary, who didn't get there for another hour. Miss Lithesome, as he nicknamed her, sat, at a desk outside his office, surrounded by a faux wooden semicircular wall from which she gazed out at the world. You had two choices of female style at Langley: matrons of honor—the librarian, schoolmarm types who could surmount any bureaucratic obstacle—or cute Mary Kay types who could find the ladies' room, but only in an emergency. DEADKEY picked the latter, considering her a tasteful office accessory like the Jonathan Adler ceramic pieces on his desk. Coming out of the elevator, Andover was startled to see someone new sitting by her desk, waiting. Banquo.

Andover headed straight toward his door and unlocked it with his keycard, Banquo following. "You couldn't even let me know you were coming?"

"I didn't want to call too late—or too early," Banquo replied.

"That's very thoughtful of you, Stewart. What do you want?" Andover commenced his usual morning routine as if Banquo weren't there. Plugging in the hot water for his tea. Turning on his computer. Spreading the front page of the *Washington Post* on his desk in front of him. Spinning the dials on his classified drawers to open them for business.

Banquo sat uninvited in the chair directly across from Andover's fortress desk, leaving on his black overcoat, and came straight to the point:

"I need someone to big-foot O'Hanlon. He needs to make some arrests. Middle Eastern men, mostly. Maybe a dozen or more. And I need them detained and at my disposal, maybe indefinitely. Today, just for starters."

Andover expelled his breath derisively, "Pffhh. You needn't have come all this way; you should have emailed. What else do you need?" he asked, a tiny crease of a smile across his thin blue lips.

DEADKEY's attitude didn't surprise Banquo, but he expected to break him down quickly. "There's something afoot. What it is I don't know, but I suspect," he paused, cleared his throat, "we have every reason to believe—"

"It's a dirty bomb," the Deputy Director filled in, completing the thought.

Banquo hesitated for a dark moment.

"In case you're wondering," Andover said, "I figure you're always going to think it's a dirty bomb. You're like the global warming people. If it's hot outside, it's global warming; if it snows outside, it's global warming. For men like you, Stewart, it's dirty bombs. The sole reason for your existence."

Banquo girded himself for another bitch-fest, then calmly tried to reestablish the previous terms of their agreement. "We had an understanding, Andover."

"Yes," the Deputy Director agreed amicably. "But sometimes conditions change." He carefully poured his hot water in a mug and swished his tea bag back and forth in the water, "we had an understanding—*had*—past tense." He contemplated his tea for a moment and directed his gaze across the wide desk.

Then patiently, as if explaining to a child: "Stewart, we've known each other many years, but I'm not going to sit here and let you start a war with Iran. You tried to kill one of their scientists; now you're hatching some scheme to kidnap one of their diplomats. And finally you want to throw some kids into jail so you can send that ugly 'Turk' of yours, that Persian thug or Iranian Jew or whatever he is—to pull out their fingernails. Well, I'm not going to let you do that."

Banquo searched Andover's face, which seemed complacent as he lifted his tea bag from his mug, held one hand with a paper napkin under it to keep it from dripping, then dropped it carefully in his wastebasket. "There," he said to himself under his breath and met Banquo's eyes.

"Yossi got out of the hospital only last week," Banquo started. "I can't imagine—"

"Ah-ah-ah," Andover said, wagging his finger, like he was shooing away a cat from scratching a sofa. "Well, I can. I can well imagine. So I don't want to hear any of your sophistry or fevered justifications. Stewart, you've always had a tendency to cast your net too widely. But the fishing expedition ends today. You've gone too far and you must be stopped. And so you will."

Banquo felt his feet slipping out from under him even as he sat before Andover's desk. In the back corner of his mind a curious thought tugged his sleeve. How in heaven's name did Andover know about his plot to briefly snatch—if all else failed—a diplomat? *Farah Nasir*. And perhaps pump her for information? Banquo always kept things vague—"Middle Eastern men, mostly"—and never used the word "diplomat." So how the hell did DEADKEY know? In this case, knowledge was power. One thing to justify such an act retrospectively, but another to make the case for it beforehand.

"Look, Trevor," Banquo started. This felt like begging.

"No, I'm not going to 'look.' Taking diplomats hostage is something the Iranians have proven themselves better at than us, don't you think? We're not going that route. Nor are you going to kidnap any of the Muslims you've been tailing . . . "

"In a lawfully sanctioned process—"

"Yes, lawfully. But if you didn't get your way, you were going to go around O'Hanlon and the law and snatch them yourself. Deny it. Of course, you can't. The last time we talked, the term 'rogue agent' came up. That would have been one of *yours*. The drunken scribbler."

"Yes, and another matter came up as well, your interest in a young . . . " Banquo knew he was losing this argument.

The wagging finger came again:

"Stewart, Stewart—you're in no position to pressure me. Can you prove your allegations? And if you can, can you do so in a way that doesn't implicate Banquo & Duncan in the use of extralegal procedures to spy on one of your superiors?" He went *pffhh* again, for emphasis. "I don't think so." Then the thin lips smiled ever so slightly again. "I hope you're not in a rush to get back to New York, Stewart. Our internal affairs people have a few routine questions, and the FBI will be sitting in with those useful 302b report forms they use, so you'll be liable to charges if you lie. Don't make us call the *Washington Post* so Ruth Lipsky can write stories like 'Troubled Agent at Nexus of Iran Flap.'"

Banquo suddenly felt hot in his overcoat. Could he really be outmaneuvered by this slippery eel? A bureaucrat's bureaucrat? Even with the threat of sexual blackmail he still couldn't bring DEADKEY to heel. The bar mitzvah boy was probably off spring skiing in the Andes. Right time of year for it. Bloody hell.

And who was the back channel to Andover, the rat? Was O'Hanlon a shrewder bureaucratic player than he seemed? Bryce? Maybe the young fink had never left his former boss? Spying on Banquo and leaking across the Potomac? God help the little prep school boy if it turned out that way.

"Andover, you don't know what you're doing," Banquo started, but he could feel himself pleading. Yes, this was begging:

"It's not *about me*. It's about what we know, and what's happened. Consider the other day. All three major New York airports are disrupted by obnoxious, belligerent passengers, ignoring security protocols on religious pretexts. WINS News shows up before the authorities. And we go on a wild goose chase. That's a *diversion*."

Banquo paused. Then for emphasis: "In the midst of this chaos a border patrol checkpoint in Nogales is overrun. Yesterday, we tracked a livery car *from Nogales* to the King of Prussia Mall in Pennsylvania. Two Iranian nuclear scientists come to America under the protection of the UN's Iranian office. And in Brooklyn we've found unemployed yet self-sufficient young Middle Eastern men lining backpacks with flexible lead aprons and taking showers in a homemade decontamination tub—"

For the first time in many years, Banquo found his voice rising. "What is it about these dots you cannot *connect*?" Mastering himself once more, the spy master tried to get this man to see the light. "It's not *about me*, Deputy Director. It's about what's going to happen, not if— but when. And when you're wrong, are you going to take responsibility? When they're calling you before some congressional committee, are you going to explain how you could have stopped it, but didn't because one of your colleagues used a drunken scribbler? Are you going to take the hit, while I become the Cassandra no one listened to?"

Banquo saw he was getting nowhere. Andover thought he had all the answers today.

"Should I put it in intragovernmental language?" DEADKEY asked with a sneer, "We non-concur. It's not worth it. It's not worth doing violence to our way of government, to our reputation, to our relations with a potentially dangerous country—and *the rest of the world*. We'll be shutting down the team as soon as I can bring this clown show to the attention of the Director. O'Hanlon will be off the case. Wallets can take a vacation. The surveillance resources will be reassigned."

Trevor Andover poured himself another cup of tea. He tried to fake some warmth, some camaraderie.

"Look, you're not the only one with back channels. We have a few down here too—so many Iranians worth listening to—because they're reaching out, because they're scared and want to be heard. And try as you may, I'm not going to let you spoil a chance for dialogue before it happens."

"*Dialogue . . .* " Banquo whispered, aghast but totally controlled. He wanted to yell now. He'd heard that word before. Always before something terrible happened. A Yellow Truck Word.

"What time is it?" Andover asked.

"Excuse me?"

"What time is it?"

Banquo looked at his wristwatch. "8:05."

"Good," Andover said. He seemed pleased about the time. He struck a speed dial button on his phone, keeping it on speaker. Banquo closed his eyes and let his mind whirl around his possibilities, not bothering to listen. Helplessness consumed him. A feeling he'd experienced only twice in his career. Once in Lebanon and then once again in the dark days of the Central American problem. Even in the bad moments, even in El Salvador, when the congressional restrictions had closed in, he had always found a work-around. What was his work-around now? He heard Andover say that he, Banquo, was in his office and they should come up and get him.

Andover hung up and rose from his chair. He approached Banquo and tossed a business card in his lap. For Skadden, Arps. "Now get the hell out of my office and let me work."

Word came down from Langley and DOJ later that day: O'Hanlon and his team were to shut down the Hung Fat van show. No more Hung Fat van, no more Jordan, no more twenty-four-hour stakeouts of all and sundry characters. No more break-ins and subway rides or King of Prussia Mall visits in the dead of night. O'Hanlon would go back to his usual fare of drug dealers, gang-bangers, fences, and the occasional sloppy mobster (as if there were any other kind these days). As for Banquo, O'Hanlon understood that he wouldn't be hearing from him for a while. If ever again.

The gang didn't take it well. A pall descended on Smith, Wesson, and Bryce when their boss brought them the news. A sense of helpless frustration. Bryce took it the worst, perhaps because he once admired Deputy Executive Director Andover. His adolescent fantasies drifted toward heroic rebellion, but he lacked the will or a plan. After he'd actually done something for once—hunting and tracking their targets—his old boss had cut off everyone's proverbials. And for what? Part bureaucratic grand panjandrum routing a rival, the other part intellectual vanity. Victory? Never heard of it. The whole business gave off the sickly reek of complacency and surrender: if you bottled it into a men's cologne, you'd name it Nabob.

O'Hanlon sat in his office, feet on the wastebasket, holding the interagency memo directing his team to stand down, displaying it to Smith and Wesson like a bid paddle at an auction, "Think of it this way: common criminals are about to get more attention from us then they'd like." His two agents stared back at him with Bambi and Thumper eyes. When they left, he placed the memo carefully at the top of his right-hand desk drawer, where he put things that annoyed him he'd rather forget.

Smith was distracted all the rest of that day. She sat with her chin on her hand staring at the computer screen, then shut it down when night came on. There was still one last thing she had to know. One last score to set straight. The Farah Nasir Lincoln. Tracked to a shady junk lot in a bad section of Queens. The team would have, assuming the judge relented on the warrant, gotten to it eventually. Not now.

Obviously there would be no return trip to Nogales, Texas, in its future, the limo soon to be stripped down and junked altogether. She had a photo of its position in the lot and took a gypsy cab there alone sometime after midnight.

By the book? Of course not. She had learned growing up with all those brothers to take what she wanted, and if she stepped over the line, some girlish coquettishness usually deflected the consequences. She justified this excursion by thinking of it as a personal thing. She wasn't going to use anything she found in the court of law, so no harm no foul. She was just . . . kitty-kat curious . . . nosy.

The junk yard lot stood in an industrialized area with little in the way of industry, out near JFK. Abandoned warehouses and dead-end streets with grass growing through cracks in the sidewalk. Smashed glass glimmering in the sickly yellow of the sodium street lights with the sound of jet planes overhead. So lonely it could have been Wichita, not the city that purportedly never sleeps.

Smith got out of the cab down the block from the lot and walked the rest of the way, her footsteps echoing around her, a sound the bustle of New York rarely allows you to hear. It unnerved her, and she couldn't help looking behind her more than once. She should have asked Wesson along. Spooky. Like when you go down into the dank basement as a kid and suddenly feel a tingle on the back of your neck and run all the way up the steps into the kitchen, panting. Flushed and embarrassed at having been scared. She jumped at the sight of something moving, across the road, waddling actually. An opossum. A damn opossum in New York City.

She chuckled at the rodent and crossed the street and knew right where she wanted to enter the lot. She took a pair of metal bolt cutters from a gym bag and started in on the chain-link fence. No way she'd climb that thing, topped with barbed wire angled out toward the street. No, she'd get in down low, forcing her way through the hole barely big enough for a kid. And damning all through her teeth as she caught her jacket on a bit of wire.

But two minutes later she was making her way through the hulks of cars in various states of disrepair, squeezing between the fender of one, almost touching the side of another, as if it were some particularly chaotic New York traffic jam in a state of suspended animation.

She arrived at the Nogales Livery Lincoln, and she went around to the trunk. From the gym bag, she fished out her Banquo & Duncan-issue Geiger counter and got a low-static reading. A little bump. She began to feel urgency now. The gym bag gave up a hammer and pry bar. She slipped them out and with her sweaty hands began to jimmy the back lock. She was good at this, but she needed to keep her hands from shaking in order to pop the trunk.

She closed her eyes and breathed for calm, and felt for that little snickety hitch within the car and finally got it. With a deep click the trunk bounced all the way open, the trunk latch hanging by a sliver of broken metal. She stuck the counter inside and began to get readings that crackled like a car radio in the middle of a thunderstorm with non-stop lightening. Off the scale. Hot as hell, very hot.

Then she heard a bark. It sent a jolt through her. She put her counter back in the bag, slammed the trunk closed, but it bounced open again. Barks mixed with snarls raced toward her through the car graveyard until they were all one long stream of canine malice, and she could hear an animal's body clambering over cars, claws against the metal adding to the mayhem. She had her back against the trunk and looked to see if she could see it coming—when it rushed right up to her. She got the trunk down and jumped on it, then up on the roof, losing an Annie Sez two-inch pump.

The junkyard dog crashed into the back of the car and jumped up, its teeth bared in an evil smile. She couldn't even tell its breed, just angry, mean, and ready to rip. The dog tried to climb onto the back again and slid off, its body twisting, all insistent muscle. Smith didn't know whether to try to make a run for it or stay put. The beast finally got up on the car and was lunging toward her again, paws slipping on the back window, when she pulled the .32 Beretta, the sissy girly gun, the one with no stopping power, and shot the mutt straight in the skull, the sound of the shot trailing off in the distance for a long time. It was the loudest shot she'd ever heard.

The dog had slipped down to the trunk, limp, its head smoking. Smith heard a voice shouting and then a siren.

O'Hanlon looked at the green numbers of his digital clock when the phone next to his bed rang. 1:43 AM. Smith's voice. "Do you want to hear the bad news or the bad news?"

"What's up?" he croaked.

"The trunk of the Lincoln is as radioactive as Love Canal."

O'Hanlon was impressed. "Shit. And the other bad news?"

"I'm under arrest." Her voice faded from the phone. "What the hell precinct is this?"

CHAPTER TWENTY-THREE

The Grunge

It started innocuously enough on the northwest corner of Manhattan, so quietly almost nobody noticed. Initially the problem surfaced at Columbia-Presbyterian Medical Center: a dozen modern steel-and-glass buildings and a few older brick ones that competed with the towering silver spans of the George Washington Bridge for the New York skyline. A small city of nearly twenty thousand medical personnel devoted to the care of its inner-city community and the science of higher medicine, where, miraculously, neither was shortchanged.

The first to show symptoms were a sixty-four-year-old granny, Mrs. Ebert Jones of Washington Heights, and a kid from a pickup basketball game, James Thomas, known on the street as Spinner. Both victims appeared at "Pres Emergency"—what the neighborhood called the emergency room of Columbia-Presbyterian Medical Center—arriving as walk-ins on a late Sunday afternoon.

Granny Jones came directly from work as a security matron at the Cloisters in Fort Tryon Park half a mile north. The reassembled European hermitage was packed to the Gothic arches with medieval treasures and owned by the Metropolitan Museum. On her feet all day in the galleries, Matron Jones was feeling faint.

Spinner came directly from his neighborhood hoops games with two of his *dawgs* to keep him company. Spinner's $200 Nike Air Force 1

Scarface Edition basketball shoes were melting off his feet. One of his friends was wearing the Adidas Intelligent Basketball Shoe that retailed for $500. These weren't looking so hot either, and all three boys were wondering loudly about where to get satisfaction in the matter of defective merchandise. But only Spinner needed medical attention. His toes were burned. He sat near the large Plexiglas window by the nurses' station in his stocking feet, his semi-melted Nikes hanging around his neck by the laces.

Unfortunately for them, that same Sunday afternoon some gang-bangers had shot two innocent children in a drive-by, while ten people from a three-car pileup on the West Side Highway had been routed to Columbia-Presbyterian. So it took two hours before either Spinner or Granny Jones received attention. By the time the attending physician came out for Granny Jones, Granddaughter Alisha had arrived, cell phone earplug in her ear. Granny felt better just to see her. The two left without the matron being treated, hand in hand, wrinkled paw in young palm, talking about the new Avon catalogue.

Spinner was given some aloe-based antibiotic topical cream and walked home in a pair of mauve hospital booties, his ruined Nikes slung over his shoulder. The attending physician cracked, "Don't step in the acid puddles."

Both were dead before midnight.

Still, in the first forty-eight hours, Homeland Security, the NYCDC, Centers for Disease Control, and the NYC Office of the Medical Examiner down on 26th Street didn't come close to connecting the dots. How could they? Granny Jones was listed at a Harlem funeral parlor as "heart attack," the family talking to lawyers about "suing the shit out of Pres Emergency," while Spinner's case was listed in the coroner's office as "undetermined cause of death," scheduled for an autopsy later in the week. Nobody bothered to check his closet, where he threw the Nike Air Force sneaks. If they had, they might have noticed all his other shoes were melting too.

Elizabeth Richards had been talking to Peter more since he'd come back—nothing like a hostage ordeal to bring estranged adults closer together. Nothing too deep, just checking in periodically. Like an old married couple, even if she was his third try. And it was that increased communication between the two, along with Peter's newfound intense amateur interest in *strange doings in the city* that prompted her to telephone him right away about a weird call she had gotten at the museum. She had picked up the phone and had to hold the traditional-style handset away from her ear because the voice on the other end was so loud:

"This is Alisha *Jones*." And irate as hell. "That's Grandmother Jones' granddaughter. She worked for you!" At first Elizabeth was confused; the only thing clear was that this Alisha was steaming at some bureaucratic runaround. "I'm calling you because the people at Personnel stopped payment of her insurance due to investigation by Equifax. I know Grandma had a heart condition, but they say they saw *burns* at the funeral. These people, these snoops from the insurance company, came to the funeral home and looked at her—right in her coffin! Right before the wake. And none of us knew!"

To her credit Elizabeth tried to get to the bottom of it. "I don't recognize the name Grandma Jones, Alisha, I'm sorry. Is it possible she worked at another department? You say she had burns on her feet?"

"Yes, on her feet. They said burns on her feet. And now the insurance detectives are trying to weasel out of paying the insurance."

"Which department did your grandmother work for?"

"Security. She worked in the security department. She was a gallery matron up at The Cloisters. Up at Fort Tryon Park."

"I'm sorry, Alisha, I think you've got the wrong department. We're the Curator's Office of the Ancient Middle East. I still think you need Personnel."

"No, you're what I wanted. A curator—curators decide things. I know you guys decide. Now curate this situation for Granny Jones!"

Elizabeth didn't lose her temper. She made a call to Personnel on Alisha's behalf and, just as importantly, the shop boss of the security guard's union, and everyone promised to look into the situation and get back to Alisha. The irate Alisha seemed mollified for the moment.

After Breuer's sudden exit and Anton's all-night train ride, it didn't take much to spook Peter Johnson these days. A hooded sweatshirt from the corner of his eyes was almost enough. So, excited and alarmed by Elizabeth's account of her conversation, he called the first member of the B & D crew he could get, who happened to be Bryce, who lost no time getting to Wallets. Tinker to Evers to Chance, and they started to grok the facts.

In an hour, Bryce and Wallets took it upon themselves to go talk to Alisha Jones. But she wanted nothing to do with them. "Burns?" Wallets wanted to ask her. But Granny was in the ground, and nobody was in the mood to dig her up again. Then Bryce, exhibiting the thoroughness required of an attorney general's son, suggested they check the Columbia-Presbyterian emergency room records for Sunday. And lo, there *was* a case of burns. James Thomas, aka Spinner. First to his apartment house; he lived with his cousin, once removed, who wanted nothing of Wallets or Bryce neither. Never mind the late young Spinner.

"Can we see his sneakers?" Bryce asked him.

"I threw them out. They're gone. All his shit."

"Sorry to bother you, Mr. Thomas."

"You're not bothering me. He bothered me. But he's not bothering nobody no more."

"Can we talk to his friends?"

"I don't *know* his friends. And you don't want to know them either."

On the way out of the building Wallets made a call to Jordan, the technician who ran the Hung Fat van; now between assignments, he was spread out on the home couch watching ESPN for the week. "Dig the Sniffer out of your toolkit and stick it in that apartment. Do it when the guy goes out to work tonight. He's got a beer concession at Madison Square Garden slinging suds. No, I *don't know* which game. And yes, I know you're not on the clock; just *bill me*."

Then down to the Chief Medical Examiner's on 2nd Avenue and 26th Street. Wallets and Bryce found Spinner just where he was supposed to be: on a sliding stainless-steel slab in a refrigerated case in the New York Medical Examiner's office. The mortuary attendant on duty pulled the stainless steel latch and slid the long metal tray out for Wallets and Bryce to admire.

Wallets took a portable Geiger counter out of his coat pocket—the thing about six inches by three in a black leather perforated case. He passed the counter over Spinner's burned feet. The needle spiked. He noticed other burns on the body. Cracked skin, blood leaking through.

"When's he due for autopsy?"

"Tonight."

"And nobody's seen him since he's arrived?"

"You're the first."

Wallets nodded for the attendant to slide the body back into the stainless-steel cold. "I think you want to tell the M.E. to do it in a hazmat suit; otherwise Do Not Pass Go; go direct to Cremation."

"Well, I *ain't* touching him!" the attendant said.

"I'd keep this close for now," Bryce told him. "Until we know what we're dealing with." The attendant shrugged. Maybe he would; maybe he wouldn't.

"If the Medical Examiner has any questions, he can use this number." Wallets handed the attendant a card. "I suppose someone will have to tell the Mayor."

The attendant shrugged again. "Ain't my call."

As he departed, Wallets remarked, "I don't know what the Workbench Boys mixed, but whatever it was didn't just burn his feet—that wouldn't have killed him. Not that fast. Maybe he ingested some."

Actually, the Medical Examiner did call Wallets, but never told the Mayor. Not that night anyway. Yeah, the kid was mildly radioactive, and yes, it had somehow gotten into Spinner's inner ear or maybe down his throat. But there just wasn't enough hard evidence. The M.E. also told the Deputy Mayor, who said, "Thank you very much," hung up, and went back to his dinner guests. Actually, His Honor was nearly the last to find out. And nearly by accident, when a science student from NYU on a field trip to the far north of Manhattan, Inwood Park, went through Christopher Street station carrying the Geology Department's Geiger counter. The thing went off like the Fourth of July as the

Uptown IRT roared through the Christopher Street station, and the student called the *New York Post*.

Well, actually before calling the *Post* the careful geology major immediately switched trains and went back to Christopher Street to verify that, *yes,* the whole place spiked his counter. *Then* he called the *New York Post.*

—◦◦◦◦—

When a phone rings in New York bearing bad news, you can be sure more than one person answers the call. They may argue about how to handle the bad news, who to inform, and who to misinform, but nobody wants to be the 911 operator who hangs up on the drowning baby thinking it's a prank. In this case, Han Lee, the thorough and alert NYU geology major, rang the city's bell. First by calling the city desk at the *New York Post*. Wisely, they brought him over to their offices to go over his story and *kept him there* for a couple of hours.

The city desk called the Deputy Mayor's Office to see if they knew anything about it. And the Deputy Mayor, slightly hung over from his dinner party, seemed to recall something about burns the night before. But not in the subway, on a slab down at the M.E.'s office. So the Deputy Mayor called the Medical Examiner for more details, and the M.E., alarmed, called Banquo & Duncan *again*, with the message "There's a kid sitting in the editor's officer over at—"

Within thirty minutes of Han Lee's first telephone call, Wallets was on his way to the midtown offices of the *Post*, and Bryce and O'Hanlon were headed there too. The Chief of Police and the Deputy Mayor were sitting in the Mayor's Office. The Mayor was still uptown near Gracie Mansion, talking to his press secretary, but en route in the limo. Smith and Wesson called the Assistant Director in charge of the greater New York field office, and somebody finally thought it a good idea to notify the Office of Homeland Security.

Nobody claimed to be in charge; nobody directed affairs from Captain America's City Command Post. And nobody called the president of the United States. Yes, the city had some sort of Crisis Center in the

Homeland Security office on Third Avenue, but the place was the loneliest office in New York, as the last one had been in the late World Trade Center. Still a gaping seven-acre hole at the bottom of the city. And yes, there *was* some sort of "secret" Command Center off Wall Street with proposed link-ups reaching into every corner of officialdom—with any luck it would cover the city sometime before the end of the century.

Later, the authorities could tell the press all about their superbly coordinated response, but right now the only thing they could do was talk on cell phones or on speaker phones in conference rooms. No real-time video links or real-time web cams. Not in a dozen different city offices, not in the Mayor's limo, or the Medical Examiner's Office—so they relied on the city's cell coverage, and you might just understand some of what they said if they talked slowly, didn't mumble, and didn't all speak at once from a secure lead-lined subbasement.

The city had a hierarchy of responses. In the best-case scenario: a prank call over public payphones claiming some sort of attack, anything from a trash fire in a rubbish barrel to the threat of an Ebola outbreak at Carnegie Hall. These calls were usually ignored. At most, the institutional security at the museum, theater, or sports arena informed. You couldn't shut the city down for every jerk who dialed the phone for cheap thrills.

In the worst-case scenario: warning of imminent mass destruction from *reliable* intel—a bomb detonation, a mustard gas attack, the dispersal of smallpox/anthrax/botox—there'd be nothing to do, just hope you were out of town. Hope they didn't nuke Jersey too, and pray the bomb squad or the hazmat team didn't get stuck in traffic.

And then there was the in-between. *Rumors* of a dirty bomb, galloping plague, the loss of electricity or water to the city, a random sniper—and whatever this *shit* was in the morgue and down in the Christopher Street subway station. The time arrived to misinform. Sit on the story. Run it down. Shut it up.

Did you think they had a plan? Federally Managed Mass Evacuation? No, *sorry.*

No evacuation plan for the city of New York existed, never would. How could it? The place is an island of millions with a dozen 1920s-era jammed choke points: six vehicular bridges, one railroad bridge, a couple of underground railways, three traffic tunnels—maybe a grand total of fourteen outbound lanes. While the whole fortress of Manhattan blocked off a very populated Long Island with millions more trapped. Three ways traversing that spit of land: the Northern State Parkway, the Long Island Expressway, the Southern State Parkway, all three roads jammed most of the day—and *no way out.* The whole mess ending at Montauk Point.

Sure, you could go west, young man. Steal a rowboat from the lake in Central Park; lug it to the Hudson River, and row to New Jersey. Whoops sorry, the currents in the Hudson would drag you out to sea, and the East River was worse.

Back in the real world, the initial phone calls were about three things. The first: to make sure somebody was going to sit on Han Lee. Second: that all the moving mouths of government knew what to say, saying the same thing for the press. And third: to find a convenient location, like a hotel, where all the principals could meet for an hour. Unnoticed, by ABCCBSNBCMSNBC et al. That was the hard part in a city of nine million people: somebody was always paying attention.

The receptionist had led Wallets through the glass doors and across the noisy bullpen toward the floor-to-ceiling glass partition of the editor's office. On a couch, Wallets could see an Asian kid playing a Game Boy. But it was O'Hanlon—already there with Bryce—who really captured his attention. The tough Irish DOJ lawyer looked like his face had been cast in black iron—angry at the world, certainly, but angrier at himself.

The editor in chief didn't mind the temporary gag order when O'Hanlon coldly explained, using the magic words, "unknown number of casualties at the city's bridges and tunnels," but did insist the *Post* have a man inside the VIP meeting.

"Nice try," Wallets told him. The boss of the paper smiled and shrugged. Then to the geology major playing Game Boy *Final Fantasy V* on the couch, Wallets asked, "Han, how would you like to earn some extra credit?"

—∞—

The VIPs decided on the Waldorf-Astoria, hotel of presidents. A massive single city block all to itself with four entrances—north, east, south, west, facilitating inconspicuous entrance and egress. The place sported the most nimble private security in the city, prepared to deal with a president's staff or a potentate's retinue.

O'Hanlon represented the Department of Justice at the table, while Bryce looked on from a metal folding chair along the wall. Wallets stayed out on the street. For what it was worth, O'Hanlon put on his best penny-loafer smile to disarm the political brutes of New York City's top governing echelon.

"Don't you think the Fire Commissioner should be here?"

Faces looked to faces; nobody had thought to call. Yes. Certainly. Right away. A chastised assistant to the Mayor's press secretary got on the phone.

"We'll wait."

—∞—

A short ten minutes later they began; unfortunately there were more questions than answers.

"Whaddaya mean you don't know what this stuff is? Don't you have a sample? What are we calling this shit, *the Grunge?* They told me you found evidence twenty-six hours ago in a Queens junkyard." This from the Fire Commissioner, already bent sideways at being the last informed and by some flunky to boot.

"No material, just traces," O'Hanlon explained; his voice got harder. "And just by freakin' *accident*, as our goddamn operation was cancelled not thirty minutes earlier." He slid the inter-agency memo across the table. "We were shut down by some bureaucrat at Langley. I'm sure you all know him." The memo made its way around the table, the name

Andover murmured. Shoulders shrugged, heads shook. Faces looked to faces once more; nobody recognized the name. And nobody wanted to be caught knowing this loser in any event.

They returned to the matter at hand, attempting to grasp the magnitude of their problem, groping its extremities. From the head of the city's Transit Department:

"You mean they coulda dumped a teaspoonful in *every* other train car? We have *miles* of rolling stock! We're going to have to uncouple every friggin' car and swab it down. I don't even think the union will allow their men inside. There's nothing in their contract about that."

From the representative of the Centers for Disease Control:

"We don't even know what the cleaning agent should be. We need a representative sample."

From the Medical Examiner:

"We're doing the autopsy now, but my preliminary finding is that the kid's brain burned up after he cleaned his ear with his pinky or touched his fingers to his mouth after touching his shoes—maybe when he retied a loose lace. In his case, there was massive capillary shrinkage in a matter of hours. That might be the nature of the particles; we just can't tell right now."

From the Chief of Police:

"Once it becomes generally known in the department, I expect a 35 percent sick out rate. Falling buildings with asbestos dust is one thing; sure, they'll go in. But asking men to patrol radioactive streets?" He wagged his head. "If it becomes common knowledge at One Police Plaza, nobody in Long Island, Westchester, or Jersey will leave their home tomorrow."

From the Chief of the Metropolitan Transit Police, his sister agency, regarding the subway cops:

"If word spreads, the Transit Authority can expect a 90 percent sick out."

Somebody asked incredulously, "You mean 10 percent will actually come in to work?"

The Transit Police Chief shrugged. "I guess the ones that just want to escape the ol' ball and chain. Radiation better than Wife. Go figure."

The Deputy Mayor was scribbling on a yellow pad. "I keep coming back to our press statement. I'm leaning toward the words 'limited exposure.' That seems safest. But those words are predicated on the idea we know what the limits are. When the hell will we know that?"

Everyone looked around the table at one another.

And O'Hanlon shined his penny-loafer smile on them, saying, "That's what we're trying to find out. A sample of the material and a general roll-up of the dispersal units. We're going to need official authorization for a general sweep. And right now we don't know how many people are involved."

"And so when the hell will we know *that*?"

———

Peter Johnson's cell phone rang. The woman's voice sounded familiar, though distant. "Turn on your laptop."

"Who is this?"

"Look at your cell phone."

A photo appeared on his cell, sent to him by text: A postage stamp–sized image, terribly clear, of a person sitting in a chair, hooded. Not like the photo taped to the back of Dr. Yahdzi's Kodak Moments back in Iran, but horribly familiar. Johnson's heart stopped.

"Will you turn on your laptop now?"

It took a moment to boot up. A window blinked for Instant Message Vid-Cam link access. Johnson hit "Allow access." The same picture again. Person in a hood. The hood came off. And this time Johnson's heart leapt into his throat and nearly came out his mouth. Giselle sat in the chair. Her eyes taped shut, her mouth taped shut. Her face looked red and bloated, tears glistened on her cheeks. The hood went back on.

Then the voice came again, and this time Johnson recognized the voice. Yasmine. The vid-cam panned, leaving Giselle in the chair and coming to Yasmine, who sat behind a table, much as she had back in Mahabad, at the interrogation.

"I'm not going to tell you twice. If I have to repeat anything, no matter how simple, we cut something off her. Understand?"

"Yes."

Here Yasmine began to explain. "My colleagues feel that the only purpose for this white American whore is to die in the service of Allah. Do you have any questions?"

"No."

Yasmine explained more. "Of course, we could execute her for pure punishment—but frankly that is not enough. We need to achieve something greater than the American whore's mere life. And alive, she can still serve a purpose. Do you agree?"

"Yes."

Yasmine asked one question, "And you will help us?"

"Yes."

"Very good. Anton will contact you. You will meet him and do what he says. Is there anything you do not understand?"

Johnson said one final word: "No."

He felt as sick as he had sitting at the interrogation table in Iran moments from wetting himself. The possibility of something like this lurked in the back of his mind ever since his fingers touched the photo of Giselle taped on the back of the picture. He felt a kind of nightmarish vindication: *dammit all to hell, he knew it.* And wanted to kneecap every bastard at B & D, castrate every authority in the city and federal government who allowed this—but, above all hated himself. He squeezed his eyes shut tight, knowing he was going to weep.

———— ❦ ————

Anton met him at a familiar restaurant, out in the open. Why not? This wasn't back-alley; this was pure blackmail and as such could be done in the light of day, or should we say the light of Il Monello once again.

Johnson sat down with a knot in his stomach and kept his hands in his lap, lest Anton see them shaking. Trembling hands, and sober too. He glared at Anton with fantasies of grabbing him by that impeccable hair, slamming his head into the table where they sat, again and again, wine glasses falling to the floor and the tablecloth slowly staining bright red from the Frenchman's bleeding forehead. In front of everyone. His hands had stopped shaking.

Anton saw none of this in Johnson's eyes, merely turning his wrists this way and that to admire his new Alfred Dunhill Onyx Coin cuff links.

Anton began, "I know what you're thinking, but . . . "

"Please," Johnson said, "no bullshit. Just tell me what you want."

He reached into the breast pocket of his jacket and took out a fold of papers. They slid across the tablecloth. "Here."

Johnson unfolded the multiple sheaves as the waiter appeared with a Shiraz and began the business of uncorking the bottle. Johnson felt horribly exposed, trying to focus on the writing in front of him and gritting his teeth at the pop of the cork and the little gurgle as the waiter gave Anton his "taste" for approval. The wine swirled in the Frenchie's glass, the required snuff of the aroma, the ceremonial sip, the nod of approval.

At first Johnson thought the papers were some kind of mistake; then he realized they were an affidavit of some sort, three copies like multiple contracts:

"I, Peter Johnson, being of sound mind and body wish to confess and testify to the details and particulars of my recent trip to Iran. First to admit that I traveled as an intelligence agent at the behest of the United States to injure the Islamic Republic of Iran in violation of the UN Charter, international laws, and comity of nations. Failing in my mission to secure state secrets and intelligence, I sought to assassinate Dr. Ramses Pahlevi Yahdzi of the University of Isfahan as per my instructions. In attempting this outrageous mission I have abused the trust of the people of Iran, a people of peace and righteousness who wish harm to no nation or race. I have sullied myself and my country in the eyes of the world and of Allah . . . " This business went on for about ten pages in a similar vein. He flipped to the second and third pages, full of dense type blurring together.

"They want a confession," Johnson said.

Anton took a snootful of the Shiraz. "Obviously." He paused from his wine to stare at Johnson across the white tablecloth. And suddenly Johnson noticed the table was only set for one.

"The affidavit will be released along with the videotapes of your interrogations, when the time comes. Everything in a nice bow." Anton made a motion with his hands, like tying a knot. "But they also want this confession in *your own* handwriting, so you'll have to copy it out and return it."

He pulled out a maroon—technically Bordeaux-colored—Montblanc Classique Meisterstuck pen from the pocket of his suit jacket, uncapped it, and held it out to Johnson: "You can sign and date the bottom of the last page there, right here. I'll take two copies now."

Were they out of their minds? Johnson wanted to shout, but kept himself in check. Yet it made a kind of sense. A kind of justification: *you hit us; we hit you.* Backdated payback. He checked the dateline— yeah, three weeks ago, while he was still in Iran. Now they could justify anything.

"*She trusted you,*" Johnson said, his voice rising despite himself.

"Don't make a scene," Anton replied, flatly.

"Don't make a scene!" Johnson hissed under his breath, his fingers curled around the tablecloth. "What about Giselle?" A couple at a table within earshot at a nearby table looked their way, then quickly averted their eyes—a domestic dispute, none of their business.

Anton reached over the table and put his hand on top of one of Johnson's. Not to reassure, but to control. He pressed it downward slightly, and his eyes widened, as his speech slowed down, deliberate, not to be mistaken: "I'm really glad we had this chance to talk."

Johnson closed his eyes and slumped in his seat, paralyzed by the image of his bound and gagged daughter. Of all the dissipations and betrayals of his life, of all the ways he had let her down, nothing, *nothing* compared to this. Had he really and truly considered the price of his decision? To go to Iran, to sit in a stinking car through a sandstorm, to pull the trigger? The answer so obvious now. He must have been crazy.

What could he do, except what the odious French banker wanted? A confession was the least of it; they had his kid. He opened his eyes, and Anton was holding the pen up again, looking bored. Johnson could see the engraving of Anton's initials at the top of it, in serif type, AHA. *Ah-hah.* He flipped to the last page of the first copy and hastily signed. Then put down the pen and handed it back, keeping the remainder of the sheaves. "When do you need my handwritten version?"

Anton settled back in his seat. "Tonight," he said amicably. "That shouldn't be too difficult."

He offered him a tiny electronic device, about the size of a matchbook. "Here, it's a wire. A little insurance. We hear everything you do, and, because it can be tracked, someone will be following your every move . . ." He paused to break a heel of bread from his roll and found the butter plate.

"As for me, I'm going to sit here and have an early dinner. After dinner I'm taking your first ex-wife to the Mamet on Broadway. That should give you plenty of time. Now go back to Brooklyn, and do what you do best—write."

———— ∞ ————

Johnson stood outside his Brooklyn Heights apartment and put the key in the front lobby door. Then wondered if Yasmine was listening to the sound of his key in the door from some obscure corner of New York, with Giselle nearby. The thought made him want to crawl away and die.

He stabbed the elevator button and waited, sinking into himself, feeling smaller and smaller. The car groaned quietly down to his level and clunked to a stop, and the door slid open. Someone inside—Johnson hardly bothered looking up. But when he did, nearly gasped. Wallets stood in front of him, with a finger to his lips in an emphatic sign to keep quiet. *Shush.*

They rode up to Johnson's apartment together in silence and went inside. Still, Johnson couldn't settle down; his eyes felt like they were going to pop out of his head. Wallets waved him toward the back of the apartment. A guy in a Padres cap and plumber's jeans came out of his bedroom. Right, the technician—Jordan? Yeah, the thorough and deliberate Jordan—from the surveillance van that early morning in Brooklyn after Johnson's wild subway ride. Jordan too held a finger to his lips. He came over to Johnson, fished the tracking device out of Johnson's pocket. He patted Johnson down and, finding his cell phone, fished that out and began fiddling with it on Johnson's desk. The technician had set up equipment: a kind of laptop with snug foam receptacles that allowed both the cell phone and Anton's little matchbook tracking unit to be pressed into the foam and hook up. Apparently the technician was making the two devices talk to each other. Wallets put his finger to his lips again. *Sheesh, he didn't need to be told three times!*

Satisfied, Jordan the Technician put Johnson's phone and electronic matchbook on the desk. Wallets led Johnson the few paces back toward the front door and paused there while the technician went into the bathroom. When the toilet flushed, Wallets opened the door and escorted Johnson out the door. Then the technician turned on the shower. Cover noise.

A few steps down the hall, Johnson blurted. "They've got Giselle."

Wallets didn't raise his voice, just nodded: "We know."

Johnson wanted to blurt a thousand expletives, but Wallets' matter-of-fact explanation pre-empted him: "We've grafted your cell phone CPU onto *their* tracking device. Cloned it, so to speak. Make some noise at this end, and it'll be picked up by the matchbook, and we'll be able to trace it back to its source. Sort of like a party line. Wherever they're listening. They track you with their device; we track them with their device. Every signal a two-way street. They'll still hear your voice but won't know we're listening in too."

"Okay. Where are we going?"

"We're not going anywhere, yet."

Jordan the Technician came out into the hall and gave thumbs up. All set.

"Now go finish your shower, scribble up what you have to for Frenchie, and wait for his call. We'll be downstairs."

Back in the apartment Johnson saw the Hung Fat van idling in front, in all its white clunky glory. *God bless Jordan.* They'd laid pen and paper out for him. And his hands were shaking again.

Anton's call came about 7 PM. So the Frenchie banker had decided to abandon Mamet. The two men arranged to meet at Carl Schurz Park, a thin strip of manicured lawn and garden that hugged the river's edge of Manhattan, overlooking the FDR Drive, the city's east-side artery.

Night cast a pall across the East River. The bell-shaped classic New York street lamps made strollers cast shadows along the paving stones and the trees in the park, their bare branches reaching to the bald faces of stone luxury apartments.

Johnson saw Anton approach from East End Avenue under the trees of the park.

The two men stood on the river promenade. The cars roaring along the roadway underneath their feet provided the thrumming undercurrent to Johnson's anger.

"Look, you *garçon de merde*, here—take your parchment." He shoved his handwritten confession and the affidavits back. "Now how do I get my daughter?"

Anton sneered at him, and Johnson could see the sneer like a yellow smile under the lights. Johnson stared back at the young man, eyes blank and challenging. As good an imitation of Wallets' gravedigger eyes as he could muster. Anton stepped away from Johnson, whispering muted words over the roar of traffic.

"We'll let you know."

Dismissing Johnson, he flipped open his cell phone and walked lightly toward the welcoming narrow strip of parkland, then the luxurious east side of Manhattan. And he didn't get twenty steps.

Three guys appeared as if by magic out of the bushes, two more from behind trees, another two were holding hands nearby and slapped handcuffs on him before he could squawk.

"Monsieur Anton Anjou? You are under arrest—"

And now Anton began to shriek in a castrato's voice:

"No, no, no! I have Rights! I have Rights!"

Back in the Hung Fat van, Anton's call was traced to a loft space on 35th Street between Fifth Avenue and Sixth. The Garment District. Rug merchants selling $50,000 Bokharas, Korean restaurants down the side streets, and crummy walk-up flats over the thread-needle houses. One-third of all clothing manufactured in the U.S. is designed and produced in this neighborhood—though the huge sweatshops are long gone to less expensive real estate in Jersey or Florida, Texas and Mexico, and further afield to the factories of Taiwan, Malaysia, all points east. The area still had a kind of 19ᵗʰ century Industrial Revolution feel about it: big square clunky buildings, block after block, squeezing the narrow cross streets. During business hours, delivery trucks, garment workers, rolling racks from cut-shop to warehouse choke the district curb-to-curb. Feeding its lace or bead sellers, textile importers, fabric shops, and of course, some of America's most famous designers, Oscar de la Fendi and the rest of the Haute Couture clans. From nine to five, Monday through Friday, the long narrow streets in the district were a roiling Hogarth print.

But at night the place became a graveyard. They parked by a fire hydrant on 35ᵗʰ Street a hundred yards west of Fifth Avenue, making the Hung Fat van stand out like the Barnum & Bailey clown mobile, and it didn't help that four police cars blocked off both ends of 35ᵗʰ Street, and two NYPD SWAT trucks parked on either side of the building entrance.

"*This? This* is the plan?" Johnson had hitched a ride, now crouched in a corner of the Hung Fat van sitting in the semidarkness next to Jordan the Technician, who smelled vaguely of Bonomo's banana Turkish taffy, Slim Jims, and Lay's Rancho potato chips, which seemed to cover all the food groups as far as the man was concerned. Smith had slithered up next to Wesson, and Bryce huddled on the opposite side, while geology student Han Lee, earning extra credit, scrunched himself on Bryce's skinny lap like Edgar Bergen's wooden sidekick, Charlie McCarthy. And finally Wallets, thinking of nobody's comfort as usual, smoked a cigarette—making the whole lot thoroughly nauseated.

"Can someone please crack the door?" Johnson asked softly; he could feel the cigarette smoke going right to his stomach, twisting it into knots.

"Will someone shut him up? I'm watching TV," Jordan said, mouth working over taffy.

Johnson snapped, "Nobody asked you—" his gratitude from earlier ancient history.

And the whole van barked, "*Shut up!*"

And so they watched TV in silence. Geology major Han using his expert's eyes to see if there were any radioactive hot spots on the colored tubes. Not that Jordan really needed the help, but another pair of eyes couldn't hurt, and besides, nobody was going to turn young Han loose on the city yet. Or back to the *New York Post* editorial offices. Double secret probation.

Three monitors stared back at them, but only two at the moment showed images, the last just a blue screen. The first monitor fed RT vidcam from a SWAT team member's helmet labeled **SWAT, Murphy**, with the cop's badge number. So on Monitor One Johnson saw what the cop saw, stifling his impulse to shout, *Hurry!* The policeman crept along, one in a line of officers down what looked like a dingy stairwell-hallway. In the van, they all watched the bobbing heads of other SWAT helmets that **SWAT, Murphy** showed them, and Johnson squirmed in silence—every sound from the hallway magnified, shuffling, waiting for orders. It couldn't have been that noisy in the hallway itself. What were they waiting for?

The second monitor gave the target apartment in microwave image and was piped over to the SWAT team leader's laptop, a map he could read. The image showed the ghostly outline of the fourth floor: a large loft space, in some places duplex-high, maybe a couple of thousand square feet. The place divided into 3-D rectangles and boxes, with a main hallway running from front door to a fire door at the back. So you had one main artery with mini hallways and rooms, some larger, some smaller, branching off on either side—and two stairways to upper-level rooms or platforms.

The red and yellow ghosts of the Iranian occupants moved from one room to another, unaware they were being watched. Some sitting at tables, others standing before the white hot burners of a stove, then opening the dark blue of a refrigerator. A bathroom showed through as a blinding green mist as someone took a shower, his body also green except for the red pumping of his heart.

"Jesus, the thing's a fucking maze," the technician commented, as he swallowed a wad of banana glue.

"No hot spots that I can see," geology major Han told them.

"See if you can locate one isolated body," Wallets said. "That may be her." Johnson wanted to crawl into the screen, go through the wires himself. *Find her.* C'mon, she's there; just look!

The third monitor suddenly blinked on with a new live feed. This from a miniature audio-video probe inserted under the front door, showing merely baseboards, and a long, empty hall. At the far edge of the camera, someone's shoes walked across the frame and vanished. Friggin' pointless. They jerked the probe back, and the monitor went blue again. Should he smash the screen? Not yet . . . *Stifle yourself.*

The technician chomped on a Slim Jim and used his joystick to traipse down halls and up stairways through the bright microwave hues. Then he stopped. A small room, upper level—a body signature. The body was curled up on the floor in a fetal position. Johnson found himself grasping the technician's armrest in a death grip. The man glanced at him, and he knew enough to let go.

"Yeah," Wallets said. Then began to speak into a headset connecting Hung Fat to the SWAT Team Leader. "We count nine. She's number ten. Up and to the right." Then listened carefully, just repeating what the Tactical Unit Commander told him. "Flash-bang? Then gas? Uh-huh. Yup. Uh-huh. Good luck. See you at the front door."

The video from **SWAT, Murphy** tilted back and forth as the SWAT team began to murmur to one another, recapping their plan: the order of clearing room by room. The extra two-man team reserved for securing Giselle both said, "Right," at the same time.

All at once the Real-Time Cam on **SWAT, Murphy** exploded with light. The loft's front door went down; flash-bang grenades whumped twice in the hallway. Then the long hiss from tear gas. And with the tear gas floating in every direction you couldn't see a damn thing. So everyone's eyes went back to the microwave monitor. They could see the tactical team members rushing down the hallway in a tight formation, then splitting off room by room. In some rooms taking bodies by surprise. In others the flash of gunfire. Some bodies fell; then men swarmed over the fallen.

The joystick followed the two tacticals assigned to Giselle up a flight of stairs, then bashing into a room. The body on the floor leapt up in fear.

And Wallets' sober voice filled the Hung Fat van: "We have her." And then to Johnson alone: "She's okay."

Johnson nodded tightly once in thanks, his face very pale. Suddenly he rose from his place. Shoving past the technician just as the man popped a bag of Lay's Rancho, and knocking the chips everywhere: "Thank you. Sorry, sorry. Thank you," breathing heavily. "I don't feel well, I'm gonna be—" And clanged past Wallets and into the street.

⸺⸺⸺

Johnson barely recovered in time to press Giselle's hand as she came out of the building on a stretcher; she looked up at him with glassy eyes and weakly pressed his hand back. "They sedated her," a paramedic explained. "Makes 'em easier to handle." Before he could reply the ambulance doors banged shut. St. Luke's Roosevelt Hospital. He'd remember that.

Then from the shadow of the Hung Fat van he watched Yasmine led from the building, hands cuffed behind her back and placed in a waiting NYPD paddy wagon along with the others arrested in the loft. She seemed of all things, mildly distracted, even *bored*—and didn't notice him. Mission accomplished?

Fifteen minutes and fifteen blocks later, the paddy wagon followed by the Hung Fat van pulled up to the limousine entrance of the Waldorf-Astoria Hotel on 49th Street between Lexington and Park Avenue. The limo entrance, reserved for VIPs, was a cavelike carport a single car wide, which ran the length of the building from 49th Street to 50th north-south. The squat car park forbidding: a low narrow tunnel that widened slightly to two lanes. A vehicle could enter and vanish from the streets, then slip out the other side unseen. The limo pass-through was low-ceilinged, cramped, and darker still, as there were almost no lights in this place—a long narrow corridor, bare concrete apron, bare concrete walls.

Recessed hotel entrances led from the two-lane limo corridor, curb-side vestibules. Oddly, the vestibules were brightly lit but illuminated nothing beyond: people could exit a limo and vanish into the hotel with no one the wiser. The west vestibule led to the Waldorf proper, the other to the "Security Tower" to the east. A separate section of the hotel reserved for VIPs, with added features—lockdown elevators, private conference areas, and quarters for private security. The two-lane limo corridor was also adjacent to a large delivery bay, a cutout, leading directly to the service elevators. A dark service bay and wide service elevator stood about four feet off the ground ever-ready for deliveries.

A phalanx of city cops entered from both sides of the street surrounding the holding vehicle, a tight wall of blue. In the Hung Fat van outside the hotel on 49th Street, Wallets offered Johnson a handkerchief and a cracked bar of Bonomo in its silvery paper.

"Nothing's going to happen to them for a while," Wallets said, nodding at the van. He meant the prisoners. "They'll cool their heels half the night. Here, wipe your mouth, have some taffy, and let's go upstairs. I have things to do."

CHAPTER TWENTY-FOUR

Spot the Idiot

Earlier that evening a fellow named Walid exited the Union Square subway at the southeast corner of Union Square Park. He had appeared inconspicuously enough under the round frilly green awning that is one of the park's signatures: an art nouveau aedicule slightly reminiscent of 1890s Gay Paree, but this one an overblown glass-and-metal translucent awning like a skylight in Captain Nemo's *Nautilus*. He walked past a young girl in a bright T-shirt trying to hand out tickets for a comedy show and a bearded guy taking signatures for some petition or other. Walid's gait was brisk but stiff.

No one noticed when he reached back with his gloved hand to feel for a Velcro flap on the side of his backpack. With practiced fingers, he pulled it open. His eyes stared straight ahead, and he never stopped walking. Up the three steps from the sidewalk toward the Union Square Park entrance, he mingled among a small crowd. Passersby were listening to a tinfoil-hat buffoon with a bullhorn standing next to a big red banner with white lettering proclaiming "9/11 Inside Job." The large banner showed the famous photo of the World Trade Center Tower collapsing on itself, and below the caption "controlled implosion."

The protestor's amplified voice echoed around the square: "This regime will never tell us the truth! This regime lives on lies! This regime staged this *so-called* terror attack! I have a physics degree from NYU, and I can categorically—"

Walid kept walking into the park, past the usually unnoticed statue of George Washington on a horse. He walked north up the park's eastern pathway, unevenly paved with pentagonal stones, benches on either side with people enjoying the early evening of a gorgeous mid-September day: couples talking or making out, a bum sitting with his grocery cart full of bags of aluminum cans, a mangy twenty-something guy strumming Dylan on a guitar, people doing a sudoku puzzle or reading the *Times* or a book.

Walid walked the length of the park down this path, occasionally looking behind him, like something was dogging him, a tail or maybe just a bad conscience. He took a left out of the park—the neon-red sign of the pretentious restaurant Coffee Shop ahead of him—and doubled down its outside perimeter southward, past a jazz band playing for dollar bills thrown in an open guitar case and the skateboarders doing their ollies and other tricks on the vacant asphalt between the iron park fence and Broadway. He walked on . . . past panel trucks from the farmers' market packing up the merchants' produce at the end of the day; past the statue of a frail Gandhi, a necklace of withering flowers around his neck; past the dog run with dogs of all shapes and sizes chasing and sniffing and barking at each other with the simple joy of life. Finally passing the exit he had just come from, making a full circuit. He kept on for another loop.

Along the sidewalk this time, past the people sitting on the steps of Union Square and among all the foot traffic of people coming from work. He stayed on the sidewalk northward, up the west side of the park along its chest-high exterior stone wall, past a newsstand and another subway exit and to the northwest entrance to the park, where he crossed the park yet again, past the people lined up for happy hour at a streetside bar called Luna Park, with tables under umbrellas and waitresses holding drink trays high in the air to squeeze between customers.

All the while a crumbly metallic grey substance fell from his backpack. A little stream of fairy dust, unnoticed in the gathering dusk.

Back on the east side of the park, he reached with his right hand and jostled the backpack, feeling it was much lighter than before. Almost empty.

He approached the steps of the nearest subway entrance, the northern one this time, and slid the backpack off his shoulders. Then looked all around and shoved it into the shiny metal trash can—*against orders*. His was lead-lined, a makeshift job with the heavy lead-laced fabric from an X-ray vest, sewn inside. All packs were supposed to be returned and not left for anyone to find, but he wanted none of it anymore.

Metro card in hand, he swiped himself through the stainless-steel turnstile and trotted downstairs toward the Downtown Number 4 platform, angling his body sideways to avoid the masses surging toward the exits.

Once on the platform Walid paced back and forth, waiting for the train, talking to himself. The hellish screech of other trains coming and leaving along the curved tracks of the station screamed into his jumbled thoughts verging on panic: telling him to get home, to get home now, right now. He pushed into the Downtown Number 4 as soon as it came, not waiting for people to exit first, as is the etiquette, as was proper, as everyone who ever rode a New York City subway knew without having to be told. Once inside, he snatched the handicapped seat at the front of the car, slapped it down on its wall-mounted hinges, and sat, elbows to knees, his head in his hands. Then started to rock his body. Rocking as if his motion would speed the motion of the train.

The other passengers took a step or two away, as New Yorkers do when they think they're in close proximity to the mad. Walid found himself alone in a safe little corner, or as alone as you could be in a crowded subway car. Rocking away the world.

Back in Union Square, a fashionable woman in her mid-thirties pulled her *Princess* away from the dog run. Time to go home, drop her off, and meet a friend for an early drink. Even with iPod buds in her ears and a Starbucks coffee cup in one of her gloved hands, she noticed something wrong. Her Shih Tzu was starting to whimper.

In the well-appointed Waldorf-Astoria conference room, various parties were still in the early stages of hashing out the question of municipal meltdown. The issue before them—a yawning abyss—and a lot of panicked officialdom was ready to jump. The answer as to *where* one stood now ranged from right on the lip of the precipice, toes over the edge—the Fire Commissioner, MTA Police Chief, NYC Police Commissioner—to a step back—Homeland Security, the city's Medical Examiner, the CDC, and the Chief of the city's Health and Hospitals Corporation, recently summoned with an entourage of six flunkies. The "secret" NYPD officer from the Wall Street "secret" Command Center, a no-show.

In the last twenty minutes, the number of "people in the know" had widened considerably and to the city's peril. Pretty soon the knowledge would spread out of control, escape the Waldorf, and start flashing on the Times Square Jumbo-Tron.

O'Hanlon walked quietly to a corner of the room and called Banquo on his cell. Without even introducing himself he whispered hoarsely, "We need you over here pronto."

"Where's Pronto?"

"Waldorf, Suite 11A. Security Tower. That's the South Tower. Everyone's here—the Mayor, everybody. It's going down. You were right, it's going down, and I just want to say, I should have ... "

Banquo's voice came back gravely, "Stop. Forget about it." When he felt O'Hanlon shake the guilt from his shoulders, Banquo gave the DOJ lawyer a clue as to where they stood:

"As you may have suspected, I'm being made something of a nonperson. Well, either a nonperson or the very prominent person blamed for everything. I've got an internal investigation on me and on B & D too. The Deputy Executive Director and his toadies at the FBI DC Headquarters are watching my every step. This morning the *Washington Post* says I'm a 'controversial mystery operative who bends the rules in what is supposed to be an era of greater accountability and oversight, sources say.'" His voice sneered at the last two words.

"Look, no one here reads the *Washington Post*; it's all the other *Post*," O'Hanlon shot back. "And this is one of those days when no one will remember what happened the day before. The slate is wiped clean. We *need* you here. Where the hell are you?"

"Close enough."

Twenty minutes later the elegant spymaster opened the conference room door, paused for a moment to take in the scene. Instead of seven people at the conference table talking reasonably, there were eighteen: a noisy murmuring gaggle of competing interests, scribbling note takers, babbling Bluetooth wireless headsets, everyone talking at once and nobody listening.

O'Hanlon got up from his spot and threw a legal pad down on the table with a harsh slap. The noise brought the group to a sudden pause. For a long moment, he held each person's eyes in his own. Then graciously gave his seat to Banquo, introducing him as an intelligence official who had been on the case from the beginning, adding two harsh words: "Pay attention."

Whatever uncharacteristic reticence that Banquo exhibited on their call together had now vanished. He pulled his chair up to the table and announced, unbidden, "We have a nuclear insurgency right here in New York City. As we speak, the populace is being poisoned by roaming Jihadis with radioactive material. Now, quite obviously, we've got to stop it."

The Mayor leaned over to mutter something to his Deputy Mayor— from the look on his face it was something like, *Who is this guy?*

Banquo's words weren't an invitation for ideas but a prelude to his own plan, now that he was fully briefed by Wallets on the street and O'Hanlon in the conference room. "The Iranians picked up in the Garment District raid *must* be interrogated. Literally right here. And right now. There's no time for crossed lines of communication."

"In this room?" someone asked.

"Of course not. We'll have the hotel secure this entire floor, and a couple of the other conference rooms will be our interrogation cells." Eyes drifted over to the Mayor, who, with his arms crossed, nodded wordlessly. An aide began relaying the order to the hotel.

"Every Workbench Boy we've already identified has to be rolled up, along with any close friends or associates, and anyone identified in our ongoing intelligence operation."

Everyone nodded.

"We need every Farsi speaker that the NYPD or the FBI has in the tri-state area up here on this floor."

"Done," said O'Hanlon. "Done," said the Police Commissioner. O'Hanlon and the Commish's aide fired up their cell phones.

"We need every member of the Iranian UN delegation detained for questioning, and one Farah Nasir arrested immediately."

"Whoa!" The Mayor held up his hands.

Another voice: "I think international incidents are above everyone's pay grade here," the city's Corporation Counsel, a lawyer in tortoise-shell Tojo glasses. Uber-dweeb.

"Well, you've got an international incident already, like it or not," Banquo told him. "Who do you need to hear from?"

"I don't know," the Corporation Counsel said meekly. "How about the Attorney General of the United States?"

"Is Washington informed and ready to act?" Banquo asked, and Bryce—his cell phone to his ear—nodded tightly.

"You're talking to your contact at Justice?" Banquo asked, a hint of a smile on his lips, knowing full well the exalted identity at the other end of the line. Bryce nodded tightly again, keeping it to himself, but quietly relishing the moment. Speaking professionally into the phone, "Yes, sir. Yes, I understand. We'll be careful." Only Banquo heard the word "Dad" at the end.

O'Hanlon elaborated, "Main Justice knows everything, and they're briefing the White House. When the Oval Office realizes the gravity and long-term repercussions of this, we're going to get big-footed, but for now we're supposed to handle it as we see fit."

Bryce approached the Mayor and handed him his cell phone, which Hizzoner looked at querulously. "The attorney general," Bryce explained. The Mayor said hello, listened, and a few moments later closed and handed the phone back to Bryce. "We're OK on the Iranian Dips," he said to everyone.

"Now," said Banquo, "we need to fix the procedures for interrogation."

"The hotel is clearing the floor now." This from the Chief of Police again. "It's all ours in about four minutes, and the Iranians from the Garment District haul are waiting behind a cordon in the limousine drive-thru. Still in the vans. Say the word, and we'll bring them to the lockdown elevators. I've assigned us a full set of suites and conference rooms on the other side of the floor."

O'Hanlon waved a piece of paper that had mysteriously emerged from a fax machine in one corner. "I've got the Department of Justice waiver authorizing us to stop this attack right here. And by authorization, we mean by *any means necessary*." He paused looking from face to face around the conference table.

"So who signs it?" The men in the room started to look from one to the other, measuring the question.

Somebody made the stupid remark, "You mean torture, don't you?" saying what wasn't supposed to be said. Everyone looked at the speaker, playing Spot the Idiot.

The Mayor.

Banquo sighed. "We mean, by *any* means."

The Mayor looked over to the city's Corporation Counsel, who said, "We'll need time to review the document, and we'll need it in triplicate."

"You've got to be friggin' kiddin' me," O'Hanlon said, dropping all his Gs, as he always did when he was upset.

Banquo looked down at the table, as if gathering himself. He didn't look at the Corporation Counsel or the Mayor, but straight ahead above everyone's heads at the wall in front of him: "We've all heard of a 'ticking time bomb' scenario, the most extreme circumstance in which a detained subject may have information to stop an imminent attack. It is widely agreed that such a context changes what questioning techniques can be used, whether or not they—'shock the conscience.' All by way of saying," and here Banquo lowered his eyes and looked straight at the Mayor, slowing down his words, "this . . . *isn't* . . . a ticking-bomb scenario . . . but a bombs-going-off scenario. Do you understand the difference?"

The Corporation Counsel stood up and walked over to the Mayor, leaning down above him to have a whispered conversation.

They both stopped and looked up when Banquo added:

"Anyone standing in the way of getting information now, in this situation, should feel obliged to personally explain to the family of every single person killed or sickened why they let it happen."

Johnson thought again back to that long-ago NYU panel: *If they didn't kill you or someone you love, it wasn't for lack of trying.*

The Mayor was back to whispering. But Banquo wouldn't let him hide in plain sight. "Are you prepared to do that, Mr. Mayor?"

The Mayor, a finely tailored bachelor known for dating actresses and models and knowing—and prizing the approval of—all the right people, looked flabbergasted. Nobody talked to him this way. Nobody.

"Or will you have your lawyer do it for you, Mr. Mayor?" The room went totally still, fixated on this quiet confrontation, this test of wills across the conference table.

"There's no need for this kind of ad hominem personal . . . " the Mayor started to say.

"Or how about your scribbler of a publicist here? Think he should do it, Mr. Mayor?"

Banquo looked away in disgust and started to give orders in preparation for the interrogations. More whispering, now furious between the Mayor and his lawyer, and the Mayor piped up to interrupt Banquo: "I can't be a party to this."

"Fine, leave," Banquo said, and kept giving instructions to those around him. The city officials in the room pretended not to be watching the Mayor's every move, but they all were. Would he actually leave? Had the man ever been talked to in this way in his life? They watched him shrink before their eyes, a political pygmy in a blue pinpoint Oxford shirt with a white collar and starched cuffs. Nervously fiddling with one gold link. He wasn't heard from for another few minutes, until the Corporation Counsel piped up on his behalf, saying, "Yes, we'll sign."

By then, no one seemed to care. The Mayor had become an irrelevancy. There was a city to save.

Information poured in from all over New York, hurriedly whispered by one aide or another around the large conference table. And orders were issued by one of the principals, the Police Commissioner, O'Hanlon, the Fire Commissioner—often by Banquo, even though he ran no department or agency. Every person looked to him; every ego in the room willingly accepted his naturally assumed authority. When in doubt, go to the Answer Man.

"We've got reports of dogs dying in Union Square."

"Chief, I suggest you cordon off Union Square from 18th Street down to 12th and from Irving Place to Fifth."

"We've got a playground—hold on. Yeah, we've got a school playground on the Upper East Side, where a young Middle Eastern man was hanging around, acting weird. Don't know if it's anything, but . . ."

"Don't assume. Bring the school principal or whoever saw him down here. If the weirdo's still there, arrest him. Find all the children who went home from school; say it's a gas leak. Take names and addresses. And get a hazmat team over there."

"Gentlemen, this is a call from Brooklyn, the King's County Medical Center. A guy showed up in the emergency room, dizzy and disoriented in a crazy getup. He had painted pants and shoes. They thought he was suffering from fumes, but they think it might be radiation poisoning."

At this Banquo's eyes flashed. "*That's* our first guy. Whatever they do, don't let the bastard die. Get agents out there now, plus the best radiation specialist in the city we can find." The Medical Examiner said, "Yessir!" and left the table.

From a nameless aide down the table: "This seems improbable, but we've got reports of an attempted suicide in the city's reservoir. Someone jumping in and out of a rowboat. Homeowners up there are suspicious."

"Which reservoir?"

"Titicus, in North Salem, Westchester."

"So what are you saying? Someone trying to suicide-bomb the water supply? Doubtful. Does the Coast Guard have a dive team for the Croton Reservoir System?"

"The North Salem Sheriff has him in holding. And yes, he's got a backpack."

"Send another hazmat team. They may have one in White Plains. If not, use the NYPD helicopter."

"Good news, they caught some guy napping. Literally napping at the Queens row . . . what should we call it? Safe house?"

"Well, that's good news and bad news. Good news, because we can pump him on site, then drag him here. Bad news: he had three roommates. And who knows how many houses like this we're talking about?"

"There's something bizarre. All the sinks were clogged with hair."

"It's not bizarre. It's ritualistic shaving—in case they die."

Silence.

The breathless, nameless reservoir aide looked up from his cell phone, hurriedly whispering so everyone could hear:

"Forget the reservoir. The Sheriff called—a domestic dispute. Husband leaves the house in fury, steals a rowboat, and rows off, no backpack—an 'asthma attack' in the middle of the lake. Cell-phoned 911. We've recalled the chopper."

The look from Banquo's eyes could have turned Medusa herself to stone. The aide wisely vanished.

⁂

Farah Nasir—Junior Service Officer, Iranian Mission to the United Nations—lived in a prewar building on Second Avenue and 48th Street, within walking distance of the UN. Wallets, together with Smith and Wesson fresh from the Garment District raid, double-parked the pistachio-shelled sedan by a hydrant. Wallets brushed down the seat and remarked, "When we're done, Banquo & Duncan is getting you two a housekeeper."

Four police cars trailed them, splitting off on either side of the street, doused their lights, and waited. A Manhattan street at night, street lamps shining down—easy to miss the curtain move at the window of Nasir's seventh-floor apartment. From the trunk of the pistachio sedan Wallets and the two federal women slapped on tactical Kevlar vests, Velcroing the cinch tabs tight. "God, I hate these things," one of the women said. Smith. Wesson made no remark. And Wallets knew what she meant; wearing the vest could save your life, but it was a clunky, movement-constricting extra ten pounds.

The three of them walked into the dark low-ceilinged lobby, where a part-time doorman asked who they were there to see. They waved him off with their badges and headed straight to the elevator. The box was old-school Otis Elevator Model B circa 1930. They had to wait three minutes—an age—for it to come down, then pull open the door and push aside the metal accordion-style gate to step inside. Only four of them could fit: the three Feds plus a cop, whose name was Carmine. The cab inched upward with groaning and whirring sounds. They watched the floors descend to meet them and disappear beneath their feet through the gate, as Wallets tapped his knuckle against metal: clack-clack-clack. Finally, the seventh floor, and they headed right down the hallway toward 7F. The cop lagged behind them watching their backs down the length of the hallway. Wesson knocked on the door, "Federal agents. Open up!"

They all heard an insistent beeping. A smoke alarm. Wesson pounded on the door again with the bottom of her clenched fist, then took a step back. She kicked the door with all her might. It was a thick dead-bolted door that didn't budge. She glanced at Wallets, who tried his luck. Nope, just a thump and a bang. Then they all looked to Carmine the Cop.

"No way. I got a Mity Mouse down in the squad car."

"Get it. And use the stairs."

Carmine talked into his radio, "Bring the Mouse. Take the stairs."

After two minutes Carmine the Cop's partner, Doleful Duane, appeared, huffing and puffing after his seven-story workout. He handed the tactical entry device, the breaching ram, off to Wallets. Who slammed it into the door, releasing its internal thumper, and blew the door open. The acrid smell of burning plastic assaulted their nostrils. The smoke alarm kept on shrieking at them and then just as suddenly died. The silence rang in their ears.

Two steps in, the sound of a pistol cocking, the hammer clicking back cut through the smoke—an unmistakable sound—and everyone pasted themselves against the wall in the foyer. "Shit," Wallets said to the others, "stay back. No matter what." Clearly, Farah Nasir was no use to them dead.

He waited a beat and swung around into the main room, his gun in front of him. Black-burned plastic filaments floating in the air like dark snow. Light came in from the kitchen and that nauseating burning plastic smell. He inched his way around the barren room and into the kitchen. A kitchen devoid of food or cooking utensils. A kitchen nobody used. The burner on the gas stove blew full blast under the smoldering ruin of a laptop. The computer's fire retardant plastic shell was refusing to ignite into a fireball but still put out a ton of smoke and a cloud of charred filaments floated across the kitchen. Something went *bang!* against his chest and knocked him to the floor.

Slumped up against the kitchen wall, it hurt to breathe, and Wallets could feel something really hot smoldering away in the Kevlar of his vest—his only thought, the supremely obvious, *Shit, I've been shot.* Hard to think about anything else, but anything else was about to intrude. Farah Nasir appeared around the edge of the refrigerator, a severe little woman with short, cropped hair and a mousey face. She still pointed the gun at him. Not a very big firearm, but did it matter? Wallets tried to lift his gun hand to point back, but it seemed a very futile gesture. And besides, neither of his arms felt like moving just then. He managed to croak, "Stay back!" Out the corner of his eye he caught the shapes of his backup moving through the smoke in the living room. He tried, *Stay back* again, but didn't really have the breath for it. All he saw now were Farah Nasir's face and her eyes. Eyes that stared at him with dead hate. The gun no longer pointed at his chest but under her own chin. He tried to tell her something, anything—to *stop, wait.* The eyes widened suddenly and once again—

Bang. As Farah Nasir blew her brains out.

The body fell to the floor. Now both G-women were in the kitchen. "Shit," Wesson said and kneeled over Wallets with a look of deep concern in her eyes. Smith reached over the dead body to turn off the stove. Neither FBI agent bothered touching the woman splayed across the floor.

Smith glanced down at the dead woman's leaking head but used a pair of oven mitts to lift the smoldering laptop and dump it on the kitchen table. The oven grate came along with the melted plastic. And it started to scorch the tabletop. "Shit," she said, very annoyed.

Last of all Carmine the Cop and Doleful Duane. The two policemen glanced silently at each other, masterfully controlling the urge to say, "Shit"; then Officer Duane spoke into the mike box attached to his shoulder.

"EMT! EMT! We got one man down and one black tag. And don't wait for the elevator—use the friggin' stairs."

———

New York City's Finest sealed off the two street openings to the Waldorf Limousine Entrance with blue wooden police barricades, stenciled over in white with the words "Police Line Do Not Cross," then added some stretchy yellow barricade tape about chest high across the entrance for good measure. Wallets approached very gingerly, like he hurt all over, as though suddenly very fragile. Then with great effort he took a deep painful breath and straightened his gait. Three cops guarding the South Entrance were in the midst of an altercation with an entourage, apparently headed there for some sort of a party. A couple of tall glamorous women, but it was the comb-over he recognized immediately. "Do you know *who I am?*" he was badgering the cop. "I could have you fired. Do you hear me? You're fired. *You're fired!*" The cop was having none of it. Wallets pulled his ID, missed once, and winced—then got it. The policeman said, "Okay," and lifted the yellow tape. Everyone had heard about the gunfight. And there were some long looks at Wallets on the order, *oh man, were you lucky.*

"Try another entrance," Wallets suggested to the comb-over and his beautiful ladies. Then past the barrier, to the cordon of policemen surrounding the paddy wagon, "Okay, let's go."

He walked deeper into the limo corridor, where the wagon was already backed into the internal delivery bay. The paddy doors slammed open. The cops yanked the Garment District suspects over the rubber-lipped transom onto the loading dock, then immediately surrounded them before the service elevator. The metal service door had seen better days: bumped and scratched, banged to hell by countless hand trucks and dollies, unloading food, flowers, laundered bedding, everything

imaginable, except—until now—Iranian agents. Wallets climbed a set
of worn concrete steps with steel edges to the side of the delivery bay,
joining the prisoners on the loading dock. Suddenly the dented metal
door slammed open with a rattling cry, and the cops prodded the Garment District haul inside. The whole event taking less than eight seconds from paddy wagon to elevator.

Wallets and two NYPD cops rode the elevator silently with their
manacled prisoners. The service door groaned open again on the
eleventh floor of the Security Tower. Nothing much to see. Just three
more cops and a service corridor brightly lit and painted taupe. The
innocuous beige hallway to hell.

"After you," Wallets said to his manacled friends.

The prisoners seemed anything but frightened. They were, after all,
under diplomatic protection and seemed confident they'd be sprung in
hours if not minutes. So none of them had any reason to cooperate. They
chatted among themselves in Farsi, derisively, making a show of their contempt for the NYPD and Wallets, who hustled them into a large guest
facility called the Astor Ballroom. The sneering smiles vanished. The ballroom was large, high-ceilinged, and fully prepped for interrogation. In the
furthest corner of the room stood a ten-foot-by-ten-foot wire-mesh
Cisco-Eagle Prisoner Holding Cell, with an L-shaped metal bench
bolted along two of the holding cell's walls. The benches had handcuff
rails, ankle cuffs on the bench legs, and manacles on eyelets attached to the
bench seat every three feet. You could throw the lot of them behind the
wire mesh and lock them down hand and foot with room to spare. While
they could still see everything else going on in the ballroom. Standing in
the cage was a very pale and frightened looking Frenchie banker: Anton
Anjou, his thin wrist handcuffed to one of the mesh walls.

As the prisoners entered, they passed a free-standing partition, a
rectangular-shaped room divider that enclosed a table and chairs; the
room divider inset with a large rectangular two-way mirror, so that
anyone sitting behind the table could look out into the room without
being observed. Notepads, pencils. A video camera on a tripod pointed
through the gray glass. Microphones, sound recorders, headphones, and
wires ran along the floor.

Plus a new addition: Wallets had been carrying something in a smelly dark-smudged clear plastic evidence bag under his arm. He placed it on the edge of the table and pulled the ziplock to reveal a charred hunk of plastic and metal: "The remains of Farah Nasir's computer. Enough of a hard drive here to get something off of?"

An FBI technician moved it to a table across the room. He sat, staring lovingly at the burnt ruin. He placed another diagnostic laptop side by side and started gently connecting the former to the latter.

As the prisoners were marched by, they could see into the enclosure of the room divider for a brief moment, but not when they reached the mesh holding cell. Once inside the cage, their reactions could be monitored without their knowing who was looking. Suddenly, they understood this.

But what really gave them pause was neither the mesh cell nor the room divider with the recording devices. Three large black booths were arranged in the center in the ballroom, more or less equidistant from each other—in a triad, like three square mausoleums. Big, black, silent, and daunting. These three black enclosures were four-foot-by-six-foot prefabricated soundproof isolation booths. Primarily used for sound recording, they were fitted with two-foot-by-two-foot custom windows so you could see inside. Their narrow doors yawned open for their first subjects.

Inside, the walls were lined with black foam soundproof cushioning, while a metal chair with more cuffs, wrists and ankles, waited patiently. Yellow-and-black caution tape ran along the saddle of the open doors, so God forbid, no one tripped going in. The wires from the interrogation table snaked into each booth. Once the door closed, no sound in the world would escape. The men behind the room dividers could give orders to the operator or ask questions, and all the prisoners in the cage would see was the subject's reactions.

This was the sort of setup designed specifically to scare the piss out of anyone watching from the mesh holding cell. You wouldn't hear a sound. Just see the pain in the subject's face, and human imagination would do the rest. You're next, Sport.

Think about it . . .

The last prisoner to pass the interrogation divider glanced inside. Yasmine. And for a second that hard veneer of hers seemed to shiver. What she had missed coming out of the loft, she noticed now. Peter Johnson sat at the desk in a folding chair, watching the prisoners enter. Casually, he tapped the eraser of his pencil on his yellow legal pad—*tap-tap-tap*—calmly waiting. His eyes met hers momentarily, but only for an instant. And what they showed her was simply *nothing*. No anger, no interest, no hate, no heat. She's arrived; that was good enough. *Dayenu*. Let's get on with it.

Though what he saw in her eyes was something a little different. The spark of doubt, shimmering for a second. But just for a second. Johnson recalled her words from his own interrogation: "Kill the mullahs; topple the regime. We'll still be in the same place. Kill me. There are millions more."

We'll see—he thought to himself. Yeah, we'll see.

Yasmine started violently when she passed the first of the isolation booths. Yossi the Turk had appeared from behind one. He'd been prepping a metal chair inside. And clearly she recognized him. Amazed that he still lived? Yossi too showed nothing. Simply pointed to the mesh cage, and the NYPD cops obligingly brought everyone inside. Locking them down, systematically, as they all started to talk—no, *squawk*—at once. The noise level in the ballroom rose. Even the non-Farsi speakers sensed the rhythm and intonation on the alien tongues.

Yossi's right eye was covered with a black patch. It had, after all, only been four weeks since he'd been shot in the high mountain valley. He didn't seem put out at his infirmity. The remaining eye managed to stare out of his skull with the same reptilian intensity. The noise from the holding cell rose to a crescendo. Half the men were banging their wrists and tugging at their cuffs. Yasmine, cool as ever, awaited her fate. Yossi spoke one word in Farsi. A soft word, and it sounded like, "Hey."

The whole cage went dead silent.

Yossi the Turk spoke again in Farsi. A full sentence or two this time. It might have been, "Who wants to be first? Any volunteers?" And several of the Dips blanched.

He went instead to where the Frenchman stood behind the mesh with his wrist cuffed to the wire. Then stared into Anton's eyes, and every time Anton looked away, Yossi shifted a little to put his broad, brutal face up close. Then finally he said one word that needed no translation. Nodding.

"You."

⸻

Looking in from behind the room divider at the interrogation table, or from the prisoners' point of view behind the mesh wire, it wasn't clear what Yossi the Turk was actually *doing* to Anton in the isolation booth. Both men were visible, Anton sitting and Yossi moving around, passing before and behind through the two-by-two window. No sound—just the Frenchman's body reacting like an eviscerated, staked-out frog in a high school science experiment, twitching every time Yossi touched him, making Anton's limbs jerk: head, shoulders, neck. The Iranian's fluttering hand moved this way and that, and the reaction on the face of his subject seemed to jump out of the isolation booth window: first contorted, wrenched in pain; the pause of fear; then after another pause, weeping. Finally the contortion once more and the muffled sound of Anton's cries inside the booth straining to escape. Was it all an act? If so, give the man an Academy Award, and that man would be the Turk, not the Frenchman, because he got results. Anton broke in three long minutes. And the team behind the see-through room divider could start asking questions.

Banquo had ordered two of the Iranian Diplomats into the two free isolation booths, and they watched the whole Anton Show, growing paler by the second, looking away, then looking back, finally pulling at their own chairs to get free.

The audio wires that ran between the interrogation table and the nearby isolation booths brought every sound to the table. The hastily assembled interrogation team had raided the minibars of adjacent hotel suites so the tabletop was quickly littered with half-consumed fruit drinks, bottled water, power bars, and the like. All swept off to the floor when the time came to do some Q & A and make use of the yellow legal pads.

The assembled team represented just about everyone involved: O'Hanlon and his team, Wallets and Johnson, a Captain from the NYPD, a Captain from the FDNY, the Medical Examiner—the top tier of people who needed answers. So the space behind the room divider was pretty scarce, leaving most watchers standing. Even Banquo, who stood silently through the whole proceedings, looking more at the heads of the interrogation team than the subjects in the booths.

No one had talked about what they were about to do, because they all knew it, they could all feel it in their bones: they were going to break down their subjects and save the lives of people, innocent New Yorkers. If such innocents had seen what the team saw, would they have let them keep it up? Would they be appalled or resolved? Or more repelled that deluded young men would poison perfect innocents just to enter heaven? No one could say.

During Anton's Q & A, Banquo occasionally whispered into Wallets' ear, who spoke softly into a microphone asking questions, his voice low and raspy. His close call with the bullet made it hard for him to breathe, and you could see his chest move slowly with each word.

The Frenchman's answers came out to their wireless headsets, so everyone plugged in behind the divider could hear. While the only thing the Iranian Diplomats saw in their holding cage was the Frenchman's tear-streaked face through the two-by-two window, lips moving, spilling his guts.

Answers going like this:

"I made transfers of $40 million in four installments."

"Yes, from Kutmar Investment Group, three other Iranian investment groups, and into an account controlled by Farah Nasir and another controlled by Yasmine Farouk."

"Accounts each woman opened several years ago, here in New York."

"Yes, both accounts in Bank of America. They applied for credit cards, multiple credit cards, each with 500K cash limits."

"Yes, that would be eighty separate credit card accounts."

"The wire-tracking device we gave Johnson—no, I don't know where Farah Nasir secured it."

"No, I don't know who manufactured it."

"No, I don't know who arranged for the parking facilities at the Valley Forge Golf Course."

"I only know of two delivery cells operating in the New York area. The one in the Brooklyn apartment and the second in Queens near the airport."

"There is some sort of central deposit for the material."

"I don't know what the material is—I'm not a chemist."

"More cells? Yes, there are more."

"The Iranians know."

Banquo made another command decision:

"All right. Enough of the Frenchman. Let's see how cooperative the Iranian Dips want to be. Start with the two sweating it out in the booths. Yossi, you know what to do."

From their manacles in the holding cell and their ringside seats in the isolation booths, the Iranian Dips watched all this with growing dread. They knew they were next, and Yasmine knew she was being saved for last.

CHAPTER TWENTY-FIVE

"A Serious Security Situation"

The Iranian Diplomats couldn't have been more cooperative. As Yossi left Anton's isolation booth, calmly closed the door behind him, and approached the other two black mausoleums, both men inside began to speak. A torrent of words streamed out their mouths as they strained against the restraints, their heads bobbing furiously in the two-by-two window. And they hadn't even been touched yet. From her place in the holding cell, Yasmine saw their fear, and contempt dripped from her like poison.

As Yossi put his hand on the first isolation booth door handle, Banquo spoke into his Bluetooth headset, "Yossi. Get to the point. We're looking for backpack cells."

And the Turk did exactly that. In quick succession the remaining Iranian Dips were run through the isolation booths like fancy women at the Elizabeth Arden tanning salon. Ten minutes at a pop, in and out. No fuss, no muss. No single individual knew the names and addresses and numbers of every additional cell, but between the seven, the interrogation team learned of four more groups of men, ranging from a five-man cell to a ten-man cell for a total of forty men.

"Think we got them all?" Johnson whispered to Wallets. But Wallets only grunted in reply. And that took some effort. So Johnson answered the question for himself, glancing at Yasmine through the two-way glass. "Unless she knows of more."

"That's enough," Banquo said. "Take all the men into Ballroom Two. There's a refreshment table set up there. Let them commingle. If someone says something interesting, we'll know, but don't count on it. If they start making love to the Frenchman without his permission, put a stop to it." To the Police Commissioner, the Fire Commissioner, and the Medical Examiner: "Why don't you take a break? Keep an eye on them." It wasn't a suggestion.

In two minutes, the six Iranian Diplomats and Anton were led from the room, leaving Yasmine alone in the mesh holding cell. Wallets left his place at the table, clutching his chest for a moment in discomfort, then came around the room divider. Both he and Yossi stood before Yasmine, staring at her. Yossi played show and tell with a small pair of pliers.

"He twists it a little. Works pretty well." Wallets measured her reaction.

The woman remained defiant. "Especially on cowards," she spat. Carefully, she unbuttoned the cuff of her shirt and slid the sleeve up. From wrist to elbow the skin of her forearm was covered in old wounds, some places cut and healed over, some burned, showing a puckered texture like cellulite. Somebody had really been at her. How much of her body looked like this?

Sitting at the table, Johnson realized that all that time in Iran, in the various facilities, the long car ride across Persian mountains and deserts, even his own interrogation—he'd never seen her forearm. In fact, like all Muslim women, Yasmine had been covered from neck to ankles.

But Wallets and those behind the room divider were more arrested by the sound of the woman's voice. It carried a primal force, so much so if you closed your eyes, you wouldn't have been able to tell who was about to interrogate whom. "If she wants to talk, let her talk," Banquo murmured into his Bluetooth. "But remember, we need to know whether there are any more cells and how the hell they got that material in here and where it is."

The two men opened the cage and stood before it. The woman jangled her manacles and imperiously held forth, like a Queen Tut whose authority has been questioned:

"You have made a dangerous error," she was saying. "And not the first time. You look down on us because our zealous students simply *held* your diplomats? But they were just students. You are government officials, torturing diplomats with your *own hands*."

Wallets looked mildly back at her, seemingly bored. This was all old history. She might have been five years old at the time of the U.S. Embassy takeover in the wake of Khomeini's Revolution.

"We're not here for a lecture."

But she wasn't appeased, more fanatic. "I'm telling you the truth. You only want to hear your truth."

"*My* truth?" Wallets repeated again, through a bruised chest. It hurt to talk. He shrugged it off as if what she said had little weight with him. "Yeah, *my* truth is simple: innocent people are dying out there, and you're responsible."

His calculated mildness seemed to enrage her. She had waited a lifetime to spit in the eyes of the devil. "The truth is innocent children die everywhere. You kill them with your bombs and missiles. The truth is whatever happens to your country is deserved. The truth is—"

Her statement was cut off by the sound of a slap. Yossi had stepped in close and slapped her across the face. His handprint glowed along her jaw. Some of those sitting at the interrogation table recoiled at the sight, especially O'Hanlon and his agents, Smith and Wesson. For no logical reason, a manacled woman slapped on the face seemed much worse than some screaming weenies in a two-by-two window. Sentimentality, perhaps. But Bryce guffawed and said under his breath, "Bitch."

Banquo didn't deign to look at him but said straight ahead: "Mr. Bryce, if you can't control yourself, you can be assigned elsewhere." Then, to Wallets, sounding disgusted, "Keep our colleague under control in there. Let's not waste time on theatrics."

Yasmine's eyes were watery with the sting, but she kept going, "*This* is your women's rights? *This* is your human rights? *This* is your—?" But couldn't find the words. Instead, she literally spit one word in Yossi's direction: "*Djjal!*" flecks of saliva reaching no higher than his waist. Yossi seemed unimpressed. At a signal from Wallets, he manacled Yasmine's hands behind her back and led her from the holding cell.

"We're totally off the books here, right?" Wallets asked in a tone of voice that made it sound almost like a challenge. The question was directed at those behind the room divider, this time the words coming out strong. He got a silence of assent.

"OK, then. Bring in the spine board."

Smith and Wesson left the room and returned nearly immediately with a bright yellow emergency rescue stretcher with straps, meant to keep someone very, very still. Like after a car accident. In the end it took Wesson, Smith, Bryce, and Yossi to strap the writhing and spitting Yasmine in place. Bryce grim, now that he was this close. The two women looked both sad and ashamed. Sad for Yasmine Farouk, PhD; ashamed for themselves to be part of this. A head strap went around her skull and was tightened. Then Yossi came with a mouth clamp to pry her mouth open and keep it that way.

"What are you doing?" Yasmine suddenly demanded, sounding scared for the first time. They lifted the prostrate Yasmine on the spine board onto a pair of trestle sawhorses so the board was up off the ground, about waist high.

"Whatever we want," Wallets said, flat and matter-of-fact. His bruised chest didn't seem to bother him so much now. He looked down at her without pity. He wanted to try to spook her before doing anything, but he also was speaking the simple truth and wasn't going to wait long for her to crumble. She kept trying to fight, but could only ineffectually flex her muscles, pinned down like that. When the mouth clamp pried her chops open, she started to mew, a pathetic sound.

Banquo's voice: "Get on with it."

"Do you want to talk?" Wallets asked, looming over her, all cold gray eyes.

Yossi flipped a latch on the mouth clamp, allowing her to move her lips. The words came out in a spitting slew: "*Djjal! Djjal!*"

"All right." Wallets signaled to Yossi, and the latch opened again, forcing her mouth open. The mewing came back. Her eyes jerked in their sockets, straining to look from side to side. Yossi had gone behind one of the mausoleums and come back with a wet washcloth and a silver ice bucket, empty of ice but filled with water. Yasmine's eyes darted as far as they could to the side to try to watch him, then closed. More of that terrible whispery high-pitched sound. Wallets assumed it was a prayer.

The sound seemed now like it was mingling with tears, a low barely audible mumble from the depths of her soul up to her Lord. Yossi with the ice bucket looked to Wallets.

Wallets gestured, but he didn't move. "Go on," he said, pointing toward Yossi like he was going to take the ice bucket himself if he didn't begin. Carefully the Turk placed the towel over Yasmine's open mouth and methodically tipped the ice bucket, pouring a stream of water over the towel. It quickly dampened, and began to choke her. Soon she began to drown. The sound went from cat-screeching-in-the-middle-of-the-night to a soft gurgle. A sound that rattled your insides. Her body straightened in a convulsion and then thrashed as much as it could under the constraints. Yossi hesitated and Wallets waited, looking at the second hand of his watch. Ten seconds, fifteen, then twenty.

"Take the towel off," Wallets said. With practiced movements, Yossi took off the towel, flipped the latch loose on the mouth clamp and both men tipped the spine board on its side, letting the water run out of her. The sound of retching, coughing, spit-up filled the room. Then deep gasps. When the spine board came face-up once more, Yasmine was still gasping for breath, her eyes streaked with red and bulging toward the ceiling. She kept breathing hard and seemed to get herself under control, starting to mutter her prayer again.

Wallets nodded to the Turk. The mouth clamp froze open, and the process was methodically repeated. From behind the room divider, O'Hanlon, Smith, Wesson, and Bryce watched, transfixed. They held their breath almost as one as the stream of water poured onto the towel, as Wallets counted off the seconds on his wristwatch. Twenty seconds, twenty-five, thirty . . .

The towel came off, the spine board flipped, and the sound of retching filled the ballroom, a thread of puke stretching to the floor.

"I can't take this," Smith said. Wesson stared back with haunted eyes. Bryce's face was very, very pale, and he looked as if he just wanted someone to relieve him of duty. The body on the spine board still convulsed, even right side up, the sound out of Yasmine's throat a death rattle. The death of her resistance. They only needed to do it once more.

One more time. The third time paid for all. No more prayers. But it seemed an age.

Wallets wrung the drenched towel back into the ice bucket. Then looked at Yasmine's face, bleached nearly white. "Talk to us," he said.

She kept her eyes closed tight, as if she hated herself for doing it, but she began to speak, through her wheezy gasps. The loose mouth clamp rattled a little. And these are the nuggets they got from her, not much considering, but helpful, especially the last:

"That's all the teams . . . unfortunately."

"Yahdzi put the titanium canisters together long before Johnson's Iran tour. That project long in the pipeline."

"The other material. Diplomatic Pouch over twenty trips, JFK and Mexico City. Trucked north to Nogales, and some direct to delivery bay, King Prussia Mall."

"In Brooklyn, DeGraw and Bond."

Wallets nodded and walked behind the room divider. Banquo pensively stroked his face. Satisfied for the present. Johnson's face had a very dark cast to it, something between resignation and reckoning. O'Hanlon was there in body, not in spirit. He'd pushed his chair back and was staring at the floor, smoking a cigarette. He didn't look up. The terrible question—was this the payoff or just more dead ends? They'd find out soon enough.

"Are we done?" he asked no one in particular, a tone of disgust in his voice.

Not by a long shot—they still had to track the bastards down.

⊶∞⊷

Outside in the real world, the great chase opened up to full throttle.

The first Workbench Boy caught napping in Queens had coughed up the location of his buddies. Two of them in a car headed to the Bronx— in a twenty-year-old Toyota Corolla with New Jersey plates, FD1357— and one of them on the subway on his way to Grand Central Station. There was some confusion as to yet another Jihadi riding the rails, but no one seemed certain as to his route or identity. Smith and Wesson got the call to go to Grand Central, while the city's powers-that-be bickered in the Waldorf over whether or not to shut down the subway.

When they descended two levels to the 7 Train platform coming in from Queens, there were so many cops on the platform, it felt like rush hour, but only for New York City's Finest. Passengers arriving on the 7 Train—despite their reading materials, their iPods, and their distracted rush—noticed all the cops, and it dawned on every passenger in a flash that something was wrong. Many passengers hesitated and began to step back into the subway car. The cops had to hustle them out, "It's all right. It's all right; keep moving."

Smith and Wesson prowled the platform like the caged cheetahs of the Bronx Zoo who run round and round the perimeter of their enclosure all day. They started at the front of the platform, near the exit, and walked down the platform as each train from Queens arrived, looking for the mark they knew so well from their surveillance of the safe house. When they moved through the crowd from each train, they scanned every face, then back to the front of the platform, following the departing passengers rushing toward the escalators. Next train ready to do it again. And quickly got tired of looking at the number 7 in a purple oval—denoting the train line—on every car. After the fifth train, they wondered if they were wasting their time hunting one lone Jihadi when there were cops here on lookout. Their new buds, Officers Carmine and Doleful Duane, had requested and been granted assignment with the Roll-Up Task Force.

On the arrival of the sixth train, they hadn't bothered to walk all the way to the front, but stood in the middle, when the train's door shuddered opened, and there he was one door away, closer to the exit. They recognized the close-cropped back of his head as instantly as if it'd been a Michael Jordan advertisement in the 1980s. The tallest and strongest of the Queens Boys. Some animal instinct made him look behind him and realize he'd been made. He started sprinting, and Smith and Wesson ran after him, dodging through the passengers who stopped to see what was going on.

He veered toward the other track, as a new Queens-bound 7 Train swooshed into the station. Wesson caught him by his right shoulder, closest to the tracks. He had one foot now on the bright yellow rubber edge of the platform. He swung his body violently around, back toward the middle of the station, and the motion—combined with her own momentum—sent Wesson flying out over the track.

The conductor had been laying on the horn, a sustained, blaring, high-pitched wail. But it did no good now. The conductor pulled the emergency brake, the wheels screamed against the rails, but the dumb flat head of the train, like a metallic worm, barreled ahead. Wesson was thrown nearly perpendicular against the front of the steel nose, and for a moment it seemed she'd be able to grasp the metal chains across the front of the car to hang on in some miraculous fashion. But she lost her grip. Then vanished under the wheels.

Smith wanted to lunge after her partner, but not against a moving train. The moving cars brought her up short. There was only the awful cacophony of the horn and the wheels—and suddenly two shots.

The backpacker was down, felled by two risky, precision shots by Doleful Duane, down in a crouch on one knee. The train had nearly stopped now, the doors still closed. Smith could tell some passengers were screaming, others had their hands over their mouths. The cops were motioning the conductors to keep their doors closed. In the third car, one face didn't look horrified, only very interested. He ducked out of sight, and Smith noticed strange movements in the car. She looked harder, and people were pressed against the doors and windows—and she saw the telltale wisps of the metallic floury powder. The other back-packer was in there.

"Open the doors," she shouted, but the cops were still signaling the conductors to keep them closed. The backpacker's head could be seen on and off moving through the car, and then he went down, three good Samaritans on top of him. Smith ran to the front of the train and pounded on the windows for the conductor to open the doors of the third car.

When he finally did, people hustled out, or just stepped out dazed, their hands up in pleading gestures, covered with the floury powder, or trying desperately to pat it off. The cops rushed in and had to pull off the good Samaritans—a burly redhead on his way to Citi Field, a skinny

Latino guy with his iPod buds still in his ears, an older, balding guy in a cheap suit—all covered in the powder and punching and kicking the backpacker, down in the fetal position.

Smith barked orders to the cops: "Quarantine this platform and corridor above. No one leaves the station." Officers Carmine and Doleful Duane jumped on it, passing their orders to the other policemen on the platform, and within fifteen seconds they established a rough cordon in the pedestrian corridor above, and began to process straphangers, scanning their clothes with Geiger counters. Getting names and addresses. Most were cooperative, but there's always one or two knuckleheads, and these mooks soon found themselves nose to dirty subway stanchions in plastic cuffs.

Smith was still barking orders: "No one leaves the station. Get a hazmat team here ASAP, and get under that train!" She crouched down and looked under the cars. No sign of her partner.

"*Wesson!*"

She died on the tracks from loss of blood before they could get her out. The backpacker on the platform, dead too. The other one, badly beaten but alive. The worst-contaminated—along with Wesson's body—were taken to NYU Medical Center and given total decontamination and iodine shots.

There was another guest of the hospital. Walid from Union Square. Someone had called an ambulance for him when he had been weaving and having trouble standing near the New Utrecht Avenue–62nd Street subway stop back in Brooklyn. He arrived at the Kings County Medical Center wearing tights under jeans that had been coated with lead-based paint on the inside, tennis shoes that were painted outside with the same paint, and a pair of grey Ultex rubber radiation-reducing gloves. The clothes dissolving.

Kings County Emergency in Brooklyn took one look at him and transferred the kid and all his disintegrating clothes locked in a hazmat container immediately to NYU Med Center—sending him right back to the Manhattan he had been so desperate to escape. Radiation cases were all to be handled at a central location as long as possible. Decontaminating the facilities in one hospital seemed better than decontaminating dozens across the city. Now the ambulance personnel who had picked him up in the first place were getting treated for radiation poisoning, right at NYU, while the Kings County ambulance was parked under the East Side Drive behind some chain-link fencing.

Walid wore a green hospital gown, propped up on a bed, with black hairs sprinkled over his shoulders. He had been losing his hair for an hour. He grimaced in pain in between muttering incoherently in response to questioning from Smith. She wore a hazmat suit now. His arms were cuffed to either side of his bed. A cop at the door and a doctor at the back of the room also wore hazmat suits. The kid had tested for radiation off the charts, "a walking Nagasaki," as the doctor had put it to the agents when they arrived.

"Why did you do this?" Smith asked. "Who helped you do this? Tell us—it's not too late. You can help."

His eyes were pleading, asking for forgiveness or understanding. And he mumbled something that sounded like, "Onion Square. I'm sorry."

<hr />

News filtered back in from the street—and Johnson marveled at the change in the Waldorf since Banquo's arrival, from the Mad Hatter's tea party to an oiled machine. The phones rang, people answered them, properly dispatched, issues resolved. Ready for the next.

A backpacker stopped outside the Metropolitan Opera.

An entire cell cornered in their row house in Jersey City, a standoff, and then a shoot out—four Jihadis dead.

A car with two backpackers—the one that had been coming from Queens—tailed by a police helicopter over the Bronx-Queens Expressway, then forced to stop at the ramp to the George Washington Bridge by two squad cars. Traffic backed up to Greenwich, Connecticut, as a tow truck was called in and the Jihadis brought into custody in the Fort Apache Precinct in the Bronx.

Matters obviously had gotten beyond the point where they could be kept under wraps. Or where doing so served the people of the city. The Mayor, the Deputy Mayor, and the Police Commissioner's faces had taken on a grayish tinge as the hours progressed. Phone calls coming into City Hall from newspapers and the rest of the media. Drudge had posted a headline, linking to stories of a few of the discrete incidents:

WORMS IN THE BIG APPLE?

With a siren flashing. Immediately, his site bent and nearly crashed under the weight of the traffic.

At last, after an eon of press-gagging, and hiding under a very large desk, those at the Waldorf conference table resolved that the Mayor must go downstairs to deliver a statement and take some limited questions from reporters—although his avail would surely occasion a melee from journalists frenzied by the cocktail drug of a world-changing story about which they as yet knew next to nothing. They'd talked to the White House, which wanted the Mayor out first—as the highest political authority on the ground—before the Feds took over. They had word the president would be making his own preliminary statement within the hour.

The Mayor would enlist the help of the general public, urging them not to flee the city, which would potentially expand exposure, but please stay inside, and make their way home on foot while authorities handled "a manageable security situation with potential public health consequences." Then, the most ticklish bit: "Young men with backpacks have been implicated in this situation. If you see someone acting suspiciously, do not engage that person, but call authorities immediately." How much more could he say? Should he mention they were of Middle Eastern or South Asian origin, or would that risk opening to retaliation every young Middle Eastern man in the city? They decided to keep it vague.

As he and the Deputy Mayor pored over the brief text one more time, word came in about what had happened at Grand Central and the loss of Wesson. O'Hanlon got up to leave for NYU Medical, but Banquo grabbed him from his chair, placed a hand up around his neck, and whispered something in his ear. O'Hanlon stayed at his battle station, his eyes glassy. Plans to house the Westchester Metro North commuters and the Long Island Railroad commuters were quickly formulated with the city's major hotels. Car traffic would not be restricted out of the city—as a safety valve—but no one could drive in. Subway and bus service suspended. All major hotel chains ordered to give stranded commuters such hospitality as available. The Mayor went downstairs, holding a printed text with scribbling on it in two different color pens.

After his brief prepared remarks, he took a few questions, then listed badly under his own inability or unwillingness to give precise answers to the shouted follow-ups.

"Is it biological? Chemical? What's this substance?"

"Anthrax? Is it anthrax?"

"How do you define 'acting suspiciously'?"

"What do these 'young men' look like and act like? And how do you define 'young'?"

"How many are there? Is this the beginning or the end?"

Every channel in America not devoted to sports, cooking, old feature films, or TV movies about women hooked on questionable men showed the same live images of the Mayor ducking back into the Waldorf, surrounded by boom mikes, frantic, pushing reporters, and a blue line of cops trying to maintain order. They didn't have TVs in the interrogation room, but someone opened the door to tell Banquo, assuming he'd want to know, "The Mayor's blowing it."

Banquo registered no surprise, nor did he feel any. He'd seen the Mayor's mettle earlier and had pegged him as a man without a chest. After this, the urban solon should go back to Hizzoner's prior obsession with transferring the entire cab fleet into hybrids and banning McDonald's as a public health risk—that is, if he survived this.

Banquo turned to O'Hanlon: "Make sure someone from DOJ gets out there to clean this up. We can't have a general melee out in the streets."

Banquo asked for a cup of coffee and braced himself for what would be a bow wave of reports of suspected Jihadis in the wake of the Mayor's presser. It would be like the aftermath of the famous radio broadcast of *War of the Worlds*—except some of the panicked calls would be reporting genuine aliens in their midst. He asked the Police Commissioner what surge capacity they had for 911 operators, and he said he'd see about diverting the operators from 311—the city's nonemergency information line—to handling emergency calls. To no one in particular and everyone, Banquo announced, "Let's buckle down, ladies and gentlemen. This is only the end of the beginning."

O'Hanlon and a team he dragooned from FBI-NYC headed out to the intersection Yasmine had given them, DeGraw and Bond, in Brooklyn. An up-and-coming neighborhood, which is an optimist's way of saying still down-at-the-heels. DeGraw dead-ended at the northern-most part of the Gowanus Canal. The barrier that the canal made to foot and other traffic meant that the half block abutting it would always be relatively blighted.

O'Hanlon didn't know what exactly he was looking for, but suspected an abandoned warehouse with red, peeling paint and the fading words "McSweeney's Machine Tools" emblazoned on this side might be it. The machine shop was chained and padlocked at every entrance, except one at the back, nearest the canal, where few people would ever have any occasion to walk.

The fetid smell of the oily, greenish-tinged water reeked especially powerfully back there. A beat-up Honda Accord was parked close to the canal, and O'Hanlon and his boys circled warily around it, unholstering their handguns. Quietly, one of the men pushed at the steel rimmed, dented security door of the warehouse, and five G-Men rushed through. In the gloom of the factory floor two more Workbench Boys looked up in surprise. They were fumbling with cumbersome industrial-strength work suits. Stunned as though caught with their pants down, they panicked. They dropped the heavy outfits and ran toward the far end of the warehouse, toward some sort of wall. As O'Hanlon's eyes adjusted to the dark, he got the impression of an empty dank vaulted room with a bare concrete floor—a metal partition toward the back, blocking their way. His G-Men took off in pursuit, when something told O'Hanlon to yell, "No! No! No!" allowing his quarry to hide behind the barrier.

O'Hanlon corralled his men back near the door and sent two agents outside to ensure that nobody went for the Honda, as God knows what might be in it—and waited for the hazmat team. O'Hanlon would've liked to have come with a hazmat, but with everything else going on, the city's twenty or so truck squads were stretched mighty thin. And as the minutes ticked by, the DOJ lawyer grew more and more annoyed. He'd given up barking into his radio, "Okay, when dammit? Gimme an ETA." After ten minutes, you could hear audible arguing from behind the partition in a foreign language and then desperate shouting. Suddenly one of the Workbench Boys stumbled out. The kid couldn't have been more than nineteen—a young Jihadi scared out of his wits, panting with an open mouth.

"Stop!" O'Hanlon yelled. "No further! No further." He trained his gun on the kid and took one step into the cavernous factory. The young man looked as if he had jumped into a huge bag of flour, except the substance on him was a shiny metallic color instead of matte white. "Get down!" O'Hanlon shouted. Cautiously, the young Jihadi dropped to his knees. "All the way down!" As the young man stretched out on his belly, he began to writhe. A moment later, convulsing in pain. Crying, no longer afraid of the gun or the G-Men—just for his life.

O'Hanlon and his four G-Men looked at one another. "What now?" one of them said.

"Don't touch him," O'Hanlon said.

"Can we use their own protective gear and go grab him?" another asked, referring to the abandoned work suits.

"Don't touch *anything*," O'Hanlon said. He looked at his radio, and a thousand curses for the tardy hazmat team ran through his mind. Ten minutes later the hazmat van pulled up, and extra protective suits were handed around. In another ten minutes, O'Hanlon, his four G-Men, and two hazmat technicians—fully suited up—walked across the concrete factory floor toward the first kid. The young man hadn't moved since the van arrived. He'd stopped thrashing and died quietly enough while everyone was putting on their gear.

There came the sound of movement from behind the metal partition. The other Workbench Boy stumbled out from behind the partition, gripping the wall edge for support. Everyone was close enough now to see what lay behind the barrier, a conical mound of metallic flour—what Landfill and Gravel men call a "yard"—about six foot by eight foot. Suddenly O'Hanlon realized they might have found the Holy Grail of Grunge. That this was where the raw fairy dust had been kept, perhaps added to secretly, kilo after kilo—only waiting for pickup by the backpack teams to mix and load into their satchels. Waiting for orders. He made a mental note to have Bryce track down who owned or leased this dump.

The two Jihadis had simply come for a scheduled pickup, about to don their protective gear to get a few scoops, when the door blew open. Then ran into the metallic pile to escape O'Hanlon and Co. Perhaps even draw the G-Men along. An act of suicidal bravery, or stupidity. Perversity? Sacrifice? Devotion? Perhaps all of the above.

The last Jihadi stepped toward them, labored step after labored step. Everyone stood frozen, horrified by the sight. His flesh was coming off his arms. He looked like the living model of a nightmare painting by Munch, and in the awful quiet of the warehouse, they heard a low crackle. He was literally melting before their eyes. All at once, he collapsed before them in a dissolving, discoagulating heap. One of the G-Men sprinted for the door, clawing at his hazmat helmet. He'd seen enough.

The Nasir computer turned out to be the mother lode. When the technician teased the raw information out of it, a Farsi speaker went through it as quickly as possible, and the intel was passed around the Waldorf conference table. Farah Nasir must have been an aficionado of modern Western art because she gave her six backpack teams the names of painters: Pollack, Klimt, Chagall, Johns, Dali, and—weirdly enough—Warhol (no one ever said she had taste). The leader of each group would call her and say the name of their painter at each crucial stage of the process; when they had their gear ready—jeans, shoes, backpacks, gloves, specially outfitted shower—they notified her they were prepared to pick up the Grunge or get a delivery of it from the Gowanus machine shop.

"Composition varied. It was up to the delivery cells to do their own mix. One part refined plutonium, one part uranium, one part calcium chloride, and one part commercial powdered baby laxative as a dispersal medium. You can breathe it in; you can get it on your skin. If you drop it on the sidewalk and it rains, the laxative melts away, leaving heavy radioactive dust. The perfect terror weapon. And the chlorine burns."

Bryce took a breath, then added, "There was a three-sentence memo from Sheik Kutmar dated five days earlier: 'You have authorization to begin the *distribution*. Any risk of capture must be met by your martyrdom. Praise be to Allah.'"

Banquo scoffed to no one in particular, "Pious pimp. Safe at home, sending his girls out to work the neighborhood."

Out in the city, cell phone service had been overwhelmed and crashed. There were a few scuffles at points of exit—when people realized, for instance, that no, they weren't getting on a ferry across to Weehawken, New Jersey. There were a couple of "citizen's arrests" of innocent, backpack-wielding Middle Eastern college students, and Sikh cabdrivers were harassed, the lot of the poor Sikhs in the aftermath of 9/11 too—the burden of their conspicuous turbans and the ignorance of their tormentors. But, by and large, the streets emptied without incident, the mass of New Yorkers making their own way, as they always do, during blackouts, subway floods, whatever else the urban gods of fortune threw their way, to be overcome with the gritty, pushy, complaining fortitude that characterized their urban breed.

Hazmat cleanup crews were already working to keep select spots in Manhattan from becoming Superfund cleanup sites for decades, while the focus of the media universe had become the Waldorf. It was surrounded on all sides by satellite trucks, their mushroom dishes pointed upward at the hotel's Art Deco towers in a kind of homage. Federal officials had shown up, but otherwise not much had changed: the Mayor was huddled with his deputy and underlings, desperately plotting what could be his redeeming second act with the press; everyone else naturally deferred to Banquo, even those who outranked him and had no real idea who he was or why he was there.

No one in the Waldorf knew what to expect next, but there was hope that when O'Hanlon found the Grunge pile, the worst might be over. Were there any Jihadis left? Were they only the first wave? How about other cities? And *where* were the canisters from Iran—never far from Banquo's mind—with their potential for something much worse? Johnson stood at a window, looking down a deserted Lexington Avenue, where red tail lights would usually be stopped at traffic lights, then flowing down the Avenue, the corpuscles of the city's life blood. The emptiness was eerie—"the very witching time of night, when church-yards yawn, and hell itself breathes out Contagion to this world."

A terrible vision of an utterly abandoned metropolis passed through his mind, a steel-and-concrete wasteland after something much worse than this, after . . . but his reverie was broken by Banquo gently tapping his shoulder. Maybe he guessed what was on Johnson's mind. Tapping his shoulder got his attention but was also somehow reassuring.

Johnson turned to him. "Peter," Banquo said. "We think you should talk to Yasmine." She had been left in the holding cage all this time, almost as an afterthought, but also because no one quite knew what to do with her. She had quickly clammed up again after the water, and no one had any appetite for pushing her anymore. "She may feel compelled to say something to you. Whether it's useful or not, who knows?" Johnson considered the man's words pensively for a moment.

"I don't know exactly what you're thinking, but a few hours ago she had a bag over my kid's head. So . . ." Johnson shrugged. "I'd be more than happy to put a carpenter ant in her ear. And stop it up with candle wax."

"Sorry, no carpenter ants. But you can keep her rattled. For reasons of cosmic justice if you like. Or as our friend Wallets occasionally puts it, 'Karma sucks.'"

After the earlier scene with Yasmine, Johnson wasn't eager to be enlisted as an interrogator, but the ever-curious journalist in him figured *what the hell,* he'd be the George Plimpton of interrogations. Not like he didn't have a score to settle.

Yasmine didn't seem surprised to see him when he entered the cage. She sat cuffed to the bench, with her head cocked to the side like a teenager with a bad attitude. Her lips were bruised, as were the corners of her mouth, her hair still wet and stringy, falling down around her shoulders. Johnson searched her face for the fantasy woman he once imagined so long ago in Iran, the noble stoic opponent of the regime. Secret Head of La Résistance. But that fantasy was long gone, replaced by the Muslim Diabolical Genius: Islamo-Nazi-Girl. Replaced finally by this bedraggled and broken scarecrow, a rag doll who'd lost her luster of arrogant, omni-competence.

"I looked up the word *Djjal,*" he told her. "It means Deceiver. The Muslim Anti-Christ. Besides Yossi, you have anyone else in mind?"

She said nothing, just shrugged.

Johnson felt contempt for her creeping in, along with anger. Just as she must have felt for him when their circumstances were reversed, the inevitable result of having power over someone so humiliated and weak.

"I was wondering about the mules with canisters lost on the Iraq border. The material from Esfahan. They weren't part of any of this, were they? Never were?" Johnson let the question hang. Her eyes were indifferent.

"Maybe they should have sent a professional," Johnson snorted. "Isn't that what you once told me? Or words to that effect? 'Clumsy journalist'? What should we call you?"

She narrowed her eyes and again ignored him. He pressed on.

"You've managed to make a bigger hash of things than I *ever* did in Iran. Remember when you told me how backwards Iran used to be? Well, happy days are here again." He leaned forward, quietly and conspiratorially, dead serious, but with a gleam in his eye:

"Y'know, I think these people are going to want to send you back to the Stone Age."

"I *am* a professional," she finally spat back, a delayed reaction.

"No, Yasmine, you're a professional *fool.* You undertook a pointless line of action in a city of innocents that can only start a war. A war you'll lose. You're either crazy or some Muslim Yamamoto of Iran, launching an attack that could only result in the destruction of your county. In the Japanese admiral's case, Yamamoto thought America was proud and just and knew the consequences of his action. Something tells me, you never thought it through that far."

Her eyes flitted away for a moment. He snorted. "And you called *me* pathetic."

"*Pointless?*" she said. "*Consequences?*" she taunted. Their eyes met, and she sat up straighter. "That's funny from the very font of surrender and appeasement." Her voice took on a sarcastic edge: "*The State Department interprets the evidence its own way. The court of International Opinion another.* You won't hit us, Mr. Johnson. The Marine Barracks, Khobar, Iraq, and now our *dirt* in your subways—they're all just a taste, just a taste of what's to come . . . "

She kept on: "Who's afraid of the big bad American Wolf? Not us. We murder hundreds and hundreds of United States' soldiers with pure impunity. We fill any country we wish with guns and rockets. Our Shahab 3 missile can reach anywhere in the Middle East, London, and the heart of Europe. Soon, even New York itself. We hold out our hand to be kissed by every aristocratic diplomat on earth. And they kiss it every time. You won't bomb us, Mr. Johnson. You can abuse me in this room all you like—you and your friends entertain yourselves with chest-thumping stories afterwards—but we know what you're made of. *Dialogue.*" The word was pure insult, making Johnson wince. "We'll kill another hundred Americans soldiers in Iraq, another thousand people in New York, and the only thing we'll grant you is an *audience* in the throne room of the world. So you may come once more on bended knee to touch our hand."

Johnson was about to give her a lecture . . . that she should never mistake American freedom for American weakness, that our vicious political debate didn't mean we lacked unity of purpose, that dissent is our true strength. All the well-worn words. But before he could, the cast of characters at a Jo von H party flitted through his mind, the West-hating, postmodern, gender-bending, self-congratulatory super-rich and talented *mediocrities*—the whole collection of "progressives" who, as the saying went, wouldn't take their own side in a fight, even if they knew which side they were on. Heaviness settled on Johnson, weariness. He didn't want to argue any more.

Then a hot flash across his brain: What was he arguing with her for in the first place? Wasn't this just a symptom of the problem, the lack of clarity and purpose? Didn't it mean she had a point? In any other society, they'd have taken her downstairs to some obscure tunnel and shot her in the head. Then left her body in the sewer—a condign punishment for a woman guilty of murder and terror. An Agent Enemy of State.

He shook his head, as if to banish the thought. Yasmine must have been mystified at his strange, prolonged silence. *No, we're civilized*, he told himself. *We're civilization*. But that carries the responsibility, the obligation to defend it.

He thought back to that Iranian van in the sandstorm. Despite everything, once more *proud* he'd pulled the trigger, and of his association with men and women who had made it possible for him to pull it. He thought of the New Yorkers killed, and the malevolence loosed on the city's streets that day. Of Wesson. The image of Giselle with a hood over her head knifed through him again. Never far away. He planned to keep the jpeg file of it in his phone, to forever remind him. His eyes filled, but he managed to control himself. Sure, he'd pull the trigger again, if that's what it took, if that's what it took to keep this woman and all her people in the darkest corners of the earth.

He finally fixed his eyes on Yasmine again: "You tried to take what's precious from me, my daughter and my city. Soon the Stone Age is coming for you, Yasmine Farouk, PhD. Don't complain. Get used to it. You're going to live in that Stone Age a long, long time."

Johnson turned his back on her. He hadn't proven to be much of an interrogator, but any lingering doubts about his role in this fight had been burned away. He left the room and the woman, but resolved never to leave the struggle, never leave the resistance, so long as there was an enemy to resist and a world to defend. For better or worse, his own civilization had come to claim him.

He punched up his cell phone as soon as he left the cage and dialed Giselle: "Honey, I'm coming home."

CHAPTER TWENTY-SIX

A Series of Unfortunate Events

Johnson sat around the apartment for the next two weeks or so, taking in the media circus around the attacks. It was a big enough deal, and deservedly so, but not quite the apocalypse. Matters might have turned a lot worse. One hundred eighty-three Americans dead, including Agent Wesson, who got a police funeral and honor guard that stretched twenty blocks. As for the city's infrastructure and public commons: Union Square, Trump Towers, parts of Grand Central, the Christopher Street subway station, J. Hood Wright Park in West Harlem, the San Remo Hotel, P.S. 158, the Bayard Taylor School on York Avenue on the Upper East Side, along with the Friends' Seminary Private School on 16th Street, and an abandoned factory near the Gowanus Canal were off-limits indefinitely. As were the safe houses and their immediate vicinity: a single family house in Queens, a ten-story apartment building in Brooklyn, a condemned former crack den on the Lower East Side, a house in Staten Island where backpackers had rented the basement, an apartment in Lefrak City, and a boathouse in Amityville. A complicated and expensive cleanup began.

Every subway car in the New York City transit system had to be scanned for the Grunge. In the end, seventeen Bombardier subway cars retired permanently. Much later, a scandal ensued when two of the cars were sold to entrepreneurs in Nevada for use as eating establishments called Manhattan Diners, one in Reno, the other in Roswell, New Mexico.

The Workbench Boys disappeared into the pocket of the federal government as "enemy combatants." Most didn't live out the month, dying of radiation poisoning in various high-security prison infirmaries. Only Banquo knew what happened to Yasmine Farouk, PhD. And the fate of the Iranian Diplomats? Actually, all requested and were eventually given amnesty and U.S. citizenship in a deal with the Justice Department, brokered by the State Department and assigned to the Middle East Desk. They were working for us now. Anton Anjou continued to live in Greenwich Village. Johnson took him out to lunch once in order to warn him off Giselle. He needn't have bothered. One of the Iranian Diplomats had moved in.

———— ∞∞∞ ————

Johnson desperately wanted to sit down with Banquo and Wallets for a debrief, and kept calling, but the word always came back that they were busy and he should keep on with "legend building"—in other words keep writing his attacks on the U.S. government and apologies for our enemies. This was getting very old, and Johnson wanted to give it up soon, but he figured for now, "Those also serve who stay at home and write vicious defenses of appeasement." The brains at Banquo & Duncan still thought him more useful with his street cred intact—indeed, bizarrely enhanced by his Iranian experience. Jo von H wanted to have a party in his honor. She thought he had been victimized by the CIA in Iran, so that's what everyone else in their circle thought too. A plausible enough fairy tale.

Speaking of which, he flipped to *Hardball* to catch the appearance Josephine had been promoting all day on *The Crusader* blog. Giselle came home from work, threw her purse and coat on a chair, and plopped down next to him. "Check it out," he said, "Jo's in fine form."

His Editrix came off the screen like an angel on fire: "After all the trampling on civil liberties, after all the money spent, all the phony alarms, *this* is what we get? No safer, no more secure. Just wall-to-wall paranoia and no security, Chris."

"Harrumph," Johnson snorted. "All of a sudden she cares about security?"

Giselle playfully hit him on his arm, "Be nice."

Johnson rolled his eyes.

Giselle reminded him, "She went all-out for you when you were in Iran, and she pays the bills, doesn't she?"

"Only some of them," Johnson replied.

Chris Matthews was asking a rambling, machine-gun–style question, something about whether Josephine von Hildebrand and *The Crusader* trusted whether the government gave them the full story, ending with this clinker:

"Do you think—we've got reports out there—do you think, you know what they're saying, those so-called neocons—although they don't seem very neo to me, con maybe, *hah-hah*—do you think—you know what I'm getting at here—and I've been around this town for a long time— do you think the Iranians were *involved?*"

Finally, the rub.

One of among many things that mystified Johnson—that he appeared to be witnessing a successful government cover-up. How easily people, like good horses, wore blinders without complaint. The administration didn't want to 'fess up to the Iranian sponsorship of the attacks. Bits and pieces about the Iranian role kept dribbling out, but the administration either stayed silent or shot down various erroneous details that tended to discredit the larger narrative, even if that narrative was true. The momentary political dynamic aided the administration's cause. The right played up the Iranian angle, but the left reflexively dismissed it, and no one was inclined to believe the right since the Iraq WMD fiasco.

The coverup was aided by hear-no-evil-see-no-evil press that seemed more concerned with the Dish du Jour—recently the revelation that a famous Hollywood actress, on the advice of a fashionable child psychologist in California, was raising her three adopted children via remote control through an elaborate system of interactive vid-cam links and talking stuffed animals.

But Chris Mathews still chewed the bit in his teeth over government spying and lying, and Josephine rode him like a gelding.

"No, Chris, I don't think the government is telling us everything. But blaming Iran—that's coming from the people who want another rush to war against another regime. No, what they aren't telling us is how they messed up, and how much they've done to make damn sure young Muslim men the world over hate us, hate us, with a passionate commitment. My writer Peter Johnson has a new piece in *The Crus*—"

Johnson hit the Off button on the remote.

He and Giselle enjoyed some peace and quiet in their lives—treasured it, actually, after all that had happened. Loving the little things. They ordered seafood Pad Thai from the local Thai place and talked over dinner, Johnson really listening for the first time in a long time, perhaps the first time ever. His mind didn't flit over the things he wanted to do the next day, or the arguments in his next piece, or the question of how soon he could extricate himself from the conversation to do whatever else he imagined he'd rather be doing: reading, drinking, skirt chasing, working, whatever. For once engaged, utterly engaged in this person across from him, who shared so much of him—of his genes, his history— but was utterly distinct, not just from him, but from anyone who'd ever graced this planet. Or ever would.

And he smiled to himself with the wonder of such simple things he'd missed so profoundly and for so long. "Dad, what is it?" Giselle asked him when she noticed his strange look. But he just shook his head.

From downstairs the lobby buzzer rang; he and Giselle shared a glance of restrained suspicion. But it turned out to be a bicycle messenger late on a delivery. A simple manila envelope. Johnson opened it. A photograph and a cover sheet. The cover sheet was a hospital form noting the death of an unknown subject due to radiation poisoning of an unknown origin. The hospital name blacked out. The photograph showed Yasmine.

No longer that alluring flower he remembered, not even the arrogant interrogator, nor even the defiant prisoner of the Waldorf-Astoria. The face was nearly black with clotted blood and withered, shrunken in on itself. At some point she must have self-contaminated as she went about her deadly tasks. Touched by the Grunge. A dead vampire. Queen of the Damned.

He slid them both back into the envelope, fingers trembling slightly.
His cell phone rang.

Wallets.

He wanted him to come in first thing in the morning.

————

The offices of Banquo & Duncan hummed like a reborn hive. When
Johnson walked off the Rockefeller elevator, it seemed as if twice as
many people worked there. The double doors to the old man's office
stood open.

Banquo waved Johnson in hurriedly without getting up, then immediately turned to his email and phone, for the moment distracted.
Johnson watched the spymaster and saw the same Banquo he'd always
known: impeccably dressed, even-voiced, but intense. Yet Johnson saw a
difference that took a while for him to pin down—an exuberance ema-
nating from the head of the firm that hadn't been there before.

Johnson thought of the Shakespeare line about there being a tide
in the affairs of men. Coming to him at last: "There is a tide in the
affairs of men. / Which taken at the flood, leads on to fortune; /
Omitted, all the voyage of their life / Is bound in shallows and in
miseries." After a long time, Banquo's tide was running again in his
favor, and he was riding the current. The dinosaur had clawed his
way out of his tar pit.

First order of business: they caught up on the press.

"Check this out," Bryce said. Somehow Trevor Andover's assistant
never managed to return to Langley and now drew a salary from B &
D. He handed Banquo the front page of the *Washington Post* and
pointed to a story below the fold in the right hand corner, bylined Ruth
Lipsky. The headline read, "Top CIA Official Ousted," and the lede:
"The Deputy Director of the CIA has resigned amid criticisms that he
ignored key intelligence in the weeks leading up to last month's incidents in New York City, unnamed official sources say."

"Unnamed *official* sources," Banquo said, smiling. "Well, that
clears it up."

Bryce laughed. "I don't know who those sources possibly could be, do you?"

"Sy Hersh has a piece in the *The New Yorker* saying you held prisoners down and tortured them with pliers with your own hands," Johnson told Banquo.

"Ah, good ole Sy. With his usual commitment to accuracy. Where did he get that?"

"He says 'former intelligence officials.'"

"Hah," Banquo smiled. "His sources are always 'former' nobodies who haven't been 'anybodies' since Vietnam."

"Watch," Johnson said, "he'll probably win a National Magazine Award for it."

Then they discussed what was happening in response to the attack. But with a warning from Banquo that Johnson couldn't misunderstand: "You're being included as a courtesy, Peter. Not for repeating *ever*—what you're about to see. In this I bind you to me."

Johnson nodded and said nothing, as he'd finally learned.

"I still think it's a job for the BFF," said Wallets.

"Uh, Giselle would think that's 'best friends forever'?" Johnson said, immediately forgetting everything he learned. This time, everyone laughed.

"The Big Fucking Fellas, the B-52s," Wallets said.

"But they want to keep it quiet," Banquo explained. "Officially, they want the attacks never solved, like the anthrax investigation. We may never know why the Iranians did it—at least not before the regime falls and we see the records. It might have been retaliation, tit-for-tat for your mission, Peter. Or maybe it's just that aggression is what they do, and killing Americans is all the same to them, whether it's on Saudi, Iraqi, or American soil. Or maybe they figured the more pain they inflict on us the likelier we are to leave their nuclear program alone. Could be a little of all of these things. My guess is that they simply thought they were good enough to get away with it—after all, the Grunge was in the pipeline long before we sent you in.

"But that's just a guess. We do know that our return delivery is not going to be by Stratofortress, but something a touch more surgical. That means the president preserves his options. He knows if it were publicly established that the Iranians did this, he'd have almost no option politically but to flatten them from the Persian Gulf to the Caucasus, and that means a lot of innocent people die and we get blamed for it internationally. He wants to do it more subtle."

"Subtle makes me nervous," Wallets shifted in his seat.

"I know, but not to worry." Banquo said. Then, "Ah, speak of the devil." All eyes went to the flat screen on CIA-SPAN. The view from space jerked down to a closer and closer view: an indistinct brown, out of which slowly there emerged brown shapes, the dominant one a long line on the ground . . . a runway. The legend at the bottom of the screen read: "U.S.A.F. Air Strip Forward Sting, Irbil, Iraq, Zulu Time: 0545."

Down the runway rolled a tiny white plane, its delicate features like a dragonfly or balsa-wood toy glider. A MQ-1 Predator, an armed unmanned aerial vehicle. Two slim dark shapes were visible perpendicular and underneath its wings, AGM-114 Hellfire missiles. The seven-inch-wide, sixty-four-inch-long, ninety-nine-pound projectiles traveled at 950 miles per hour when launched, with an eighteen-pound shaped charge high explosive anti-tank warhead—the business end of American 21st century precision warfare. From Lockheed Martin, with love.

The scene shifted courtesy of the Long Eye Satellite system. First: a grid of a city, a main thoroughfare, then a stretch of two blocks, and finally the top of a black sedan. The sedan bumped the car in front of it hard. A common traffic accident.

"Time to get out," Banquo said to the screen.

As if he heard those words, the driver of the sedan got out and looked at the damage from the fender bender, then began arguing with the other driver, waving his hands. You could almost see his face.

"Look familiar?" Banquo asked Johnson; squinting, he couldn't tell. Then shook his head no.

"No, why should you?" Banquo said to the screen. "Just one of the men who beat you. Sheik Kutmar's chauffeur. But I imagine you were rather distracted at the time."

No, Johnson didn't recognize the man.

Banquo continued talking to the screen: "Keep him in there; let him make his cell phone calls. And you make your own. Time to get out of the way." The driver made a gesture like a traffic cop as if to say, "Don't bother to get out," toward the passenger in the back of the sedan. Some more talking through the rolled down window: as though suggesting the passenger should just sit there, he'd fix it, call for another vehicle. Then the driver walked toward the side of the street with his hand up to his ear like he was making his own cell phone call.

"Another couple of steps. Go inside the café. Buy a coffee."

The driver ducked under the awning of the café, ostensibly going inside.

Twelve seconds later, the screen went all white in a flash and then cleared to show a plume of black smoke and fire where the sedan had been. Window glass in the street. The terrible pause when no one moves those first few moments.

"Real subtle," said Wallets, smirking.

"Where's our guy?" Johnson said. "Is he still there? The driver, I mean. There he is."

The driver was one of a number of people crawling out into the street from the various shattered storefronts around the explosion. He staggered toward the car and threw his hands in the air, putting them on top of his head in wailing grief. Even from a satellite you could tell.

"Give him the little gold statue now."

The sedan was a mangled, flattened piece of burning metal.

"What does it look like to you, Wallets? We get our man?"

"Sheik Kutmar," Wallets pronounced. "Officially with the virgins."

Then Banquo did something utterly unaccountable. He got up from his desk, came over to Johnson's chair, spread his arms wide, and hugged him. Wallets looked down out of embarrassment but couldn't suppress the beginning of a smile that steadily grew. And Johnson saw Wallets smile—really smile, broad and easy—for the first time since the Iraq/Iran border.

Banquo seemed to catch himself, sat back down, and said in his usual, calm understated tone of voice, "That's partly thanks to you, Peter. What started five years ago in these offices just ended on TV."

Seeing Johnson's confusion, Banquo explained: "During your incarceration, we kept busy and took out a little insurance." Banquo went on, "We spirited the chauffeur's family to Dubrovnik on the Dalmatian Coast. Then kept them in a small villa. His choice was silver or lead, as the saying goes. His family getting the lead first. Naturally, he chose silver. So the driver helped us arrange a fender bender in a busy street. Then made a cell phone call. Our final targeting sequence painted the sedan. Couldn't miss, and—as you saw—Sheik Kutmar's car happens to blow up."

"That's still a hell of a hole in the street to explain," Wallets said, gesturing toward the smoldering scene on the screen.

"Well, yes," Banquo said. "We won't be able to do that again. There'll be all sorts of crazy reports from the scene—flashing lights in the sky, UFOs. But they'll figure it out. The thing is, we've had UAV flights over Iran since '04. And the Iranians have never tracked them on radar because they were afraid we'd learn too much about their defense systems if they did. Now, that'll change."

He clipped the end of a cigar, as the CIA-SPAN shifted to something else. But no one bothered to watch. "So, we'll be on to the next thing," Banquo explained, looking first at his cigar as he rotated it in his fingers, then up over everyone's head, as if he were addressing a memory. "One down, twenty-four to go. The top echelons of Iranian intelligence and the people who run the nuclear program are about to suffer a series of unfortunate events."

What was there left to say?

⸺◦⊰⊱◦⸺

After Johnson left, Banquo and Wallets sat alone for some moments. A brief quiet time, each lost in his own thoughts. At last Banquo sighed.

"Well, shall we get on with it?"

Wallets nodded silently, and they both rose from their chairs, Wallets taking a briefcase with him.

They returned to the same office once used to introduce a much less worldly Peter Johnson to his quarry and target, one Dr. Ramses Pahlevi

Yahdzi. Now, Yossi sat at the very same desk, looking like a swarthy, petulant Yul Brynner, called to account for some indiscretion. The eye patch added to his coldness, looking out at the world with the same bored insolence as ever.

"Yossi, a recap of recent history if you don't mind," Banquo began. "I want to thank you personally for extracting Johnson from the bazaar, for arranging the safe house, for stocking the trunk of our getaway car. Your forethought allowed the team to heal up and then pass the bandit roadblock in Kermanshah. A brilliant bit of soldiering. But there are certain things still troubling us."

The spymaster paused. "For instance, there's the untimely death of Jan Breuer."

Yossi had an elbow on the clear desk, his chin propped on it. He didn't say anything or make a gesture.

"This look familiar?" Wallets asked, opening a brief case and pulling out a Leupold Night Vision rifle scope.

"Rifle sight," Yossi said.

"Very good," Wallets said, calmly. "Very useful for dropping some unlucky bloke standing on Second Avenue, no?"

"Depends on how good you shoot," with a shrug.

Wallets nodded. "Well, we all know your skills."

Yossi looked unimpressed. What did it take to get this guy's attention? Wallets grew impatient, drew a Marlboro out if his pack, and lit it, annoyed. But Banquo made a tiny sweeping motion to him with his hand: *take it easy, not yet.*

Yossi sometimes reminded Banquo of that prisoner described in Primo Levi's *Survival in Auschwitz*, whose innate bestiality allowed him to thrive in the camp, a world better suited to him than any sane one. For Yossi, the world of intelligence was something like that—double-crosses, uncertainty, and violent opportunism his most natural element.

"We don't want this to get ugly," Banquo said, glancing to a corner of the office. The black soundproof isolation booth from the Astor Ballroom waited for a chance to prove its worth again. Wallets saved one from the Waldorf as an afterthought, sensing a day like this would eventually arrive.

Yossi snorted in disbelief. "You want me torture myself?"

Banquo ignored the aside. "We have the scope; we have the rifle that you lodged in a gutter in a corner of the roof and the ballistics. We have a witness who saw a large bald man headed down the fire escape around 8 PM at 345 East 76th Street, catty-corner from Il Monello. We can always add your fingerprints at a later date. What we don't have is a motive. Care to provide?"

"He bother people," Yossi said.

Now it was Wallets' turn to show incredulity. "*Lots* of people bother people."

Banquo hushed him with his hand again. "Who, Yossi?"

"He annoy people whose money he steal," Yossi said.

Typical and plausible. Breuer had skimmed too much from his corrupt transactions, and someone had finally demanded final payment. But who?

"Jan Breuer was a contemptible human being in many ways," Banquo said, in a confiding tone. "But he was important to us. Indeed, we couldn't get anything done without contemptible human beings. He kept us apprised of who was taking what money, giving us an opportunity to use vulnerable marks for our own purposes or publicly discredit them if they wouldn't play along. How do you think all the George Galloway bribes went public? This also gave us one Peter Johnson. He turned out to be ripe for the plucking for the right reasons, but knowing he was on the take first brought him to our attention. A good résumé detail if you will. And if he double-crossed us, well then it would have been more than just bloggers pointing out his dubious investments in Nigerian parking garages."

Yossi looked at him as if to say, *Your point is?*

"So you killed a very valuable asset to us. And now you're going to tell us why, or you'll face a capital murder case. The strongest we can arrange."

"No," Yossi said, shaking his head and smiling. "No. Then I tell everything, everyone."

Banquo knew what he meant. And he was right, of course. A public trial would be a disaster, and Yossi would become the hero of the press corps just as soon as he started singing about tormenting people for the United States government. Banquo had hoped Yossi wouldn't think it through so well. Too bad. Plan B.

"You should be a lawyer in your next life, Yossi," Banquo smiled. "Put the legal proceedings aside; there's still the matter of a certain girl-friend." A zaftig beauty from Morocco. "One Miss Esmeralda? And a ten-year-old son living in Jersey City with a very uncertain immigration status. It might be that they could be unceremoniously deported, to say . . . any number of countries with no fondness for the kith and kin of a rogue agent who betrayed them, killed their operatives, stole their money," Banquo paused. "Well, you get the idea."

Yossi took his chin off his hand. The spymaster had his attention. Here Banquo paused to hit the intercom button on a phone on a small table between him and Wallets: "Bring him in."

Bryce escorted in a very pale, ashen-faced Deputy Executive Director Trevor Andover looking as though he missed at least one night's sleep, his suit rumpled. He clutched a Vitamin water bottle, labeled "Rescue Green Tea." He didn't make eye contact with anyone but sat in the chair Bryce pulled out for him and took a slug of his drink. A scared man. And easy to scare. It wasn't even fair.

Banquo looked from Andover the conniving bureaucrat to Yossi the thug—an unlikely match. But somehow it fit. Then he continued, demanding of Yossi, "Why in heaven's name would you ever, ever leak anything from this office to this man? What unlikely promises did he make you?" but didn't wait for an answer. Irrelevant now. Then to DEADKEY.

"Trevor," Banquo said, "I want you to read the confidentiality agree-ment you signed with the Agency once again. You're not the Director; you don't get a free pass, a Medal of Freedom. Or a brass plaque on the wall of a conference room. You're a hired soldier, like Wallets. Like me. You have to be competent and, failing that, at least loyal. And inter-rupting satellite feeds when my people are in jeopardy in Iran doesn't count as either."

DEADKEY's eyes clouded, then glazed over. Banquo's voice kept on: "Come now, that wasn't so long ago. Our team's in the safe house tracing Nantanz nukes and working their escape. Suddenly there's no satellite feed, the laptop blanks out—they're trapped; they're blind. That *was you*, no? Betray them; make them bolt in panic; maybe even get them caught?" Banquo's voice took on a kind of sadness.

"For what price? To what end? To disembowel my operation? Or was it simply a matter of non-concur? A principled difference in policy?"

Trevor Andover shrugged, as if to say *all of the above. Whatever you like*. Banquo's eyes fell on the sad gray man drinking tea in the chair, and Andover kept staring at the floor.

A tired voice. "That's about it, Stewart."

"In addition, I have here on speed dial"—Banquo's voice slowed down as he pushed a few buttons on his cell phone and then held it up for Andover to see—"Ruth Lipsky. 202 334 9532. I'm sure the *Washington Post* would be eager to do a follow-up on the suspect CIA Deputy Director who just resigned 'amid criticisms.' You know how the press can get when there's blood in the water."

The pale DEADKEY nodded silently but made no remark. Another sip of Rescue Green Tea.

With everyone in a proper frame of mind, Banquo prepared to begin the questions in earnest, and Bryce switched on the recording equipment. The sad gray man in the chair just stared at the floor.

Banquo turned once again to Yossi. "Sometimes you worked with our office and sometimes against us. You had more than one master. The Israelis first. Then me. Iranian Intelligence was another. And the Deputy Executive Director, at least your fourth. So we need to know at which points you, Yossi-Djjal-Deceiver, worked with whom and for what reason. We have lots of time, so we can start from the beginning, when Wallets met you for the first time in 2001, in Istanbul, just after the Mossad sprang you from the Yemeni prison—

"But, before you answer," Banquo said, letting it hang in the air a bit, "I should make one last stipulation, Yossi. After this, if you're straight with us, I'm sure we can get that immigration situation squared away . . . Provided you continue to do us occasional favors. We'll need your help getting close to one of your contacts in Iran."

Wallets smiled to himself, glancing at his boss—always focused five moves ahead on the board, returning from the dead so many times, both literally and career-wise, relentless in serving The Cause. Banquo had just set the predicate for another Grand Panjandrum somewhere in Iran to experience a very unfortunate event.

—◦◦◦—

Johnson rented a movie to watch with Giselle as was his wont lately. Harmless fare—*The Pursuit of Happyness* with Will Smith. But when Giselle came out of her room, it was obvious she wasn't going to stay home and watch a movie. Shortish black skirt, a heart pendant her stepmom Elizabeth Richards had given her, tall heels. She saw his look. "Dad, I have a date."

He shrugged. Even though he wanted to let loose with a torrent of overprotective warnings, he checked the urge. She added, quietly, "I don't think you're going to like it."

That pushed him over the edge, "What do you mean? Where are you meeting him?"

"I'm not. He's picking me up here. He's very . . . traditional."

Oh crap, Johnson thought. His imagination immediately settled on a Saudi. He no sooner had gotten the Iranians out of his hair than now he'd have to deal with a Saudi prince, who would have her pregnant and back in the Kingdom before he knew it, minus a driver's license and a passport. "Look, honey, I love you and want you to be happy, but there are so many nice boys in this city. Can't you find one of them?"

She seemed nervous and popped into the bathroom for a final look at her hair, before she answered him. "Don't worry, Dad; he's American."

The doorbell rang. Johnson beat her to the door and opened it to see—gray eyes, looking sheepish. First time he'd ever seen them sheepish.

"Oh! I didn't expect you. Come on in. What's going on? Something up?" Clueless.

Wallets didn't move from the hallway. Giselle came out staring through the open door. "Hi." Very shy.

"Hey there," Wallets said. More shy than her. Then to Johnson, "I won't keep her out late."

Johnson stood there speechless but managed to croak, "Okay."

He closed the door slowly and padded back toward the couch. Put his feet on the coffee table and threw his hands behind his head, still stunned. Then laughed out loud. "Sonofabitch," he muttered. Wallets would be good to his word—nothing to worry about. He looked out his big window at the glimmering Manhattan skyline. He breathed in its beauty for a long time with a dumb smile on his lips and thanked God to be alive.

⁂

Jo von H's Party Day arrived. Johnson walked from his apartment down to the corner of Henry and Montague to look for a cab. A dark feeling had grown on him all day after he noticed a limo parked downstairs— parked for hours. You didn't see many limos in this neighborhood, and this long black Cadillac 2009 limousine was so shiny it looked as though the driver stopped at every other intersection to get out and polish it. The rear window descended, and Johnson felt like he was in a rerun of a bad movie he'd seen too many times.

"Mr. Jon-sohn, Mr. Jon-sohn," the guy in back called to him. Impossible to ignore him—too ridiculous. So he stopped and came over to the car. The Asian gentleman, in a grey suit, crisp white shirt, and red power tie, didn't look very threatening. "Can I give you a ride, Mr. Jon-sohn?"

"Upper West Side?" Johnson asked, conscious that he was acting as though he were negotiating with a gypsy-cab driver.

"Anywheh," the man said, and Johnson climbed in, his nostrils filled with a scent he had known before—new limo smell. A razor-thin Asian man in a tuxedo slid over the couch, making room, gave a sharp head-bow in greeting, and asked, "Drink?" Johnson looked at a bar that took up most of one side of the vehicle, bristling with multicolored bottles and glasses of all kinds. He could get used to this—at least until they hit Central Park West in the 70s.

Johnson settled with his bourbon into the back seat next to his mystery host and did everything he could not to demand, *What the hell?*

The man began, "A Mr. Anjo from Bank Ruxonburg recommended I get in touch with you . . ." And Johnson's mouth stayed agape for most of the rest of the ride. Turned out there really was a Japanese industrialist—sitting right there. Turned out he did want to bid on New York real estate. Turned out he did need someone to do some quiet banking on the side for him to keep his name, Yoshimi Matsui—printed on a two-sided Japanese-English business card—out of the transaction.

Turned out, in short, that Johnson's belief that the Iranians had wanted to funnel money into the West through him, of all people, had been a fantasy based on inference. He enjoyed his bourbon and some conversation about the vagaries of commercial real estate and, as they got near Jo von H's place, began to consider the possibilities. Yet another unusual financial transaction? The industrialist offered him a carrying fee, *naturally*. So could he really turn the man down? No one was asking him to do anything criminal. Just helpful and deceptive.

He gave a crisp head-bow of his own to Mr. Matsui and declined an offer to take the bourbon glass and all for the road. Stepped out onto the street, saying politely, "Let me consider it." And thinking for the second time in two days, *Sonofabitch.* Then took a deep breath and girded himself for what was ahead.

⁓⁓

The long mile down Josephine von Hildebrand's vanity hallway seemed to last an hour, as if the hallway itself extended geometrically at each weary step Johnson took. The stale *Crusader* covers marched by in silence. Neville Poore at his elbow talked an incessant stream, excruciating in his familiarity. Johnson tried to listen, his boredom competing with his contempt. Even the thought of a good bourbon at Hallway's End held no allure. He'd drink one anyway.

Now behind *The Crusader* podium his Hostess with the Mostest sallied forth. In a fantastic moment Johnson saw her growing directly from the podium base, part of her, her true anchor. After she was done talking, they'd unplug her and wheel her out. Yet a new Lancelot looked on with admiration.

"In an age of fear and aggression, Peter Johnson offers us understanding and peace," Jo von H said.

"Peter has not only talked the talk, he has walked the walk. He was put in jeopardy on assignment recently by the recklessness and lies of our own government. And we almost lost him. But now he's come back for good."

Yeah, he'd come back all right, just not the way Jo von H thought.

". . . So please welcome the ultimate crusader, Peter Johnson."

The clapping and bravos washed over him and offended his ears. He climbed the first step of Josephine's spiraling staircase, avoiding the podium, and looked at the crowd, the mass smiling, inching forward in anticipation of the knowing and sneering putdowns Johnson would inevitably deliver against all the people and things they hated. Time to feed the beast. Neville Poore winked at him, and Johnson pretended not to see.

"Thank you, thank you very much," he began. "I can tell you I've learned a lot about the nature of Iran, about how our government works, and—especially—who my *real* friends are."

A titter of laughter rippled through the crowd. Johnson raised his glass and, way off in the back of the room, met Robert Wallets' sober gray eyes.